A JIM HIGGINS DRIFTLESS MYSTERY NOVEL

Driftless IDENTITY

SUE BERG

LITTLE CREEK PRESS
MINERAL POINT, WISCONSIN

Copyright © 2025 Sue Berg

Little Creek Press
5341 Sunny Ridge Road
Mineral Point, Wisconsin 53565

All rights reserved

No part of this book may be used or reproduced in any manner whatsoever without written permission from the author.

Follow Sue on Facebook @ Sue Berg/author
To contact author: bergsue@hotmail.com
To order books: www.littlecreekpress.com

ISBN-13: 978-1-967311-01-9
LCCN: 2025907476

Cover photo: The Bend, La Crosse, Wisconsin © **Phil S Addis**

Book Design by Little Creek Press

This is a work of fiction. References to real places, events, establishments, and organizations in the Driftless area are intended only to provide a sense of authenticity. They are used fictitiously and are drawn from the author's imagination to enhance the story being told.

ACKNOWLEDGMENTS

As we age, surprises await us on the road of life. In December 2024, I had unexpected open heart surgery to replace an aortic valve. For those who wonder how a book is transformed from idea to manuscript to edits to final proofs while the author is in recovery mode, I think the saying "It takes a village!" would apply to this book.

I want to thank my husband, Alan, and my four children for their help during my surgery, hospital stay, and recovery at home. Thank you to my church family and teacher friends who brought wonderful, home-cooked meals to us during my recuperation. I was concerned for several weeks that my book production schedule would have to be changed and a later release date selected, but thanks to my family and the professional, amazing staff at Little Creek Press, you are holding *Driftless Identity* in your hands. Kristin, thank you for being a steadfast and enthusiastic advocate for Wisconsin authors. I have found a home at Little Creek Press, and I never want to leave! Thank you, Shannon, for your expertise in editing and revision. My books are so much better with your eagle eye!

I am always thrilled to meet readers who have enjoyed my books. Without you, our stories would lose their meaning and purpose. I am truly grateful to the many who have read my books and continue to look forward to the new installments. You make my heart sing!

A verse that sustained me during my recovery gives me hope for the future: "Even to your old age and gray hairs I am he, I am he who will sustain you. I have made you and I will carry you; I will sustain you and I will rescue you." Isaiah 46:4 NIV

Praise for the Jim Higgins
Driftless Mystery Series:

DRIFTLESS GOLD

"… an irresistible tale of lost treasure and the scoundrels who will do anything to get their hand on it."

~Jeff Nania, author of the Northern Lake Mystery Series

DRIFTLESS TREASURE

2021 Finalist Award in The Independent Author Network

"Descriptive scenes and well-drawn characters in a story of crimes with international implications."

~Greg Peck, author of *Death Beyond the Willows*

DRIFTLESS DECEIT

"Berg creates a smorgasbord of subplots with characters confounded by real-life issues from family loyalty and faith to forgiveness and love, both lost and found.
~Patricia Skalka, author of the Door County Mystery Series

DRIFTLESS DESPERATION

"An honest portrayal of the crime and rural poverty that exists beneath the bucolic veneer of this unique landscape."
~John Armbruster, author of *Tailspin*

DRIFTLESS INSURRECTION

"… a solid cast of multi-dimensional characters in a plot that kept me guessing. The novel's storyline and characters are as good as anything on the mystery/suspense bestseller list today. Give this author a chance."
~Christine DeSmet, author of the Fudge Shop Mystery Series

OTHER BOOKS BY SUE BERG

Solid Roots and Strong Wings—A Family Memoir

The Driftless Mystery Series:

Driftless Gold

Driftless Treasure

Driftless Deceit

Driftless Desperation

Driftless Insurrection

FOREWORD
THE DRIFTLESS REGION

The name *Driftless* appears in all of the titles of my books because this region of the American Midwest where my novels take place is a unique geographical region, though relatively unknown. The Driftless Region—which escaped glacial activity during the last ice age—includes southeastern Minnesota, southwestern Wisconsin, northeastern Iowa, and the extreme northwestern corner of Illinois. The stories I write take place in and around La Crosse, Wisconsin, which is in the heart of this distinct geographical region.

The Driftless Region is characterized by steep forested ridges, deeply carved river valleys, and karst geology, resulting in spring-fed waterfalls and cold-water trout streams. The rugged terrain is due primarily to the lack of glacial deposits called drift. The absence of the flattening glacial effect of drifts resulted in land that has remained hilly and rugged—hence the term *driftless*. In addition, the Mississippi River and its many tributaries have carved rock outcroppings and towering bluffs from the area's bedrock. These rock formations along the Mississippi River climb to almost six hundred feet in some places. Grandad Bluff in La Crosse is one of these famous bluffs.

In particular, the Driftless portion of southwestern Wisconsin contains many distinct features: isolated hills, coulees, bluffs, mesas, buttes, goat prairies, and pinnacles formed from eroded Cambrian bedrock remnants of the plateau to the southwest. In addition, karst topography is found throughout the Driftless area. This landscape was created when water dissolved the dolomite and limestone rock resulting in features like caves and cave systems, hidden underground streams, blind valleys and sinkholes, and springs and cold streams.

About eighty-five percent of the Driftless Region lies within southwestern Wisconsin. The rugged terrain comprising this area is known locally as the Coulee Region. Steep ridges, numerous rock outcroppings like the Three Chimneys northwest of Viroqua, the classic rock formations of Wisconsin Dells, and deep narrow valleys contrast with the rest of the state, where glaciers have modified and leveled the land.

The area is prone to flooding, runoff, and erosion. Because of the steep river valleys, many small towns in the Driftless Region have major flooding problems every fifty to one hundred years. Farmers in the region practice contour plowing and strip farming to reduce soil erosion on the hilly terrain.

Superb cold-water streams have made the Driftless Region a premier trout fishing destination in the country. A variety of fish, including brook and rainbow trout, thrive in the tributaries of the Mississippi River system. The crystalline streams are protected by Trout Unlimited, an organization that works with area landowners to maintain and restore trout habitat. In addition, abundant wildlife such as deer and turkeys provide excellent hunting for the avid sportsman.

La Crosse is the principal urban center that is entirely in the Wisconsin Driftless Region, along with small cities, towns, and numerous Amish settlements. Cranberries are grown and harvested in bogs left over from Glacial Lake Wisconsin. At one time, cigar tobacco was grown and harvested throughout the Coulee Region, but foreign markets decreased the demand for Wisconsin-grown tobacco. However, tobacco barns or sheds are still found throughout the landscape and are an iconic symbol of a once-thriving industry. The region is also home to Organic Valley, the nation's largest organic producer of dairy products, organic vegetables, and fruits, particularly apples. Winemaking and vineyards have popped up in recent years, and apple production continues to be a staple in the Driftless economy.

After describing the area's geographical features, you can see why Wisconsin is the perfect setting for a mystery series! It's a wonderland of unparalleled geographical beauty, impressive wildlife, and friendly, memorable people. Enjoy!

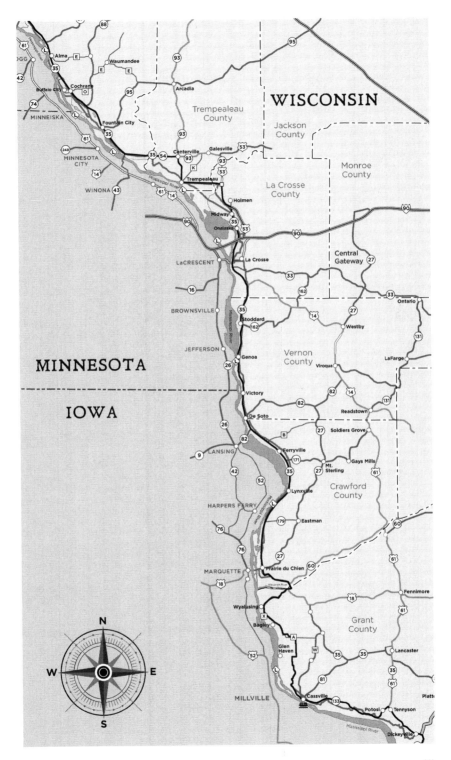

DRIFTLESS IDENTITY

THURSDAY, AUGUST 28

A SIMPLE TEST TO FIND OUT WHETHER YOUR MISSION IN LIFE IS FINISHED: IF YOU'RE STILL ALIVE, IT ISN'T FINISHED. YOUR MISSION GOES ON.

1

The heat during the last few weeks of August had been stifling and unrelenting in the Driftless region. The trees wilted in the hot sun for lack of water; the grass had turned brown and crackled underneath your feet. A dusty haze in the air left a fine grit across the surface of everything. Farmers were worried about their crops; golf courses were pumping water on their lawns and greens. People were crabby and short-tempered. Where was the rain?

Late on Thursday evening, lightning streaked across the sky in brilliant blue fingers of incandescent radiance. All day the humidity had been building, and now it seemed about to smack its big fist across the landscape. The air smelled of ozone and moisture.

Leslie Birkstein draped her hand across her swollen belly and restlessly tucked her feet under the quilt. The air conditioning was turned too low again. Her husband, Sam, who was scrunched in an awkward position on the couch, sat up suddenly when a growl of thunder rattled the windows of their hilltop cottage on U.S. Highway 35 along the Mississippi River south of La Crosse, Wisconsin. The light from the TV filled the darkened room with a blue hue. Sam got up, walked to the large window as lightning bolts danced on the horizon of the Mississippi River bluffs.

"Hey, will you go to Gas & Go and get me some maple nut ice cream?" Leslie asked, trying to keep the whine out of her voice.

"Another craving?" Sam asked. He turned and looked at Leslie. "It's almost eleven, hon. I was thinking about going to bed."

Leslie smiled shyly. "Yeah, I know what time it is, but just think, in another couple of months my cravings will be gone, and then you'll have to listen to our baby fussing and crying. You might even be walking the floor, trying—"

"Okay, okay. When you put it like that, I guess I can indulge your cravings," Sam said reluctantly.

"You're a good man, Charlie Brown," Leslie said, walking up to him and hugging him around the waist. Paco, their black lab, got up from the rug and stretched in a lazy movement reminiscent of a yoga pose. He let out a groan accompanied by a huge yawn. Then he stood and wagged his tail, looking expectantly at Sam.

"No, Paco. I'm not taking you with me. You have to stay with Lez," Sam said, holding up his hand in a stay position. Paco's tail drooped like a flag being lowered to half-mast. Sam walked to the entryway and grabbed his rain jacket off the hook. "Be back in a half an hour," he said.

The door slammed shut. Leslie stood by the window and watched Sam back the Jeep out of the garage into the rain that had just begun to fall. He headed down the steep bluff driveway toward the gas station in Stoddard, seven miles north on the Great River Road.

In the quiet cocoon of the Jeep, Sam could barely hear the threat of the rumbling thunder. He thought back over the events of the last six months. So many things had happened—the first being their surprise pregnancy, which they'd found out about in April. Now Leslie's expanding abdomen was a taut ball of muscle and growing baby.

Sam was fascinated with the pregnancy, frequently laying his hand on Leslie's belly to feel the active life within her. He read about the baby's development, poring over a medical nursing textbook he'd bought at Goodwill. The only thing he found scary was the delivery, although taking childbirth classes with Leslie had helped alleviate some of his anxiety.

Then another surprise development landed in their lap. Bobby Rude's childhood home, perched beneath the precipice of Warner's Bluff in Genoa along the Great River Road, came up for sale. Bobby, now a junior at Logan High School in La Crosse, had gone to live with Jerome and Sara Knight after his alcoholic father had died in April at the Tomah Veteran's Hospital. Bobby had been instrumental in gathering crucial evidence in a couple of tough cases facing the investigative team at the La Crosse Sheriff's Department. His dream was to become a cop—more specifically, a detective.

Sam and Leslie hadn't planned on purchasing a home, but they were tired of city life and wanted a place in the country to begin raising their family. The Rude house was situated at the top of a steep hill beneath the sandstone bluffs that rose above the tiny river town of Genoa. The buildings of the tiny fishing village were scattered like pebbles on a sand beach beneath the ridge of bluffs just south of the house. The view of the majestic Mississippi from their front window was worth every penny they'd paid for it, although the house had fallen into disrepair over the years and needed substantial improvements.

They purchased the riverfront property for a modest sum, but the dwelling was small and needed new plumbing, electrical work, and a roof. While remodeling, they decided to add an expansive wing to the north, including an art studio for Leslie and, above it, two bedrooms with a master bath on the second floor. Sam revamped the kitchen with new appliances, IKEA cupboards he'd purchased online, and granite countertops. They freshened up the rest of the house with paint and new flooring.

Despite the responsibility of a mortgage, Sam and Leslie enjoyed the panoramic views of the river from their home every day. The wide, silent waterway flowed south while barges ferried their cargo up and down the river when it was open. A variety of wildlife passed through their backyard: white-tailed deer, turkeys, foxes, coyotes, and multitudes of birds, including their favorites, bald eagles and red-tailed hawks. Sam had discovered several mountain biking trails in the area, giving him and Paco some much-needed exercise and recreation. Their daily runs alleviated the stress of Sam's detective work at the La Crosse Sheriff's Department.

Things at the law enforcement center on Vine Street had been slow throughout the summer. The investigative team was still gathering and organizing the evidence from the ball club killings, their last major case. Lori Lifto, the ax-wielding assassin of the victims, was dead, but the other perpetrators were alive and incarcerated in the La Crosse County jail until their trials began in the fall. In the months since the last sensational murder case, the investigative team had been busy with low-level crimes—cuffing and stuffing drug dealers, tracking down the perps of small-time robberies and house break-ins, and conducting interviews with victims of sexual assault and domestic abuse.

As Sam drove north on the Great River Road and rolled into Stoddard, the storm intensified. The wind and rain began to pick up, and lightning crashed every few seconds. The trees along the river road whipped in a circular pattern as if in a blender. Leaves and small twigs blew across the town streets, and the gusts of wind shook Sam's Jeep from side to side. Several cars pulled over on the shoulder of the road, waiting for the pounding rain and ferocious wind to ease up.

Sam parked along the Gas & Go building. When the storm showed no signs of abating, he pulled his hood over his head, opened the driver's door, and dashed inside the store. A young teenage girl looked up when he entered. She smiled tentatively as Sam pushed his hood back.

"Nasty out there?" she asked, taking in his brown curly hair and hazel eyes.

"Yeah, you might say that," Sam said, shaking the rain from his coat. It dripped on the floor and formed a messy puddle. "What's the forecast anyway?"

The girl shrugged her shoulders. "Don't know. I get off at midnight, so I hope it settles down before then. That's all I care about," she said, disinterested in the weather.

Sam walked to the freezer section and pulled out a carton of maple nut ice cream. On his way to the checkout counter, he grabbed a bunch of bananas and a gallon of milk. Sam set the items on the counter, paid for them, and waved to the clerk as he exited the store.

Back on the road, sheets of rain continued to beat against the Jeep. Sam drove slowly, inching his way south on the deserted river road highway, noticing the absence of traffic. Several miles out of town, his Jeep coughed and hiccuped. Sam eased the car over on the shoulder of the road, where the engine completely died. He tried to start it, but nothing happened. He groaned with frustration.

"What's goin' on?" he rasped to himself. "Did I run out of gas?" he asked himself. He slammed his fist into the steering wheel, then slumped back into his seat. "I don't believe this!"

After a few moments, he made a plan. He reached for his cell, then let out another frustrated groan. He'd left his phone on the kitchen counter. Now he had fewer options—none of them pleasant. Trying to hitch a ride back to Stoddard in a raging thunderstorm was not appealing. He was about a mile from home, an easy walking distance.

After a few more minutes, the rain seemed to ease up. "I guess I'll just have to walk back to the house," he said softly to himself. "Lez is never going to let me live this down."

Sam decided to leave the groceries in the Jeep. Leslie would have to bring him back with some gas anyway so he could get his vehicle off the road before morning. He opened the car door in disgust and stepped out into the storm, locking the Jeep with his key fob. The wind whipped rain into his face, blowing his hood back. He grabbed it angrily and pulled it back on his head, tying the strings firmly. Then he ducked his chin to his chest and started walking.

Sam had been in thunderstorms before while camping, hiking, and biking. Outside in the elements, the noise of the electricity passing through the atmosphere was deafening and scary. As he walked, his anxiety grew. He recalled an incident in Canada when his family was tenting, and the wind and rain were churning the woods around them. He'd been terrified. Those memories always created uneasy feelings when thunderstorms and high winds barreled across the land.

During the lightning flashes, he noticed the wide Mississippi River had taken on the look of a raging serpent, complete with whitecaps and sloshing waves. He was almost to the scenic turnout above Genoa when suddenly, without warning, a tree about a hundred feet in front of him was struck by a lightning bolt. The brilliance of the electrical current supercharged the atmosphere around the tree. The current traveled through the ground along the highway in a microsecond to where Sam was walking. He was blown off his feet and out of his shoes. He tumbled to the ground face down, unconscious, his heart thumping in an irregular rhythm. The rain continued falling for fifteen minutes until finally easing into a gentle shower. Sam lay on the side of the road oblivious to the raindrops that fell softly upon him.

2

Jim Higgins, chief investigator for the La Crosse Sheriff's Department, was just about to shut off his bedside lamp at eleven-thirty and snuggle up to his wife, Carol, when his cell buzzed on the nightstand.

"Now what?" he mumbled under his breath as he reached for the phone. "Higgins," he answered bluntly.

Carol stirred beside him and sat up. Jim leaned over and gently kissed her on the cheek. Her hair was mussed, and she wore a frown. He covered the phone with his hand as he continued to listen. Whispering to her, Jim said, "Go back to sleep. I have to go out on a call."

He focused his attention on the female voice coming over the phone. "Yes, Sheriff Turnmile. You need me at the Stoddard Gas & Go as soon as I can get there. I've got it, ma'am."

The sheriff's abrupt manner and rude voice grated on his nerves. He tempered his inclination to tell her that he wasn't some rookie. That he had over thirty-five years' experience on the force. That he had just about seen it all when it came to crime in the Coulee region. But he knew that would get him nowhere with the new sheriff, who saw everyone and everything as a direct assault on her authority and leadership.

Is she ever gonna change? Jim thought angrily, whipping off the quilt and setting his feet on the floor. *After four months on the job, she ought to be able to trust me by now,* he thought. An image of his friend, former Sheriff Davy Jones, made him sigh with regret. *Boy, I sure miss Davy.*

He focused on the voice coming over the phone as he sat on the edge of the bed.

"We're going to need the crime scene people here and at least one more detective. Right away! We need to get a leg up on this," the voice ordered. "You got that, Higgins?"

"I know the drill, ma'am. I'll be there in fifteen minutes," Jim said politely through gritted teeth.

"Good. See you in a few minutes," she answered. "Oh, by the way, the young cashier was critically wounded. She might not make it. If that's the case, then this whole deal becomes not only a robbery but also a murder. You got that, Higgins?"

"Got it. I'm on my way," Jim said, and he hung up before she could insult him again.

"I take it that was the infamous Sheriff Elaine Turnmile giving you orders and getting under your skin, messin' with your mind," Carol said from her side of the bed. She rolled over on her back and looked up at the ceiling.

"Don't even get me started, honey," Jim began. "Turnmile tests the boundaries of my conduct every single day. Sometimes I feel like I'd be better off in a deep, dark cave, somewhere far, far away from her. I don't need any more reminders about how rude and irritating she can be."

Carol cuddled up to his back and kissed his neck. "Poor baby!" she said teasingly.

Jim climbed out of bed and started getting dressed when the bedroom door creaked open.

Lillie, his eight-year-old daughter, walked into the room, squinting in the light of the lamp.

"What's up, toots?" Jim asked, taking a blue golf shirt out of his closet. "Did the thunder wake you up?" He slipped the shirt over his head.

Lillie remained silent. Her blonde curls tumbled over her shoulders in disarray, and Elsa, her favorite doll, hung limply under her arm.

"What's the matter? You need something?" Jim asked, slipping on a pair of blue jeans. A twinge of anxiety passed through him when she continued to stare him down. "Did you have a bad dream?"

"Sam's in trouble, Bapa," she said seriously.

"Oh, yeah? How do you know that?" Jim cringed since he knew the answer before asking the question. His daughter, Lillie, *knew* things. Not facts and information—although she knew plenty of mundane tidbits about history, music, science, and nature. No, Lillie had premonitions. She frequently *saw* events and predicted them before they happened. Jim and Carol were awed and, at times, terrified by the ramifications of their daughter's gift. It often made their lives complicated and fraught with emotional angst.

"Sam's hurt, and he's in big trouble," Lillie reiterated quietly. By this time, his daughter stood directly in front of Jim. He stopped pulling on his sock and looked into Lillie's azure blue eyes. *She's doing it again. Makin' another prediction,* he thought. His heartbeat cranked up a couple of notches.

"Okay. I'll check on Sam when I get to Stoddard," Jim said. "I'm sure he's at home—probably sleeping in his bed." He smiled weakly. "I have to roust him out anyway to go on this call with me, so don't worry, Lillie. I'll handle it."

Lillie looked at her dad with a wisdom beyond her young years. Jim almost felt foolish about his comments when she continued to stare at him with a penetrating gaze.

"You can try, Bapa, but he's not home. He's in the dirt," Lillie said.

At this statement, Carol sat up in bed and stared at her daughter. "Lillie, you know Daddy will do everything he can to make sure Sam is safe," she said, giving Jim a look out of the corner of her eye. "Won't you, honey?"

"Of course I will," Jim said resolutely. "Hey, I've gotta go." Kneeling in front of Lillie, he pecked her on the cheek. "You go back to bed. I'll check on Sam." He knew ignoring her prediction was the last and least effective of his choices.

"You have to find him first," she said cryptically. Lillie climbed into Jim's lap and threw her arms around his neck. "Can you do that, Bapa? Can you find Sam?" she asked, their blue eyes locking in a stare.

"I'll try," Jim said.

"Promise?"

"Absolutely. I always try to do my best." Jim felt like he was reporting to Sheriff Turnmile.

When did I lose control around here? he thought.

Lillie scooted across the bed and climbed in beside Carol, snuggling against her. Carol smiled and kissed the top of Lillie's head. Jim stood up and watched the two most important women in his life nestle together against the raging storm outside. He leaned down and kissed Carol and brushed Lillie's curls away from her face. She yawned and closed her eyes,

"Looks like we dodged that bullet," Jim whispered to Carol.

"Don't count on it, Bapa," Lillie said quietly from beneath the quilts.

3

By the time Jim arrived at the tiny village of Stoddard along the banks of the Mississippi River, the worst of the storm had passed, but the atmosphere at the Gas & Go convenience store was crackling with tension. Someone was loaded into an ambulance, and several police cars surrounded the convenience store, their blue and red lights flashing with synchronized regularity. Another officer was staking out the parking lot in yellow crime scene tape.

Sheriff Elaine Turnmile stood inside the entrance of the gas station directing the CSI crew, pointing and giving orders. She turned when Jim approached her. Her blonde hair, styled in a loose French knot, barely touched the crisp collar of her tan shirt. Her shirt was bedecked with award pins, and a small U.S. flag was attached to her collar. Her stout hips filled her trousers to capacity. She wore a pair of clunky, scuffed cowboy boots.

"What do we have?" Jim asked as he walked up to her. She scanned Jim's casual slacks and blue jeans with a scrutinizing eye.

"A robbery and a shooting," she snapped succinctly. "The young cashier—Vicki Invold—was unconscious when we arrived, so we weren't able to get any information from her. She's lost a lot of blood. Shot three times with what looks like a small caliber pistol at close range. Her vitals were very weak. I don't think she's going to survive."

"How much money was taken?" Jim asked, his face clouding with anxiety.

"Not sure yet, but they didn't get into the safe, so whatever they got was in the till—probably several hundred dollars. Not enough to shoot someone over. The idiot!" The perpetual frown she wore deepened. She turned when another police officer approached her and asked a question.

Jim took the opportunity to escape her critical eye.

He pulled a pair of blue paper booties over his shoes and snapped on a pair of latex gloves. Then he stepped into the crime scene. He walked up and down the store's aisles, peeked into the bathrooms, and then had brief conversations with some of the crime scene technicians. Behind the checkout counter where the young cashier had collapsed from the gunshots, the floor was stained with a large puddle of blood, and a few dollar bills lay scattered in the puddle and nearby on the floor—a somber reminder of the degenerates who resorted to violent crime for a few lousy bucks.

After looking everything over, Jim went outside and stood under the eave as a gentle rain fell softly on the roof. The air that had been stifling just an hour ago was sweet, washed clean of the dust and oppressive heat. Jim breathed deeply and thought about the young girl who now was fighting for her life—all over a few measly dollars. He grunted in frustration and took out his cell to dial Leslie Birkstein, one of his investigative officers.

"Chief. What's up?" Leslie answered. She sounded awake and alert.

"I'm lookin' for Sam. He around?" Jim asked. There was a moment of uncomfortable silence.

"Leslie? Is Sam there?"

"No, he's not, and I'm getting a little bit worried."

"What do you mean?" Jim asked. In his mind, Lillie's prediction of disaster came back to him. *He's in the dirt.* Jim recalled his daughter's words and the crisp, confident way she'd said them. Her disturbing prognostication stuck in his mind as he listened to Leslie explain.

"Well, he went to the Gas & Go in Stoddard about forty-five minutes ago to get some ice cream, and he hasn't come home yet. This storm has been awful, and I'm—"

"Leslie, I'm at the Gas & Go in Stoddard right now," Jim interrupted.

"You are?"

"Yeah. That's the reason I'm calling. There's been a robbery and shooting here. I wanted Sam to assist me. That's why I called. If he's not home yet, I must have just missed him," Jim said, giving her the sketchy details of the crime.

"A robbery? Well, I don't know where he could be. I think I'll take the Prius and drive along 35 and see if I can find him," Leslie suggested. "Maybe he ran out of gas or had car trouble or something."

"Yeah, you might want to do that. An hour to go get ice cream is a little too long," Jim said. "Let me know if I can help." He put his cell in his pocket, but the uneasiness about Sam had snaked into his mind, and his stomach did a flip-flop. He couldn't seem to shake off a feeling of dread.

He dialed another member of the investigative team, DeDe Deverioux, who lived on the south side of La Crosse near Gundersen Lutheran Hospital.

"This is DeDe," a voice said. Jim heard some rustling and mumbling in the background.

"DeDe, it's Jim. I need you down at the Gas & Go in Stoddard. There's been a shooting and robbery. How fast can you get here?" Jim asked brusquely.

"Be there in twenty minutes, Chief," she answered.

Jim hung up. He wandered back into the convenience store again, found the coffee pot, and poured himself a cup. A CSI tech, Carl Ettinger, looked up and caught his eye as Jim stood nearby watching him work. Carl had worked for the sheriff's department for a couple of years. A tall, slim athlete from eastern Minnesota, he had a reputation for being thorough and competent, but it was his ability to interpret the facts of a scene into a workable scenario that had caught the attention of Jim and the other investigators in the department. Like Sam Birkstein, he was an avid biker and loved working out in the bluff country around La Crosse. Now he looked up at Jim, his blue-gray eyes frank and curious.

"Anything interesting?" Jim asked, taking a sip of coffee.

"Too early to tell," Carl began, "but it looks like the clerk was shot at point blank range, three quick shots, all in the center of her chest. Some kind of small pistol. I don't think she's going to make it. Looks like she had a drink in her hand, and when she fell it spilled and mixed with her blood on the floor. The necklace she was wearing is interesting. Filigree heart. The chain is broken like someone ripped it from around her neck." Carl held up a clear plastic bag. Inside was a heart necklace on a silver chain. A few drops of blood lay at the bottom of the bag. The heart was open in the center, and a series of tiny diamonds were embedded in the swirling lacework around the edge of the heart. Jim took the bag and studied the jewelry. "Did you look at the CCTV tapes yet?" Carl asked.

"Nope, haven't seen them," Jim said, laying the bag back on the counter.

"There should be an image of whoever did this. That'll make your job a little easier," Carl said, holding up a piece of hair in tweezers. He meticulously placed the sample in another clear plastic bag.

"Any other thoughts?" Jim asked. Carl looked briefly in the space over Jim's shoulder where Elaine Turnmile was talking with another cop. After a moment, he shifted his gaze back to Jim.

"Yeah, why the hell did Davy have to go and die on us?" he asked, his tweezers poised in midair.

"I don't know, but I hear you," Jim said soberly.

Carl's expression of heartfelt sorrow was familiar to Jim. It helped to know that he wasn't the only one who missed Davy Jones, the laconic sheriff who'd led their department for over ten years.

Jim shook his head, the memories of the former sheriff and college buddy still fresh in his mind. He would never forget the day just four months ago when the harried sheriff stood up from his desk, walked out to talk to his secretary, and dropped on the floor from a massive coronary. He'd never recovered consciousness. Jim still caught himself reaching for the phone every now and then to discuss the details of a new case with him. And Carol was using every opportunity since Davy's sudden demise to watch their diet—even twisting Jim's arm into walking each evening along Chipmunk Coulee Road where they lived.

"Honey, I'm perfectly healthy," he said recently, defending his lifestyle on one of their lopes along the quiet road.

"Not good enough," Carol said, huffing. "Watching your diet and getting some exercise is a little extra insurance that you're going to be around to help raise our family."

"Now you're treading on God's territory," he said gruffly. "He's in charge of the time clock."

Carol stopped and turned to face him, her finger stabbing the air between them, her brown eyes flashing. "You always say something like that, so here's one for you. Isn't our body supposed to be a temple of the Lord? Whose job is it to keep the temple up to snuff, huh?" she said huffily.

Jim leaned over and kissed her cheek. "Point taken." He'd learned when to argue and when to acquiesce in the last five years of their marriage, the second one for both of them. A voice next to his ear made him jump. Startled, he turned.

"So, Lieutenant, what's your take on all of this?" Sheriff Turnmile asked. She propped her hands on her wide hips and waited, watching Jim with skepticism. Somehow she made Jim feel like a newbie, but he bit his tongue and swallowed the urge to level her with a critical barb. Instead, he took comfort in Eleanor Roosevelt's statement: "No one can make you feel inferior without your consent."

Despite his resentment at her rude behavior, Jim gazed calmly at

Turnmile and began. "I don't have a take yet, ma'am. I'm trying not to let my presuppositions cloud the actual evidence left at the scene, but if you want my opinion, I'd say off the top of my head that this was planned and carried out by an individual who, for some reason, panicked and ended up shooting the cashier. She may have resisted his demands for money, and he didn't know what to do about that. Or they got in some kind of verbal battle. Instead of ditching the robbery plan, he went through with it, shooting the girl to prevent her from calling the police. If that girl dies, this is gonna get a lot worse." His blue eyes searched the sheriff's face. Getting nothing but a blank stare, Jim had no idea what she was thinking. He decided to quit while he was ahead.

Turnmile looked at Jim with cool detachment. Without speaking a word, she suddenly spun around and walked deeper into the store toward the manager's office.

Carl, the CSI tech standing next to Jim and hearing his exchange with the sheriff, leaned toward Jim, studying the side of his face in the harsh fluorescent lighting. "Like I said, I miss Davy," he quipped sadly, watching the sheriff clomp toward the back of the store.

A few minutes later, Jim heard loud, argumentative voices coming from down the hallway. He walked that way until he came to the manager's office. Stopping in the doorway, he asked, "What's going on in here?"

Turnmile swiveled and faced him, her cheeks flushed pink, her eyes blazing with anger. "Apparently, someone disabled the security camera," the sheriff said. "The tapes only show customers who entered the store until ten-thirty this evening. After that, there are no recorded images." She let out a groan of frustration and blew a stray lock of hair out of her face. "Where the hell is the manager of this place? He better be able to explain this."

"He's in one of the squad cars outside," a police officer answered. "He's pretty shook up."

"So we have no images of the customers who were in the store leading up to the time of the robbery?" Jim asked.

The sheriff harrumphed. "That's right, Sherlock. None after ten-thirty," she said, her words dripping with sarcasm. "This is gonna be a real conundrum—a regular shit show." She turned sideways as she brushed past Jim and walked briskly out of the office, her bristling attitude on full display.

"Great. Just great," Jim said sourly, biting off his words. He turned to the officer who was scanning the video images. "Listen. Call the owner of Gas & Go. Get him out of bed if you have to," Jim ordered. "Find out how someone might have disabled the camera. We may be dealing with a perp who's very savvy in electronics or an employee who was involved in the planning and execution of the robbery."

"An inside job?" the officer asked, surprised.

"Possible," Jim answered bluntly.

"What about the lightning storm? Maybe it knocked out the security system somehow," the officer suggested.

"That's another possibility," Jim said.

"I'll get on it." The officer took out his cell phone and punched in a number.

Jim left the office and walked to the front of the store. His cell beeped in his pocket.

"Higgins."

There was a moment of silence, then a soft, muffled sob came over the phone. "Chief. It's Leslie. Sam was struck by lightning. Someone found him along the highway. I'm at Lutheran Hospital. He's still alive, but he's in trouble. Can you come?"

"What?" Jim gasped. "When did this happen?" A picture of Sam, healthy and vibrant, came into Jim's mind as if Sam himself had walked through the door.

"It must have happened about an hour ago. Can you come, Chief?"

"Yes, of course, Lez. I'll be there as soon as I can." Jim stared into space as Lillie's words pounded through his head. *Sam's hurt and he's in big trouble.* Once again his daughter's prediction preempted any knowledge Jim had of the perilous situation confronting one of his team members. All Jim could do now was hope and pray that Sam would live through the night.

4

DeDe Deverioux arrived at the convenience store fifteen minutes after midnight. She walked up next to Jim, eavesdropping on his conversation with Sheriff Turnmile.

"Sam was struck by lightning? When did this happen?" the sheriff asked. "What are the chances?" Her mouth hung open in astonishment as she tried to comprehend the news.

"What! What are you talking about? Did you say Sam was struck by lightning?" DeDe asked, alarmed at what she was hearing. Jim turned at the sound of her voice. The sheriff glared at DeDe as if the information was only for their ears, but DeDe stubbornly refused to back down, waiting for someone to explain.

"Leslie called me fifteen minutes ago," Jim began explaining. "Information is sketchy at this point, but apparently Sam was struck by lightning as he walked along the highway. Leslie asked me to come to the hospital. I'm leaving you here, DeDe, to pull the team together and finish up the collection of evidence. The manager has to be interviewed—"

"I've already done that," Turnmile rudely interrupted.

"DeDe will complete an interview with the manager at my request," Jim said sternly, his blue eyes flashing. "Interviews are crucial for getting a sense of what happened." He could envision an argument developing that he was sure would center around Turnmile's authority and chain of command. He held up his hand in a stop gesture. "Work with me, Elaine. I'm not asking you—I'm telling you—my team will be interviewing all store personnel who were on the scene during the shooting. End of discussion." *Sometimes the bullshit just has to end,* he thought.

Jim was surprised when the sheriff conceded without an argument. "Fine. Being thorough is better than being sloppy. Go for it," she finished as she stalked off toward her SUV.

DeDe laid her hand on Jim's arm. "You'll let me know about Sam?"

"Absolutely. You're in charge here, DeDe. I'll call as soon as I know something." Jim turned and walked briskly to his Suburban.

The hospital parking lot was almost deserted when Jim arrived just after one o'clock. He pulled his Suburban close to the ER into an empty spot, threw his sheriff's department sign on the dash, and jogged to the entrance.

The young lady at the lobby desk looked up when the door swished open.

"One of my officers was brought here an hour ago. He was struck by lightning. Sam Birkstein.

What room is he in?" Jim asked in rapid-fire style. He leaned over the counter as the girl quickly tapped the computer keys, grabbed a sticky note from the counter, and scribbled the room number on it. "Third floor, room 3875. Elevators are over there," she said, pointing behind her. "But visiting hours have ended, sir."

Jim ignored her. "One more thing. Vicki Invold is here somewhere. She was the victim of a shooting in Stoddard. I need to check on her, too."

Her eyes scanned Jim's civilian clothes, and she raised her eyebrows. "I'll need to see some identification, please." Jim huffed in frustration, then dug in his pocket and pulled out his police ID, which he showed her. "Thanks," she said.

After scanning the patient list on her computer, she informed Jim that Vicki Invold was still in surgery. "The surgical waiting area is right above us. Her number is 54908. You can keep up-to-date on her status through the monitor mounted on the wall," the girl informed him.

"Yes, I know how that works. Thanks," Jim said. He walked quickly to the elevator.

Stepping onto the third floor, Jim walked past the nurses' station and proceeded in the direction of Sam's room. A nurse intercepted him.

"Excuse me, sir. Visiting hours are over. Who are you here to see?" she asked.

Jim stopped and walked back to the station. He leaned over the counter and spoke in a low, intense voice as he flashed his ID at the nurse.

"Sam Birkstein is my partner at the sheriff's department. His wife, Leslie, called and asked me to come over. He was injured this evening, and it's really important that I talk to her."

"Let me check and see how Mr. Birkstein is doing now. He's been sedated and was sleeping fifteen minutes ago, but that may have changed," she said. She stepped from behind the counter and swished down the quiet hallway. In a few minutes she was back with Leslie.

"Hey, Chief. Thanks for coming," Leslie said, stepping into Jim's arms. After a brief hug, Jim pulled back, and their eyes met. He noticed Leslie's solemn stare, a stare that asked, "Is this really happening?"

"So what's the prognosis?" Jim asked, folding his arms across his chest. He scanned Leslie's face as he waited for her explanation.

"Well, it's pretty serious," Leslie began. She swallowed hard, but a sob escaped from her throat, and she began to cry. Jim waited patiently while she got herself together. She started again. "The officer on the scene told me that a tree was struck and exploded along the highway. They think that the lightning traveled through the ground to where Sam was walking on the side of the road," she said. "The ER doctor said that explains the burns on the bottoms of his feet and the redness that branched up his legs from the current—and his missing shoes."

Jim's heart broke for Leslie. He grabbed her hand and held it firmly. He knew from police training that lightning injuries were problematic and could affect a person for the rest of their life. "So, what other physical injuries does he have?" Jim asked.

"The doctors really aren't sure yet. He'll have a battery of tests tomorrow to assess the full extent of the damage," Leslie explained. "Right now they're just trying to stabilize him. They told me the intense heat of the lightning expanded his lungs and cracked some of his ribs. He may have some hearing loss, and his heart rate is irregular right now. That could be a permanent condition, or it may clear up on its own. They're trying to get that under control with medication. It's all damage control now." Leslie shook her head and brought her hand to her face, covering her eyes. Jim gave her space, knowing she was trying to be brave and still be realistic about her husband's injuries. "They'll have a nurse with him for the remainder of the night."

"Hey, you know we're all here for you," Jim said gently. "Sam's still alive, and that's the important thing right now. What about the psychological effects?" he asked.

"The doctor warned me that he may have some emotional ups and downs, and his behavior may change since the current basically fried his nerves. Loss of coordination and muscle pain are possible, too, but right now it's too soon to tell." Leslie stopped talking and looked down the hall. "This is so unbelievable," she whispered, and she started crying again. "All over a stupid carton of ice cream. Me and my dumb cravings."

After a moment, Jim asked, "Can I see him?"

"I guess so," Leslie said hesitantly. She checked with the nurse.

"Fifteen minutes max," the RN said with authority, looking over her reading glasses.

Leslie and Jim walked silently down the hall. When they entered the room, Jim was shocked at Sam's pallid appearance. He was as white as the sheet that covered him. Jim's eyes misted with tears as he watched Sam, silent and mute like a body in a coffin. That someone so athletic, intelligent, and engaging could be reduced to a silent, corpse-like figure left him speechless. An IV dripped into his muscular, tanned arm, and an EKG machine measured his pulse and blood pressure. The red numbers blipped irregularly across a small screen near the head of the bed. A nurse hovered in the background typing on a computer, keeping an eye on the machine's data.

Jim thought back to the first time he'd met Sam Birkstein. Breezing into the interview at the law enforcement center, his Hollywood good looks, slightly irreverent attitude toward life, and decent understanding of human nature had made a distinct impression on the interviewing committee. In addition, Sam had a quirky sense of humor—a jauntiness and cocky self-assurance. Underneath it all, Jim recognized Sam's deep desire to fight the cancer of crime that had penetrated all levels of society.

Sam's college record was impressive. He was obviously intelligent and hardworking. Jim sensed a toughness just below the surface despite Sam's innocent demeanor and protected, religious upbringing. Jim sensed Sam would be a tough investigator. He had the grit and determination of a junkyard dog defending his territory. Over the last five years, he had proven his mettle in a number of sticky situations. His drug arrests alone were enough to impress even the most severe critics of which there were several in the department, the most recent being Sheriff Elaine Turnmile. Much of the criticism centered around his outlandish wardrobe, which Sam claimed he needed for his undercover drug surveillance. And then there were his crazy theories about complicated crimes. Most of the time, however, his theories proved insightful and on target—much to the chagrin of his detractors.

Fighting back tears, Jim leaned over the bed and grabbed Sam's hand. To his surprise and Leslie's delight, Sam opened his eyes.

"Sam, it's Lez. I'm here, honey," she said gently, stroking his hair. She kissed him tenderly on the cheek as her eyes filled with tears.

Sam looked at them, dazed with confusion. A frown crinkled his forehead. "Where... am I?" The words seemed to stick in his throat.

"You're in the hospital," Leslie answered, her blue eyes studying his face. "You were struck by lightning. Do you remember anything?"

Sam shook his head. The motion was so slight that Leslie wondered if she'd really seen it.

"Don't remember... anything," Sam croaked. "Everything hurts. My feet." Sam turned his head, and his focus drifted to Jim standing along the opposite side of the bed. His eyes softened in recognition. "Chief?" he asked. "How come you're here?"

"Don't worry about that now," Jim said softly, purposely slowing down his speech. "Just rest. Go back to sleep."

Leslie laid her hand on Sam's chest. "I'll be right here, honey. All night. Don't worry," she said. Sam closed his eyes in exhaustion. Jim and Leslie exchanged a glance and stepped away from the bed.

"Do you want me to call someone to be with you tonight?" Jim asked. "I can sit with you for a while, but I've got this robbery—"

Leslie waved a hand in front of her. "I've already called my parents in Decorah. They're on their way. Sam's parents are driving from South Dakota, but it will take them until tomorrow evening to get here. The nurse is going to make a bed for me tonight in the recliner, but I need someone to check on Paco tomorrow morning. Can you do that?" Leslie asked. She dug in her purse and handed Jim her house key. Paco had served with Leslie in the U.S. Army, sniffing out IEDs in Iraq and Afghanistan. Although he was not an official canine cop, his escapades taking down perpetrators were well-known in the La Crosse law enforcement community.

"It's as good as done," Jim said, offering a tentative smile as he put the key in his pocket.

At that moment, someone knocked lightly on the door. Leslie and Jim looked up.

"Excuse me. Are you the wife of the patient, Sam Birkstein?" the young man asked.

Leslie nodded. "Yes, is there something you needed?" she asked.

"Well, no, not exactly," he said. He handed a plastic bag to Leslie. It was heavy and contained some awkward items. "These are some items we recovered from your husband when we picked him up along the road on Highway 35. The bag was left in the ER, so they told me to bring it up to his room."

"Thank you," Leslie said as she took the bag. The ambulance attendant turned and left. Curious, Leslie peeked into the bag and then sucked in a breath. "What in the world—? Where did this stuff come from?" she asked, turning to stare at Jim.

"What do you mean? What's in there?" Jim asked, bending over the bag. He saw money, quite a lot of it, and at the bottom of the bag was a small handgun—a nine-millimeter pistol, stainless steel with rosewood grips, and a pair of muddy, high-top boots.

Leslie started to reach into the bag, but Jim stopped her. "No. Don't touch anything," he warned, laying a hand on her arm. His mind was racing with the possibilities of this revelation. *It couldn't be,* he thought. "Does Sam own a small pistol like that?"

"Not that I'm aware of," she said. Then in a firmer voice, she said, "No, he doesn't have a pistol like that. He's just got his department-issued gun. I'd have known about it if he had something like that."

"Did he take cash to the store when he went this evening?" Jim asked.

"I don't know, but I doubt it. We don't use much cash; Sam usually just uses our debit card." Leslie paused. "What are you thinking, Chief?"

Jim continued firing questions. "What about those shit-kicker boots? He have anything like that?" Higgins's piercing blue eyes made Leslie squirm with discomfort. She'd seen that stare and heard his quick, intense questioning techniques many times during interrogations. Was the chief conducting an informal interrogation about Sam?

Leslie thought for a moment. "He's got a lot of weird shoes, but no, I'm sure he was wearing his running shoes—Nikes—they were by the door. They're always sitting there. That's where he parks them when he comes in the house from his runs. He slipped them on when he left the house to go to the store."

"You're sure about that?"

"Yes, I'm sure," Leslie answered, pulling her shoulders back and standing straighter.

"I don't like the way this whole thing is setting up around Sam."

"What thing?"

"The robbery and shooting at the Gas & Go," Jim said.

Leslie's eyes popped open in surprise. "Excuse me? You think Sam had something to do with the robbery and shooting at Stoddard?" The silence in the room seemed deafening until she finally found her voice again. "Chief, that's impossible! Sam would never do anything like that! How could you even think something—"

"Leslie, right now I don't know what to think, but you've got to admit, this doesn't look good for Sam. A gun, cash from an unknown source, and—"

"Wait. Those clothes in the corner of the room," she said as she walked over to a chair and picked up the clothing that Sam had been wearing when he was admitted to the emergency room. She spread the clothes on the end of the hospital bed. "These are the cutoffs and T-shirt he had on," she said as she fumbled in the shorts pocket and pulled out Sam's wallet and car keys, "but I've never seen this jacket before. When he left the house tonight, he was wearing an old, navy L.L. Bean rain jacket he's had ever since I've known him. Where did he get this ragged thing? And those rubber boots are not his," she said forcibly, pointing to the bag. "Where are the Nikes he was wearing?" Jim watched her carefully as she compared the clothing Sam had on when he left the house to the clothing lying on the end of the bed.

Leslie held up an oil-stained, tattered jean jacket that was missing two buttons. "I've never seen this before." Her eyes held a panicked look, like a kid caught in a lie. "What's going on, Chief?" she asked again.

Jim's stomach rolled. "I don't know, but this doesn't look good. This doesn't look good at all."

5

At three o'clock in the morning, Jim was sitting in the small chapel of the Gundersen Lutheran Hospital introducing himself to Harry and Julie Invold, parents of the young girl who had been shot at the Gas & Go convenience store. A young teenage boy and girl sat in a corner clutching hands, crying, and talking softly to each other.

"Can you tell me about your daughter's condition?" Jim asked gently once the introductions had been made. He noticed the mother's tear-stained face and the father's disbelieving stare. Their clothes were rumpled and disheveled; their expressions looked as if someone had slapped them across the face. A rosary was clasped in Julie's fist, the beads trailing into her lap.

Julie stared at Jim. He'd seen that look before, and he could almost read her thoughts. *I can't believe my child is probably going to die.* The incongruity of the situation struck Jim with a tremendous sense of sadness and defeat.

"She's not expected to live through the night," Julie whispered weakly. "Her injuries were too severe. They tried to patch her up, but—" She began crying again. "She lost a lot of blood. The priest just administered last rites, but they're still working on her."

"I understand. I'm so sorry," Jim said, and he meant it. Underneath his calm exterior, his anger was building. "I want you to know my staff will do everything we can to find this perpetrator and bring him to justice."

"What is this world coming to?" Harry asked hoarsely, staring at the wall. "My daughter was only nineteen years old. She had her whole life ahead of her. She wanted to be a nurse." His voice trailed off. Jim noticed tears glistening in Harry's eyes, his jaw rippling with pent-up emotion. At that moment, Jim knew that any words of comfort he could offer would be like skipping a stone over the surface of a pond. Instead, he asked, "Did you know of anyone who would want to harm your daughter?"

Julie and Harry exchanged a perceptive glance. An awkward silence ensued.

"You tell him, Harry," Julie said despondently.

Harry's face lit up with anger, the emotion carving out a rough visage. "Vicki had a loser boyfriend a couple of years back, but she finally got rid of him. We hoped that part of her life was finally over."

"How long ago was this?" Jim asked, listening carefully to the information while jotting notes in his memo pad.

"Two years ago. She had a real nice guy now, BJ LaPointe," Harry said, the faraway look spreading over his face again. He pointed to the corner where the two kids were hunched together. "He's over there in the corner with our other daughter. He's a nice guy," he whispered.

Jim looked down at his notebook and added a few details. "What was this old boyfriend's name?"

"Devon something," Harry said. "Do you remember, hon?" He looked at his grief-stricken wife.

She turned to Jim and said, "Devon Williams. That was his name."

"Is he still in the area?" Jim asked.

Harry shook his head. "I don't know," he said, shrugging his shoulders, but underneath he was smoldering with unresolved emotion. Jim didn't want to think about the anger these parents would feel in the coming months.

"Did you have a problem with him?" Jim asked, noticing Harry's angry disposition.

"Well, Lieutenant, how would you feel if your seventeen-year-old daughter was dating some twenty-three-year-old dude who doesn't even have the balls to come up to the door of your house and introduce himself?" By now, Harry's eyes were little black, glittering embers. "Most guys over twenty are sexually experienced, and a young, naive girl wouldn't have a chance of keeping her virginity intact with somebody like that."

Julie stared at her husband, shocked at his attitude. "Harry! That's kinda judgmental, don't you think?"

"Our daughter is dying from multiple gunshot wounds, and all you can say is I'm being judgmental! Get real!" Harry snarled.

Jim held up his hand, attempting to fend off a domestic dispute. "I get it, Harry, I really do. I've got four kids—two daughters. I understand where you're coming from."

Jim tried to fast forward to the time when Lillie would begin dating, but somehow his mind refused to go there. Still, if some older guy came snooping around Lillie when she was only seventeen, Jim knew where he'd be—he could see himself on the front porch with his 30-06 loaded and ready. His older daughter, Sara, had been abducted a few years back, and the torment and anguish from that experience still haunted her and cast a long shadow on her relationships with men. Jim had walked the line for her in a gravel quarry down in Vernon County, where he'd been shot up in the process. He'd do the same thing again if anyone threatened any of his children.

"What's this Devon look like? Can you give me a physical description?" Jim asked.

Harry said, "We don't really know. We never actually met the guy. Sorry."

Jim began explaining the dire circumstances surrounding the

shooting of their daughter. "We have a problem. The closed-circuit TV cameras at the gas station were not working during the robbery, so we have no images of who might have done this. We really need to find anyone in the vicinity of the gas station during the robbery, someone who might have seen the perpetrator, so if you think of anything later, or hear something—anything—here's my card. Please call."

Julie took the card. "Sure, we can do that," she said sadly.

Jim got up from his seat, briefly shook hands with the young girl's parents, and expressed his condolences again. Then he turned and left.

When he reached the hospital lobby, he sat on one of the couches and dialed DeDe Deverioux. He noted the time—three-thirty in the morning. His eyes watered as he stifled a yawn. He leaned back on the couch feeling like he could sleep on his feet if he had to.

"Chief, what's up?" DeDe asked. "Any news about Sam?"

"I've seen him and talked with Leslie. He's hurtin', but something weird is going on," Jim began.

"What do you mean? Are you talking about Sam's injuries?"

"No, not really. His injuries are typical of a lightning victim—disorientation, muscular pain, burns, and an irregular heartbeat. He has a few cracked ribs and some lesions on his legs where the current traveled through his system." There was a significant pause. "No, I'm talking about something else," he said. Jim began to tell DeDe about the strange items in the bag: the money, the gun, and the clothing that Sam was wearing when he was transported to the hospital.

"That is weird, Chief," DeDe said when he was done explaining the circumstances.

"Have they determined how much money was taken during the robbery yet?" Jim asked.

"There were several thousand dollars in the safe, which is all still there. The manager estimated that the perp got about twenty-two hundred dollars at the most," DeDe said. "But, getting back to Sam. You don't seriously believe Sam had anything to do with this robbery and shooting, do you, Chief?"

"No. I don't believe Sam would do something like that. It goes against everything he believes as a cop and what he was taught as a child." Jim thought about one of his favorite Bible verses: "Train up a child in the way he should go, and when he is old, he'll not depart from it." Then he continued, "But the money, the clothes, the gun, and his missing jacket and shoes seem to paint him as a prime suspect in the robbery. Somehow, whoever did this must have found Sam lying by the side of the road after the heist and decided to use the situation to his advantage. When he saw Sam, he stopped and exchanged some articles of Sam's clothing with his own and then planted some money and a gun under him when he was unconscious. He's being framed." There was an intense moment of silence.

"Is that your theory, sir?" asked DeDe cautiously.

"Well, we don't have Sam to help us build a premise for the crime, so right now, yes, that's my theory... for the moment," Jim said stubbornly. "What other theory explains the circumstances Sam is in?" More silence. After a few uncomfortable moments, Jim asked, "So what evidence did the CSI people find at the scene?"

"Hair in and around the vicinity of the cash register, a broken heart necklace, some pieces of dried material that Carl thinks might be some type of animal manure—probably from a pair of boots—and a few dollars from the till that fell on the floor. The cash in the register was gone except for the coins. And there was considerable blood from the victim, of course."

"What about your interview with the store manager?" Jim asked.

"He was shook up, sir," DeDe continued. "I find it hard to believe he's involved in any way with this robbery. He said he was about to go home and lock up when a couple of people came in the store during the storm. He looked briefly at the images on the CCTV camera but then went back to his work when everything seemed normal. When I showed him a photo of Sam from Facebook, he was adamant he hadn't seen him in the store last night, but he wouldn't have because the camera quit working by ten-thirty, at least half an hour before Sam was in the store. He only noticed one other kid come in, but he said there were probably more customers he didn't notice. When the storm hit, they briefly lost power for a minute or two. He continued preparing his order of supplies he needed the next day when the power came back on, and then he sent his report to the owner in La Crosse via email. Apparently, he didn't notice that the cameras in the store weren't working."

"What about the shooting and robbery? What did he tell you about that?" Jim asked impatiently.

"He said he was sitting at his computer when he heard a customer speaking rather loudly. He was about to get up and investigate when he heard the three gunshots. He hesitated going out to the front of the store. Instead, he stayed in his office and called 911. He thinks he waited a couple of minutes at the most, and then he ran out front and tried to help Vicki. In the meantime, while he was in his office, the perpetrator hightailed it outta there. The manager said one interesting thing. He didn't see or hear a car leave the parking lot, but he thinks whoever robbed the store might have been on foot or parked his car some distance away—maybe a few blocks away. Anyway, his impression was that the robber escaped on foot."

"Okay. We need to establish a timeline. That could be crucial in proving Sam's innocence," Jim commented, but something about the manager's account didn't sit right with Jim. He knew that frequently, the time that passed during a crime could be wildly inaccurate according to those who witnessed the crime. People often thought more time had elapsed during the crime, or in the heat of the moment, time seemed to stand still. So when the manager said he waited a few minutes before going out to the front of the store, in reality, it could have been seconds. "We need to interview all the people who live in close proximity to the store. Stoddard's not that big. I don't care if we have to canvas the whole community. Someone may have seen something. That's the first thing we need to do."

"The Stoddard police are out patrolling the city, but they haven't found anyone wandering around," DeDe said. "I sent some of our people out as well. Getting back to Sam, sir. I understand your concerns, but what proof do you really have?" She was still trying to wrap her head around Jim's theory of Sam's involvement in the robbery and shooting.

"Well, you'd be surprised. I am in possession of evidence that looks suspicious at the least and downright incriminating at its worst." Jim thought about the bag that held the money, gun, and shoes. "His rain jacket and Nike running shoes that he was wearing when he went to the store are missing. They may be at the scene of the lightning strike, and no one noticed them, but I doubt it. His Nike shoes were replaced with a pair of rubber boots, and his rain jacket was exchanged for an old jean jacket. And then there's the money and pistol. Until I have an interview with Sam and establish his whereabouts at the time of the robbery and shooting, I have to draw some conclusions about the items that the ambulance attendant gave Leslie at the hospital. At the very least, I will be recommending Sam hire a good attorney. He'll probably need one. Right now, Sam's our only suspect… and there's something else."

"What's that, Chief?" DeDe asked, her sense of horror growing.

"Frequently, lightning victims have temporary memory loss. Sometimes it's permanent. So Sam may not even remember what he was doing before he was struck," Jim said, "but I have to interview him as if he were a suspect—because he is." He waited. Finally, DeDe responded.

"I'm beginning to see why you're worried," she said softly.

FRIDAY, AUGUST 29

TEAMWORK CAUSES COMMON PEOPLE
TO ACHIEVE UNCOMMON RESULTS.

6

Lila LaPointe grabbed the edge of the duvet and pulled it back in one sweeping motion, exposing her sleeping son, BJ, still lying in bed at seven-thirty in the morning.

"Mom! What the hell are you doing?" he said angrily, grabbing the duvet and pulling it back over his head with an indignant jerk.

"You need to be to work in half an hour. I've called you at least four times. You need to get up and get ready," Lila said, her voice barely civil behind her outrage. She was sure this confrontation would escalate into another obnoxious row with her son. *How many fights have we had this month?* She'd lost track.

"Leave me alone," BJ mumbled, his voice muffled by the blanket over his head. Her son's response angered Lila even more. She poked the body beneath the blanket. *Poke, poke, poke.*

"Knock it off, Mom."

Lila quit poking and tipped her head back, staring at the ceiling. Tears formed in the corners of her eyes. She blinked them back and continued her harangue. "Listen, young man. You are going to work today if I have to drag your ever-lovin' little ass across the floor and into the car. You need to get up right now!" she yelled.

Suddenly the covers flew back, and BJ jumped out of bed, practically knocking her on the floor. "I'm up! Are you satisfied now?" he said, spittle flying. He was red in the face, and his expression was dark with exasperation. "Why can't you leave me alone?"

Instead of backing up a couple of steps, Lila leaned in, crowding BJ against the mattress. Her index finger tapped her son's chest as she talked.

"I'll tell you why. Because I'm your mother, and I'm going to ride your tail until you understand that getting to work on time is important. Your dad wasn't late one day in the twenty years he worked at Trane. Being on time is important. That's why," Lila said in an ominous tone.

She suddenly felt embarrassed as her eyes swept over BJ's half-naked body. She stepped back as she scanned her son's physique. He'd filled out over the summer. His chest was broad and deep, his arms muscled and strong. But it was the masculine line of his jaw, the whiskered face, the deep determination of his eyes that unsettled her. He looked just like Jack, her deceased husband. Jack hadn't been dead more than three months, and here she was looking at a replica of her former husband in his prime. BJ wasn't a kid anymore—he was a man. The realization left her with a deep, disturbing feeling.

She remembered something she'd read somewhere: "If what you're doing isn't working, stop doing it and do something else." The advice seemed apropos to this moment in time. She took a deep breath and, in a gentler voice, said, "Listen, I don't want to fight anymore. You still live under my roof. And as long as you do, I expect you to work at something, get in at a decent hour, and be respectful of the way I run my home."

She paused, expecting him to fire another verbal salvo igniting the whole ugly scene all over again. They couldn't seem to get by their arguments and disagreements. The hostility continued to loop over and around into the same fight without an ending. But she was surprised when BJ stayed silent. Lila tilted her head, taken aback by his sudden mute demeanor. She looked into his eyes and noticed her son's blank stare.

"Is that clear? Do you get what I'm telling you?" she asked, pushing a stray strand of hair away from her forehead. BJ stared into space. Gradually he focused his attention back on his mother, and his body coiled with tension. "By the way, where were you last night until three o'clock in the morning?"

Her son's shoulders slumped, and the hostility he'd displayed just a minute ago deflated like a limp sail without wind. Suddenly he looked like a teenager again. There was a sadness in his eyes that Lila hadn't seen before.

"Something awful's happened, Mom," he sputtered. "Something really awful."

Lila's eyes widened, and she felt a catch in her throat. She found her voice and asked, "What? What's happened?"

"Vicki was shot and killed in a robbery at Gas & Go last night down in Stoddard," BJ said, his voice cracking with emotion. "She's dead, Mom."

Lila stood transfixed, not quite comprehending what he'd said. When she failed to respond, BJ's shoulders began to shake, and he covered his face with his large hands and sobbed softly. Lila wrapped her arms around her son as he continued to sob into her shoulder. "Oh, my darling. How did this happen?" she whispered.

7

On Friday morning, Donavon "Doc" Wycowski was busy sanding some pine boards that were lying across a couple of sawhorses. He leaned over the lumber and put some muscle into it, creating a cloud of sawdust. Doc was working on some fascia boards for a houseboat undergoing restoration at Stoddard Boat and Marine. After half an hour, he stopped sanding and looked at the dark waters of the Mississippi River in the distance, sparkling in the sunshine. He'd love to be out on the water today catching a mess of walleyes. He spent a few moments daydreaming. Was there anywhere in the world as beautiful as the Mississippi? Well, not to him. At this crossroads in his life, the river was what got him through each day.

Doc thought of the friends who'd given him advice during his recent trials and troubles. Just take one day at a time. The journey of a lifetime starts with one step. Yada, yada, yada. All the platitudes that he had previously scoffed at and fundamentally rejected as being trite and overused had now become his mantras. He felt the eyes of his boss on his back, and he turned away from his daydream of the river and went back to sanding boards. When he looked up, Doogie Baumgartner, the proprietor of Stoddard Boat and Marine, was staring at him.

Doc—as the guys at work called him—pushed the electric sander across the weathered wood. The fine sawdust floated in the air, landing on his arms and clothing. At one time in his life he would have considered this kind of work simpleminded monotony—the kind of work that lowlifes did. Now his hands were calloused, and his nails were chipped, but deep inside he felt an enormous pride in what he accomplished every day using just his hands and a few simple tools. He wore casual clothes—a T-shirt, a pair of khaki shorts, and boat shoes—a far cry from the thousand-dollar suits he'd worn previously as a professional plastic surgeon. But that seemed like eons ago, before his world had disintegrated.

He ended up in the tiny river village of Stoddard six months ago, hungry, looking for work, living out of a pup tent he'd snaked out of a dumpster. He had no money to pay for a campsite in a campground, so he'd developed a routine of pitching the tent at the edge of a field toward dusk and leaving early in the morning before anyone discovered him and kicked him off their land or began to ask questions. Walking through the small river town of Stoddard six months ago, he came upon a Help Wanted sign in the boat restoration office window. He went in, applied, and landed a job.

Ernest Baumgartner, aka Doogie, the owner of the boat refurbishing business, watched him carefully during the job interview. The application hung limply from Doogie's hand as he listened to Doc fruitlessly trying to explain his skill set. The proprietor's kind, brown eyes were filled with questions. Despite his rugged work clothes, Doogie had a confident air about him. He wasn't someone you could easily bullshit. He'd been around the block, dealt the hard blows that life often handed out, and he was still standing. During the interview, Doc was making his own assessments of Doogie. He had always been impressed by credentials, education, and possessions, but suddenly he was beginning to understand that those things did not necessarily make a man. Rather, a man's beliefs and values made the man.

"It says on your application that you've used precision tools," Doogie said, pointing to the paper with a thick, greasy finger. Doc noticed Doogie's dingy, wife-beater tank top beneath the Oshkosh bib overalls, all overlaid with a raggedy, flannel long-sleeved shirt that hung open over his massive, hairy chest. If he was trying to impress someone with the success of his boat refurbishing business, it wasn't working.

Doc made a wry face. "I used a lot of specialized tools in another line of work in my previous life," he tried to explain. Doogie didn't look impressed or convinced.

"So, when did you switch over to carpentry tools?" Doogie asked, his hazel eyes full of doubt. He'd heard a lot of down-and-out stories in his day, but this guy's story was pretty unbelievable. He leaned against the counter of the office watching Doc's face, taking his measure.

"I've always messed around in my garage with woodworking stuff," Doc explained. "My dad was a natural, and he taught me pretty much everything I know."

Doogie paused for a long minute having a debate with himself as he studied the man standing in front of him. He tilted his head and squinted a little bit, then crossed his arms across his huge chest. With lightning speed, Doogie made a decision he hoped he wouldn't regret.

"Okay. You're hired," Doogie said, standing up straight. "We'll see how things go. I'll pay you fifteen dollars per hour, no benefits, and after six months we'll talk about a raise—if you last that long. By the way, you got an address?" His eyebrows crinkled above his brown eyes like two caterpillars arching their backs.

"Not yet. I'm still trying to find somewhere to stay." Doc said, his gaze steady and calm.

"Old lady McCann has a small cabin behind her house over on Lake Road that's empty. You might need to clean it up, but she'll rent it to you if I give her a call. You want me to do that?" Doogie asked, tipping his head and looking at Doc through squinted eyes.

"That'd be great. Thanks," Doc said, averting his gaze when his boss continued to stare at him. Somehow, Doogie couldn't quite get a handle on this guy. He'd had plenty of dead-end employees who worked for a week and then disappeared. Finding people willing to work with their hands nowadays was almost impossible. It seemed like nobody wanted a job.

He looked Doc over again—dark hair, a firm, unlined face with deep brown eyes, and a medium build with a hint of untapped physical strength beneath his exterior. *Something's off,* Doogie thought. Was the guy normally that shy? Was he afraid of something? Where'd he come from? Was he on the run from the law? Nothing on his application gave the slightest hint of his past other than his previous occupation, which seemed pretty incredible. Plastic surgeon? Highly doubtful. Somehow this newest employee reminded Doogie of Dr. Richard Kimble, the star of the TV show *The Fugitive* back in the seventies. *Jeez, I hope he didn't kill someone,* he thought.

Throughout Friday afternoon, Doc continued cutting and sanding the intricate wood pieces that would make up the refurbished interior of the 1971 Nautaline houseboat cruiser. The boat was old by anyone's standards but a classic just the same. When the restoration was complete, it would be a fine river-worthy vessel. Doc even thought of trading his work on it for a chance to purchase it. Living on a houseboat for six months of the year would be an interesting life.

At the end of the workday, around five o'clock, Doc punched out and walked slowly down Prairie Edge Avenue to his small cabin on Lake Road. He breathed deeply of the towering pines that lined the road to the river. The sharp scent of the evergreens made his eyes mist with unexpected tears. Memories of his idyllic summers spent in a palatial log home in Fish Creek up in Door County, Wisconsin, came back to him with surprising clarity.

A painted turtle crossed the road in front of him and humped lazily into the tall foxtail growing along the edge of the road. Black-eyed Susans and Queen Anne's lace bloomed in profusion in the nearby fields. Doc was tempted to pick some flowers for Mrs. McCann, but he sensed the old lady would probably belittle him, take another puff on her cigarette, and scrutinize him with those hard, frosty eyes. He wasn't in the mood for any more suspicion, so he passed up the flowers and continued to walk.

In the quiet cul-de-sac at the end of the road where his cabin was located, he noticed a huge bald eagle sitting on a branch about ten feet off the ground in a sturdy oak. Doc stopped a moment taking in the sunshine that was sifting softly through the trees. As his eyes moved upward to the sky overhead, he spotted the eagle's mate, a smaller male, about ten feet higher in the same tree. At some invisible signal, the two eagles lifted off their perches and flew out over the slough, their flight a coordinated ballet of grace and majesty.

Doc turned and strolled down the narrow footpath to his cabin. He thought about the evening hours ahead of him. No television. No computer. No internet. No cell phone. Just time and the flowing current of the big river. Maybe he'd take the boat out and catch a mess of crappies for supper. Or maybe he'd just have a bologna sandwich and a beer and sit on the bench under the massive white pine tree near shore and take in the gorgeous scenery. The blue bluffs and deep silence of the river had a mesmerizing beauty when the sun set in the west. They filled his heart with a peace he couldn't seem to find anywhere else. Either way, he planned to leave the problems of the past behind him. But getting rid of the dull ache of loneliness that welled up in his chest every evening was easier said than done. *Good luck with that,* he thought.

8

Jim woke up about eight-thirty Friday morning. He sat up in bed suddenly, trying to get his bearings. Then the gruesome events of the previous evening flooded back into his brain. He lay down again and listened to the morning sounds filtering into the dark bedroom—the gentle cooing of doves on the roof of his pole shed, the rumble of Lillie's and Henri's feet on the wooden floors as they chased each other through the house, and the intermittent buzz of a chain saw from his neighbor to the south on Chipmunk Coulee Road.

He got up and took a shower. Walking into the bedroom with a towel wrapped around his waist, he raised the blinds on the big, low window and peered out at the sunshine cutting brilliant paths through the massive oaks and maples onto the thick carpet of grass in his expansive backyard. Even with all the natural beauty around him, he could sense the shadow of depression hovering at the edges of his consciousness.

In April, after the ball club killings, he'd suffered a substantial bout of despondency. This bone-deep melancholy was "the direct result of mental and emotional trauma suffered from confronting death and fighting nefarious criminals and perpetrators," according to Vivian Jensen, Carol's psychologist sister, who ran a counseling service in Holmen. It had taken him a couple of months of desk duty, a prescription for Zoloft, extensive discussions with Vivian and his pastor, and a long, lazy vacation with Carol in Charleston, South Carolina, to regain his sense of health and equilibrium.

Toweling off, he stood in front of the closet viewing his considerable clothing collection. He finally selected a pair of navy dress slacks, a pink shirt in a Herringbone pattern topped with a gray worsted wool sport coat he'd bought in Paris on his honeymoon. A Tommy Hilfiger checkered tie in gray, navy, and light blue set off the muted colors of the shirt and jacket.

Walking into the sunny kitchen, he poured himself a cup of strong coffee and whipped out a cast iron frying pan. He scrambled two eggs and popped two slices of whole wheat bread into the toaster. He had his head crammed into the depths of the refrigerator, searching for his favorite raspberry jam, when a voice interrupted him.

"Daddy!" Henri shouted. He tackled Jim's legs from behind, which pushed him farther into the depths of the fridge.

"Hey, you little bruiser. Whatcha doin'?" Jim grabbed the jam and set it on the counter. Then he turned around and held out his arms. Henri jumped into them. The little tot grasped Jim's neck in a bear hug, and his brown eyes sparkled as he bubbled with the latest news.

"Daddy, I got a new backpack for school. Wanna see it?" the little tyke asked.

"Sure, you go get it and bring it out here," Jim said. Henri got down and ran from the room while Jim dished up his eggs and toast and sat down at the dining room table. Piano music wafted down the hall from Lillie's bedroom. Mozart. Jim smiled at his ability to identify the composer of the pieces Lillie was playing these days. She was advancing rapidly in her piano performance and music composition, thanks to the guidance and work of Sister Maria at Viterbo University in La Crosse.

While he ate breakfast and drank his coffee, he marveled at the time that had elapsed—almost five years since the surprise pregnancy that had produced their son. Now Henri was preparing for kindergarten at St. Ignatius Catholic School in Genoa, just five miles down the Great River Road.

"What time did you get in?" Carol asked, bending down to kiss Jim's cheek.

"About four," Jim said. "The young girl who was shot at the gas station died this morning."

"I can't imagine," Carol whispered, staring absentmindedly into space. "Are you going into the office?"

"Only after I check on Paco and then on Sam. If I leave in the next half hour, I should get to the office by eleven."

"Why don't you bring Paco here?" She paused and thought. "Or better yet, I could go down and get Paco and bring him here until Sam and Leslie get home," Carol suggested.

"You sure you're ready for that? That dog is a handful," Jim said. His eyebrows puckered in a frown as he spread raspberry jam on his toast.

"The kids love Paco, Jim. Lillie can take him down by the creek. It's the least we can do to help out, don't you think?" Carol sat across from Jim at the table and made little circles with her finger on the tabletop. When Jim didn't respond, she looked up at him and covered his hand with hers.

"Okay, if you say so," Jim said. "But I think we'll take him home tonight. He's not very comfortable out of his element. He's connected to Leslie and Sam at the hip."

Once they'd made a plan and Jim handed off Leslie's house keys to Carol, he drove up the Great River Road and stopped briefly at the site of the lightning strike. The tree that had been struck in the storm was being cleaned up by county highway workers. Nothing that seemed pertinent to the investigation stood out, so he got back in his Suburban and headed into La Crosse, stopping at Gundersen Lutheran Hospital to check on Sam.

At the nurse's station on the hospital's third floor, Jim was informed that Sam was undergoing tests and wouldn't be back in his room until noon. Jim left and drove to the law enforcement center on Vine Street. He pushed through some paperwork he'd put off, answered multiple phone calls from law enforcement personnel who were concerned about Sam's condition, and fended off reporters who were trying to piece together the robbery and murder. Jim stayed busy replying to numerous emails and texts about current and previous cases that demanded his attention. Beneath all the activity, he kept thinking, *How did Sam get himself in this predicament?*

9

While Jim worked in his office Friday morning, DeDe Deverioux and Paul Saner, detectives on Higgins's team, plodded door-to-door throughout the neighborhood near the Stoddard Gas & Go. The air was brisk—cool with brilliant sunshine and a cloudless sky. Neighbors were outside picking up twigs and branches, and one resident down the street was running his chain saw cutting up a birch tree that had blown over in the intense storm the previous evening. The streets were still damp from the torrential rains. Cars sloshed through potholes that were filled to the brim with rainwater.

Knocking on the doors of the neighborhood homes, DeDe and Paul conversed with residents near the vicinity of the gas station. Many were not aware of the robbery and shooting, and they were shocked and saddened when the two detectives shared the news.

"These things just don't happen in our little town," Mrs. Marge Litchfield said emphatically. Her white hair was piled on her head in a compact beehive style. She wore a blue print house dress peppered with red roses. A pair of white fuzzy slippers decorated her tiny feet, and an apron with embroidered pockets was tied around her ample waist. "We love our little community. I've lived here all my life. We're not violent people." Her eyes flicked back and forth between DeDe and Paul.

"I believe you, ma'am," Paul said politely. "My question is whether you saw anyone walking along the street last night around eleven o'clock? Did you notice a strange vehicle parked near here about that time?"

"No, I was in bed the whole time," she said. "I took my hearing aids out when I went to bed, so I didn't even hear the storm."

Paul nodded. "I understand. Here's our card if you remember something later. Thank you." Mrs. Litchfield shook her head sadly, took the card, and quietly closed the door.

Birch Street was lined with majestic oaks and a few enormous white pines but not many birches. The sidewalks were a bit crooked, some corners of the slabs had heaved up due to frost, and several were cracked and needed replacement. The two detectives continued their rounds. Higgins had been adamant that they knock on the door of every home within a three-block radius of the gas station or the whole village if they had to, following up on any leads that might give them information about the crime, especially anyone who had been to the gas station about eleven o'clock that evening.

"Well, we've covered twelve houses so far," DeDe said, referring to the village map she'd copied off Google Earth. She checked off Mrs. Litchfield, then wiggled her toes crammed into a pair of low pumps. *I should have opted for my Skechers running shoes this morning,* she thought. "At least it's not a hundred degrees today. It's actually a beautiful day, but..." DeDe said, her voice trailing off in a wistful sigh.

"Yeah. I know. The death of that young cashier makes this whole thing a lot more disturbing,"

Paul said sadly. "Now we're looking for a killer, not just a perp who robbed a gas station and shot the attendant. And then there's Sam. You heard any updates this morning?"

"I talked to Leslie about seven-thirty this morning. He's going to have a bunch of tests today. I'll talk to her later and let you know what I find out."

It was ten o'clock. They'd almost finished canvassing the designated area when they knocked on the door of a Victorian mansion set back from the road and surrounded by huge mature trees. Getting no answer at the front door, they stepped off the porch just as the owner came around the corner of the house to the front yard. He had been working up a sweat gathering stray branches that had blown off the trees during the storm. He threw the branches into a cart pulled by a John Deere UTV. His face was red with exertion, and his T-shirt was sweat-stained under the arms. His irritation with the mess in his yard was obvious in his expression. As Paul and DeDe approached him, the middle-aged man shut off the UTV watching them carefully, his hazel eyes alert under the bill of a Milwaukee Brewers baseball cap. They introduced themselves and showed him their IDs. He identified himself as Seth O'Connor.

"I heard about the robbery on the early news this morning," he said, squinting into the sun. "Terrible thing. That girl died, huh?"

"I'm afraid so," DeDe said. "It is a terrible thing. That's why we need everyone's help. Did you see or hear anything out of the ordinary last night between ten and twelve?"

The man continued to study her, then looked at Paul, dismissing DeDe's presence with a glance and ignoring her question. *Is it because I'm a woman or because I'm Black or because I'm a Black woman?* she thought. *Go figure.*

"I didn't notice anything last night, but last week a guy in an old blue Dodge pickup was hanging around Zabolio's Bait and Tackle store down by the public boat ramp. A bunch of us guys go there every morning for coffee, and he's been coming in every morning for worms and minnows. Quiet, but kinda different. Know what I mean?" Mr. O'Connor asked, tilting his head to one side.

"Not really," Paul said, wondering what he meant by the phrase "kinda different." "Can you describe him? Do you know his name?"

"Medium height and build but athletic, seemed kinda down on his luck, wouldn't tell anyone where he was from. But now, when

I think about it, he's probably just some dude who's here on a fishing vacation and is renting a cabin for a week." Seth shrugged nonchalantly and said, "I'm sure he's harmless. It wouldn't be fair to suspect him of a robbery and a murder, now would it?"

"Well, you're not accusing him of anything. He's not a local, but he may have seen something that the locals didn't notice," DeDe said.

"Hadn't thought about that," Seth said, giving DeDe a second look as if he'd just noticed her. "You could ask at the bait shop. Curt could probably tell you more about him," he said.

"We'll do that. Thanks," Paul said. They went down to the bait shop and talked to the owner, Curt Zabolio.

"Seth O'Connor mentioned a guy who was in your store last week buying bait every day. He wasn't a local. Can you tell us about him?" DeDe asked after they'd introduced themselves.

"It's best not to believe everything Seth O'Connor tells you. He's kind of a windbag. The guy he's talking about was just a fisherman from Illinois. Paid cash for his bait, was quiet, seemed to like his privacy. Why you askin'?"

"Did you hear about the robbery and shooting at the Gas & Go?" Paul asked.

"Yeah. What's up with that?" Curt said. The bait tank bubbled quietly next to the counter, the little fingerling fish moving languidly in the water.

"We're just trying to find out if there were any visitors in Stoddard in the last week or so," DeDe said. She immediately noticed his skeptical expression.

Curt chuckled under his breath and said, "Listen, when you live along the biggest river in the United States, you're bound to get people passing through—people fishing, boating, vacationing, that sort of thing. If I worried about every new face that came in my shop, I'd be a worse gossip than Seth O'Connor. And I wouldn't make much money. Friendliness counts in this business."

"That makes sense," Paul said as he slid his card across the counter. "We understand. If you think of anything, just let us know."

By noon, Paul and DeDe were headed back to the law enforcement center in La Crosse. Paul swiped his badge at the secure entrance, and they headed to the third floor. Emily Warehauser chirped a friendly greeting as they stepped off the elevator.

"Mornin', you two. Jim's in his office," she said. Her fingers flew over the computer keys as she typed and conversed at the same time. "Any breaks on the Stoddard thing?"

"Nothing yet," Paul said despondently.

"It's early. Hang in there," Emily said, smiling wanly.

DeDe and Paul walked into Jim's office and pulled up two chairs. Jim finished his conversation, hung up the phone, and swiveled toward the two detectives.

"Whaddya find out?" he asked bluntly. DeDe noticed his crisp pink shirt and complementary tie, but his brusque response was out of character with his normally polite, patient demeanor. Everyone in the building was aware of Jim's latest struggles with depression and anxiety. Among the officers, it was a hot topic of discussion, with plenty of gossip floating around the department.

"We knocked on twenty-two doors and basically came up with zip," Paul said. "How's Sam?"

"I stopped at the hospital on the way here, but he's having tests, so I didn't get to talk to anyone," Jim said. "What I want you to do today is start investigating Vicki Invold's associations: friends, coworkers, family, teachers, anybody who knew her. This robbery might have been a one-off in which the perpetrator didn't know her, but there's also the possibility that he did know her. Try to get an idea of her personality, that kind of stuff. Something happened during the robbery that caused her to be shot. What was it? Did she get smart with the guy? Did she recognize the guy and threaten to report all she knew? Did she physically resist him in some way?" Jim stopped his rapid discourse, gathered his thoughts, and started again. "That necklace she was wearing appeared to be torn from her neck. That sounds to me like she was arguing with someone. Her parents mentioned some loser boyfriend she'd had a while ago. Who knows? Maybe he came in the store, and they argued about something. There are things about the shooting that don't sit right with me, that necklace being one of them." He stopped briefly and leaned back in his chair. Then he posed a question. "Why shoot someone if you don't have to unless you're just a sadistic SOB, which is also possible, I guess. Was the perpetrator someone Vicki knew? Did they argue and it got out of hand? That's what I'm thinking right now. Get my point?" Jim asked. He stared at Paul and DeDe. An uncomfortable silence descended on the room.

Finally, Paul nodded. "Yeah, I get that. So what about Sam as a suspect? Where are we on that?"

Jim drew in a deep breath and began. "I stopped down on Highway 35 this morning where the lightning strike happened and looked around. There's nothing there that's going to help us. If Sam was wearing his Nike trainers, they've disappeared. Also, his L.L. Bean raincoat is missing. I think whoever switched the clothing took the raincoat and shoes and disposed of them somewhere. They could be from here to Timbuktu." His shoulders slumped at the thought.

DeDe thought Jim looked battle weary, and they hadn't even started the investigation yet. Then she said, "I can't believe that Sam would ever be involved in something like this. That's just not possible knowing his character and core beliefs in law enforcement."

"Of course, he's not involved!" Jim said loudly, laying his palms on his desk. His blue eyes burned with intensity. "None of us believe that!" He paused and toned down his rhetoric when he saw the shocked expressions on the faces of Paul and DeDe. He took a deep breath. *Get a grip,* he thought.

"Sorry," he said. "That was unprofessional. My apologies." He waited a few moments, tamping down his sense of anxiety, and then he continued in a calmer tone. "For what it's worth, I agree with you.

Sam's character and belief system don't support the theory that he could commit such a heinous crime, but the circumstantial evidence is not comforting. Disproving Sam's involvement while finding the real killer is not something I'm looking forward to. Physical evidence and witnesses who can corroborate Sam's innocence might be hard to come by."

Good luck trying to prove a negative, Paul thought. "You do realize the press is going to have a heyday with this, don't you?" Paul asked, crossing his legs. Paul's and Jim's eyes locked in a stare for a moment.

Jim groaned ominously. "What do you think I've been doing all morning? I'll tell you what," he said, answering his own question. "I've been fending off the press's requests for interviews. Nothing like a crime supposedly committed by a police officer to get reporters fired up, especially in this woke culture," Jim said disgustedly, throwing a pencil down on his desk. He stopped and gathered his thoughts, trying to rein in his sense of panic about Sam's predicament. Everyone sat silently for a moment thinking about the strange circumstances facing them.

"We need to find Sam's original clothing," Jim continued, leaning forward across his desk. "I want every dumpster from here south to Prairie du Chien and north to Trempealeau checked out." He pointed at DeDe. "I want you to call every landfill in the tri-county area and give them a description of Sam's shoes and jacket. That clothing is somewhere, and we need to find it. Call Goodwill and Salvation Army, too." Paul and DeDe stared at him, doubt written all over their faces. "I know—it's a super long shot, but we've got to try. We can't just sit here and wait for the evidence to show up on our doorstep."

"Yes, sir," DeDe said. Then, with a look of hesitation, she continued, "I hate to bring this up, Chief, but we're going to be shorthanded with Sam injured. Leslie's going to have to take care of him at least for a few weeks until they get a normal routine established and the doctors get a handle on his injuries. What about Mike Leland? Could he help us out right now?"

Jim started to answer. "Well, that depends on Sheriff Turnmile—"

"—and how threatened she is by the suggestion," Paul said, rolling his eyes. "What a—"

"Don't say it," Jim warned darkly. "We all have our own opinions about the new sheriff. Let's just leave it at that."

Paul stood up and walked to the narrow window overlooking Vine Street. He felt his temper simmering beneath the surface every time the new sheriff was mentioned in a conversation. He listened at the window with his back turned while Jim and DeDe continued their conversation.

"So where is the bag of items that was found under Sam when they picked him up at the accident scene?" DeDe asked.

"I walked it down to the crime scene people on second floor this morning. Carl Ettinger will take a look at it in the next few days," Jim said. "I hated to do it since it incriminates Sam, but ethically, I had to. At least the press won't be able to accuse me of complicity. They're already suspicious of a cover-up, and if a cop's involved somehow, the media exposure is gonna kill us." Jim swiped his hands over his eyes, leaned forward, and rested his head in his hands. Then he whispered dejectedly, "How did Sam get into this mess?"

"He was in the wrong place at the wrong time," Paul said as he turned, walked back to his chair, and plopped down. He loosened his tie and ran a hand through his thick, dark hair. "I don't know how this happened, but we need a plan, Chief. Time is ticking by."

Jim straightened up. "You're right. Let's make one."

A half an hour later, everyone had their assignments. DeDe and Paul left to begin their tasks, and Jim took the elevator to the first floor. Walking down the hallway to the sheriff's office, he felt like he was walking the plank.

This will not go well, he thought. *Be prepared to be belittled and challenged at every turn. Davy, where are you when I really need you?*

10

Jim walked into Sheriff Elaine Turnmile's office on the first floor of the law enforcement center. The place that had once been so familiar he could have found his way around it blindfolded—where he'd spent considerable time discussing cases with his former boss, Davy Jones—now made him feel like a fish out of water.

The disarray of Davy Jones's office had been comforting in an odd way; the piles of file folders stuffed with case information, the loose pencils that he doodled with, the stray Coke can sitting on the corner of the desk, all had been swept clean of any masculine influence. In its place, a sterility devoid of human warmth pervaded the office. Jim felt like he'd entered a laboratory in which he was the rat and the sheriff was the technician who was about to perform her gruesome experiments on him. He found it unnerving that someone so regimented and full of braggadocio could intimidate him so easily. *Why do I let her push me around?* he thought. He shrugged his shoulders. *Must be the depression.*

Jim waited patiently for Turnmile to finish a phone conversation. When she looked up, the civility Jim had hoped for dissipated.

"Yes? What do you need, Higgins?" she asked curtly. She clasped her hands together and laid them on her desk. Jim noticed there were no personal mementos or photographs gracing her office. No family. No sweetheart. No children, not even a pet. Just a blotter pad, a cup of writing utensils, and a stackable black paper holder with a few folders in it. Not even a coffee cup. The place had no human warmth. A chill ran down Jim's arms. Was it the air conditioning or the cold, dehumanizing stare of Sheriff Turnmile that unnerved him?

He cleared his throat. "I need to bump up Officer Mike Leland to my investigative team since Sam will be out for a while. I don't think his condition has been fully diagnosed yet, but he's going to have some serious repercussions from this lightning strike accident. I can foresee a substantial leave of absence coming down the pike. That means Leslie will have to be home with him until they figure something out. The situation needs to stay fluid, considering everything that's happened. I'm going to—"

"Not a problem. I totally understand," Turnmile interrupted.

"You do?" Jim asked, his mouth falling open in surprise.

Turnmile went on as if he hadn't spoken. "I'll talk to Chief Pedretti at the city. You contact Mike and have him begin reporting to you immediately until we know where this thing with Sam is going. It may or may not turn into a permanent assignment. That will be determined later." She gazed at Jim with a placid expression. Shocked that she had not resisted his request or given him a numbskull excuse for opposing the suggestion, Jim stood mute in front of her.

"Anything else, Higgins?" she finally said, staring at him with her cold, green eyes.

"No, ma'am," he muttered. "And thank you."

"Not a problem. Keep me up-to-date on the Stoddard robbery."

"And murder," Jim added.

"Yes, that, too." Her phone rang. Jim turned and escaped into the hallway before she could nail him with another wintry stare.

Puzzled by the lack of interest in a fellow officer, Jim contemplated

Turnmile's concession about adding Mike Leland to the team. It seemed very odd to him. She hadn't asked one question about Sam's condition or shown any empathy for Leslie. *How in the world did we elect a sociopath as sheriff?* he thought. *The fickleness of the voting public.* On the way upstairs to his office, his cell beeped.

"Lieutenant Higgins," he said crisply, relieved he'd escaped the sheriff's scrutiny.

"Hey, Lieutenant Higgins. It's Bobby Rude," a familiar teenage voice said.

"Bobby! How are things going?" Jim asked. Bobby had recently moved in with Jim's daughter, Sara, and her husband, Jerome Knight, the former priest at St. Ignatius parish in Genoa, after the death of his alcoholic father in April. "Life treating you okay?"

"Oh, everything's good with Miss—oops—I mean, Sara. It feels really weird to call her by her first name, but I guess I'll get used to it." Jim's daughter, Sara, had been Bobby's fifth-grade teacher at St. Ignatius Catholic School in Genoa. Now the teenager was a junior at Logan High School in La Crosse.

"So, what's up? Something on your mind?" Jim asked. He punched the third-floor button in the elevator as he listened.

"Well, I know this is going to sound crazy, but something's going on with this group of guys at school, and I think it might tie in with the robbery and murder last night in Stoddard."

"Really?" Jim doubted it, but the skin on the back of his neck prickled, and he stored away the sensation in his brain, interpreting it as some kind of forewarning. "Tell me about it."

"There's this group of kids that do parkour—"

"Par—what?" Jim asked, trying to keep his voice reasonable. *Nothing like a teenager's jargon to make you feel really old,* he thought. He stepped off the elevator and walked down the hallway, listening carefully to Bobby's explanation.

"Parkour. It's a training program that involves getting from one place to another by running, jumping, rolling, climbing, swinging—stuff like that."

"So it's a type of martial arts?" Jim asked, trying to sharpen the picture forming in his mind as Bobby talked.

"Yeah, it's like martial arts, but it's more complicated than that. The kids who do parkour use their environment, both city and country, to put themselves through obstacles that sharpen their physical and mental skills."

Jim walked into his office and plopped his haunches on the corner of his desk. "So they swing from the rooftops and trees? Is that what you're saying? Like some kind of survival training and obstacle course combined into one?" Jim said. Emily walked in with some paperwork and handed it to him. He casually threw it on his desk, much to Emily's displeasure.

"Yeah, it's sort of like that, but there's more to it." Jim could tell Bobby was frustrated by his limited understanding of the sport, so he continued explaining. "If one member of the group completes a challenge, then everyone in the group has to do that challenge, too. Kinda like Horse in basketball. Adapting physically and mentally to the environment is also part of the deal." Bobby stopped a moment. During the interlude, Jim wondered about the relevance of this to the robbery case.

"So how does this relate to what happened last night?" Jim finally asked, during a pause.

"It's complicated, but some of my friends have heard some dirt in the hallways about some kids who are into small-time crime around town. Anyway, it's too involved to talk about over the phone. Can we meet tomorrow morning? Common Ground Café? North side? About nine?" Bobby asked. "I'll explain it then and bring a few of my friends."

"Sure. That's fine," Jim said.

"Great. I'll meet you there." And he hung up.

Jim stared at nothing in particular, thinking about this new twist. *What else is gonna happen? We haven't even got a theory of this crime yet, and now Bobby's suggesting some kids practicing parkour are involved.* It didn't seem likely to him. In fact, it seemed downright impossible.

However, Jim couldn't dispel Bobby's hunches as teenage melodrama since he'd been instrumental in a couple of previous cases that had led them to witnesses they didn't know existed. Jim thought about the old possible versus probable argument he'd already thoroughly debated with his team of young upstarts. It never really got them anywhere. Jim shook his head, got up, and walked out to the lobby.

"Leslie called, Chief," Emily said. "You must have had your phone turned off for a while. She wants you to return a call to her as soon as you can." Emily looked Jim over with a critical eye. Although he was snappily dressed today, she wondered about his mental health. This last round of depression was a little too familiar for comfort. She'd seen Jim hurting six years ago from the death of his first wife, Margie. Back then, Emily felt like a tugboat guiding a large ship into a harbor without the benefit of a rudder. She didn't care to repeat the experience. "Everything okay, sir?"

Jim leaned over the counter and whispered, "That's a loaded question."

"I care about you. You can't blame me for being concerned," Emily said, her brown eyes soft with affection. She couldn't hide her apprehension that Jim might be sinking into another black funk.

"Well, for your information, the last time I met with my therapist, Vivian, I wasn't excessively fatigued, aggressive, reckless, or feeling hopeless. My sex life with my beautiful wife is still on par for a fifty-six-year-old. My two small children remind me every day in numerous ways that I have a lot to live for. I plan to continue tracking down the murderers, perpetrators, and sleazeballs who continuously challenge our laws and threaten the safety of our city and state, throwing the populace into a tizzy and wondering what in the world the police are doing. Although rumors floating around this building may suggest otherwise, my depression is over. Period. End of subject." Jim dipped his chin and met her stare with a resolute gaze.

Emily rolled her eyes and looked up at her boss, a smile flashing across her face.

Jim finished with a flourish. "I appreciate the concern, Emily, but I'm fine. Really." He turned and strolled down the hall.

"Whatever you say, Chief," she said, watching his back.

Turning and giving her a dimpled grin, he pointed his index finger at her and said, "I say."

"Got it," Emily said under her breath.

11

The examination room in the neurological department at Gundersen Lutheran Hospital was predictably sterile, although a lovely painting of Grandad Bluff hung on the wall opposite Sam's bed. Leslie Birkstein stood next to her husband, Sam, who was lying on an examination table with a pillow propped behind his head. His brown wavy hair was streaked with blond, and his tanned complexion was evidence of his love for the outdoors. But the upshot of the accident last night told a different story. Unshaven, his five o'clock shadow made him look rough like the drug punks he usually dealt with in his work as a detective, and his anxious demeanor indicated he'd suffered a major trauma.

Sam had become more animated and complained of a severe headache during the night. As Leslie watched him struggle to understand what had happened to him, she wondered how their life would change—had changed—in the flash of a fifty million jolt of white-hot electricity.

"Where was I again?" Sam asked during a quiet conversation last night.

"You went to Gas & Go in Stoddard to get me some ice cream," Leslie repeated.

"I did?"

"Yeah. On the way home you ran out of gas, and you must have decided to walk to our house." Leslie watched her husband's face. Confusion and doubt passed over Sam's handsome features.

"I don't remember that," he muttered. He closed his eyes and appeared to be sleeping. Leslie wondered how much of his convenience store visit he actually remembered. The loss of recall would be a significant factor if he were charged with the gas station robbery and murder. She still couldn't believe the bag of items found by the ambulance crew. All of it seemed to point to Sam's involvement in the crime somehow, but that was impossible. *So how did that stuff get there?* she wondered.

There was a faint knock on the door, and Dr. Sig Thompson came into the room, a group of medical students fluttering around him like bees on honey, their clipboards and pencils at the ready, their eagerness oozing from their pores. Sam wanted to bat them all out of the room.

Dr. Thompson was six feet tall, had an amiable, friendly face, and was dressed impeccably in a crisp white shirt, a fleur-de-lis blue tie, and navy dress slacks. Sam gave him a cold stare, his eyelids at half-mast. He remained silent as Leslie gently rubbed his arm. Sam glanced at her for reassurance.

"Good morning, Mr. Birkstein," Dr. Thompson said crisply as he stood by the side of the examining table.

"What's good about it?" Sam finally asked softly. Leslie lifted her eyebrows conspicuously.

"You're still alive. That's the good part. You came very close to being killed," Dr. Thompson reminded Sam. "In fact, it's something of a miracle that you're still here."

Sam reached for Leslie's hand. She was struck by the desperation and panic in his eyes as he held onto her. She gave him a comforting glance. "It's okay, honey," she said. "Dr. Thompson is going to explain what we can expect the next few weeks while you recover."

Sam held onto those words—*while you recover.* Would he recover and get back to normal? He didn't know, but the confidence in Leslie's blue eyes and her gentle touch calmed him, and he relaxed his grip on her hand a little.

"I want to explain a few things to you before we start your examination," the doctor began. "You were struck with a cosmic direct jolt of electricity—that's the technical term for the power in lightning bolts. And it explains the feathering redness we see on your legs and chest and the burns on your feet." Dr. Thompson pulled away the sheets, exposing Sam's legs. The medical students leaned over Sam's body trying to get a good look at his legs. Dr. Thompson ran his finger along the swirling patterns under Sam's skin. "These will eventually disappear. They were caused by an electron shower that broke the capillaries beneath the skin's surface."

"What about my headache?" Sam asked weakly. "When's that going to go away?"

"You may have lingering effects from the strike, your headache being just one of many. You may also develop migraines, which could continue for some time. We'll give you some medication to help with that. You'll also be on a medication for your irregular heartbeat, which was a result of the jolt. When the electrical current passed through your heart, it caused spasms called atrial fibrillation—a condition in which the upper chambers of your heart beat at an irregular pace." There was a brief pause in the conversation. "How do you feel otherwise?" Dr. Thompson asked, his brown eyes gently assessing Sam.

"Like I'm in a fog," Sam said slowly. "I can't believe this has happened to me."

The physician nodded. "That's typical. The fogginess is a very common symptom. What about your feet? How do they feel?"

"They hurt when I walk, but I can manage... I guess," Sam told him.

The medical students crowded around the end of the bed as Dr. Thompson gently removed Sam's socks and pointed to his red, blistered soles. After a few moments, he continued his prognosis. "In the next few weeks, you should try to return to your normal, daily activities. However, anxiety and other personality changes may cause you and your wife some concern. You'll probably be very tired, and you might sleep a lot. Don't worry about that; it's pretty normal. Just continue to take it easy and return to the things you enjoy when you feel ready."

"Will I be able to do the stuff I used to do?" Sam asked. "You know, like running and biking?"

"That depends—" Dr. Thompson began. But Sam interrupted.

"On what? God? Because in the end, Doc, God's the one who controls the whole healing process," Sam said, the anxiety in his voice building. His eyes flashed with defiance.

Dr. Thompson gave Leslie a perceptive glance. Sam's rude response was totally out of character. Leslie reddened with embarrassment. *Here we go,* she thought. *This is what the doctor's been warning me about. The friendly, empathetic person I used to know has been replaced by someone who's rude and caustic.*

"Don't bullshit me, Doc," Sam snarled. "I need to know what I'm up against."

"Okay, I won't. Religious beliefs can certainly play a role in your recovery," Dr. Thompson said, watching Sam's face. His voice had changed from sympathetic to authoritative. "I agree that prayer and a belief in a higher power are all beneficial things, which can aid in the healing process." He looked at Leslie and held her gaze. "Let me be honest here. You have suffered a tremendous shock to your neurological system. At this point, you've survived," he dipped his head toward Sam, "by the grace of God, to use a religious term. Now you must focus on recovering as much of your former function as possible. You seem to have a good support system, and that will be a key factor. But I must warn you that your life may change in ways you hadn't anticipated. Be flexible, be patient with yourself, maintain your sense of humor, keep doing the things you like to do."

"I like my job. What about that, Doc?" Sam asked brusquely.

"I am recommending a leave of absence from your job for at least a month until you have a better handle on the areas of your life that have been affected by your accident. We'll have another consultation then, and together we'll determine if you're ready to return to work. You work at… ?"

"The La Crosse Sheriff's Department. I'm a detective," Sam said. By this time, Sam had crossed his arms over his chest in defiance and challenge. His hazel eyes, normally warm and friendly, were blazing with an irritation that filled Leslie with foreboding. She closed her eyes briefly, thinking about the challenges ahead.

"Hmm, an interesting occupation," Dr. Thompson said, but the hesitation in his response made Leslie suspicious. Did he doubt that Sam could carry on his duties as a detective? Would his injuries affect his ability to process information and make decisions—skills critical to apprehending perpetrators of criminal activity? During the night, Leslie had browsed the internet for information about what changes she could expect in Sam's personality and functioning. None of it was the least bit comforting. The doctor's response seemed clouded with skepticism as well.

Sam interrupted Leslie's thoughts. "There's something else I want to talk to you about, but I don't want these other people in here. Just you and me and Lez," he demanded. He pulled the sheet back over his legs, made a shooing gesture at the students, and lay back on the pillow while the students filed out into the hallway.

"So… what's on your mind, Sam?" Dr. Thompson asked when the room was quiet.

"Sex. Will I still be able to make love with my wife?" Sam asked. Leslie stared at him, her cheeks coloring with a bright, pink blush, appalled at the in-your-face audacity of Sam's question.

Dr. Thompson calmly regarded Sam and Leslie. Then he said, "I don't know. Sexual intimacy can be affected by a lightning strike; after all, it relies on the nervous system, but more than that, it relies on the love and trust you have in your partner. So, I can't really answer that except to tell you to go for it and see what happens. If your ability to have sexual relations is affected, we can do some other things that might help."

Despite Dr. Thompson's reassuring comments, Sam shook his head and slumped back on the pillow. "That's what I thought you'd say. I guess there's nothing we can do but wait to see what happens—if anything happens."

12

On Friday afternoon on the north side of La Crosse, Mike Leland, a La Crosse police officer, was sitting on Hager Street off Copeland Avenue in a city cop car filling out a speeding ticket. The young girl he'd stopped was stewing in her car, a basket case of tears and drama. Mike hadn't heard this much bellyaching since his former girlfriend had a fender bender in the parking lot at Target. But then, what did the teenager expect when she drove forty-five miles per hour in a twenty-five miles per hour zone? Dah. That was almost twice the legal limit. In Texas, that would land you in jail.

Officer Leland finished the ticket with a flurry of his signature, got out of the black and white cruiser, and walked to the passenger window of the sporty Nissan 370Z. He handed the ticket to the distraught girl through the window.

"Am I supposed to thank you for this?" she asked, tears streaming down her face.

"You don't have to," Mike replied calmly. "What I want you to remember the next time you're behind the wheel is the speed in designated areas. Always follow the speed limit, and you'll be just fine."

"My parents are going to take away my license!" she pouted. "And probably my car, too!"

"That's not a bad idea," Mike said. "I hope they make you pay the fine, as well." The girl shot him a belligerent look. Mike held up his hand in a stop gesture. "A few weeks of deprivation might improve your appreciation for the privilege of driving."

"What a bunch of crap!" she exclaimed. She rolled up her window in disgust and gingerly pulled out into traffic.

"Enjoy the rest of your day, miss," Mike said to the rear window as the girl drove away from him into the flow of traffic. *Teenage drama. Go figure,* he thought. When he heard his radio squawk in the police cruiser, he walked back to the car, got in, and listened to the message from the dispatcher.

"To any officers in the George Street area. A citizen has called in a vehicle that he believes belongs to his neighbor, which was stolen last week. The caller did not approach the driver of the vehicle. The driver is still with the car. Please respond. The citizen is in the 3500 block of Loomis Street," the dispatcher said.

Mike called in to dispatch headquarters and said he was on his way. Driving farther north, he came to Loomis Street, where the stolen vehicle, a white, rusty 2006 Chrysler Town and Country van, was sitting by the curb. The male driver had gotten out of the vehicle and propped the hood open. He was dressed in a woman's halter top, three-inch high heels, and a pair of skinny, faded jeans with conspicuous rips down the legs. Casually leaning against the car, he looked at Officer Leland out of the corner of his eye when he approached him.

"Afternoon, sir. Are you having some trouble here?" Mike asked. He watched the man's eyes and hands, looking for any quick movements that might indicate he had a weapon.

"Well, other than the fact that my heels are killing me, yeah, I'm having trouble. I guess I must have run outta gas. My car don't go, so that must be what's wrong." The man's eyes were darting here and there, and the scabs on his face and arms made Mike wonder about meth.

"Is this your vehicle, sir?" Mike asked.

"Well, of course it is," the man said impatiently, pushing his shoulders back, adopting a truculent attitude.

"You might want to reconsider that statement since we've received a call that this vehicle could be stolen," Mike said, giving the man a cool-eyed stare. The driver of the van briefly adjusted his halter top, which was sagging for lack of breasts. As Officer Leland looked over the man's driver's license, another cop car rolled up and parked in front of the stolen car, hemming it in.

The other city police officer approached the scene and continued the conversation with the van's driver while Mike ran the license plates through the system confirming the vehicle was indeed stolen. The cross-dresser was cuffed and taken downtown without incident.

Mike returned to his squad car. He sat inside and began filling out a report about the arrest at 3597 Loomis Street. He was just completing it when his cell rang. Absentmindedly, he cradled the phone to his ear.

"Officer Mike Leland," he said, his mind still on the details of the arrest.

"Mike. It's Jim Higgins. I just finished talking to Sheriff Turnmile and Chief Pedretti, and I have permission to bump you up to our investigative team. You heard about Sam, right?"

Mike sat up straighter and cleared his throat. "Yes, sir. How's he doing?"

"Hard to tell yet, but he's going to have some major hurdles getting back to normal life and the job. We're investigating that robbery and shooting at the Gas & Go in Stoddard. Be in my office at nine Monday morning. We're having a meeting to consolidate all the evidence and see where we're at."

"Yes, sir. I'll be there."

"See you then," Higgins said, and he hung up.

Mike stared out the windshield. *There must be a God in heaven,* he thought. Then his stomach did a little dance, and he let out a whoop of excitement.

13

As Jim drove home through the secluded, shaded valley, the sun was sinking toward the horizon. He reviewed the facts of the robbery and shooting. Without surveillance video, the possibility of identifying the perpetrator was much more difficult and would make the case against Sam even harder to disprove. DeDe and Paul had not uncovered any witnesses who might have noticed something amiss in the neighborhood. Vicki Invold's sketchy boyfriend, Devon Williams, hovered in the background. Right now he was simply a person of interest, unless something else came to light. Jim reassured himself that the investigation was in its infancy, and as they moved forward, something would break the case open—that was his hope anyway.

Jim turned into his driveway on Chipmunk Coulee Road Friday evening. He parked and strolled in the house, smelling something delicious. Walking into the dining room, he stopped briefly at the antique buffet and sifted through the day's mail.

"Nothin' but bills," he said under his breath, laying the pile back down. Entering the kitchen, he popped the oven door open. Roast chicken and smashed potatoes. One of his favorites. Nobody seemed to be around despite the dinner fixings warming in the oven.

"Hey! Where is everybody?" he yelled, slipping off his necktie.

He walked through the living room to the back porch and stepped onto the limestone terrace, which overlooked his ten-acre property. He listened for a minute. Then he heard faint squeals of glee coming from the small creek that passed along the border of his land toward the back of his property. He walked across the lawn toward the creek.

Most of Jim's property was mowed and trimmed by a landscape service, but the acreage along the creek was kept natural. Now, in late August, the area bloomed with tall vegetation, including sandbar willow, gray dogwood, viburnum, and false indigo interspersed with black-eyed Susans and wild bergamot, which partially hid the creek from view. He waded into the undergrowth and came out by the pristine creek. The gurgling of water over the sandstone rocks provided the perfect playground for the children.

Lillie and Henri were catching crawdads while Paco, Leslie and Sam's big black lab, stood watch over the children. When the dog saw Jim, he woofed a greeting and bounded up to him. Jim leaned down and pounded his broad side, ruffling his ears. Paco seemed to remember him and wagged his tail in elation. Then the canine shook his fur in a tremendous convulsion and sprayed Jim with a boatload of water. Jim laughed. "Hey, you big lummox!" Then to the kids, "I thought I'd find you pipsqueaks down here!"

"Bapa! Look! We've got a whole bucket of crayfish!" Lillie shouted. Her blue eyes blazed with excitement. She held the bucket crawling with crayfish up in the air as proof of their afternoon activities. Her wild blonde curls framed her flushed face, and her shorts and shirt were spattered with mud. Standing next to her, Henri looked up at Jim with big brown eyes, his head of hair a tumble of wet ringlets, and an irrepressible smile lit up his cherubic face. Jim's heart swelled with tenderness at the sight of his children's innocent exuberance.

"Come and see, Daddy!" Henri said in his high-pitched voice.

Jim walked toward them thinking about his childhood days on the farm. The idyllic setting in his backyard was exactly like the one he'd shared with his brother Dave on the farm in Blair, Wisconsin. What he'd hoped to provide for his second set of children—peaceful surroundings, places to explore, and hours discovering the secrets of nature—was a reality. Mud, water, dirt, bugs, rocks, worms, and plenty of space to run were all part of the package. It seemed to align with a book Carol had been reading recently entitled *Let Your Kids Play in the Dirt*.

"Jim, let's make sure Lillie and Henri are exposed to all the normal stuff we enjoyed when we were growing up. Things like digging for worms, fishing, camping, building forts, collecting leaves and bugs, picking wildflowers—stuff like that," she said, looking over her half-moon glasses at him.

Jim looked up from a John Sanford novel he was reading and focused his attention on the title of the book she was devouring with enthusiasm.

"You know I will, hon, but you don't need to read a book about it. You lived it. You're already an expert. And besides that, I had a perfect childhood," he said pompously, "so I know the kind of environment that will produce great kids." He went back to his reading.

Carol's eyes flashed. "Well, it wasn't exactly perfect, Jim. After all, you discovered a sister you never knew about until you were fifty-three years old," she said, her mind suddenly remembering the moment of that bombshell information.

Jim felt a surge of anger, but he kept his voice level. "That didn't affect my childhood because I didn't know Juliette existed back then. So I *did* have a perfect childhood. End of discussion," he said, irritated that Carol had reminded him of the traumatic discovery of his lost sibling. He would never forget the day when Juliette, his sister, had been found dead near Riverside Park with four-year-old Lillie in tow. After an uncomfortable silence, Carol got up and walked over to Jim, placing her hand lightly on his arm. She leaned down and kissed his cheek.

"I'm sorry. I didn't mean to trample on your memories," Carol said softly.

Jim looked up at her and shut his book. "Not a problem. It's water over the dam now. Besides, we gained Lillie in the whole process so how could it possibly be a bad thing?" He smiled at her.

"Well, when you put it like that, I guess it wasn't a bad thing, although it sure got your cork out at the time," she said, smiling back.

A tugging on his pants leg brought Jim back to the creek.

"Daddy! Look! We have seventeen now," Henri said, proud of his counting abilities.

"What are you going to do with them? Make crawdad stew?" Jim asked, grinning.

Lillie's eyes widened in shock. "Never, Bapa! We're just going to look at them and then let them go. We could never eat them!" She screwed up her face in disgust.

"Hey! What's up?" Carol asked, walking up behind Jim. She was dressed in a sleeveless top, a pair of ragged cutoffs, and knee-high rubber waders.

"Where've you been?" Jim asked, looking at her getup. Carol gave him a quick peck on the lips.

"Just enjoying a few hours with the kids before supper. Come on, time to clean up," she reminded everyone. "Let the crayfish go." When groans of disappointment threatened the carefree atmosphere, she teased them with the promise of chicken and potatoes and chocolate cupcakes for dessert.

Suddenly Paco turned, stood alert, his ears erect, and looked toward the house. Then he let out a sharp bark and hightailed it toward the two figures standing on the patio.

"Oh, it's Sam and Leslie!" Carol said, waving. Henri and Carol headed for the patio, but Lillie grabbed Jim's hand and pulled until he leaned down. Her eyes were serious—her voice quiet yet uneasy.

"Bapa? Is Sam okay now?" she asked innocently, her eyes pools of azure blue.

Jim knelt in front of her. "Not really, but we're not going to talk about that in front of Sam, okay?"

"Leslie looks worried," she said, glancing toward the house.

"She is, but I want to tell you something—" Jim started to explain.

"I already know," Lillie interrupted confidently. "We should just love them and be their friends and help them."

Jim smiled and kissed his daughter on the cheek. "You got it, toots," he said proudly.

"… and pray for them," Lillie finished seriously.

"Exactly," Jim agreed, taking her hand.

They walked up to the patio. Sam found a comfortable spot in an Adirondack chair. Paco slobbered him with wet kisses, his tail wagging furiously. Carol embraced Leslie and held her for a long moment. When they disengaged, Leslie brushed away tears. Sam sat stoically, avoiding eye contact, concentrating his attention on Paco.

After an awkward pause, Lillie tentatively walked up to Sam, reached out, and took his hand. She gave him a gentle hug. Sam smiled uneasily. Jim noticed the dark circles under his eyes and the tension beneath his tanned complexion. Carol and Leslie went into the house to find some refreshments, and the kids followed to get cleaned up for dinner.

"Hey, they finally let you out, huh?" Jim said, plopping down next to him. "Can you stay for dinner?"

Sam's eyes wandered to the woods along the backyard. "We had a sandwich on the way home," he said slowly. Paco nudged Sam's arm with his nose looking for more affection.

"Somebody missed you, from the looks of it," Jim said, filling in the empty space. Sam absentmindedly caressed Paco's velvety ears. The dog relished the companionship, his eyes at half-mast, his pink tongue dripping saliva.

"Lez told me about the robbery and the stuff they found underneath me when I was lying along the highway half dead," Sam said despondently. "It doesn't sound good, Chief."

Jim leaned forward and rested his elbows on his knees. Their eyes met, and Jim steadily held his gaze. "Listen, Sam, nobody in the department believes you're capable of doing something like that. We're doing our best to figure out where the stuff in the bag came from. But I've got to tell you, unless you can give us some clues, we're in a world of hurt. I'm afraid you are the only person of interest in this case so far, and I wouldn't be surprised if, in the coming weeks, you'll become the main suspect if no new evidence comes to light or other witnesses come forward. So my advice to you right now is that you hire a good lawyer," Jim said. Sam's eyes widened with apprehension, and his mouth opened in a slack expression. He seemed flabbergasted at Jim's suggestion.

"A lawyer? I haven't been charged with anything yet!" he hissed angrily.

Jim pumped his hands up and down in a gesture meant to calm Sam. "I know, I know, but that may be just around the corner. Do you remember anything before or after you were struck by the lightning bolt?" Jim asked.

"No. I don't remember being struck or anything after that until I woke up in the hospital. Some of the other stuff is hazy, too." He suddenly seemed confused. "Were you there?" Sam asked. His brow crinkled above his hazel eyes, and the fogginess of the event hung like a cloud in his brain.

"Yes, I was there when you first woke up. You were pretty disoriented, which is understandable considering what you'd been through."

Sam said, "I've started to remember a few things about my trip to Stoddard in the storm. But that's about it. I've been wracking my brain ever since I found out about the robbery." Sam looked at Jim, his eyes moist and shining with tears. "You gotta help me, Chief. I don't have anyone else I can count on."

"Hey! That's not true!" Jim laid his hand on Sam's arm. "Everyone on the team is working very hard to figure this out, and you know Lez will always be here for you, and so will our family. We're always going to be here for you."

"You gonna be here for me when I end up in jail for armed robbery and murder?" Sam asked indignantly, but beneath the anger Jim could see Sam was terrified. "That's a nice sentiment, Chief," Sam continued, his jawline hardening, "but the reality is usually a little different." Jim hesitated in his response, not wanting to fuel Sam's anxiety.

"The best thing you can do right now is go home, let Leslie take care of you, heal, and try to relax," Jim said gently. "Maybe that will help you recall what happened. In the meantime, DeDe, Paul, and I will be out beatin' the bushes trying to figure out who committed this crime and then framed you for it."

"Framed me?"

"Yes, that's what I think happened. Whoever committed this murder drove south on 35, and when they saw you lying on the side of the road, they stopped and exchanged clothing, left money and the gun, threw all of it in a bag, and escaped unnoticed," Jim explained.

Sam continued to stare at his boss with a look of astonishment. "That's pretty unbelievable, even for our team, and we've seen a lot of crazy stuff, Chief," Sam said. "Good luck with that theory," Sam's shoulders sagged in disillusionment. "I feel like I'm brain dead, but even I know that proving my innocence is going to be almost impossible," Sam said. He leaned backward and rested his head on the back of the chair, studying the green foliage of the trees that surrounded the patio. He sighed deeply, his desperation on full display. Jim thought about telling Sam that Mike Leland would round out the team in his absence, but from the looks he was getting, he knew Sam would not be able to handle the news, so he stayed silent.

Leslie appeared at the door of the porch and walked over to Sam on the terrace. She leaned down and kissed him tenderly on the cheek.

"Ready to go home, honey?" she said. Paco woofed as if he understood the word *home*.

Sam looked up at Leslie with a childlike trust. Jim was taken aback by the way things had already changed in their world. He wondered if Leslie was prepared to meet Sam's needs—his unrelenting questions, his spotty memory—because right now, from where he sat, that seemed like an impossible job.

"Yeah, whatever you say," Sam said. With Leslie's assistance, he slowly rose from the chair. He turned and began limping through the house. Jim thought he looked like a ninety-year-old man rather than the rough-and-tumble, athletic detective he knew so well.

Jim walked the couple through the house and helped Sam into Leslie's Prius. Shutting the passenger door, he reminded Sam to buckle up. Then he looked past him and locked eyes with Leslie.

"You call me if you need anything," Jim reminded her. "Anything."

"I will, Chief," she promised wistfully. "My parents are at the house now, so we're good." Paco swiped the side of her face with an exuberant swish of his tongue. "Well, at least someone is glad to see me," she said with a wan smile.

"Take care," Jim said, waving to them as they drove down the driveway.

Later that evening, Jim and Carol cuddled together on the couch. The children were asleep, and the TV was turned down low. Jim was reading the preliminary CSI reports from the gas station in Stoddard while catching snippets of an old movie Carol was watching on television. In the back of his brain, he was turning over the facts of the case, analyzing their chances of freeing Sam from the suspicious mess he was in.

During a commercial, Carol hit the mute button and asked, "Anything new on the robbery?"

"Nothing much. I'm meeting with Bobby Rude and some of his friends tomorrow morning. What do you know about parkour?" Jim asked. Carol's face was a blank.

"Never heard of it. What is it?" she asked.

"From my limited understanding, it's a martial arts discipline that's refined and perfected using your surroundings. Participants apparently leap from buildings, jump fences and creeks, run like the wind, roll under and around obstacles, stuff like that. Nothing I could do anymore at my age," Jim said gruffly.

"You mean like those American Warrior competitions on TV? That kind of stuff?" she asked.

Jim vaguely knew what Carol was referring to. "Probably, or something close to it anyway," he said.

"So what's this have to do with the robbery?" Carol asked. "Doesn't sound like it could even be related."

"It probably isn't, but we haven't been able to find one resident in Stoddard who saw anything remotely strange the night of the robbery. No unfamiliar vehicles. No speeding cars leaving town. Nothing. I guess the thunderstorm was the perfect cover for the crime. Everyone was so fixated on the storm that nobody noticed anything out of the ordinary." Jim paused, then held up his index finger.

"But..." Jim locked eyes with Carol, "the manager of the station said he didn't think the perp had a getaway car—that he might have been on foot. So maybe our suspect used his parkour skills to escape from the scene undetected." Carol gave him a dubious look. Making a disgusted face, Jim blew out a puff of air. "I know," he said, "it sounds pretty stupid. That's not much to go on."

"No, it's not."

"But Bobby did tip me off to this group of kids from Logan who do these parkour antics, so I arranged to meet with some of them. It's probably a dead end. But Bobby's heard some rumblings among his friends about some kids who are into small-time crime—break-ins, trespassing, stuff like that. It's probably a total one-off." *You've stooped pretty low if that's all you've got to go on,* he thought.

Carol kissed his cheek, turned the television off with the remote, and stood up. "I'm going to bed. Tomorrow we've got to clean the garage. It's a total mess with all the kids' summer toys in there."

"We?" Jim pointed at his chest.

"Yes, we." Carol was silent for a minute, then she said wistfully, "Can you believe Henri is already five years old and going to kindergarten?"

Jim reached for her hand, and she sat back down on the couch and snuggled up to him. "Time flies when you're havin' fun," he said.

"Speaking of fun... we did have a good time makin' the little twerp, didn't we?"

"A whole year of fun, as I recall. And hey, the fun's not over. Come on, let's go to bed," Jim suggested with a grin.

"Imagine that. You still haven't learned your lesson."

"Just remember you're talkin' to the guy who had a vasectomy, so the fun can continue!"

"Oh boy! That's a word picture for ya. No pain, no gain. Is that the idea? Well, in that case, I guess I'm in for it."

Nuzzling her neck, he moved up to her mouth and kissed her long and fervently. When he pulled back, Carol looked into his eyes, grabbed his hand, and said, "What are we waiting for?"

SATURDAY, AUGUST 30

INNOCENCE HAS A SINGLE VOICE THAT
CAN ONLY SAY OVER AND OVER, "I DIDN'T DO IT."
GUILT HAS A THOUSAND VOICES,
ALL OF THEM LIES.

LEONARD PELTIER

14

Despite Jim's misgivings about the parkour idea, he got in his Suburban on Saturday morning and drove into La Crosse to a small restaurant on the north side called Common Ground Café. He parked his car around the corner from the restaurant, walked a half block, and swung the door open.

Inside, the place was bustling. The smell of bacon, pancakes, and freshly baked cinnamon rolls made Jim's stomach cramp with hunger. The tables and booths were filled with patrons clutching their coffee cups as they studied the menu. Jim waved to the owner of the establishment, who was busy behind the grill, sidestepped a bustling waitress with a loaded tray of food, and strolled down the hallway past the bathrooms to a small meeting room in the back. Bobby Rude and two other teenagers were standing along the wall in a huddle, engaged in intense conversation. When Jim walked up, the talking stopped. The boys looked at him expectantly.

Bobby rushed forward. "Hey, Lt. Higgins! We're here like I promised."

Jim nodded at the group. "Anyone want anything to drink? I'm buyin'," he said with a grin.

The boys put in their orders. Jim retraced his steps and found a waitress who promised to deliver their drinks and a plate of cinnamon rolls to them. Everyone passed the time with small talk, getting settled around the table. Jim and Bobby sat on one side of the table, and the other two boys sat across from them.

Bobby Rude's two friends could not have been more different. Toby Erickson—a skinny beanpole dressed in camo sweatpants and a loose black sweatshirt—had dark eyes and medium brown hair in a shaggy style. The other boy, Jerrod Fleming, had a splash of red freckles across his wide face, which reminded Jim of the old *Howdy Doody* cartoon character—a head of carrot-colored hair and striking green eyes. He had the body of a medium-weight wrestler crammed into a pair of ripped blue jeans and a long-sleeved T-shirt that said JUST DO IT across the front.

The clink of dishes and the hubbub of conversation from the front of the café drifted down the hallway along with the smells of breakfast food. The waitress delivered their drinks and rolls, and Jim got started.

"Okay, guys. Bobby tells me you're parkour enthusiasts. Is that right?" he asked, taking a bite of his cinnamon roll.

Toby and Jerrod exchanged a glance.

"Yeah, we're members of the club here in town," Toby said. "Our teacher is from Holmen, and we meet every Thursday night."

"So you practice these parkour skills on a regular basis?" Jim asked, licking frosting from his finger.

"Oh sure, but it's not competitive like other sports. It's for discipline and to stay in shape. We work out in different neighborhoods and sometimes out in the country on public land. County parks and stuff like that," Jerrod said.

"As Bobby might have told you," Jim explained, "my team is investigating the robbery and murder of Vicki Invold, the cashier who was shot and killed at the Gas & Go in Stoddard the other night. Did you guys know Vicki?" Jim made eye contact with each teen, skirting around the parkour issue.

"I knew her in a roundabout way—had a few classes with her and saw her in the halls," Bobby said. "She went to Logan and graduated last year. I think she was going to Western Tech to become a nurse. She was nice, I guess."

Toby picked up the story. "The biggest thing you need to know about Vicki was this guy she hung around with. Devon Williams." Jim's head jerked up at the sound of the name, the same name Vicki's parents had mentioned the night of her death, but he refrained from making a comment that might influence the boy's account. Toby went on.

"He was older than her by maybe five years. Her parents disapproved of Vicki going with someone so much older, and Vicki told me her parents wanted her to break it off with him. After a couple of months, she finally did. Her parents thought he was out of the picture, and I guess he was... for a while."

Jim leaned back and asked, "What do you mean?"

"Well, they thought Vicki had finally gotten him out of her system," Jerrod said. "That she was finally done with him."

"Was she done with him?" Jim asked.

"Seemed like it, but the rumor was she still had some contacts with him, although everyone I talked to said she had a new boyfriend who was a nice, normal guy—some dude from Aquinas," Toby said.

That jibes with what Vicki's parents told me, Jim thought.

"Why didn't the parents like this older guy?" Jim asked, even though he already knew the answer to his question.

Toby began to speak, but Jerrod held up his hand in a stop gesture to his friend. "Are you kidding?" Jerrod said, his eyes widened as he leaned over the table. His body had tensed up like someone who was being threatened. Jim thought if some other teenager had asked the question, the kid might have thrown a punch at him. Jim sat up straighter and intently watched Jerrod's face.

"He was a scumbag," Jerrod began, his voice dark with desperation. His friendly vibe disappeared as he talked. "Into drugs, drank a lot, provided booze and other stuff for kids' weekend parties, hung around the school parking lots and the mall looking for fresh recruits. Vicki deserved better than that. She was a nice girl from a good family. He was nothing but a total loser."

"Plus, girls who thought they could handle him found out in a hurry that it was all about him. He got what he wanted and left them in the dust," Toby added.

"Are we talking about sex?" Jim asked.

The boys nodded affirmatively. Bobby watched the exchange between Jim and his two friends with a laser intensity.

"So he had sex with these girls, took their self-esteem, got them pregnant, and then abandoned them? Is that what you're telling me?" Jim said, listening to the teen's version of things.

Jerrod stared at Jim. "Pretty much," he said quietly. "Probably paid for their abortions."

Jim was not surprised by the implications the boys were suggesting. Still, even after thirty years in law enforcement, his blood boiled when he thought of the sexual trauma experienced by these young girls. Jim noticed the intensity of Jerrod's attitude—hostility mixed with a sense of loss. Then he thought about Devon Williams. *Predators. We'll never get rid of them.* An image of Vicki, young, defenseless, and naive, falling under the spell of a con artist like this Devon, formed in his mind. The muscles in his jaw rippled with anger as he listened to the boys' story.

"So where is this Devon Williams now?" Jim asked calmly.

Both boys shrugged their shoulders. "I don't know and don't care," Toby said sourly. "Haven't heard about him for quite a while." He leaned back in his chair, thrust his feet out in front of him, and stared at the floor, lost in angry thoughts.

Jim swiped his hand across his cheek. "Well, this is all interesting information, guys, but without some clue as to this Devon's whereabouts—what he looks like, where he hangs out—it doesn't leave me much to investigate. You get my point?" he asked, although he'd jotted down the basics of the conversation in his small memo pad. The tension in the room seemed to hinge on something unresolved.

"Was Vicki pregnant?" Jim asked brusquely, out of the blue.

The boys gave Jim a blank stare. Toby summed it up with a shrug as he crossed his arms over his chest. When it came to the sexual context of things, the boys had clammed up.

Jim tried another tack. "How did you get to know this Devon? Was he into parkour, too?"

"For a while, when we first started the club, he came pretty regularly. But eventually, he slacked off and quit altogether. You can't do amazing physical feats and be hungover or smokin' weed and expect your body to cooperate," Jerrod said. "Your coordination goes out the window. Honestly, he never really fit into the parkour group. He was just a burned-out wannabe who was always high on something, looking for new admirers."

Everyone sat there for a minute or two reflecting on what had been said. Jim asked another question.

"So do you think Devon might have had something to do with the robbery and shooting of Vicki?"

After a significant silence, Bobby Rude spoke up. "Well, Chief, we've been hearing rumors around school that Devon befriends kids who are on the outer fringe of things—you know, kids who don't quite fit in or kids who are needy for attention or kids whose parents are drunks like my dad was—and he recruits them to go with him on raids."

"Raids? What kinds of raids? You mean criminal activities?" Jim asked. In spite of his misgivings, this was getting interesting.

Toby offered more information. "From what we've heard, the raids were little practice runs—stuff like shoplifting, purse snatching, breaking into garages and stealing tools. You know, weed whackers, hand tools, some house entries, that kind of stuff," Toby said. "But—"

"Lately, we've heard about more serious stuff," Jerrod interrupted, leaning across the table. "Drug drop-offs around town, small-time robberies of businesses, that kind of thing. Like the robbery at that gas station in Stoddard. That's got Devon's name written all over it."

"So you think this Devon is the head honcho of a group doing his dirty business so he can keep his hands clean? Is that it?" Jim asked.

"Yeah, pretty much," Jerrod said. "He likes to paint himself as the mastermind behind the crimes. What a joke!" Jim thought a minute about what the boys had told him.

"Describe him," Jim demanded. He scribbled the description in his memo pad as the boys talked.

"Dark curly hair, wide face, a smashed-in nose, 'bout six two, athletic," Toby said.

"Race?" Jim asked.

"He's Black," Jerrod said. "One more thing. He's intense—you know, like just really intense."

"Okay. Here's what we're gonna do," Jim said. "You're all gonna keep your heads down—this Devon character sounds dangerous—but keep me informed about anything else you hear. Contact me but don't—" he stopped and eyeballed each boy, and his voice hardened, "don't try to do something on your own." He gave Bobby a particularly serious look. "This is a police investigation. We appreciate your help, but the tough stuff is our territory. Understand?" He pointed to each boy. They nodded, their eyes wide with the consequential nature of Higgins's request.

Jim dug into the pocket of his jeans, pulled out some business cards, and handed them out.

"Here's my card. My work and home phone numbers are on the back. Call me whenever you think something might be going down. I'll handle it from there."

"Thanks, Lt. Higgins," Bobby said. "We'll let you know."

As the boys shuffled out of the room, Jim called Bobby back. When he was sure the other boys were out of earshot, Jim said, "Something else is going on here. What's the deal with Jerrod?"

Bobby's eyes grew wide. "Well, Jerrod used to go with Vicki. He's really shook up about her death. She dumped him for this Devon guy."

"Thought so," Jim said, watching the other boys exit the building. "Is Jerrod the kind of guy who's looking for revenge?"

"Oh, Chief, I don't think he'd…" His voice trailed off, and his face grew thoughtful. When he looked back at Jim, there was an uneasiness, his confidence eroding. Bobby's expression toughened. "On second thought, sir, if Devon did even half the stuff we've heard he does to the girls he gets, then revenge wouldn't ever be enough."

Jim sighed and ran his hand across the back of his neck as he studied the floor. Then he looked up and smiled at Bobby. "Thanks, Bobby. You did the right thing in coming forward. Keep an eye on your friends, okay?" he said, his smile disappearing.

"I'll try, sir, but I can't guarantee they won't do something stupid," Bobby said seriously.

"Call me if there's trouble," Jim said. *And there will be,* he thought. *Somebody will do something stupid.*

15

Devon Williams sat three stories up on the roof of the W.T. Johnson building on the north side of La Crosse. At one time, the building had been a popular north side department store—a destination for the latest in clothing and accessories. The store front was designed in an eclectic style, one articulated with a metal Italianate cornice and frieze accented by a Romanesque round arch. Each floor of the three-story building had trios of arched windows decorated with intricate brickwork. The building sat kitty-corner from the Common Ground Café. The 1897 multifaceted Victorian monstrosity was slated to be razed in a few months, but it was the perfect perch to watch the comings and goings of the teens and that pesky detective, Jim Higgins.

Devon used the considerable climbing skills he'd honed to perfection on the sandstone bluffs in and around the La Crosse area to scale the walls of the building in the back alley. He was a natural athlete, lithe and strong with quick reflexes. Climbing the shell of the building had been challenging, but he had an uncanny ability to find a hold where none seemed to exist. He snaked his way up the naked wall until he reached the old fire escape, then athletically boosted himself up, climbed the rickety, rusted stairs, and stepped onto the roof.

Since the murder of the Invold girl at the Gas & Go Thursday night, Devon had waffled about staying in the area. Should he leave? If he stayed, what were his chances of becoming a prime suspect in the investigation? He'd thought about dressing down his army of miscreants for their failures in other robberies around town, but he decided that would only draw attention to himself and the botched misdeed in Stoddard. After all, if one of the little rugrats was interviewed by the cops, they were bound to cave and start chirping like a canary, revealing the parameters of his operation. Too risky. He'd take care of the problem himself.

He lay on his belly on the roof, the heat from the morning sun warming the black shingles. He grabbed a pair of binoculars from his jacket, zeroing in on the front door of the café. It was busy—always was on a Saturday morning. Customers floated in and out. He watched and waited.

Suddenly, he noticed a tall man walking briskly toward the café. Gray-blond hair, strikingly handsome, dressed casually in jeans, a long-sleeved plaid shirt, and running shoes. He pulled the door of the café open and waited for a granny with two small children to exit the restaurant. He smiled widely, revealing dimples. Friendly. Confident. Sure of himself.

Watching Jim Higgins arrive at the café, Williams felt his stomach turn over with anxiety, a leftover quirk from his childhood days when he'd dodged and ducked the fist of his alcoholic and abusive father. Devon had heard some rumblings about the detective, none of it comforting. The veteran cop had been on the force for over thirty years. Intelligent, hard-driving in his pursuit of criminals in the Driftless Area, and fearless in obtaining justice for the victims of crime.

Devon's resolve wavered. Did he want to take on this legendary cop and his formidable skill set? He heard his team was competent and hard-driving. He thought about it for a moment. At this point, he really had no choice. His operations around town had been lucrative; he hated to give up and leave the area when things were just starting to be profitable. Besides, he had an idea. Something was brewing in the back of his mind like a pot of chili simmering on the stove. A duplicitous grin appeared at the corners of his mouth. He crouched over and slinked to the edge of the building. Then he carefully lowered himself over the edge until his foot found the old fire escape. When he reached the ground, a plan crystallized in his mind. He jogged down the alley, climbed on his fat wheel bike, and pedaled furiously toward the river.

16

The sunlight was sifting into the bedroom through the sheer curtain, leaving ribbons of radiance on the thick gray carpet. Since the ferocious storm on Thursday evening, the air had changed. Now it felt as if fall had arrived on the doorstep. The temperature in the bedroom was cool, thanks to an easterly breeze wafting through the window. Sam groaned and cuddled down beneath the quilt, burying his head in his pillow.

Since returning from the hospital to their home overlooking the Mississippi River near Genoa on Friday evening, everyone was trying to adjust to the reality of Sam's injuries. To Sam, things seemed chaotic and out of sync. Things moved too fast. He moved too slowly. Nothing felt right. Everything hurt. His headache banged away unabated despite the medication the doctor had prescribed.

To top it off, Leslie's parents had arrived from Decorah, Iowa, with their little schnauzer puppy in tow. Paco was not a happy camper; he didn't take kindly to sharing his turf with a little ankle biter. During the night, the black lab had found his way into Sam and Leslie's bedroom. Now, Paco rolled over on his side in the early morning light and scratched an ear with his back leg. He walked over to the bed where Sam lay sleeping, his arm flopped over the edge of the mattress. Paco nudged it with his wet nose, licking his skin.

"Go away, Paco," Sam muttered softly. When the big brute refused to quit, Sam cracked one eye open and threw his arm around the dog's neck. Paco's tail began to wag excitedly. "What's with you this morning?" Sam asked.

"He's just feeling protective," Leslie commented, coming out of the master bathroom. "He knows you're hurting." She rubbed a towel over her wet hair.

Sam groaned. "Well, if he wants to go for a jog, that's not happening. Not with my feet as blistered as they are." Sam rolled on his back, grimacing from the pain of cracked ribs.

"Tell me one thing, Lez: When is everybody going to quit fussing over me?" Sam asked. "I'm not an invalid, you know." He stretched out on the mattress and stared at the ceiling. After a few moments, he crossed his arms behind his head, then grimaced when his blistered feet rubbed against the sheets. "Everybody was practically tripping over each other last night getting me things." His voice mimicked a whine. "Need a glass of water, Sam? More hotdish, Sam? Maybe it's time for more medication. Jeez!"

Leslie lay down next to him, watching the side of his face. Already she felt the pressure of gauging his moods—managing her responses to the disturbing changes in the man she knew and loved.

"Please, Sam. Don't push everybody away. They mean well," she said softly. "We all love you."

"Well, if you got asked every ten minutes how your headache is and how you're feeling and all that bullshit, you'd get sick of it, too," Sam said, his voice taking on a roughness Leslie hadn't heard before. "I feel like I'm in a damn cage in my own home, and everybody paid a ticket to come and stare at me."

"My mom and dad will be leaving tomorrow, so—"

"So I can be asked a thousand questions when my parents arrive," Sam rudely interrupted. "Dad will be spouting Bible verses, and Mom won't quit talking until they're five miles down the road on their way home."

Leslie worried about the changes she'd seen in her husband since the lightning injury. Usually she was the one who would not tolerate a coddling attitude from family or friends. *No pity parties. Buck it up. Stand tall and take whatever life dishes out.* The old military mantra. But now, she wasn't sure how to handle the same attitude in Sam. This was the man who had the patience of Job, the man who could tolerate the crassness and rudeness of just about anyone, the man who had the self-confidence to handle almost any situation he found himself in, the man who could dress in drag and tease the men who tried to pick him up. He'd certainly changed—into what she wasn't sure—and she didn't know what to do about it.

Leslie touched Sam's shoulder tenderly and pulled him over on his side so she could look into his eyes.

"Please, Sam. Try to understand how scared everyone was when they heard the news. You're going to be a father pretty soon. Imagine how concerned you'd be if your child faced a major life-changing situation like the one you're in."

Sam stared into his wife's azure blue eyes. He knew she was right, but a wedge of irritability kept him from appreciating her words. Instead, his hand caressed her swollen belly. He kissed her tenderly.

"Mmm, you smell really good." He kissed her neck and nibbled on her ear. "I'll try to be a better boy," he said under his breath.

Leslie stiffened. "This isn't funny, Sam."

He pulled away from her suddenly, his temper flaring. "See what I mean? Everybody's walking around poop-lipped. Well, somebody better find a sense of humor in all this pretty soon, or I'm goin' to go nuts." He sat up on his side of the bed. His head began to throb, and he squeezed his eyes shut and lay back down. His ribs felt like they were on fire.

"I'll get your medication," Leslie said somberly as she stood up and headed to the bathroom.

Sam lay back on the bed, his thoughts turning to the charges that would likely be filed against him for the robbery and murder of Vicki

Invold. Unless someone came forward and admitted to the crime—fat chance—the physical evidence found beneath him after the lightning strike would definitely be enough to convince the district attorney to move forward in the investigation with the ultimate goal of charging Sam with the crime.

Sam closed his eyes and thought about the things that he might face in the coming days: a robbery charge and murder rap, the possibility of a search conducted at his home, the scrutiny of the entire investigative team digging into every detail of his life, being put on administrative leave (hopefully with pay), and the media's attempt to uncover the juicy details of a police scandal. Nothing could be more appealing to a raft of investigative reporters than a cop up to his neck in subterfuge and serious criminal allegations.

But I'm innocent, Sam's brain screamed. He brought his fist down and punched the mattress in frustration. *I have no idea how those clothes, money, gun, and boots came to be on my person during a raging thunderstorm. How did that happen?* The failure of his memory left him nauseous with fear and incessant panic.

Leslie appeared at his side of the bed, holding a glass of water in one hand and three colored pills in the other.

"Lez, tell me again about the stuff they found," Sam demanded for the umpteenth time. He was convinced if his memory could function adequately, he could clear this whole thing up in a few minutes. He could point the police to the real killer, the person who actually committed the crime.

"I told you, honey, Lt. Higgins is trying to figure that out. The shoes, jacket, money, and gun are not yours. I told Higgins that, but there's not a lot of wiggle room on that subject. What I think or say right now does not carry a whole lot of weight," she explained, "since I'm obviously going to defend you come hell or high water." She brushed a strand of damp hair away from her face. "Here, take these," she said gently, offering the pills to him.

He swallowed the pills and drank half the water. Sam stared ahead with a vacancy in his eyes, making Leslie's heart skip a few beats. He looked up at her with a troubled expression. Then he grabbed her hand and hung on. "What are we gonna do, Lez?" he asked quietly.

"We're going to find the killer and nail him to the wall." Sam took comfort in her words, but it was the look of determination in her blue eyes and the steely quality in her voice that calmed his racing heart and kept his hopes alive.

MONDAY, SEPTEMBER 1

DWELL IN POSSIBILITY.

EMILY DICKINSON

17

At nine o'clock sharp on Monday morning, Lt. Jim Higgins stood in front of the investigative team in a classroom on the third floor of the La Crosse Law Enforcement Center on Vine Street. As usual, Higgins was dressed to the nines. He wore a lightweight cadet gray suit jacket and pants made of fine Irish wool, a crisp blue and white pinstriped shirt, and a Michael Kors blue and gray paisley tie.

In front of the classroom was a whiteboard with a picture of Vicki Invold taped in the center. Besides the teen's picture, the board contained little else except the skeletal facts of the crime: time, place, location. Everything else—motive, suspects, and possible leads—was up for grabs.

As Jim looked over the small team of detectives, a few city cops straggled in and grabbed seats around one of the long white tables. He wondered what evidence they had collected. For his part, he had little to show for his efforts—he seriously doubted they did either. The only encouraging bit of news was that Sam hadn't been arrested as a suspect—yet. However, Jim knew that wouldn't last long. To top it off, Sheriff Turnmile was hunched in the back of the room, ready to listen and evaluate the evidence, her familiar scowl reflecting her current disposition. Her presence, although completely appropriate, left Jim fighting off the urge to ask her to leave. He huffed at his misgivings, cleared his throat, and fiddled with the knot of his tie.

Higgins looked at each detective, trying to get a feel for what might be in store. DeDe and Paul were calm and focused. Higgins's gaze drifted to the newest member of the team.

Mike Leland, the young street cop, felt the weight of Jim's serious demeanor settle on him. Higgins had notoriously high expectations. Professionalism and integrity were not merely words meant to impress the public; they were principles that guided the decisions and actions of the team during every investigation. Mike looked down at his hands in an effort to escape the chief's penetrating scrutiny.

Despite his outward show of confidence, Jim felt he could just as well have been locked away in a dark closet with no key. Never in his thirty years on the force had he confronted such a bewildering set of circumstances: a young girl murdered in cold blood for a few bucks during a raging thunderstorm, one of his cops facing a debilitating injury who was being framed for a crime Jim was sure he hadn't committed, and a confused jumble of seemingly unrelated facts which muddled rather than clarified the direction the investigation should take. Everyone was exceptionally quiet and subdued. No one offered any interesting information. In addition, Sam and Leslie's conspicuous absence made things feel off-kilter. Everything seemed unfocused and ambiguous.

"Okay, everybody, let's get started," Jim began with more confidence than he felt. The room quieted, and discussion among the cops stopped. Jim felt the weight of the investigation shift to his shoulders. "Since the robbery and murder of Vicki Invold at the Gas & Go in Stoddard on Thursday night, we have collected very little evidence as to who the perpetrator of the crime might be. We have a lot of work to do."

From the back of the room, Sheriff Turnmile's voice startled the group. "Looks to me as if you have a perpetrator—and the evidence as well. What about Officer Birkstein? Where are we on that aspect of the investigation?" The group turned and stared at the sheriff. Jim lifted his chin in her direction. Then, as if watching a tennis match, the cops turned back and waited for Jim's reaction and response to the sheriff's challenge.

"Pardon me for being blunt, ma'am, but the probability of Sam committing a crime of this magnitude is preposterous. I base my opinion on the past five years of working with Sam, during which time I've watched him in almost every conceivable law enforcement situation: tracking down evidence, developing a workable theory of the crime, interviewing hundreds of witnesses and suspects, planning stings and take-downs, shooting and getting shot at. You name it, Sam's done it. His moral fiber and his unwavering loyalty to the safety of the citizens of the La Crosse community is evident to anyone who's had contact with him. I intend to address the articles that were found beneath Officer Birkstein along the highway in a moment. But I repeat—I do not believe now, or ever, that Officer Birkstein was involved in this crime." Jim's hands rested on his hips, his blue eyes blazing at the sheriff's suggestion.

Paul thought Jim looked like a gunslinger who was preparing to fire a volley of bullets at an assailant. *Showdown at the O.K. Corral.* Paul found himself squarely on Jim's side in his defense of Sam. But then he had a series of uncomfortable thoughts. Wasn't justice supposed to be blind? Nobody is above the law, right? Everybody is innocent until proven guilty. What exactly was the sheriff insinuating? How were they supposed to prove Sam's innocence when the evidence so strongly suggested his participation in the crime? Paul squirmed at the implications of his own thoughts, and his disparaging opinion of the sheriff plummeted to a new low.

Elaine Turnmile and Jim locked eyes and continued to stare at one another for a long minute. Finally, Sheriff Turnmile said, "Just checkin'. Carry on, Lt. Higgins."

Everyone remained silent. Jim cleared his throat and continued. "The storm was used as a smokescreen for the crime. I don't have to tell you that Sam is in a terrible position, although I am convinced he was not involved in any of this." Jim threw the sheriff another hostile glance. "Furthermore, Sam is facing another set of formidable physical challenges from the injuries he sustained during the lightning strike. To put it bluntly, he's in a world of hurt on multiple fronts." He paused for effect, glancing at the sheriff seated in the shadows near the back of the room. *Like you give a shit,* he thought bitterly. "However, that does not magically eliminate the evidence that seems to have gravitated to his person. So first, let me address the items found beneath Sam after the lightning strike incident down on Highway 35."

"You know something, Chief?" Paul asked, his eyes wide with concern.

"Something... yes," Jim said hesitantly. "I've talked to Carl Ettinger from crime scene down on second floor. He's analyzed the clothing Sam was wearing when he was found along the road, namely the blue jean jacket. Sam's DNA appeared on the collar of the jacket, but basically, that's the only place it was detected. There's a lot of controversy surrounding secondary touch DNA. You might remember the case of Amanda Knox." Jim noticed the sheriff shaking her head in the back of the room. Jim waved his hand as if to dismiss the vacillating gesture of the sheriff. "The point is, according to Carl, the jacket was not something Sam wore or handled on a regular basis. Because of that, Carl believes the jacket is not Sam's, despite the fact he was wearing it when he was found along the road." The team listened carefully, reserving judgment.

"However—" Jim began.

Paul let out a groan and muttered under his breath.

"There were significant amounts of DNA material from another source, supposedly the owner of the jacket. When we find the perp, we might be able to use the DNA from the jacket to draw some conclusions. But in all likelihood, the DNA on the clothes will become a non-issue and won't be used as evidence to prosecute anyone.

Judges today usually sustain defense motions that make use of touch DNA evidence since it's confusing and misleading. Often, it puts people at the scene of a crime they were never at." Jim paused, gave Sheriff Turnmile a withering stare, and took a deep breath. "So... the upshot of the whole thing means we have to ignore the clothes issue altogether for now. But I still want to find the clothes Sam had on when he left the Gas & Go station."

"Doesn't Leslie know what Sam was wearing when he left the house?" Paul asked.

"Absolutely. She swears Sam was wearing an L.L. Bean rain jacket, a pair of cutoff shorts, a T-shirt, and a pair of Nike running shoes," Jim said. "I have no reason to doubt her."

The group let out a collective sigh of relief, tentative as it was. "What about the boots?" DeDe asked.

"The boots had a distinctive sole pattern which really doesn't help us much since the rain washed away any footprints that might have been left on the side of the road. However, the boots did have some interesting material stuck under the heels, and Carl confirms the same material on the boots was found in the store near the counter." Jim stopped momentarily. "Whoever was wearing the boots was definitely in the store on Thursday night." The team stared at Jim.

"So what was on the boots?" Mike asked after a few uncomfortable moments.

"Manure," Jim said unceremoniously.

"In cow country, that's not much help, is it?" Mike Leland repeated. *And I thought I would be on the cutting edge of solving a difficult crime.* His mouth froze in a lopsided grin.

"If it was just cow manure, you're right. It wouldn't be much help," Jim said. "But, believe it or not, DNA can pinpoint animal feces to a specific animal. In this case, a donkey."

"You've got to be kidding, Chief," Paul said, surprised. "Really?"

"Really," Jim said, straight-faced. "But listen, this is actual evidence that could give us some direction. The original owner of the boots might be a farmer—maybe someone who owns some animals, namely donkeys—so we can start checking that out. Can't be that many donkey owners in the Coulee region, right?" Jim paused. He glanced at his team, then shook his head. "I know it's not much to go on, but right now it's one of the few pieces of solid evidence we have that might lead us to the perpetrator."

The silence from the team was deafening. He felt like he'd gone out on a very shaky limb that was about to break and crash to the ground. "So guys, what have you found out?" he finally asked.

At that very moment, a bustle at the door attracted the group's attention. Carl Ettinger, the CSI tech from second floor, knocked and stepped into the room. He looked straight at Jim and held up a small metal object in a clear ziplock bag and another similar bag that contained a crumpled piece of paper.

"What's that?" Jim asked bluntly.

"Well, we're not sure, but we found it in the pocket of the blue jean jacket. Maybe a car part? A piece of something mechanical?" Carl said. "Thought the team might have some ideas, so I brought it up." He handed the bag to Jim.

"Any prints on it?" Jim asked, turning the bag over to get a good look at the object.

"Yeah, we got a partial thumbprint from it," Carl reported. "It also has a tiny serial number on one side. Other than that, your guess is as good as mine."

Jim looked at Carl as he continued his explanation of the contents in the second bag.

"This one contains a receipt from the gas station. Apparently, someone crumpled the slip and stuffed it in the pocket of the blue jean jacket. It was a little wet, but we dried it out. Gas & Go's store ID number is on every receipt. Somebody bought a candy bar and a pack of Marlboro cigarettes at the Stoddard Gas & Go at 11:34 p.m. on the night in question. Might help establish a timeline of the crime. Did you talk about the necklace?"

"No, not yet," Jim said. The team looked at Jim, waiting for an explanation. "Vicki was wearing a unique open filigree heart necklace the night of the robbery. The chain was broken and was lying on the floor next to her. It appeared to have been jerked off her neck, making me think she might have had an argument with the perpetrator."

"I've got the necklace with the other evidence if any of you want to look at it," Carl said. "Otherwise, that's it for now." Getting no response, he shrugged nonchalantly, turned, waved over his shoulder, and left the room.

Each team member carefully examined the objects in the bags, turning them and examining the contents through the clear plastic. No one had any ideas where the silver ring might have come from. DeDe handed it back to Jim.

"I'll take this with me when I go and talk to Sam this morning," Jim said, rolling his shoulders as if he were trying to remove a heavy weight. "Okay, moving on. Anybody have anything? DeDe, did you find out anymore about Vicki's friends?"

DeDe Deverioux was the newest member of the La Crosse investigative team, although she had already served more than two years on Jim's staff. A native of South Carolina, she grew up in the bayou low country with her grandparents. Upon their deaths, she decided she needed a change and headed north. Her husband, Jude Delaney, followed her. The former owner of a five star New Orleans restaurant and James Beard nominee, Jude had recently opened a new establishment, Si Bon, on the south end of La Crosse. The refurbished barn had become a sensational success throughout the region and featured a combination of fresh, locally grown produce, meats, and cheeses made in the area, and fresh caught fish from the Mississippi River. While her husband cooked and built his reputation as a chef in the city, DeDe worked at the La Crosse Sheriff's Department untangling criminal activities throughout the Coulee region. The pace of crime in La Crosse was nothing like New

Orleans, where she had worked previously, but crime was crime no matter where you went.

DeDe leaned forward and rested her elbows on the table. "Over the weekend, I had a long conversation with Vicki's current boyfriend, BJ LaPointe. He was pretty upset about her death. They'd been going together for about a year. BJ claims they had a loving and stable friendship. He shared his Snapchat and Instagram accounts with me. In his texts and tweets, he said their relationship was Gucci."

"Sorry?" Jim said.

"Things were good, cool," DeDe said.

Jim nodded in understanding. "Any text references to a Devon Williams?" he asked.

"Devon who?" Paul asked.

Jim told the team about his meeting Saturday morning with Bobby Rude and his friends, gave a brief description of the discipline of parkour, and listed the activities Devon Williams was supposedly engaged in, according to the boys.

"Vicki had a relationship with Devon a couple of years ago, according to her parents," Jim explained. "They strongly disapproved since Devon was almost five years older than Vicki. Right now, he's a person of interest in the case simply because of his association with her. But, according to Bobby and his friends, this Devon has a following—a bunch of outsider-type kids on the fringe of school culture who were attracted to him—kids needy for attention and acceptance, including a number of girls who had sexual relationships with him. The kids I talked to say he offered them alcohol and drugs and a listening ear. Apparently, the kids are loyal to him and seem to gravitate to his leadership. He must be pretty charming. The boys described him as intense." Jim lifted his eyebrows as he finished. Not getting a response from anyone, he continued.

"Once this Devon gains their trust, he begins to introduce them to the world of crime. So, for starters, Mike," Jim turned his attention to the newest member of the investigative team, "I want you to check out the petty crimes that have happened within the city limits in the last six months—purse snatchings, house break-ins, vandalism, small-time thefts, things like that. Then categorize them, talk to the kids who were caught, interview them, and get back to me. We need to find some of Devon's followers."

Mike nodded enthusiastically. *Finally, something concrete. Anything's better than manure,* he thought. "Will do, Chief."

Jim turned to Paul. "Let's get a handle on the gun, Paul. You can talk to crime scene and see what they've come up with. Try to find out who it belongs to, when it was purchased, prints on it, like that. You know the drill," Jim said.

"Got it," Paul said seriously.

DeDe interrupted. "Oh, by the way, I sent out a description of Sam's L.L. Bean jacket and Nike running shoes in an email to La Crosse, Vernon, Monroe, Richland, and Trempealeau County recycling centers with a sidebar to inform the personnel who empty trash receptacles and dumpsters at highway waysides to be on the lookout for the clothes. Leslie was able to find two photos of Sam wearing the items, so I included those, too. It's a long shot, but we might get lucky," she concluded, although Jim picked up on her sense of doubt.

"Good. That's great, DeDe," Jim said. "I want you to call every vet center in the area and ask about people who own donkeys."

Paul and Mike looked at each other and squelched the urge to laugh. DeDe's eyes flashed with irritation, and she threw each of them a scathing glance but smiled at Jim. "I'd be glad to, sir," she said through clenched teeth. "I'll also follow up with the school counselors and see who may have been in a relationship with this Devon fellow in the last year."

"Good idea," Jim said. "I have a request into the DOJ for a background check on Devon Williams, but I haven't heard anything yet," Jim said, seemingly unaware of the nonverbal exchange between his team members. "Paul, we'll do a press conference tomorrow morning specifically asking for the public's help in identifying anyone who might have been out and about on the evening of the storm in the Stoddard area near the vicinity of the Gas & Go along with an artist's rendition of Williams as a person of interest." Jim paused, then asked, "Anyone have anything else?" Not getting a response, Jim gathered his folders. "Let's meet again Wednesday afternoon, one o'clock, and see where we're at."

After Jim left the room, Paul leaned over and whispered to DeDe, "Good luck on your donkey hunt."

DeDe gave him a subtle smile. "Just remember this—somethin' my Memaw taught me." Her Southern drawl slipped in as she spoke.

"Oh yeah. What's that?" Paul asked, smiling as he leaned over the table. DeDe looked into his hazel eyes, a lazy grin on her face.

"There's a lot more horses' asses than there are horses," she said in a silky, smooth voice. DeDe stood up and walked confidently down the hall to her office.

"Hey, what's that supposed to mean?" Paul shouted after her.

DeDe turned, throwing Paul a mischievous glance. "Here's another one: If the shoe fits, wear it," and she quietly closed her office door.

18

DeDe Deverioux leaned back in her chair, stretched her hands toward the ceiling, then rubbed her neck and moved her head from shoulder to shoulder, getting out the kinks. It was already noon, and she'd completed ten calls to local veterinarians in the area inquiring about owners of donkeys. So far, she had three names, all in the vicinity of West Salem.

"You wanna know what?" Dr. Harter asked rudely.

"I'm looking for any customer in your practice who might own a donkey. I know it sounds crazy, but it may play a significant role in a criminal investigation in La Crosse County," DeDe explained. She rolled her eyes and swiped her hand across her forehead. *This has got to be the worst assignment I've ever had,* she thought.

Dr. Harter chuckled. "Did ya have a bank robber who escaped on a donkey?"

DeDe gritted her teeth. "Not exactly, but the robber had donkey manure under the heels of his boots." A significant silence followed. "Dr. Harter, are you still there?"

"No kiddin'? Well, of all the stupid things! Don't that just beat all," he said. "I guess jackass jokes wouldn't be appropriate right now, huh?"

"Not really," DeDe said wearily. "So back to donkey owners..."

"I can only think of one guy in my practice who has donkeys that I know of—Jerry Lancaster. He's got a small hobby farm out by the Amish, north on Highway 16. He actually raises donkeys and sells them to Amish sheep farmers. The donkeys are trained to protect the sheep from coyotes and other predators. He makes pretty good money selling them. I've been there a number of times and done vaccinations and health checks on the animals. You might give him a call." Papers rustled in the background as he searched for Jerry's phone number. "His address is 2891 Jorstad Coulee Rd."

"Thanks, Doc. I appreciate it." DeDe hung up the phone, looking at her notebook with the addresses and phone numbers of the donkey owners. She packed up her leather satchel with her notebook and cell phone and wandered to the lobby.

Emily looked up from her administrative duties when DeDe paused at her desk.

"Have you ever had an assignment that absolutely tests your commitment to your profession?" DeDe asked sourly.

"I know. I heard about the donkey thing," Emily said in a low, sympathetic voice.

"Does the whole building know?" DeDe asked, her voice loud with agitation as her arms flopped at her sides in a frustrated gesture.

Emily noticed DeDe's brown eyes were smoldering with resentment. "The news went through the place like wildfire," Emily said. She tipped her head to the side and made an apologetic face. "Sorry. By now, everyone knows. That's a given."

"Paul. Paul and Mike," DeDe said angrily under her breath. She softly pounded the desk with her fist.

"How can I help?" Emily asked, studying DeDe's reaction carefully.

"You can't," DeDe grumbled. She picked up her bag and turned toward the elevator. "I'm leaving and heading for Jerry Lancaster's place over near West Salem somewhere. Then I might head to Cashton. There's another guy over there with a beast of burden. I

DRIFTLESS IDENTITY

won't be back in my office today." She heaved the heavy leather bag onto her shoulder and walked dejectedly toward the elevator, muttering complaints to herself.

Emily watched her go. "First time for everything, I guess," she said as she returned to her work. "Donkey poop. Go figure," she whispered to herself.

At one o'clock in the afternoon, Sheriff Elaine Turnmile sat in her office crunching absentmindedly on a handful of Cheetos. Little orange flecks of baked cheese escaped her mouth and fell down the front of her tan shirt. She was mulling over a number of personal issues. As she thought, she absentmindedly licked the yellow powder from her fingers.

It couldn't have been a more beautiful day—brilliant sunshine, seventy-five degrees, white puffy clouds in a blue sky all framed in the rectangular window of the sheriff's office like a painting. In the distance Elaine could see the soaring sandstone bluffs, the hardwood trees beginning to turn color. The gorgeous weather outside should have cheered her up, but it didn't. Soon, it would be fall, then winter. *Ughhh! Cold and snow,* she thought. She shivered just thinking about it.

Think positive thoughts. Be in the moment. "That's what Dr. Rayholt told me to do," she said softly to herself.

Dr. Rayholt had also given her suggestions about her interactions with staff, family, and the few friends she had. "You need to make some changes, Elaine, or you're going to be a terribly lonely woman. I can recommend some therapy and medication. That might help."

Elaine closed her eyes as the doctor's words rattled around in her head. She inhaled a deep breath, held it for ten seconds, and exhaled slowly. She swiveled in her chair, reached for the desk phone and dialed. "Here goes nothing."

"Jim Higgins," the familiar deep baritone voice crackled over the phone a few seconds later.

"We need to discuss some issues. Can you break away for a half an hour?" she asked, the rudeness lying beneath her words like a snake loitering in the grass.

Jim heard the irritation in her voice. "I'll be down in fifteen minutes, ma'am," he said.

"I'll be waiting."

During the fifteen minutes Elaine waited, she wondered where she'd gone wrong. How could she have so badly misjudged the duties of sheriff?

Six months ago she was interviewing for administration jobs in law enforcement agencies around Wisconsin: Wausau, Superior, Eau Claire, La Crosse. Although she was only forty-five years old, she had a boatload of experience, both as a street cop in Milwaukee and as an instructor at the Madison Police Department Training Center. In those days. she was confident and full of herself. She beat down the doubters and contenders who were waiting to see her fail.

But instead of feeling the glow of success when she landed the sheriff's position in La Crosse, the ensuing responsibilities discouraged her and filled her with skepticism. Fear of failure haunted her every waking minute. Doubts loomed each day like a man-made Everest. Now she was the one who wondered when she was going to trip and fall flat on her face. When she woke up and put her feet on the floor, she wanted to crawl back in bed and hide under the covers. This latest case—the robbery and murder at the gas station—was her first big test as sheriff, and she was sure she would fail miserably. She was surprised to feel tears welling in her eyes.

A quiet knock on the door made her jump. Higgins. She hurriedly wiped away the tears and sat straight and tall.

"Come on in," she said loudly through gritted teeth.

Lt. Higgins opened the door and stepped into the office. He noticed her flushed face. *Had she been crying?* That didn't seem possible, but everyone had a side no one knew about. "You wanted to see me, ma'am?" he asked.

"Yeah, have a seat," Elaine said coldly. She pointed to a battered leather chair that sat against the far wall. Jim walked over and pulled the chair closer to her desk.

"Let me just say this, Sheriff Turnmile," Jim said as he got comfortable, "I know we haven't gotten off to the best start, but—"

"Don't worry about that," Turnmile rudely interrupted. "I expected as much. I know Davy Jones was very competent and a popular leader with the police force here in La Crosse County—and one of your best friends." She hesitated a moment, temporarily at a loss for words. "To be completely honest," her voice wobbled and caught in her throat, "I'm really struggling with how to handle this mess that happened at the gas station on Thursday night..." She watched Jim's face, wondering how her confession would play out. Jim stared at her. "Maybe you've got some ideas?"

After several moments of uncomfortable silence, Jim ventured into the fray. "You heard our discussion this morning. We're kickin' around some possibilities, getting some feelers out on the street. I've called Mike Leland—he's on board. All of my investigators are out right now tracking down various leads." Jim cleared his throat, then charged forward. *Nothing ventured, nothing gained,* he thought. "To be honest, Elaine, you've pissed off just about everyone in the department. I'd suggest you try a little kindness, some common courtesy, and once in a while, fire up your sense of humor. *If you've got one,* he thought. "I think you'll find those things will take you a long way in the right direction."

"Point taken," she said, feeling a sudden urge to call Higgins *sir*. "This morning, I could see you'd taken the bull by the horns. That's good." She watched Jim carefully, trying to think of a way to broach the next subject. "Your experience showed."

"Well, I've been doing this a long time," Jim commented humbly.

"So... what are we gonna do about Sam and this sack of stuff they found underneath him? I'm feeling some pressure about filing charges. People are wondering what's going to happen."

Jim leaned back in his chair, resting his ankle on his knee, studying the gruff sheriff. He wondered who she was referring to. But the sudden turnaround in Elaine's attitude pleased him. He'd expected a shouting match when she called him to her office. Instead, she seemed to be making a concerted effort at repairing her reputation as a hardcore veteran from the inner city.

"We're working on that, too," he said, referring to Sam's predicament. "I was just heading out to Sam's to do a formal interview. Crime scene came up with a few things I want to ask him about. According to Leslie, the jacket and boots don't belong to him, but until we have more conclusive evidence, it looks bad. You can help. Get out in front of the rumors and deal with the press directly. Get ahead of all the insinuations and suspicions. Give them a few morsels they can gnaw on while we try to get a handle on the gun and the clothes."

"That's your advice?" Elaine asked.

"Yep. That's my advice right now," he said simply. *What else do you want?*

"Okay. I'll run with it. Keep me informed on the progress of the investigation," the sheriff said brusquely.

Jim stood. "Will do," he said. "Anything else, ma'am?" Turnmile shook her head and picked up her phone. Jim interpreted the gesture as a dismissal, and he left her office and headed south along the Great River Road to interview Sam Birkstein.

19

On Monday morning at nine o'clock, Sara Knight stood in front of a sophomore American Lit class at Logan High School and eyed the students' sleepy faces. She glanced at the clock. *Nobody should have to teach American Literature at nine in the morning.*

Without their phones in front of them, the students seemed dead to the real world. *They might actually have to make eye contact... and carry on a conversation,* Sara thought. *How in the world am I going to engage them in a discussion about Walt Whitman when they won't even acknowledge my presence?* Fortunately for her, the dogged determination of the Higgins family was not in short supply. *I will find a way,* she thought, grinning to herself. *After all, I am my father's daughter. The acorn hasn't fallen too far from the tree.*

Sara pushed a lock of blonde hair behind her ear as the bell rang. She wore a muted orange sweater over a cream-colored blouse with a brown pencil skirt and tall, brown leather boots. Despite her misgivings on the third day of class, her clear blue eyes sparkled with optimism, and she gave the students a friendly smile.

"Mornin', everyone. Please hand in your reaction paper to the poem you selected from *Leaves of Grass,*" she said.

There was a flurry of noise; students reached into folders, shuffled through papers, tore paper from their notebooks. Suddenly, the door flew open, banging against the wall. Everyone jumped and looked startled. Two teen boys rolled across the floor, a living ball of thrashing arms and legs. Spit flew. Muffled curses accompanied the fight, and some well-placed punches ripped through the air and landed with dull thuds on muscled flesh.

Sara stepped from behind her podium and shouted, "Boys! Stop it!" Students in the front row of desks jumped up and retreated to the perimeter of the room near the wall of windows. Sara was about to reach over and grab Jerrod Fleming's shirt when a random kick from one of the boys tipped over her podium, and her notes about Walt Whitman went flying. The papers fluttered to the floor like autumn leaves drifting to the ground.

Meanwhile, the fight continued. Sara yelled again, louder this time, "Jerrod! Lyle! Stop it right now!" This time she was able to grab Lyle around the waist. She hung on as he heaved himself in the direction of Jerrod. Sara and Lyle landed on the floor. Jerrod stopped for a moment, poised in a wrestling stance, and emitted a vicious snarl like a wild dog. He was promptly grabbed from behind and hauled off his feet by Sherman Granville, the math teacher from the classroom next door.

"What the hell is going on in here?" he yelled, his voice loud and strident. Everyone stopped and stared. Suddenly a deathly quiet descended in the classroom except for the huffing and puffing of the two teenage fighters. Still grasping a fistful of Jerrod's shirt, Granville shouted, "I asked a question, and I want an answer! Now!" His nostrils flared, and his friendly brown eyes blazed with anger as he eyeballed the two fighters.

Sara lay crumpled on the floor. "Are you hurt?" the math teacher asked, giving her a concerned look as he let go of Jerrod's clothing. Sara shook her head. Granville extended his hand, and Sara grabbed it and hauled herself up to a standing position.

"No, no, I'm fine. Let's all calm down." She took a deep breath and got her bearings. Boys," she finally said, her eyes like cold granite, "you will accompany me to the office so we can sort this out. Now!" She pointed her shaking finger at the door.

Sherman leaned over. "I'll watch your class. I've got prep, so you just go." He began picking up the papers off the floor.

Sara shook her head in disbelief. "Thanks," she whispered as she walked by him, accompanying the hostile boys. "Nothing like starting the morning out with a fistfight."

Back on the second floor of the law enforcement center, Carl Ettinger was explaining his findings from the crime scene to Paul Saner. Ettinger stretched his long, lanky figure back in his chair, which creaked ominously from the extra tension like a fiddle string being tuned a little too tightly. The CSI tech eyed the pistol that lay on the long counter against the wall.

Paul Saner leaned over the counter and looked at the number on the pistol. "Yeah, I see where it's been scratched out. It's probably stolen," he said. "Anything else I should know?"

Carl tugged on his nose, then said, "It's a Kimber 9-millimeter. Nice gun. Probably cost six or seven hundred. Single action. Might want to check with firearms dealers in the area. Maybe it was purchased recently, and the dealer might remember the buyer, but that's a long shot. Three bullets were fired—all three at the victim's core, according to the coroner. He wasn't aiming to injure—lethal intent all the way. Whoever did it wanted the girl dead." The CSI tech looked over at Paul and raised his eyebrows as he finished his recitation of the dire facts.

"That's grim," Paul commented thoughtfully as he took a picture of the gun with his cell phone.

"For someone who deals in the hard truth of incontrovertible facts, that is an opinion, for what it's worth. Fact or not, I'd say it's all pretty tragic. She was a pretty girl. So sad," Carl concluded. His shoulders slumped in defeat.

"Tell that to her parents," Paul said as he turned to exit the lab.

Carl swiveled quickly, pulling his long legs under the chair. He held up an index finger. "One other thing—actually, a good thing—Sam's prints are not on the gun."

"I didn't expect them to be," Paul said sternly as he stared at Carl. "But that *is* a good thing."

Paul took the elevator to the first floor, walked through the lobby, hung a left, and walked down a long corridor devoid of any artwork until he came to a door labeled La Crosse County Morgue and Medical Examiner. He pulled the door open. Carol Higgins looked over the top of the computer screen and smiled warmly at Paul. She had worked in the morgue for several years and now worked part-time.

"Paul! Good to see you. Looking for Luke?" she asked.

"Yeah. He in?"

"Yes. He's finishing the autopsy on the Invold girl. Let me see if he's got time to talk to you," Carol said. She got up, walked through her office down a short hallway, and pushed the button on the side of the double swinging doors. One door swung open, and she walked through. Several minutes later, she returned.

"He'll be done in fifteen minutes. So how's Ruby and the kids?" she asked as she sat down behind the counter.

Paul and Carol visited and shared kid stories, family news, and other law enforcement gossip. Finally, Luke Evers, La Crosse County medical examiner, appeared and waved Paul into his office. Paul found a chair and looked expectantly at Luke.

"So, what do the results look like on the Invold girl?" he asked. "Anything unusual?"

"Not really, but I'm not completely done yet. Three shots to the center of the chest with a 9-millimeter handgun of some kind. We retrieved all the bullets, two from the body and one from the wall behind the cash register. The striations on the bullet are being microscopically analyzed, but they're not finished yet. The shooter was at close range, not more than ten feet away. The girl really never had a chance, even after the first shot. One shot went straight through the heart, the rest came in rapid succession, close proximity. Lethal intent all the way, I'd say," he finished, looking sad.

"Never gets any easier, does it?" Paul said.

"No, it actually gets harder, especially after you have children of your own. It's not something you'd ever want to happen to your kid."

For an instant, Paul could picture his children, Melody and Max, all grown up, on the threshold of adult life, full of optimism, exuberant about the possibilities that stretched out before them. The office grew quiet as both men got lost in their own thoughts about their families and kids for a few moments. Thoughts about life. Thoughts about the reality of violence and evil let loose in the world.

"Okay. Guess that says it all." Paul hoisted himself from the chair. "Thanks, man."

"No problem. It's what I do," Luke said.

Paul turned and left the morgue. *No surprises there,* he thought.

20

Higgins had intended to head down the Great River Road to Sam's in the morning, but the sun was high in the sky when he finally got on the road. In the distance, the surface of the Mississippi River sparkled with sunshine like a diadem of jewels. The spectacular blue sky lifted Jim's mood. Opening the car window, he rested his arm on the frame and breathed deeply, the lingering traces of office staleness chased away. The strong smell of brackish water and the musky smell of vegetation that grew along the riverbanks cleared his head.

Birksteins' driveway was just a couple hundred feet north of the Highway 56 turnoff to Genoa. While Jim waited for the oncoming traffic to clear so he could turn up the driveway, he noticed a huge barge, the *John McHenry*, sitting in the water near shore. A couple of guys were out on the decks working the ropes and laying rigging, preparing the barge for its passage through Lock and Dam Number 8. Someone leaned over the railing scanning the water, checking the tow for deformation and broken studs. Another man, puffing on a cigarette, sat on the edge of the huge steel cover that protected the grain within. Beyond the barge, the steep blue-green hills and the dramatic sandstone bluffs were beginning to show hints of gold and orange. *Fall's just around the corner*, Jim thought.

When the traffic cleared, he turned into the driveway, proceeded up a steep incline, and parked near the garage. He got out of the Suburban and turned to look at the Mississippi again. Sam and Leslie had certainly chosen a house with a spectacular view. Jim thought of the song by The Who, "I Can See for Miles." You could literally see for miles up here—Minnesota was just two miles west, Iowa about twenty miles south.

While Jim stood there humming The Who song, his cell buzzed in his pocket.

"Higgins."

"Dad? It's Sara."

"Yeah, sweetheart. What's up?" Jim was back on speaking terms with his daughter. Since Sara's recent marriage to former priest Jerome Knight in June, their father-daughter relationship had righted itself, the stormy waves of distrust and resentment that had developed during Sara's abduction had been beaten back, and now they seemed to be on a more even keel.

"Dad, I need you to come over to Logan High School as soon as you can or send someone over here who can help," Sara said calmly, carefully choosing her words.

"Why? Aren't the city cops there?"

"Yeah, they are, but let me fill you in. Two boys in my American Lit class had a terrific row this morning. Fists were flying, and one of the boys has a nasty-looking black eye, and now they're sitting in the principal's office. One of them is Jerrod Fleming. He said he met you the other day."

Jim moved his hand over his eyes and moaned. "Let me guess. He did something stupid," he said, not hiding the disgust in his voice.

"Well, using your fists to solve a problem could be called stupid, but I'm more concerned that something criminal could be involved," Sara said.

"In what way?"

"Dad, I don't have time to go into a detailed explanation; it's just a sixth sense that something is wrong. My next class starts in five minutes. That's why I need an investigator to get over here and talk to these two kids. Jerrod refuses to talk to anyone unless it's someone who's investigating Vicki Invold's murder. This fight had something to do with the robbery and shooting in Stoddard the other night."

Jim's stomach turned over, but he felt like a knot of suspicion was beginning to loosen. *Jerrod knows something he didn't tell me the other day.* "Okay. I'll get a hold of Paul or Mike Leland," he said tersely. "I'll try to get them over there in the next half hour. Then I'll follow up with them. How does that sound?"

"Sounds good. Thanks, Dad," Sara said and hung up.

Jim made a quick call, dispatching Paul to the school, promising to head up there as soon as he was done with Sam.

Disconnecting from the call, Jim stood in the warm sunshine and thought back to Sara and Jerome's wedding in the backyard at their home on Chipmunk Coulee Road in June. A beautiful evening, seventy-five degrees, stars twinkling above the patio, the little string band playing music, people getting happy and a little tipsy, dancing and swaying together. Crickets chirped in the high grass by the creek, candlelight lanterns glowed along the patio, Sara was beautiful in her lovely gown, and Jerome appeared handsome and happy. By ten o'clock, Lillie and Henri had petered out, exhausted from the day's activities, and Carol took them into the house to get ready for bed.

Jim looked among the guests, and when he didn't see Carol or the kids, he traipsed in the house searching for them. Carol was just coming out of Henri's bedroom. She put a finger to her lips, then grabbed his hand and headed down the hall to their bedroom. When they arrived, she turned, leaned against the wall, and pulled Jim to her. She kissed him fervently, her hands running up and down his back under his tux. She hooked her leg around Jim's thigh, and when she came up for air, Jim saw that look in her eyes.

He'd never loved anyone like he loved Carol. Oh, he'd loved Margie, his first wife. He loved their life together, and he'd always treasure the memory of her in his heart. But Carol was so unpredictable and sassy. She ignited his romantic flame like no one else he'd ever known.

"Honey, we have a hundred guests out on the patio. You can't be serious," Jim whispered hoarsely, her passionate caresses and kisses arousing him.

"Oh, Jim," she said, kissing him again, tugging at his cummerbund, moving up and nibbling on his ear. "It's just that you're so handsome in that tux, and everything's so romantic. That little band is terrific and..."

"How much have you had to drink?" Jim interrupted while he kissed her neck.

Her head jerked back. "Hardly anything. A couple of glasses of wine."

Suddenly, a deep voice penetrated the dim recesses of the hallway. "Jim? Carol?"

"It's my brother Dave. So much for your sexy ideas," Jim whispered. "Don't worry. We'll have plenty of time when everyone leaves." He grinned and kissed her again. "Yeah, we're right here," he said, grabbing Carol's hand and pulling her into the hallway. "Just tucking the kids in for the night."

He smiled to himself. She'd made it worthwhile later. Very worthwhile. The memory of it made him warm all over.

He heard the creak of a screen door opening. Sam hobbled down the driveway, walking painfully across the gravel. Suddenly the happy wedding night capers fizzled as he watched Sam limp toward him, his face taut with tension, his eyes shadowed with worry. Jim missed Sam's friendly smile and easygoing demeanor. Although his physical features hadn't changed—the brown, curly hair streaked with blond, his handsome, tanned face, and deep-set hazel eyes— the trauma of the lightning strike had changed his countenance.

Something ugly was brewing beneath the surface, and Jim didn't like what he saw. However, he cut Sam some slack, knowing he was still in the grips of recovery. The healing process was just starting.

"Hey, Chief," Sam muttered. He stopped walking and stood in front of Jim, studying him as if a message had been written on his forehead. He wore a pair of black sweatpants cut off at the knees, well-worn leather sandals with red and black striped socks to cushion his burned feet, and a red T-shirt that said, "Not everyone likes me, but not everyone matters."

After Sheriff Turnmile's withering stares, Sam's expression of curiosity didn't bother Jim in the least. He was used to the funky clothes, especially the running commentary on the shirts. The warm sunshine beat down on their backs, and Jim wished he could be out on the river on the *Little Eddy*, the boat he inherited from his dad, cruising over to Lawrence Lake near La Crescent, Minnesota, casting for a mess of crappie and walleye instead of dealing with this mess.

"So... how are things going?" Jim asked, his friendly blue eyes taking stock of Sam.

Sam squirmed under his steady gaze. "Not much different than yesterday. Lez's parents left this morning, and my parents will probably be arriving about suppertime."

"Can we find a place to talk? I've got some news and some questions for you," Jim said.

Sam turned back to the house, waving Jim forward. "Let's sit on the patio out back. It's nice and quiet there," Sam said.

They walked through a breezeway that connected the house and garage and stepped through a wrought-iron gate that led to a small brick patio in the back of the house. It was a cozy little nook decorated with pots of geraniums and petunias. Four pine Adirondack chairs surrounded a fire ring at the center. A tall evergreen tree and a couple of mature maples shaded the patio, making it pleasantly cool. Sam and Jim made themselves comfortable. Jim laid his cell phone on the arm of the chair.

"How are you feeling?" Jim asked again, settling back in the chair.

Sam groaned. "Not you, too?"

"Well, you never answered my question the first time I asked it."

"Yeah, I know," Sam said dejectedly. "I know I'm being a pain in the ass, but all this attention just doesn't suit me. I've never been someone who dwells on my shortcomings or physical limitations. I guess I just don't know how to handle all the attention since the accident." Sam rubbed his hands together as if he were chilled, then looked toward the bluffs that rose majestically into the blue sky a hundred yards behind the house.

"Well, get over yourself," Jim chided gruffly. "People mean well, Sam. Once you get back on your feet, they'll quit asking."

Sam propped his elbows on his knees like a pouting teenager and scowled.

"Anybody contact you from the press?" Jim asked.

Sam sat up straight and nodded vigorously. "Oh, yeah, but Lez has managed to fend them off so far. They're like a pack of wolves who smell blood, and as you can imagine, Lez is the she-wolf protecting her cub." The word picture Sam painted made him grin, the first smile Jim had seen in a couple of days.

"She'll always be in your corner. I can't think of anybody better to fend off the shysters. By the way, Sheriff Turnmile is having a press conference right about now," Jim said, tapping his phone.

"And?"

"Not sure of the upshot yet. We'll see what develops, but she's supposed to be beating back the gossip about your involvement in the case. I told her to give them a few tidbits to chew on until we can get a handle on what might have happened. As you can imagine, I don't have a whole lot of confidence in her ability to charm anyone, least of all a bunch of rabid reporters intent on nailing a cop suspected of a crime. You know what reporters are like when they smell blood."

They sat quietly for a moment until Jim felt the pressure of minutes slipping by.

"Listen, Carl Ettinger at crime scene discovered a few things that I want to run by you." Jim fumbled in the pocket of his suit jacket and pulled out two plastic bags. He stopped. "Before I start, though, I have good news: Paul just told me that your prints were not found on the gun. That's a major deal."

Sam tipped his head back, looked at the sky, and muttered, "Well, I could have told you that."

Jim continued. "The next thing is this ring." He handed the bag to Sam. "It was found in the pocket of that denim jacket you were wearing, and I wondered if you'd know where it might have come from."

Sam took the bag and turned it over in his hand, examining it closely as if his life depended on it—which, at this point in the investigation, was a distinct possibility. He stood up suddenly, winced, and motioned Jim to follow him.

They walked to the garage and entered the side door. Sam pushed the button on the automatic door opener, and the wide overhead door creaked up, filling the dark interior with sunlight. Jim noticed three mountain bikes hanging on large hooks against the south wall of the garage. Although he was no expert, he could see they were well-cared for and seemed to be treasured possessions of Sam's.

"I bought this Cannondale Trail 5 this spring. Had to lay out nine hundred fifty bucks for it, but it's really a nice bike. Gonna try to get out on it in the next few weeks. Maybe take Paco for a run."

Sam held up the ring in the bag and compared it to a ring found between the handlebars and the head tube. "I could be mistaken," he said, "but I think this is a headset ring for a mountain bike." He looked closer, then stood up straight. "There's a serial number on it—it's super small—but with a little help from a bike repairman, I think we could identify it."

"Really?" Jim asked.

"Really. Let me give my bike guy a quick call." Sam slipped his cell from his pocket, scrolled to find the number of Buzz's Bike Shop on Rose Street, and had a quick, intense conversation with a guy on the other end.

When the conversation ended, Sam looked over at Jim and said, "Yep. He's pretty sure it's from a mountain bike. If you take it into the shop, he thinks he can identify the make and model."

We've gone from donkey poop to mountain bikes, Jim thought. *I didn't see that coming.*

"Okay, that's good. Something anyway," Jim said.

"What's the other thing?" Sam asked. "You said you had a couple of things to show me."

Jim pulled out the other ziplock bag and flattened it, pressing it out between his thumb and finger so they could read the print through the clear bag. "This receipt was found in the jacket pocket, too. It shows the purchase of a candy bar and a pack of Marlboros at the Stoddard store at 11:34 p.m. Do you remember if you were still in the store then?" Jim wasn't hopeful that Sam would remember the series of events leading up to the lightning strike, but he had to ask. If nothing else, it established the reality of Sam's amnesia due to his injuries.

"I left my house, according to Leslie, at 11:02. You know she's kinda weird that way—got a memory like an elephant. It took me about seven minutes to get to Stoddard. Although I don't remember specific details, things are starting to come back a little. I sat in the truck for probably a minute or so, hoping the rain would quit. When it didn't, I got out, went in the store, got milk, bananas, and ice cream, paid the girl, and was back in the car in about ten minutes. Tops. So I'd say that I was out of the store no later than 11:20."

"Still have your receipt?" Jim asked. Sam nodded.

"Lez probably has it somewhere."

"Good. Find it and hang on to it. Without the CCTV video, that slip establishes the window of time when you were there."

"I've made that trip every day over the last couple of months, so I know how long it takes me to get up the river road. Since I hate runs to the store, especially at night, I don't waste any time doing it. It's in and out. I'm sure that's what I did Thursday night."

"You don't remember meeting someone inside the store, in an aisle or something, or maybe at the door when you were going out?"

Sam thought, then shook his head. "Nope. I don't remember meeting anyone. It was raining hard, and the storm was pretty intense. There weren't any other people around that I remember."

"So the perpetrator must have entered the store sometime after 11:20, made his purchase at 11:34, and the shooting was a few minutes after that, possibly between 11:34 and 11:37, give or take a minute or two."

"How is that important?" Sam asked, confused. "Does it tie in with something else?"

"Well, establishing a timeline might make finding witnesses more probable. We have a smaller window to work with. It might not mean anything yet, but it could be crucial down the road," Jim explained.

"Or not," Sam said despondently.

"Or not," Jim echoed.

21

Paul Saner hurried down the curved sidewalk that led to the front entrance of Logan High School on Avon Street. The commons area was quiet between classes, sunlight streaming in on the ceramic tile through the huge front windows. Paul greeted a school police officer who was roaming the halls and followed the signs to the administrative offices. Opening the door, he approached the counter and flashed his ID.

"Paul Saner. I hear you have a couple of students who want to talk to someone in law enforcement."

"Just one moment. I'll get Mr. Vistad," the secretary said. She stood and walked down a short hallway, turned into an office, and when she came out, a tall man was following her. He wore black dress pants and a white shirt, and the knot of his burgundy tie was loose, the top button of his shirt undone. He looked tired, but when he came to the counter, he smiled and shook Paul's hand.

"Paul, good to see you," he said. Drew Vistad was a familiar fixture in the educational hierarchy of the La Crosse School District. He'd worked his way up through the ranks, first as a classroom teacher, then through numerous administrative positions until finally landing the principal position at Logan some fifteen years ago. He had a penchant for the classroom teacher, a fierce admiration for the way each instructor influenced the direction of their students' lives.

Paul said, "So, my understanding is you've got a couple of kids I need to talk to."

"They're in here," he said, turning and waving Paul through. "We've been waiting for you."

Mr. Vistad led Paul into the depths of the administrative wing, turned right down a short hallway, then stopped abruptly in front of a closed door with a long rectangular window above the doorknob. Paul glanced through the window and saw a scrawny teen sitting in a chair, holding an ice bag against his eye.

"We've separated the two boys for obvious reasons—the main one so they wouldn't kill each other," the principal said in a sour tone. "I won't muddy your questioning with a bunch of irrelevant information except to say the student is Lyle Leverentz. I'd like to sit in, if I may," he said, tipping his head to the side as if to ask permission.

"Absolutely. Let's get at it," Paul said, turning the knob.

As the two men entered the room, Lyle looked up and slowly lowered the ice from his face. His eyes were hard and dark, his face shadowed with anxiety. The black eye had turned a deep purple despite the ice. Paul guessed he was about sixteen, but he had the brittle look of someone much older, someone who'd already experienced the rough-and-tumble jolts of adult life. He wore all black: black T-shirt, black jeans, and black combat boots laced tightly at the ankles. Paul was sure he would have carried a handgun if he'd been allowed to. That would have probably been black, too. Color-coordinated to blend in with his black spiked hair. At the moment, Paul didn't have a lot of faith that the interview would produce the information he was hoping for.

Sitting down opposite Lyle, the two older men got comfortable in the cushioned chairs and studied the kid in front of them. Paul had a feeling this interview might devolve into a staring match—a contest of wills; many of these tough kids had the resolve of a hardened warrior like the heroes in the fantasy video games they played. Paul wasn't interested in a power struggle, so he skipped the I-want-to-get-to-know-you-and-be-your friend chat. Instead, he said, "Lyle, I understand you had an altercation this morning with another student. Can you tell me what happened?"

Lyle dipped his chin to his chest, thinking and calculating. Then he lifted his head, his grim expression laced with resistance. "Why should I?" he asked, his lip curling with contempt.

Paul smoothed his tie, leaned forward across the table, and pointed his index finger at Lyle's chest. "You should tell me because I'm a police officer, and I might be able to unravel the conflict you're having with this other student, especially if it involves Devon Williams," he said, keeping his voice flat and professional.

At the sound of Devon's name, Lyle's eyes changed from hard to wary. Although the conversation had only begun, the mention of Devon Williams moved the discussion past the trite details of the fistfight into more complicated territory.

"How do you know Devon?" Paul asked. "Where did you meet him?"

"Who says I have?"

"I know more than you think." Paul was taking a risk with his assumption. Nevertheless, as Higgins liked to say, nothing ventured, nothing gained. Higgins also reminded his team regularly that when you assumed things, you could end up looking like the first three letters of the word. But Paul was surprised when the kid began asking him questions. It was a gutsy move that reminded Paul of a move on a chessboard.

"Well, maybe I should ask—what do *you* know about Devon?" The teen looked down his nose at the principal and the detective. Paul marveled at his composed attitude, but his physical antics told another story; the corners of his mouth twitched, and he puckered his lips together. His knuckles were white from grasping the arms of the chair, and his leg jiggled up and down. He was nervous, but he put on a good act.

"No, no, no," Paul said, his index finger ticking back and forth like a metronome in time to the words. "I get to ask the hard questions. That's how this works." He crossed one leg over his knee in a casual move. Continuing in a conversational tone, he said, "But, since you're the curious type, I'll play your little game." Paul cleared his throat and began. "To answer your question, here's what I know about Devon Williams. I know he recently dated Vicki Invold, the girl who was shot to death at the Gas & Go in Stoddard. I know he has a group of kids around him who seem to admire his criminal activities, who hold him in high regard, despite the fact that he's nothing but a two-bit hoodlum and bully. I know he charms young girls into his lair, and then when he's taken all their self-respect, he dumps them and leaves them to pick up the pieces." Paul's voice hardened. He leaned forward over the table and dipped his chin downward, watching Lyle's reaction. "I know he's been encouraging his little band of brothers to commit petty crimes throughout the city. Burglary, house break-ins, shoplifting. That kind of stuff. Sound familiar?"

The teen was obviously conflicted. He sighed and looked out the window, stalling, but his leg continued to jiggle up and down.

"What makes you think I'm doin' that kind of stuff?" Lyle sneered, looking back at Paul.

"Officer Mike Leland has a list of kids who've been involved in some delinquent activities around town. You're on the list, according to the La Crosse juvenile court proceedings from the last few months. And he talked to your court-appointed social worker—a Jackie Dreves. Sound familiar?"

Lyle slumped forward, propped his elbows on the table, and cradled his head in his hands. He sat like that for several minutes, during which time Paul and Principal Vistad exchanged knowing glances. The silence continued for several moments until Lyle lifted his head and slouched back in his chair. His confession tumbled out.

"I met him on a houseboat on the marina over by French Island in May... I think," Lyle mumbled.

"You mean where the Black River dumps into the Mississippi?" Paul asked. "That place near Veterans Freedom Park off Clinton?"

"Yeah, that's the place," Lyle said.

"Why were you there?"

"Buyin' weed."

"And?"

"We got talkin'. Devon was—" Lyle looked directly at Paul and squinted, "charming." He spat out the last word like it was a piece of rotten meat. Then the kid grinned and lifted one eyebrow in a sarcastic expression.

"You find this funny, Lyle?" Paul asked.

The teen shrugged his shoulders, his smile faded, and his eyes turned hard again.

Paul continued. "We believe Devon may be involved somehow with the robbery and murder at the Gas & Go last Thursday night," Paul explained, unfazed by Lyle's surly attitude. "What do you know about his relationship with Vicki?"

"She came runnin' every time he whistled, he conquered, and she disappeared in the weeds," Lyle said, his lip curling in a malicious grin. "He has an appetite for sex—the younger, the better."

Paul thought about his daughter, Melody. Although she was only five, he knew how fast the years would pass. Soon she'd be a teenager—a vulnerable, innocent teenager, if he had anything to say about it. Someone ripe for the likes of Devon. Someone easily buffaloed by his empty flattery and contrived platitudes. Paul felt a knot of anger growing in his gut, but he took a deep breath and focused his attention on the information Lyle offered.

"When did you meet with Devon?" Paul asked brusquely.

"Last month, I think," Lyle answered.

Paul frowned. "I'm confused about something. I thought Vicki and Devon broke up over a year ago," he said.

Lyle thought for a few moments. "Well, they did break up," he finally said, "but they were seeing each other on and off since then. I'm not really sure, but I remember seeing them behind a bar on Third Street just a little while ago—like a month ago. They were having some kind of argument—a discussion about something. But it wasn't friendly."

"Okay. Do you remember the name of the boat you were on when you met Devon?"

"Nah. Just a houseboat. Kinda dumpy. No idea whose it was."

"When was the last time you saw him?"

"A week ago."

"Where?"

"In an alley off George Street behind Motel 6."

Paul considered everything Lyle had told him. Some of it lined up with what he already knew. Some of the information was new, like the houseboat on French Island and the recent contacts with Vicki. But it was clear from the conversation with Lyle that a conflict existed between Devon and Vicki. What were they arguing about? Was that why Devon had come to the Gas & Go on Thursday night? To resolve an argument that had started in the alley?

Paul felt his phone vibrate in his pocket. He fished it out and answered.

"Paul. It's Luke at the morgue. Listen, I wasn't totally finished with Vicki's autopsy when you stopped in. There's more."

"Yeah. What's that?" Paul asked.

"Vicki was pregnant—about five months along, give or take a few weeks."

"Oh boy," Paul said, closing his eyes briefly, feeling like he'd been sucker punched.

"Who's gonna tell her parents?" Luke asked. "Paul, are you still there?"

22

Seth O'Connor lifted an expensive dirt bike out of the weeds near the alley behind his house in Stoddard. He couldn't remember seeing any kids in the neighborhood who owned a bike like this. This one looked like something that somebody might race with—wide tires with deep treads, beefy construction, no back suspension, and a high seat set at a steep angle.

Huh. Wonder where this came from. Have to ask the wife, he thought. He leaned the bike against the wall of his garden shed at the back of his property along the narrow alley. He puttered in his garden cleaning out dead refuse and plants beaten into the ground by the driving rain from the storm Thursday night. He wheeled the dead material to his compost pile, then walked to the house.

"Esther? You here?" he yelled into the kitchen, hanging his hat on a hallway hook.

"I'm here. Where else would I be? You want some lunch?"

"Sure. Whaddya got?"

"Egg salad sandwiches and apple pie."

Seth walked into the kitchen and gave his wife a peck on the cheek. She had developed a significant tire around the middle, but he was no Romeo anymore, either. They had fallen into a familiar and comfortable acceptance of one another's warts. Middle-aged spread, graying hair, a few wrinkles here and there, Seth's bald crown—it was all part of the package now.

Esther busied herself with the sandwiches, cut a couple of wedges of pie, and laid the table with plates, forks, and coffee cups. They sat down together and began to eat. The sunlight streamed into the kitchen, leaving streaks of light across the round oak table.

"Did you notice a bike back in the weeds by the shed this week?" Seth asked as he chewed on a bite of sandwich. He reached for a sweet pickle.

"A bike? No, I haven't been back there for a couple of days. When did you find it?" Esther asked.

"Just now. I was working in the garden, and when I went into the shed to get a rake, I noticed the bike leaning up against the wall next to the alley."

"The neighbor kids have bikes, but they've never left any of them in our yard." Esther was puzzled by the news. "Where do you think it came from?"

Seth shrugged. "I don't know where it came from. Looks expensive. I wonder…" His voice trailed off.

After several minutes of silence, Esther asked, "What were you wondering?"

Seth looked at her, then harrumphed. "Probably nothin', but I was thinking about that robbery at the Gas & Go Thursday night. You know, those two detectives who stopped to talk to me."

"Who? You didn't tell me that," Esther said accusingly.

"Yes, I did. Don't you remember?"

"No, you didn't tell me. I would have remembered that," she insisted.

And so it went for several minutes, back and forth, until Seth finally called a truce. "Okay, maybe I didn't tell you, but that's not the point. I have a feeling that bike might have something to do with that robbery. I think I'll call that detective."

"If it makes you feel better, do it," Esther said.

"Yeah. That's the least I can do. It might be helpful," Seth finished. He looked relieved.

"You want pie?" she asked.

"Sure," he said. While he waited for Esther to serve his pie, he dug in his wallet. Looking at the card, he remembered the name, Paul Saner. *I'll give him a call,* he thought.

23

By three o'clock Monday afternoon, Jim was back in his office on the third floor of the law enforcement center on Vine Street. He sat staring out his long, narrow window at the traffic below, his feet propped on the windowsill. A verse from Proverbs he'd read that morning drifted into his mind: "He who sows injustice will reap calamity, and the rod of his fury will fail." Whoever carried out the crimes against Vicki Invold was heading for disaster—and a big slice of justice. He'd see to it. A fresh breeze wafted into the office, lifting Jim's mood and reviving him. He turned back to his desk and stared at the copy of the DOJ's background check on Devon Williams.

Jim scanned the materials rapidly: Devon Williams, age 24, Black, social security number, fingerprints, arrests in Iowa, Wisconsin, and Minnesota. The arrests involved two traffic violations for speeding in Iowa, a misdemeanor theft of property in Minnesota, which was dismissed due to a mistake by the arresting police officer, several counts of harassment and aggravated battery against gays and lesbians in Minnesota and Wisconsin for which Devon had spent a year and a half in jail, and resisting arrest in Wisconsin which landed him in the La Crosse County jail for three months in 2019. Jim added up his fines, totaling over $8,000. Finding funds to pay the fines would be enough for a guy with criminal tendencies to begin venturing into serious crime. In addition, he had failed a drug test for a job at Sam's Club in Onalaska in 2019. Since the time of the background check six years ago, his residence had changed eleven times, and currently his address was unknown. His job history and address disappeared from the report in 2019, leaving Jim to conclude he had been living on the street and probably was involved in nefarious activities to survive.

Jim sighed and flipped the papers on his desk with a flick of his wrist. Although misdemeanor charges didn't land you in state or federal prison, the fines and jail time were backbreaking and depressing, to say nothing of the blemish on your job resume and the smear on any credible reputation you might have had.

Jim's cell rang.

"Higgins."

"Hey, it's Paul. Just found out from Luke that Vicki was five months pregnant.

"Oh boy, that complicates things," Jim commented.

"Yeah, it does, and I also found out a few things when I talked to the two kids at Logan who got in a fistfight this morning."

"Let's hear it," Jim said gruffly.

"Lyle Leverentz revealed that Devon has been dealing drugs— cocaine and weed out of a houseboat over on French Island. Apparently, Devon's sexual preferences run to young girls. The younger, the better, according to Lyle. He might entertain them there, but Lyle wasn't sure about that."

"Not surprising," Jim commented laconically. "What else?"

"He must be living off drug sales and small-time heists around the city, pawning the stuff his little cohorts bring to him. But I'm also wondering if he's trafficking some of the girls he's been involved with. Lots of guys pay big money for young flesh." Paul's voice hardened as he related the facts to Higgins.

"So where is Devon now? Did Lyle say?"

"He told me he doesn't have a vehicle that he knows of, but get this, he rides some kind of fancy bike around town. The only place Lyle knew he'd been was the houseboat, although he has met him in a few alleys on the north side to buy drugs."

"That's interesting," Jim said. *Maybe the perpetrator did escape on a bike the night of the robbery and murder.* "All right, where is this Lyle kid now?"

"At school," Paul said. "One more thing. Devon and Vicki had an argument down behind a bar on Third Street about a month ago. Lyle thought it was about something serious. So I'm thinking maybe he hunted her down and visited her while she was working at the Gas & Go in Stoddard to continue the conversation. They argued, and it got out of hand."

Jim suddenly sat forward in his chair. "That fits with what I think might have happened at the gas station. That broken necklace bothers me. An argument would explain how it might have ended up on the floor. What else did you talk about?" Jim asked.

"Before the principal sent him back to class, I warned him that we would be checking in with him regularly, so he better keep his nose clean and stay the hell away from Devon."

"Good advice, but he won't follow it, most likely," Jim concluded.

"I'm heading over to French Island right now to check out the houseboat thing," Paul said.

"Wear your vest. Be careful," Jim warned.

"Got it. Talk to you later," and Paul hung up.

24

While Paul traveled north to French Island, Jim decided to head over to Buzz's Bike Shop to check on the ring found in the pocket of the blue jean jacket. Traffic was busy. People were heading home from work. A mangy dog wandered in front of Jim's vehicle, forcing him to brake suddenly to avoid hitting it. The car behind Jim honked at him and flipped him off. Unperturbed, Jim waved out the window and drove on.

Buzz's Bike Shop was on the corner of Rose and River Valley Drive, just two blocks from the Mississippi River and the marina where Devon had supposedly been hanging out, according to Lyle. Buildings like these were familiar to La Crosse residents. They were scattered throughout the old logging and brewery sections of town. Many of them had been converted to storefronts or apartments for college students.

The bike shop was a Victorian red brick monstrosity with a forest green turret and arched brick windows. A plaster Napoli cornice ran along the eave of the roof. Four or five expensive bikes were padlocked in a bike rack outside the shop. Jim parked, got out, and walked into the shop.

As he opened the front door, the smell of rubber tires, plastic, and metal overwhelmed him. He was transported back to the machine shop on the farm in Blair, where his dad had serviced, repaired, and tinkered on farm machinery. Several customers were milling about the store. A few waited patiently at a service counter in the center of the shop. Jim browsed, amazed by the selection and quality of the bikes on display.

The bicycle world had certainly changed since he'd saved all his chore money for his first Schwinn pedal bike. He could still remember that bike: the red and white paint, the cushioned leather seat, and the red, white, and blue streamers that dangled from the end of the handlebars.

A young man approached him and interrupted his reverie. He was muscular and in top physical shape. *Reminds me of Sam,* Jim thought.

"May I help you, sir?" he asked, fixing his gaze on Jim.

Jim reached into his jacket pocket and pulled out his ID, flashing it for the clerk to see. The young man looked at the ID, then raised his eyebrows in surprise.

"Don't have too many detectives coming in here," he said in a friendly way.

"I can believe that," Jim said, smiling. "I need to talk with a bike mechanic. Is that what they're called these days?" he asked.

"Yep. Come with me," the young man said, crooking his finger over his shoulder.

Jim followed the clerk through the store to a large back room with high ceilings and walls lined with tools, some familiar to Jim and some he supposed were specific to bike repair. A counter ran along one wall, and two young repairmen were hard at work adjusting the bikes' mechanisms. The young clerk introduced him to a middle-aged man examining a Giant mountain bike. The man, Rory Feldstein, had curly brown hair, large owl-like glasses, and hands that were rough and stained with grease.

Rory wiped his hands on a grease rag while he looked at Jim's badge with interest. "So, do you know Sam Birkstein? He's a detective, too," he said.

"Absolutely. He's on my team. I work with him every day," Jim said.

"That was an awful thing that happened to him. I knew a golfer once who was struck by lightning. How's he doing?"

Jim turned solemn. "He's doing. It's hard to tell the extent of the damage yet. Hopefully each day will get a little better for him. Thanks for asking," Jim said, and he meant it. "Listen, I have this ring," Jim pulled the bag out of his pocket, "and we're trying to identify what it might have come from." He handed the bag to Rory. "Sam thought it might be a bike part. Do you recognize it?"

Rory turned the bag over, carefully inspecting it. He held up a finger, then turned and walked to a computer sitting on a counter along the wall. He typed a bunch of stuff, brought up a bike parts website, typed in the serial number on the ring, and pointed at the screen.

"This ring is from the Kona mountain bike line, a model called Process 153. The serial numbers match perfectly."

"How sure are you?" Jim asked.

Rory stared at him, then said, "One hundred percent." He turned the computer screen toward Jim. "Look, you can see for yourself."

"No, that's okay. I'll take your word for it," Jim said, waving his hand at the screen. "Can you run a copy of that brand information and a photo of the part?" Jim asked.

"Absolutely."

They conversed for a few minutes. Jim was about to leave, but before he did, he pulled out a mugshot of Devon Williams.

"Ever seen this guy hanging around the neighborhood?" Jim asked as Rory inspected the photo.

"No. But can I make a copy of this?" he asked. "I'll inform my staff, and we'll keep an eye out for him."

When Jim left the store, he had two thoughts. One—Devon Williams was quickly becoming *the* person of interest in the robbery and shooting death of Vicki Invold. And two—they were getting closer to discovering his whereabouts in La Crosse. *We need to find this guy before another tragic event occurs.*

Before Jim left for home, he straightened his desk and filed the background check and bike information in a manila folder. Then he picked up his phone and called Tanya Pedretti, the La Crosse chief of police.

"Tanya, Jim Higgins," he said.

"Hey, Jim. Haven't talked to you in a while. What's up?" Tanya said.

Jim admired Tanya. She was one of a growing number of women police chiefs around the state. She was tough, fair, and ran a tight ship. Then he thought of Elaine Turnmile. *Well, there's really no comparison, is there?*

"We're trying to track down a person of interest in the Stoddard Gas & Go robbery and shooting. For some reason, a guy named Devon Williams keeps floating to the surface of this quagmire. Does his name ring a bell?" Jim asked.

There was a quiet moment. "Sorry, Jim. The name doesn't sound familiar to me," Tanya said.

"Well, I need a favor. I have a suspicion that this Devon character is getting around town on a mountain bike. And some of the evidence from the crime scene seems to suggest the same." Jim felt a little guilty that he did not mention that the bike part in the blue jean jacket was found on one of his own detectives. But he was sure Tanya was aware of the situation, so he continued. "The last time he was seen was over on French Island near the Black River where those houseboats are by Veterans Freedom Park. I really need all of your officers on the street to be on the lookout for a Black guy, mid-twenties, riding an expensive mountain bike around town. I'll get a photo to distribute to your officers. If somebody spots him, I need him brought in for questioning."

"Fair enough. I can do that," Tanya said.

"Thanks. I appreciate it." Jim hung up. A quiet knock on the door interrupted his thoughts.

"Lt. Higgins?"

Jim looked up. Emily was standing in the doorframe with a sealed envelope in her hand.

"Yes, Emily. Did you need something?" Jim asked, reaching for his suit jacket.

"The law enforcement staff got a get-well card for Sam and some gift cards. We wondered if you could drop it by his house before you go home this evening?" Her brown eyes were sympathetic and misty with tears. "We all feel really bad for Sam, Chief."

"I know. We all do. I'll be glad to drop it off," Jim said, taking the envelope. He hadn't really planned on stopping again at the Birksteins, but it was on his way home, and he was glad to do it.

After sending a photo of Devon Williams to the police chief, Jim read through his notes, organized his desk, and filed everything the team had collected that day. It was already after five o'clock. He strolled wearily to his Suburban across the warm blacktop parking lot. The weather was gorgeous: sunny, baby blue sky, warm but with a hint of autumn in the air. The trees were just beginning to show hints of red and orange hues. Traffic zipped along Vine Street, and down the street from the law enforcement center he could see a group of little boys playing baseball in someone's backyard. He climbed in his Suburban and drove south until he came to State Road, then worked his way through a maze of ranch houses until he came to Green Bay Street. He turned right and pulled up to a modest ranch home painted gray and decorated with black shutters. The yard was small but was overshadowed by a massive maple tree, which hovered over the house, casting its dappled shadow on the roof. He walked up to the dark red front door, rang the bell, and waited.

After a few moments, Jim could hear footsteps inside, and the door opened. Jerrod Fleming stood in front of Jim, his eyes wide with surprise.

"Lt. Higgins. What are you doing here?" he asked.

"I need to talk to you about what happened at school this morning. May I come in?" Jim asked politely.

"Sure. My mom's at work, but my dad is out back puttering in his shop. Do you want me to get him?" Jerrod asked nervously. He stood in front of Jim and shuffled his feet. Jim noticed a bruise along his jawline and a significant scrape on his right upper bicep.

"You can get your dad, but only if you haven't been honest with him," Jim said, giving the nervous teen a perceptive stare.

"I told him about what happened at school. Is that what you mean?" Jerrod asked.

"That and anything else about Devon Williams."

Jerrod sighed loudly. "I came clean with my dad and mom about Devon. So I guess we're okay, huh?"

"If you say so," Jim said.

"Let's go in the kitchen. Can I get you a Pepsi?" Jerrod asked.

"Yeah, that'd be great." Jim stepped into the house and followed Jerrod into the small but cozy kitchen. He found a seat at the table. Although the house was small and decorated conservatively, it had a warm, lived-in feeling. Jerrod placed a cold Pepsi in front of Jim and sat down in a chair opposite him across the table. Jim popped the tab on the Pepsi and took a long drink. Jerrod watched the lieutenant nervously.

"So, whaddya want to know?" Jerrod asked. The look in Lt. Higgins's eyes made him pause.

Jerrod decided there was no point in trying to buffalo the detective. This guy was sharp, determined, and focused. No bullshit here.

Jim set his Pepsi on the table. "On Saturday, when we talked at the café, I got the sense you were more involved with Vicki than you let on. Is that right?" Jim asked.

Jerrod looked down at his scraped knuckles and silently shook his head. "We dated our junior year. I thought we were a couple, but I guess I was too stupid to see what was really happening."

"Which was what?" Jim asked brusquely.

"That Vicki was cheating on me—going out with Devon on the side." He looked out of the kitchen window, unable to hide the pain in his eyes. Jim let the silence do its work. Finally, Jerrod blurted, "I got really mad when I found out. I threatened to tell the whole school what a slut she was. It wasn't a pretty sight, I can tell you that."

"What did Vicki say? Did she defend herself?" Jim asked.

"She told me that Devon was really insistent. He *expected* her to give him all the sex he wanted. She seemed scared, and yet, in an odd way, she seemed attracted to him, too. Does that sound crazy?" Jerrod stared at Higgins, and for the first time Jim could see how confusing the situation had been for the teen.

"Listen, when men use their power and sexual prowess to lure girls into a relationship for their own enjoyment, that's as wrong as wrong can be. If a relationship is authentic, then sexual coercion of any kind should never be needed. The fact that he was threatening her tells me their relationship was not a healthy one," Jim said in a fatherly tone.

Jerrod huffed and shifted uneasily in his chair. "You can say that again. She was scared of him, scared of what he might do to her."

"So we've established that Devon and Vicki's relationship was coercive. What happened this morning that brought on the fistfight?" Jim leaned back in the chair and watched the teenager closely.

"I was in the hall by my locker right next to Mrs. Knight's room getting my books for first hour. Lyle Leverentz is a scuzzball—he's one of Devon's minions. He's been throwing his weight around at school, always going on about Devon. Devon this and Devon that. He came up behind me and..." Jerrod blushed, "started humping me. And when he did that to me, I just lost it, and we got in an all-out pounder."

"Okay, I can understand that. Anything else?" Jim asked.

Jerrod leaned forward, intense and focused. "I'm not sorry I beat the shit outta him. He deserved every punch I gave him," he said hoarsely, tears pooling in his brown eyes. His clenched fists sat on the kitchen table as if he had unfinished business.

"I can understand how you feel," Jim commented. He thought about teenage boys and their first love. He remembered the intense feelings he'd had for Jenny Timberton during his senior year of high school. That first kiss. His first foray into a sexual encounter. He could still conjure up those feelings, still remember her innocence and sweet, tender trust in him.

Breaking the silence after Jerrod's intense outburst, Jim asked, "What do you know about Devon that you didn't tell me Saturday?"

"Lyle knows a lot more about Devon's operation than I realized. He's one of his inner circle. Lyle thinks Devon trusts him, but he's just too stupid to realize he's being manipulated."

Suddenly the sliding glass door opened, and Mr. Fleming stepped into the kitchen from the back deck. When he saw Jim, he looked puzzled, but Jerrod interrupted before he could speak.

"Dad, this is Lt. Higgins from the sheriff's department," Jerrod explained.

Jim stood and shook hands with Mr. Fleming. "I've been having a conversation with your son about Vicki Invold and Devon Williams," Jim explained.

"That punk! If I ever get my hands on him, I'll tear him from limb to limb!" The immediate anger that surged out of Jerrod's dad was surprising and revealing. Mr. Fleming waved his arms in exasperation, and his big, bulky body tightened with anger and frustration.

Jim held his hand up in a stop gesture. "Easy. Easy. Calm down. I understand your frustration, Mr. Fleming."

But Mr. Fleming was on a roll. "Can't you cops keep these creeps off the street?" he shouted. "Vicki was a nice girl, and now she's dead, all because of a smooth-talking jerk who wouldn't hear no for an answer! Us parents of these teenagers are worried these riff-raff are going to target our kids next!"

"Believe me, I understand your anger and frustration. I've been trying to locate Devon, too, but he seems to be almost invisible. Any clues, Jerrod, where he might be?" Jim asked, looking back at the teen.

"I don't know where he hangs out. I've heard kids mention French Island, but..." His voice tapered off, and he shook his head, then shrugged his shoulders.

"All right," Jim said, turning to Mr. Fleming. "I want you to make sure you know where your son is at all times," Jim said soberly. His serious expression captured Mr. Fleming's attention, and he backed up a couple of steps. Fleming's eyes grew wide. He could sense Jim's concern woven into his words. "Don't let him go anywhere alone. This Devon character is dangerous."

Then Jim turned to Jerrod, his blue eyes blazing, his finger pointed at his chest. "And you, young man, are to honor that. Keep your parents informed about where you're going and who you're with. Carry a cell phone with you all the time. Don't try to be a hero, and quit using your fists to settle your problems. Understood?"

The teen hung his head and mumbled, "Yes, sir."

"You still have my card?" Jim asked brusquely.

"Yes, I do... sir," Jerrod said.

"Don't do anything stupid, and if you hear from Devon or Lyle, call me immediately."

25

After his interview with Jerrod Fleming, Jim made his way through the south side of La Crosse, connecting with Highway 35 along the Mississippi River. The great waterway shimmered in the afternoon sunlight. A couple of fishing boats bobbed on the waves near Stoddard, the occupants of the boats casting their reels in a relaxed style, their poles arching and flexing. Perched near the river's edge in an old craggy oak tree, a bald eagle watched the surface of the river for its next meal. Up ahead, a couple of bikers dressed in brilliant red and yellow silky shirts and shorts pedaled furiously along the river road. Although Jim admired their dedication in keeping themselves fit, biking near live traffic didn't appeal to him. He'd witnessed too many mangled bodies—those who'd collided with a vehicle and lost—for the sport to have any appeal.

As Jim drove south, he pondered the information they'd recently collected. That was the crux of the problem. The information about the robbery and murder at the Gas & Go was circumstantial evidence that could not be corroborated by eyewitness testimony. It was a bunch of unrelated facts that left them all scratching their heads. To Jim, it seemed like the entire population of Stoddard had disappeared into thin air the night of the incident. Where the heck were all the people who needed gas or milk or ice cream on a Thursday night? Of course, the storm probably discouraged anyone from going out, especially when food or gas was not a necessity and could wait until morning.

The teenage boys Jim and Paul talked to testified about Devon Williams's ability to direct and plan multiple crimes in the La Crosse area. Although some of the young upstarts had been caught, none of them had confessed to knowing Devon. If Devon actually was coordinating these crimes, then they were a faithful lot, mute and silent, pledging their loyalty to the miscreant.

The malfunction of the CCTV camera at the convenience store in Stoddard the night of the crime left police without a recording of the customers who had come to the store between ten-thirty and eleven-thirty. None of the crime scene evidence had yielded any DNA, fingerprints, or mobile phone records. They had some cash, a gun, a jacket, and a pair of boots. But that was found on a cop, not on a criminal. Devon Williams, or someone working for him, was apparently good at staying in the shadows and turning the spotlight on others—namely Sam. Jim softly pounded the steering wheel as he drove, his frustration mounting, hoping something substantial would soon move the investigation forward.

Coming to Birksteins' driveway, Jim roared up the steep incline the second time that day and parked his Suburban in front of the garage. He climbed out, walked to the front door, and rang the doorbell. Leslie appeared, surprised at the unannounced visit.

"Chief! Good to see you. I'm glad you stopped," Leslie said, smiling widely. "Come on in."

Jim stepped into the living room and immediately noticed a huge painting on the wall opposite the door hanging over the leather couch.

"One of yours?" he asked, pointing to the painting.

"Yes. I was going to put it at Arterio's gallery over on Losey Boulevard in town, but Sam insisted we keep it. Now I'm glad we did."

The painting was impressive—morning on the river, misty, an ethereal quality to the light, a blue heron in sharp, exquisite detail in the forefront, cattails poking their heads above the swampy shoreline in the background. Jim loved it.

"Did you work from a photograph?" he asked, moving closer to the painting, studying it intently. The colors, the brushstrokes, and the composition all worked together to create an evocative painting that drew you in and made you feel like you were right there. It stirred memories in Jim about everything he loved about life along the river.

"No, I didn't have a photograph. I wish it would've been that easy," Leslie said. "I was in our little dinghy and rowed along the shore for a couple of miles between here and Victory very early in the morning. I sketched while I was in the boat and used my memory for the colors. It turned out good, I think," she pondered, the pride coming through in her voice.

"It's more than good, Lez," Jim said softly. "It's great, and if it was for sale, I'd buy it."

"Really?"

"Yeah, really. Will you do a river scene for me sometime?" he asked.

"For you, Chief, of course."

"Price?"

"Twenty-five hundred," Leslie stated without hesitation.

Jim swallowed hard. His Norwegian frugality bubbled to the surface. "Consider it a done deal," he finally said. He thought about the money Carol had spent updating their living room recently and decided she wouldn't think twice about spending a chunk of change like that for a beautiful painting.

Jim studied the painting some more until Leslie turned to him and asked, "So, did you need something, Chief?"

"Oh, I forgot." He dug into his inside jacket pocket and pulled out the card. "The office staff wanted to give Sam something and wish him well." He handed the card to Leslie.

"Well, that was sweet. I don't know how Sam will take it, though," she said hesitantly.

"Things still rough?" Jim asked, frowning and crossing his arms over his chest.

"More than rough, if you want to know the truth."

"Where is Sam, by the way? And Paco?" Jim asked, looking around the room.

"Well, that's a good question. When I came home from getting groceries, Sam, the Jeep, and Paco were gone. That was about four o'clock. I don't know if I should be worried. I don't think he's ready to drive yet, but I don't want another blowup so… I guess I'll let it go. What do you think?" Her blue eyes were filled with concern. She laid a hand on her distended belly, waiting for an answer.

Jim studied the floor for a few minutes, then lifted his head and met Leslie's troubled gaze.

"I think Sam is trying to find his way back to some kind of normalcy. He needs some solitude to think things through, to find some inner strength. Maybe even some time to pray. I wouldn't worry too much—yet," Jim said carefully.

"Yeah, you're probably right, but it's so hard to see him struggle." Leslie's eyes misted with tears. "Hey, thanks for stopping. I really appreciate it," Leslie said. "And I hope Sam will, too."

"Not a problem. Listen, I need to get home. I've been late every night this week, and the kids get pretty difficult when I'm not home to tuck them into bed." Leslie smiled shyly at her boss. "Just wait," Jim continued, "in a couple of months, you'll totally understand." He gave her a big grin and opened the front door.

"Thanks, Chief," Leslie said.

"No problem." He stopped and turned. "Hey—I'm praying for you," Jim said seriously. He walked to the Suburban, got in, and headed back up the river.

26

Being promoted to detective status at the La Crosse Sheriff's Department was something Mike Leland had dreamed of and had worked hard to achieve. Though his office hours had officially ended for the day, he continued to stare at the spreadsheet he'd created about petty crime in La Crosse. As he scanned the columns and numbers, he tried to make sense of what he'd found.

In the category of property crime, motor vehicle thefts were up slightly—a 1.4 percent increase since last year. Burglary and general theft had held steady. The crime scene hadn't changed much when you considered the size of La Crosse. His afternoon of evaluating the statistics seemed relatively benign in the general scheme of things. It wasn't until he sorted through the juvenile court records and looked at the individuals who had been through the system that Mike began to feel a sense of accomplishment. He was surprised to find that nine kids had admitted they were recruited by a more experienced perpetrator. *Someone like Devon Williams,* he thought. *But don't jump to conclusions without evidence.* He knew that was Higgins's pet peeve.

He made a list of the nine teenagers and picked up his phone.

"La Crosse County Juvenile Detention Facility, Brenda speaking. How may I help you?"

"Hey, Brenda. It's Officer Mike Leland. Can I talk to one of the social workers who deals with offenders? Somebody around there yet today?"

"Hmm, actually, I think the only one still here this late is Julie Bronke, but she's the one you'd want to talk to. Let me connect you," Brenda said politely.

The phone rang three times, and finally, a weary voice came over the line.

"This is Julie. How can I help you?"

"Well, I'm not sure yet," Mike said. He identified himself, explained his situation, and suggested a strategy. "I'd like the opportunity to talk with some of these kids about how they got involved in crimes around town. Is that possible?"

"I can try, but many of them have counseling sessions and other therapy that cannot be changed," Julie said. "But late in the afternoon might work, although you probably won't be able to meet all nine boys. I'll get back to you, but don't count on hearing from me until at least noon tomorrow."

"That's great. The sooner, the better. Thanks," Mike said and hung up.

He sat at his desk thinking until he noticed the sun dipping low in the sky. Glancing at the wall clock, he groaned. He'd worked right through lunch, and now the cramping in his stomach told him it was time to eat. He grabbed his phone from his desk, shut the door of his tiny cubicle, and walked out into the late afternoon sunshine. When he got settled in his truck, he texted his friend, Anastasia.

"R U busy?"

"Cooking supper. Wanna come over?"

"B there in 20."

The sun was sinking toward the horizon when Detective Paul Saner pulled into a parking lot off Boathouse Drive on French Island.

He stared at an enormous Army tank sitting on a cement pad in a large section of lawn. Red, white, and blue flags snapped in the breeze next to the tank, and a sign labeled Veterans Freedom Park arched over the entrance to the field. Paul got out of his F-150 Ford pickup and walked slowly across the grassy lot toward the water. The sky was clear now, but on the western horizon, a bank of clouds was gathering, just a hint of gray in the distance. *Might rain later*, Paul thought.

When he got to the riverbank, he stopped and gazed from one end of the small inlet to the other. A tidy row of houseboats lined the banks of the Black River. Some were neat as a pin; others looked like they were barely holding together and would disintegrate if a strong wind blew. But there was a rustic charm to the little river community that Paul found appealing. *Kinda like Huck Finn,* he thought. *Life on the river.*

He turned and began walking along the shore, noticing some of the names plastered on the houses: The Rat Hole Retreat, The Pack Shack, John Boy's Place, Wishin' and Fishin'. Noticing some activity on one of the floating houses, Paul waved. A woman waved back.

"Hi. I'm looking for someone, and I was wondering if you could help me?" Paul hollered.

"Come on over. We're out back," the woman said, waving at Paul as she disappeared around the corner of the houseboat.

Paul crossed the gangway and walked around the side of the houseboat to a deck that faced the water, where he found a middle-aged couple sitting comfortably at a patio table.

"Sorry to disturb you," Paul apologized, holding out his ID.

"You didn't tell me the guy was a cop," the older man said, scowling at the woman. He scanned Paul up and down with a contemptuous glance, then turned up his nose like someone smelling a dead fish. His beady eyes were framed by a pair of horn-rimmed glasses, and his gray hair was trimmed and neat. He crossed his scrawny legs and continued to stare belligerently at Paul.

"I didn't know he was a cop," the woman explained. "I was just being friendly." She held out her hand. "Rose Becker," she said, smiling. Her gray hair was tied up in a bun on the top of her head, and she wore a broom skirt and a colorful top. "Just ignore him. Horatio hasn't had his gin and tonic yet," she said with a grin. Paul shook her hand.

"I was wondering if you might be able to identify someone who is a person of interest in an investigation we're conducting," Paul said. He reached into his jacket and held out a picture of Devon Williams. The older man grabbed the photo and studied it intently. Then he handed it back to Paul, his scowling demeanor like a permanent expression as he watched the surface of the river.

"Well?" Paul asked. "Do you recognize him?" The man's cranky attitude was getting under Paul's skin.

Horatio pointed downriver. "There's a young guy six houseboats down who comes and goes all hours of the night, but he's never here during the day. Don't know his name, but he looks like that guy," he said, pointing to the picture in Paul's hand. Paul's stomach did a little dance.

"How do you know that?" Rose interrupted, her eyebrows raised in surprise. The men looked at her.

"Well, how do you think I know that?" the man snarled. "I gotta get up and pee at least twice every single night, and while I'm peeing, I've seen him coming and going."

Rose looked skeptical. "It's dark. How did you notice all that activity in the dark?"

"There's a security light right down by that dock," Horatio said, pointing downriver. "You'd be surprised what you can see with just a security light once your eyes adjust."

Rose shook her head. "And you think you know someone. Go figure," she said.

"So how certain are you that this guy in the picture is that guy on the houseboat?" Paul asked, giving the grumpy man an intense stare.

The man hesitated, then said, "About ninety percent. That good enough for you?"

"That's very helpful. Thanks," Paul said, although he felt like biting Horatio's head off.

"Can I get you something to drink?" Rose asked.

"No, no thank you," Paul said, waving his hand at Rose. "I'd appreciate it if you didn't mention my visit to anyone. We're trying to locate this fellow, and we don't want to spook him."

"Is he dangerous?" Rose asked. Her hand moved up to her throat. *Why do women always do that when they're frightened?* Paul thought.

"He could be," Paul said carefully. "If you notice anything more, here's my card. Just give me a call anytime, day or night."

Rose reached out, took the card, and turned it over, studying the number on the back. "I will. I'll call you if I see him," she said softly. The older man continued to stare belligerently at Paul.

Paul turned and left the boathouse, strolling casually along the shore in the direction the man had pointed, counting off the floating houses until he came to the sixth one downstream from the older couple's river residence. There was nothing that would make it stand out from any of the other houses. It was a vintage model, a small raft of treated two-by-fours floating on blue plastic barrels. A fifteen by twenty foot enclosed cabin sat on top. The cabin was sided with white vinyl siding and had a padlocked door. Nothing fancy. Nothing that would attract any attention. Perfect for a place to sleep or to have illicit sex with minor girls or to store a stash of cocaine.

Paul stood on the shore and thought. *Might have to conduct some surveillance on this place. Get Sam to help me.* After a few minutes, he turned and walked back to his truck. He sat there and wrote some notes in his notebook. When Paul drove out of the parking lot, the curtain covering the back window on the boathouse door flicked aside, and then it was quiet again.

27

Around four o'clock on Monday afternoon, Sam climbed in the Jeep with Paco and drove north on the Great River Road to Stoddard. When he came to Rocky's Supper Club on the main drag, he turned left and crossed the Burlington Northern railroad tracks, then wove his way through a residential area until he came to the Stoddard Public Marina. He parked the truck in the lot. In the seat next to him, Paco woofed with excitement at the river flowing silently in the distance. Sam sat for a minute in the Jeep, savoring the quiet, peaceful surroundings. Despite the splendor of the scenery, Sam continued to brood on the recent harrowing events of his life, but try as he might, he failed to come up with a reasonable explanation for the things that had happened to him. He mumbled a few worn-out platitudes to himself, which elicited a look of canine concern from Paco. *In this world you will have tribulation… that's what Jesus said,* Sam thought. *I guess He was right.*

Sam unhooked his seat belt and stepped out of the Jeep. Paco jumped down next to him, sniffing out this new environment. Sam heard the laughter of children on the twirling merry-go-round in the little playground that was part of the city park, and he thought about becoming a father in just a few short months. *How am I going to handle that?* he thought sourly. *I can't even manage my own life, let alone somebody who is helpless and totally dependent.*

Walking slowly onto the pier, he watched powerboats and small fishing crafts moving about on the calm water. Someone with a young boy in a cramped dinghy pulled in a nice bass near the pier. The sun was brilliant in the west, sinking toward the crimson horizon, leaving long glittering reflections on the water's surface. Paco nuzzled Sam's hand, and Sam absentmindedly stroked the dog's silky ears and neck.

Sam turned, walked along the pier, and then slowly meandered down a pathway leading to a shaded street and a row of small cabins and homes nestled along the shoreline. As Sam walked along the street, he took in the atmosphere of the place. One guy was remodeling his house, installing new windows and doors. Sam waved to him and continued his leisurely stroll through the neighborhood. It was quiet, and the people he met were friendly. The smell of grilling food made Sam's stomach growl with hunger. Residents of the neighborhood greeted him with a simple wave of the hand as if he belonged there. No one could have ever guessed the trauma he'd been through in the last week, and that was just fine with him. He'd had his fill of everyone and their fussy mollycoddling over him.

Sam's first week at home after the accident had been rocky and difficult. He'd had several tense exchanges with Leslie, something uncharacteristic of their marriage. He'd said a number of hurtful things, and he cringed when he remembered the wounded look in Leslie's kind, blue eyes. His parents' frazzled expressions and overworked colloquial phrases had forced him into the Jeep and down the road in search of some quiet and solitude. His mother had been cooking up a storm, and his dad simply walked around the house thinking deep thoughts. He knew they meant well, but his fried nerves could not absorb any more pity. Leslie was blessed to have her artwork. She had been working on a new painting, and her interest in it kept her from hovering over him. He, on the other hand, would normally have gone biking or hiking, but his physical prowess had gone through a major overhaul when he was struck by lightning. He simply was not ready to tackle a demanding physical regimen.

What's wrong with me, anyway? he thought. He just couldn't seem to get a handle on his tongue. Every hurtful thought that came into his mind spewed out of his mouth. At times, he felt like a raging lunatic rather than the loving husband he'd once been. He was sure the gracious forgiveness and grace Leslie and his parents had extended to him wouldn't continue much longer. He thought of the Bible verse his mother had taught him as a child: "A soft answer turns away wrath." Sam knew sooner or later, despite the truth of the Bible verse, they would get sick of his attitude and fight back. Then the fireworks would really begin.

He'd walked almost a half mile with Paco at his side when suddenly the big lab stiffened and stood alert. A man sat on a bench by a pine tree next to a small crude cabin near the water's edge. Before Sam could stop the big brute, Paco had bounded across the long, dry grass. He stood by the man's side, his tail wagging furiously.

Sam strolled over to Paco and the man. "Sorry about my dog. He's got a lot of energy."

"Oh, don't be sorry," the man commented, resting his bare feet in the sand below the bench. "He seems friendly. He's a beautiful animal." He held out his hand to Sam, and they shook. Paco looked up at Sam expectantly, his tail pumping energetically as if to say, *Don't you want to make a new friend?*

"Doc Wycowski. Have a seat. It's a beautiful evening." He slid over, and Sam sat down on the weathered gray bench next to him. The sun was dropping lower in the sky, and the river reflected the rays until it seemed the surface of the water was on fire, with reds, golds, and oranges in a riotous swirl. They sat like that for a while, the two of them together on the bench, soaking in the peaceful sunset and the beauty of the river. Even though they didn't say anything, the silence was comforting.

Finally, Doc spoke. "From around here?" he asked Sam while he stroked Paco's big, majestic head.

"Just down the road near Genoa. You?" Sam asked, turning to get a good look at the man.

"I'm new to the area. Came to town about six months ago. Beautiful place," Doc said. The golden sunset reflected off his tanned arms and face. Sam thought he was quite handsome.

"Yes, this area is very beautiful. The river is special. You live here?" Sam asked, pointing to the ramshackle cabin.

"Just renting, for the time being."

You can't be paying much for that shack, Sam thought. They fell into another long silence. Sam had an eerie feeling this man understood him, even though he hadn't told Doc one thing about himself, not even his name.

Finally, Sam said quietly, "I was in an accident last week."

Doc's sympathetic eyes seemed to invite him to tell his story like a priest inviting a sinner to confession. "Tell me about it," Doc said simply. He turned toward Sam in a gentle manner, crossed his legs, and waited.

As the minutes ticked by and the sun hung in the evening sky, Sam told the man about the lightning strike, the residual effects he was experiencing from the accident, and the fallout he'd had in his relationships as a result of his altered personality. The details of the suspicious items found under him as he lay along the side of the Great River Road he kept to himself.

"I feel like I finally understand what the apostle Paul meant when he said: 'What I want to do, I don't do, and what I don't want to do, I do,'" Sam said, his expression troubled as he thought about his recent behavior. "That's a lazy man's paraphrase, by the way."

Doc continued to stare at the surface of the river. "I don't know much about the Bible, but I've been through some trouble myself," he said, his voice wistful. "There's no education like adversity." To Sam, those words felt like a soothing salve and an admonition all rolled into one.

He waited for Doc to continue, but he stayed silent. Sam finally asked, "What happened to you?"

Doc let out a sigh and kicked his feet out in front of him, crossing them at the ankles. He leaned back, tucked his hands behind his head, and began to tell his story.

"I had my identity stolen a couple of years ago, and in the process, my bank accounts were wiped out in one fell swoop. Nobody could trace where they'd gone or who'd stolen them. The police tried, and I hired a private detective, but it remains a mystery to this day. Without the influence of my money, my wife lost her confidence in me, and a couple of months later, she filed for divorce. Six months after that, my job as a plastic surgeon was called into question when several patients claimed I wasn't competent. Their surgeries had not turned out the way they thought they should, and rather than adjust their opinions based on realistic expectations, they threatened to sue. I was fired and ended up homeless. So much for malpractice insurance."

"Are you serious?" Sam asked, his eyes widening in disbelief.

"Unfortunately, I'm dead serious," Doc said, looking at Sam with a sad smile.

"You sound like a modern-day Job. How can you still smile?" Sam asked.

As if to prove it could still be done, Doc turned and smiled at Sam, a smile so genuine that it lit up his eyes and energized his face. "Live and learn, I guess. This whole experience taught me some important lessons. You see, I've lived my whole life based on the importance of image—having the right education, landing a good job, marrying a beautiful woman, making lots of money, possessing impressive things like houses, boats, cars, and lavish clothes, enjoying the prestige of an important job that bestows power, celebrity, and status. All of it disappeared overnight. I was left with nothing. Like that," he snapped his fingers in midair, "it was gone." Doc's eyes misted with tears. "My family and friends deserted me. I hit the road with nothing but a backpack that held the sum of my earthly possessions, and believe me, there wasn't much left when the system gobbled me up and spit me out."

Sam stared at Doc, speechless. "I... I can't believe that."

"Believe it. It's true," Doc said. "Why do you think I'm living here? What I've learned from all of this is to keep it simple." He lowered his arms to his side and continued to stare at the river. Sam noticed Doc's frayed sweatshirt and worn cutoff jeans.

Doc continued rolling out his philosophy. "Appreciate the little things in life—a cold drink of water, the golden glow of a sunset, the warmth of someone's hand in yours, the velvety fur of a dog, the regal flight of an eagle in the sky, the beauty of a poem. You don't know when you get up in the morning whether you'll live through another day, so just live in the moment and try not to think too much about tomorrow."

Sam listened carefully, comforted in an odd way, knowing that someone else's life had been turned upside down, too. He didn't know if he agreed with Doc's philosophy, although it seemed like a simple way to approach life. *Didn't Jesus tell us not to worry about clothes or food?* he thought. For a kid of a Lutheran pastor, he'd learned plenty of Bible verses, and suddenly one came to mind: "Consider the lilies of the field, how they grow; they neither spin nor toil yet Solomon in all his glory was not arrayed like one of these." Did he believe what Jesus promised—that God would provide everything he needed if he had faith? Doc's authentic confession felt like an open door to a confession of his own failures.

"I don't know how to handle my ugly moods and thoughts," Sam said. "Everything I say gets screwed up and comes out vicious and hurtful."

Doc nodded gently, listening to Sam explain his dilemma. "Forgive yourself," he said quietly.

"What?" Sam asked, crinkling up his forehead, turning to study this strange man.

"You've been through a tough time. Forgive yourself," Doc repeated.

"How am I supposed to do that?" Sam said tersely. "Especially when none of this was my fault to start with." Doc noticed the anxiety that had crept into Sam's voice.

"When things don't turn out like you expected or come up to your standards, forgive yourself. Move on. Try again."

"Why would that work?" Sam asked, totally confused.

Doc shrugged. "I don't know if it will. But what you're doing now obviously isn't working, so do something different. You might be surprised at the results."

Sam sat on the bench with Doc a while longer thinking about what he'd said. He had nothing to lose—and it *might* work. It was starting to get dark. The street lights blinked and then glowed with an orange iridescence, spilling light into the deepening dusk. Sam stood and thanked Doc for the visit. He called Paco, who had been wandering along the shoreline of the river. Walking away from the cabin, Sam suddenly turned around and asked, "Could I come back again sometime?"

Doc smiled. "I'm not going anywhere. You know where to find me."

As Sam strolled back to his Jeep, he suddenly realized he felt lighter, more relaxed. The hard knot inside of him was loosening and unwinding. Something had changed, but he had no idea what it was. And that was okay with him.

The back door to the Birkstein house slammed loudly. A few moments later, Paco appeared in the studio where Leslie worked on the new painting. The basic outline of shore, water, and horizon was taking shape. Muted blues and pinks against a gray background hinted at an early morning scene. In the reeds by the shore, an old, forlorn rowboat was etched in charcoal. Paco padded up to Leslie and nudged her swollen belly, laying his head on her knee, searching for attention.

Leslie leaned down and kissed the top of the big lab's head. "Hey, you big brute. Where have you been?" she asked softly. "Is Sam with you?" She continued studying the composition in front of her, squeezing a few more blobs of paint on her palette, dabbing her brush here and there, building the layers that would create the mood of the painting.

Sam stood in the doorway of the studio quietly watching Leslie paint. His emotions, which had been so wildly unpredictable just a few hours ago, had quieted. Instead of anger and frustration, he felt repentant about his crotchety attitude and the pity party he'd been throwing for himself the last few days. He kicked off his shoes by the door and padded in his stocking feet over to Leslie's stool. Leaning over her, he wrapped his arms around her shoulders, pushed her blonde hair back, and tenderly kissed her neck. Leslie was surprised by the subtle affection since he'd been avoiding intimate situations since he'd gotten home from the hospital. *Probably scared the sex is going to fizzle,* she thought.

"Hmm, do I sense an apology coming?" Leslie asked, finding Sam's touch arousing. Sam kneaded her shoulders. After a few moments, Leslie turned toward him. She sat on the stool and watched his face.

"An apology is long overdue. But I'd rather show you instead of using my words," he said, his eyebrow hitching up. His hazel eyes were warm and sensual. "Mom and Dad around?"

"Nope. They drove into La Crosse to get a bite to eat and do a little shopping," Leslie said. She got up from the stool and stood in front of him. "Was that some kind of an invitation?"

"Yep. I mean... it's worth a try, don't you think?" Leslie wasn't sure what he meant by "it." She sensed he was far from confident about the outcome, but she loved him for his intentions.

"Lovemaking with you is always worth it," she said, interpreting his hint. A smile teased the edges of her lips. Sam kissed her, and her belly bumped up against his. He found her hand and pulled her toward the stairway that led to the upper bedroom. Paco's ears perked up, and his eyes brightened.

"No, Paco. You stay," Sam said sternly when the faithful canine tried to follow them up the stairs.

"I love it when a man takes charge," Leslie giggled.

"You ain't see nothin' yet, baby," he said, kissing her again.

28

The children's squeals and giggles from the backyard filled the evening air on Chipmunk Coulee Road with a lighthearted sense of security and happiness. Just what Jim needed after a frustrating day of chasing the shadowy existence of Devon Williams. *Why can't I find him?* He took another sip of his Leinenkugel's and firmly grasped Carol's hand. Her expression was animated with love and satisfaction as she watched the children romp in the yard.

"How you doin', honey?" he asked softly. He knew that her middle-aged life had taken a major turn when they'd found themselves in charge of two young children five years ago—a newborn son and a four-year-old waif deposited on their doorstep by Jim's lost sister. He'd had a major shift in his plan for middle age as well, but amazingly, it had been a tremendous blessing, albeit one that frequently left them gasping for energy at the end of the day.

Carol continued watching Lillie and Henri chasing the fireflies that had started flashing their sporadic blinks out in the yard. "I'm fine, Jim. Those little twerps give me a run for my money, but I wouldn't have it any other way. Why are you asking?" She turned and looked at Jim.

"Well, you're always reminding me that we're not young anymore.

But I have to say you've never been more beautiful to me than you are right now," Jim said, lifting her hand to kiss it tenderly.

Carol's eyes suddenly misted with tears at the unexpected sentiment. "Jim, really? Are you serious?" She brushed a hand over her eyes and turned to look at him. "I'm tired, my hair's a mess, I'm dressed in clothes you probably couldn't find at a good secondhand store, and I desperately need a shower. Beautiful?" She shook her head and rolled her eyes. "You have an odd perception of beauty, honey."

"Just say thank you, sweetheart," Jim reminded her.

"Okay. Thank you, sweetheart," she whispered softly, then she giggled quietly.

"Would there be a possibility of a soak together in the tub this evening so I can regale you with more compliments?" Jim asked. He watched the outline of Carol's face and noticed a subtle smile.

"Oh, I see where this is going. Why didn't you just suggest the sex right off the bat?"

"You know me. I like the intrigue of romantic interludes."

"It's getting a little deep out here on the deck, isn't it?"

"Well, we can skip all that and get right to it, if that's what you want," Jim said, suppressing a chuckle. He turned his attention back to the kids' antics out on the lawn.

Carol laughed. "Well, we'll have to wait until the kids are in bed. But I have to say, I do enjoy your attempts at romantic foreplay, and you know me, I always enjoy our romps in the bedroom."

After the kids had been bathed, read to, and tucked in for the night, Carol and Jim retreated to the kitchen to make a pot of tea. Carol cut pieces of apple cake and squirted a dollop of whipped cream on each one. Then she gathered the tea things on a tray and carried them into the living room, where she set the tray on the coffee table. Carol was pouring mugs of tea when Lillie appeared in the wide, arched doorway of the living room.

Jim looked up, surprised to see his daughter standing there in her nightgown.

"Lillie? What now?" Jim asked, somewhat irritated. "Do you need something, peanut?"

"I smell smoke, Bapa," Lillie said seriously.

"Smoke?" Carol repeated, raising her eyebrows at Jim.

Lillie nodded.

"Well, it's all in your head. We didn't even have a fire on the patio tonight," Jim said sternly.

"I'm not lying, Bapa," Lillie insisted loudly, stomping her foot on the hardwood floor, her classic gesture of aggravation. "I. Smell. Smoke."

"Well, we don't smell anything, do we, hon?" Carol said coolly, looking at Jim over her mug of steaming tea.

"Not a thing," Jim said, rising from the sofa. He walked over and took Lillie's hand. "Come on, toots. You have school tomorrow."

Lillie stood stock still. She looked up at Jim. "Are you trying to calm my fears?" she asked.

"As a parent, I always try to calm your fears, especially when they seem unfounded and unsupported by the reality of the situation. I don't smell smoke, and neither does your mother. Come on. Bedtime," Jim said, marching Lillie down the hall.

Jim tucked Lillie in and leaned over to kiss her good night—again.

"You really don't smell smoke?" she asked tentatively. Her crystal blue eyes tugged at Jim's heartstrings. Knowing her predilection for the dramatic, he tried to balance that with her precocious intellect and her odd premonitions. It was a mix that would challenge any normal parent, and sometimes it sent him into a breathless panic.

"No, I don't smell smoke," he said reasonably, "but I appreciate your vivid imagination." He leaned over her and kissed her nose.

"Does that mean you think I'm smart?" Lillie asked, tilting her head on her pillow.

"I think you are the smartest eight-year-old I know, Lillie," Jim said. Lillie started to speak, but Jim put a finger across her lips. "Good night. I love you, and I'll see you in the morning." Jim rose and walked out of the room. He closed the door quietly and went back to the living room.

29

A couple of hours after his conversation with Lillie and a relaxing soak in the tub with Carol, a deep slumber washed over Jim. Normally when he was working on a demanding case, he slept fitfully, his subconscious mind busy and active with the problems confronting him. But occasionally, his body's need for rest overrode his inclination to think deep thoughts, and he slept the sleep of the dead. Monday night was one of those nights. It wasn't until he was awakened around twelve-thirty by Carol's shouts and the desperate shaking of his shoulders that he became fully conscious of his surroundings.

"Jim! There's smoke!" Carol shouted, whipping off the quilts and sheets. "It's a fire! Get up!" She grabbed her robe as the bedroom began filling with a thick, smothering haze. She began coughing fitfully.

Although Jim was groggy from the deep slumber, he was upright on his feet in a few seconds. He stood by the bed feeling a desperate panic deep in his chest. Was he dreaming? No, this was no dream. Lillie's concern came back to him. *I smell smoke.* His eyes burned, and he felt claustrophobic, like a drowning swimmer coming to the surface of the water, gasping for air. He could hear the high, ear-piercing beeps of the smoke alarm sounding a warning throughout the house.

"The kids! We've got to get the kids!" he shouted, his voice hoarse with panic. He beat Carol to the bedroom door and felt the knob—still cool. He threw the door open. Red-hot flames were being sucked down the hallway toward the children's bedrooms. The heat was intense, the smoke billowing, the fire getting worse every second. They had to move fast.

"You get Henri! I'll get Lillie!" he shouted, pushing Carol in the direction of Henri's room. Jim sprinted down the smoke-filled hallway toward the flames and burst through Lillie's bedroom door. Lillie was sitting upright in bed, her eyes wide with panic and confusion. She began coughing.

"Bapa! I can't breathe!" she shouted. She started to cry.

Jim swooped down and lifted her into his arms. He turned and ran down the hallway toward the garage. Carol got to the door first and opened it. She grabbed Henri out of his bed, and he sleepily grasped her neck.

Jim punched the garage door opener. They loaded the kids in the back seat of the Suburban, and Jim turned to Carol. "Back the truck out, go to the end of the driveway, and call 911," he ordered loudly.

"What are you going to do?" Carol yelled.

Jim was already lifting a large fire extinguisher from the garage wall. "I'm going back in to try and tamp down the fire," he shouted over his shoulder. "Go, Carol, go!" he shouted, waving her out of the garage.

Carol backed the Suburban out of the garage as Jim re-entered the house. He slipped on a pair of running shoes near the back door and walked down the hallway toward the flames. The furious blaze had turned his beloved home into a raging inferno. Pulling the lock pin on the extinguisher, he began spraying the retardant on the swelling wall of flames. The heat was frightening, sucking the oxygen out of the room, the inferno licking at the ceiling. The walls and furniture were snapping and crackling, the fire hissing like a demonic force.

Jim continued to advance on the conflagration, his face glowing from the intense heat. The thick smoke and the fumes from the fire extinguisher choked him, robbing him of oxygen. He didn't know how long he continued spraying the fire. It seemed like hours, but his rational mind told him it had only been about fifteen minutes. Soon he heard the whining of the fire engine in the driveway.

Seconds later, someone tapped his shoulder. He turned, and a masked fireman took the extinguisher, strapped a mask over Jim's face, and led him out of the house through the garage. Other firemen rushed into the house past him. He heard glass breaking and the dull thud of an ax hitting a wall.

Outside the house in the driveway the fire crew were unrolling hoses, and a pumper truck began humming loudly as water was forced through the hoses and sprayed on the smoking roof into the interior of the house. Jim threw his arm over the fireman's shoulders as they stumbled over the maze of hoses. They walked through the crew to an ambulance that sat at the end of the driveway, its lights flashing red blips against the dark silhouette of trees surrounding Jim's house. The fireman turned Jim over to an EMT.

"In here, sir," the EMT said, grabbing his elbow and helping him into the vehicle. Jim was sweating profusely, and his face felt seared as if he had a bad case of sunburn. His T-shirt was soaked with sweat, and his pajama pants were blackened and scorched by the intense heat. Jim began coughing, deep hacks that tasted like smoke. The attendant helped him onto a gurney and began administering oxygen. Lying down, Jim breathed the oxygen deep into his lungs, and he began feeling better almost instantly. He removed the mask and asked, "My wife and kids? Where are they?"

"Your wife and children are fine, sir," the EMT said, gently replacing the mask on Jim's face. "They're waiting in the Suburban at the end of the driveway just like you told them to do."

In the quiet, insulated ambulance, Jim felt like he was in a cocoon.

He closed his eyes, but all he could see was flames. His eyes popped open again. He heard the banging of car doors and voices shouting. Outside, neighbors began showing up concerned by the loudness of the sirens and the flashing red and blue lights at Higgins's residence. The orange glow out the ambulance's back door reflected off the pole building. Hearing the chaos outside, Jim realized the fire was far from over.

"I need to talk to my wife and make sure my kids are okay," Jim said hoarsely. He coughed again, a prolonged deep hack that made his lungs hurt.

The attendant bent over Jim and talked softly. "You're going to be okay. As soon as your oxygen levels come up and we get your cough under control, I'll dress the burns on your hands, and you can go see them. Just relax. Everything's going to be okay."

There was a commotion at the door of the ambulance and suddenly Sam and Leslie Birkstein and Sheriff Turnmile burst through the ambulance door.

"Chief! What happened?" Leslie asked, kneeling next to the gurney. Sam stood behind Leslie with the sheriff, his face a mask of shock and anger. Sheriff Turnmile gave a weak wave.

Jim ripped off the oxygen mask. "Somebody tried to burn down my house! That's what happened!" he shouted. He began coughing again.

The EMT stepped between Leslie and Jim. "Please. You have to let me take care of this guy. He's suffering from smoke inhalation, exhaustion, and burns. Your questions will have to wait a while longer." Leslie started to argue, but the attendant held up her hand in a gesture of authority and pointed at the ambulance's back door.

"Okay, okay," Leslie conceded, although she didn't feel very cooperative. "We'll just be outside, Chief." She gave Jim a sympathetic gaze, turned, and exited the ambulance, taking Sam and the sheriff with her.

By three-thirty in the morning, the hoopla and chaos of fighting the blaze at Higgins's residence had died down. The neighbors huddled in groups around Jim and Carol and offered sympathetic handshakes and hugs while Jim moved among the crowd and reassured everyone they were unharmed. Sara and Jerome, Jim's daughter and son-in-law, showed up with Bobby Rude, their eyes clouded with fear and concern.

"Dad, are you sure you'll be all right?" Sara asked, giving Jim a hug.

"Yeah, I'll be fine. But someone started this, and I intend to end it—with an arrest!" Jim's nostrils flared with anger.

"What do you mean, Dad? You mean—" Her eyes widened with the implications of Jim's statement. "Someone intentionally started this fire?"

"The fire chief thinks so, and so do I," Jim said. "But we'll meet with the arson investigator tomorrow and find out more."

Carol walked over to the little group. "You go home now. There's nothing more we can do tonight," she said sensibly. She grabbed Jim's arm and held on.

Once the crowd had dispersed, Jim loaded Carol, Lillie, and Henri into the Suburban and began the drive to Gladys Hanson's farm. When he thought about Gladys, his long-time friend and prayer warrior from the Hamburg Lutheran Church, his eyes filled with tears of gratitude.

Gladys only lived about five miles from his house, as the crow flies, but he had to negotiate some back country roads to get there. He pulled into the driveway and parked near the back porch of the house. After a few moments, Gladys opened the back door and stood on the top step in her fluffy pink bathrobe, her hair rolled in curlers, her wrinkled face creased with worry.

The yard light created a halo around the Suburban as if they were in a circus spotlight. Jim and Carol stunk of smoke. They were absolutely devastated by the damage to their beautiful home. But more than that, they were reeling from the thought of their close brush with death. The shocked silence in the Suburban continued until Carol spoke.

"How much of the house was destroyed?" she asked softly, staring out the front windshield.

"The fire pretty much gutted the kitchen, dining room, and living room. The bedrooms, my study, and the master bathroom just have smoke damage," Jim said. "I can't believe we got out of there alive." Jim leaned back in the seat, a swell of exhaustion washing over him. Gladys waved at them. Jim waved back. "Let's get the kids inside, and then we'll clean up and get some sleep," he said.

"How did something like this happen, Jim?" Carol asked. "We could have all been killed!" The anger in her voice triggered Jim's memory of their narrow escape from the burning house.

"I don't know how it happened. I have some suspicions, but right now," Jim said calmly and authoritatively, "we're going to try and get some rest. The fire chief is looking everything over, and we'll meet with him tomorrow." He leaned over and tenderly kissed Carol's cheek while tears spilled over and ran down her face. "Come on, honey, let's get the kids inside."

Jim climbed out of the Suburban and opened the back door, cradling Lillie in his arms. Carol lugged Henri up the back steps of the house, and they tromped into Gladys's familiar kitchen.

"Come on in, you poor things," Gladys said, clucking over them like a nervous hen. "I got the beds all ready, Jim. Just take the kids upstairs."

Once the children were tucked in bed, Jim and Carol took showers and slipped into pairs of old cotton pajamas that Gladys had found in a dresser drawer. They sat around the kitchen table and talked softly.

"What are you going to do now, Jim?" Gladys asked gruffly. "Rebuild?" Her hazel eyes were steady and reassuring. Jim thanked God for this no-nonsense friend who'd been like a mother to him for many years.

He sighed heavily. "Absolutely, we'll rebuild. We'll go over in the morning and meet with the fire chief. But first, I want to know how this fire started."

"Do you think someone did this intentionally?" Carol asked, her eyes widening with the horrid thought.

"There's lots of sick minds out there, Carol," Gladys said brusquely, "and Jim's work makes him a pretty big target." She locked eyes with Jim. "Of course, I'm not tellin' you anything new, am I?"

Jim shook his head forlornly. Gladys continued. "Now listen, you two. I'll keep the kids here tomorrow while you get your bearings and check on the house. Lillie and Henri love feeding the chickens and goats, and we'll make some chocolate chip cookies. That'll keep them occupied." Gladys smiled for the first time. "They're going to need some normal activity to erase the memory of the fire from their little minds."

"We can't thank you enough for taking us in and helping with the kids," Carol said, squeezing Gladys's hand. "Again."

"Uffda. Don't even think about it," Gladys said, waving off Carol's thanks. "And just so you know, you're staying here until your house is ready." Jim began protesting, but she stopped him with a stern look. "We're not arguing about it, Jim. That's the way it's gonna be. Period."

"Okay," Jim said quietly, acquiescing. They sat silently around the table until Gladys stood up.

"You two need to go to bed," she ordered. "You look exhausted. I'll wash and dry those clothes you brought from the house. Get the smoke smell outta them. We'll talk more in the morning."

Jim stood up, leaned over, and softly kissed Gladys on her wrinkled cheek. Carol and Jim climbed the steep, narrow stairs to one of the bedrooms and crawled beneath the soft, sweet-smelling sheets. Carol snuggled up to Jim, laying her head on his chest. The eastern horizon was just beginning to lighten when they both fell into a restless sleep.

TUESDAY, SEPTEMBER 2

ALL YOU'VE GOT IS ALL YOU CAN GIVE AND
THAT WILL ALWAYS BE ENOUGH.

SARAH MUELLER

30

The morning after the fire at Higgins's residence, Devon Williams sat in a sixteen-foot Discovery cruiser on the Mississippi River just off a small island outcropping a couple of miles downwind from Stoddard. In the distance, the smokestack from the defunct Genoa nuclear power plant rose into the air, punctuating the morning sky like a giant exclamation mark. Along the shore of the tiny island, a belted kingfisher sat in the brush cocking his head, peering into the shallow water, looking for its next meal. Something startled the bird, and he flew away suddenly, screeching a loud warning rattle to the occupants in the nearby anchored boat.

Lyle Leverentz sat across from Devon in a captain's chair, sullen, beat up, and sporting a black eye. He wrapped his arms around his rib cage and complained loudly about his altercation with Jerrod Fleming the day before.

"God, I hurt all over," Lyle whined pathetically. "That little son of a—"

"Quit bellyaching!" Devon warned, leaning forward in his chair. His dark eyes flashed with irritation as he listened to Lyle's litany of injuries. "Why can't you keep your nose clean? Your fight with that Jerrod kid resulted in another cop on my tail. Now I not only have

Higgins chasin' me, but some other guy has been snooping around the houseboat. You need to learn to shut up and keep your head down until this whole thing quiets down!"

Devon was in a foul mood, and he nervously picked his teeth with a toothpick. After a few moments, he tossed the toothpick over the side of the boat in disgust. He walked to the rear of the craft, opened a cooler, and took out a beer.

"Thanks to you, I had to sleep on this boat last night, and that wasn't my idea of fun," Devon said sourly. He popped the lid on the beer and took a guzzle. Lyle dipped his head to his chest and looked up at Devon, his expression a petulant moue.

"Don't look at me like that! And wipe that stupid pout off your face. Grow up!" Devon shouted. He stopped yelling, took another swig of beer, and gave himself time to calm down.

"I've got another job for you, and this time you better get your act together and do it right. There's a little jewelry and coin store on the corner of Moore and Kane Street—some gal who has a private showroom in her house..."

Donovan "Doc" Wycowski hadn't meant to eavesdrop—it just happened.

He'd taken the little, beat-up skiff with the fifty horsepower motor out on the river early Tuesday morning just as the sun peeked over the horizon. He liked to putter in the boat among the numerous islands and inlets of the Mississippi River just below Stoddard. Morning on the river before sunrise was like nothing else he'd ever experienced.

Doc had spent some time studying the map of the river that was thumb-tacked to the office wall at the Stoddard Boat and Marine shop the last few months. The map reminded him of a child's drawing, complete with squiggles and doodles jumbled together in a haphazard arrangement—blue for the river, green for the land. River navigation along this part of the Mississippi took some getting used to. Now, after several months, he was finally able to orient himself to the formations within the river and the silhouettes and contours of each land mass. He hoped his little adventure farther downstream this morning would result in a nice catch of walleye and panfish.

The air was fresh and bracing. A slight westerly breeze ruffled his hair. He leaned forward, watching closely for wing dams hidden just beneath the surface closer to shore. The river's water level was normal this year, so he wasn't too worried about hitting one. Still, it paid to be cautious.

The little island called Small Fry was in a grouping of islands just south of Stoddard where the Coon Creek emptied into the Mississippi. The spot of land was charming in the early morning light. On its east side, a sandy beach was populated with a wedge of cattails and purple milkweed. Toward the middle of the tiny patch of land, a few scraggly trees, windblown and hardy, clung to the soil. A colony of muskrats nearby were energetically diving and swimming in the patch of cattails, building a lodge in the swampy area that hugged the shoreline.

Farther down the river, Doc Wycowski saw a powerful speed boat hanging around one of the several U.S. Aids to Navigation System river buoys, or USATONS. He was becoming better acquainted with the navigational aids in the river, and he knew that the number of the buoy was 684. The speed boat seemed to be engaged in some sort of activity near the buoy, but Doc couldn't make out what they were doing.

Doc cast some chub into the water. He rested the end of his fishing pole in a holder he'd attached to the lip of the boat's edge. He baited another hook with a large night crawler on a different pole and threw it into the current. About fifteen minutes later, he heard the powerful inboard motor of the speed boat rumble along the other side of the island. Through the cattails and tall grasses, he caught a glimpse of the expensive craft and the two men in it. After a moment, someone killed the engine, and Doc heard the splash of an anchor being thrown in. Everything was exceptionally quiet, the kind of quiet that only happens on the water in the early morning. The dialogue between the passengers in the big boat traveled across the water and the small island toward Doc.

He listened carefully. The whole conversation sounded hostile, filled with anger. Were the boat's occupants friends? It didn't sound like it. As Doc continued listening, he wondered. He heard some phrases about a cop, but he couldn't catch every word. Were the two men in the boat partners in some kind of crime? The whole exchange reminded him of the wild gossip and rumors floating around the clinic when he was on the precipice of financial ruin. An undercurrent of suspicion and distrust clouded every exchange he'd had with friends and office staff until he couldn't bear to walk into a room and carry on a conversation.

More malicious exchanges came from the expensive boat. Doc strained to hear the words, but he couldn't make out the gist of the conversation. Fifteen minutes later, the powerful motor started up, and the driver gunned it in a westerly direction. Doc watched the churning white trail in the water, the two occupants' faces grim and hard. What were they talking about? He wondered where they were headed. They seemed to be in a hurry, and the desperation in their voices left him feeling uncomfortable and filled with suspicion.

He thought again about the wall of silence he'd experienced from trusted colleagues and friends when his reputation had come into question. The distrust had driven him into isolation and finally into a desperate flight to escape their furtive stares and frigid distrust. He blew air through his lips in disgust, but not before he jotted down the boat's registration number. Who knew? It might come in handy. It seemed to him that the tables had turned. Now he was the one filled with misgivings and doubt. *Who were those two men, and what were they talking about?*

31

The light dawned misty and gray in the early hours of Tuesday morning, but by ten o'clock, the fog lifted, and buttery sunshine filtered through the large maple trees on Gladys Hanson's yard, leaving deep shadows on the green lawn. Somewhere a rooster crowed loudly. Jim rolled over, rubbed his face, and glanced at the clock. He groaned when scenes from the previous night roared back into his brain—the panicked escape from the house with the kids, the smoke, the heat, and the devastation to his home. His burned hands felt clumsy beneath the white bandages, and he picked at them, distracted.

"Carol, it's already ten o'clock," he croaked, clearing his throat loudly. The smoke he inhaled the night before made his voice raspy and hoarse. He cleared his throat, trying to get rid of the rough edge. He sat up briefly, then lay back down next to his wife, grimacing at the acrid taste in his mouth.

Carol rolled on her back and pushed her dark hair away from her face, staring at the tiny cracks on the white bedroom ceiling. "I can't believe this is really happening," she said softly, her voice wobbling with emotion.

"Believe it. It's real," Jim said somberly, studying her profile intently in the morning light.

"It's like waking up from a bad dream, but the dream is reality."

"I know. My thoughts exactly," Jim said. He pulled Carol to him and kissed her tenderly.

Carol draped her arm across his chest. They cuddled quietly for several minutes until Jim suggested a plan.

"Let's have breakfast, leave the kids with Gladys, and head over to the house."

Everything was quiet when Jim and Carol descended the steep stairs to the cozy kitchen. The scent of fresh cinnamon rolls filled the air and made Jim's stomach cramp with hunger.

"Where are the kids?" Carol murmured to herself. She walked to the window and pulled the curtain back. She looked outside, and her depressed mood lifted a little.

"Oh, look, Jim," she said. "Gladys is already entertaining Lillie and Henri if you can call feeding the chickens and gathering eggs entertainment."

"It's entertainment if you don't have to do it every day," Jim said gruffly, pouring a cup of coffee and balancing a roll in his hand.

After breakfast, they headed to Chipmunk Coulee Road. Absorbed in thoughts about what lay ahead of them, they spoke little on the way to the house. Jim drove up the driveway and parked. The burned-out center of their home sat like a black lump of coal, desolate and cold in the morning light. Wispy puffs of smoke were wafting from the debris into the cool morning air. Two men were picking through the rubble, putting burned material from the house into metal canisters and taking notes.

Carol began crying softly. Jim reached over and grabbed her hand. "It'll be all right, hon. We'll get through this, and in a couple of *months*, we'll be back home. We have a lot to be thankful for. We could've all been killed."

She turned her gaze to Jim. Her eyes were red from crying, and her face was dark with disappointment. The memory of their chaotic escape during the night was only hours old, and she felt panic rising in her chest at the thought of carrying the children to safety amid the heat and smoke. She stayed silent, but Jim could feel the weight of her thoughts.

"I remember you told me once you weren't a shrinking violet," Jim continued quietly, meeting her stare. He studied Carol's face, looking for reassurance. "I think your exact words were: 'I'm more of a steel magnolia.'"

Carol slumped against the car door and focused on the house again. Jim could see her anger building, and he waited for an outburst he was sure would come.

Carol sighed deeply. "I do remember saying that, but it kind of pales in the morning light considering everything that's happened, don't you think?" After a few more moments, Carol angrily wiped away more tears. She sat up abruptly. "I don't know who did this, Jim, but you better figure it out!" she said through gritted teeth.

"Listen to me, honey. This is not going to defeat us," Jim said, his voice gritty with resolve. "We'll rebuild and we'll survive." There was a gloomy pause as he absorbed the damage of the charred remains for several moments. "But I can't do this without your help." His voice cracked with emotion.

When Carol saw the deep sorrow in Jim's eyes and the look of defeat on his face, she reconsidered what she was about to say knowing a tirade would benefit no one. Still she couldn't hide her frustration as the words tumbled out.

"I'm sorry, but I'm just so angry." She clenched her fists in her lap, a desperate attempt to control her emotions. She continued to gape at the scene.

"So am I, but that will only get us so far," Jim said curtly.

"I know. You're right but—" She turned toward Jim, and he held up his hand in a stop motion.

"If we're going to start arguing," Jim interrupted, "then whoever did this has already won. Their goal was evil, pure and simple. You can't fight evil with evil, Carol. You've got to fight evil with good. And don't worry, I'm not going to surrender one inch to the degenerate who did this. I will find out who did this—somehow. Trust me."

Carol's emotions were careening like someone on a roller coaster ride. Calm was needed, but what she really wanted to do was pound something—anything.

"I should have known how you'd react to this," she said angrily. "Are we supposed to just forgive whoever did this? Skip down the Christian path and go on our way like nothing's happened," she blurted, waving her hand toward the house, "because right now that seems pretty impossible." Jim let her stew, and after a few moments, she calmed down and slid over in the seat. Jim pulled her close to him, wondering what was coming next.

He tentatively offered advice. "Forgiving people is never easy. The one who forgives pays the price. God knows that. He also knows all about the frustration and anger we're feeling. Just remember one thing: As bad as this looks, God is for us. He's with us, and He'll help us."

Carol grasped his hand, and Jim relaxed a little. "I'm sorry for going off on you," Carol said contritely. "I guess I need an attitude adjustment, but that might not come until we start rebuilding." She brushed her lips against his cheek. "Come on, let's find out what we're up against."

"Is this the shrinking violet or the steel magnolia talking?" Jim said, a ghost of a smile on his face.

"Think steel, baby," Carol said, climbing out of the Suburban.

Dave Thompson, the fire chief, walked up to them as they stood in front of the torched house. "It looks like the fire started from diesel fuel that was poured through an open window in the dining room. By my estimate, it was a couple of gallons." Chief Thompson explained.

"I remember I left the window open about six inches," Carol said. "Why didn't we hear an explosion or something?"

"If you ignite diesel fuel right away before the fumes begin to evaporate, there isn't much sound. I think that's what happened here," Thompson explained. "Whoever started the fire dumped a couple of gallons of fuel through the window after they cut the screen, and then they poured a trail across the driveway. When they lit the trail of fuel, it traveled to the house, up the wall, and into the dining room. Once there, it began burning rapidly, spreading through the center of the house."

"What kind of dollar figure are we talkin' about?" Jim asked another man who had walked up silently and stood beside them listening to the conversation.

Willis Grady, their insurance agent, had visited with them last night. Seeing the home in broad daylight, Jim thought it was a total loss, but Grady took it in stride. A short, stout man with a drooping walrus mustache, his brown eyes were kind and empathetic. He'd seen a lot of disasters in his years as an insurance adjuster. Part of his job was to reassure the homeowners that everything was not a total loss.

"I know it looks horrendous in the daylight," Grady said, "but the fire was contained to the center of the house. That was due to your efforts with the fire extinguisher, Jim, which saved your home from being a total loss. The kitchen, living room, and dining room suffered extensive damage, and your office has some smoke and water damage. The rest of the house is intact, just smoke residue. I would estimate the cost to rebuild and clean up the damage will be over $200,000—all covered by your homeowners' insurance, of course."

"How much time will it take to do that?" Carol asked softly.

"Depends on the availability of carpenters, but I think it'll take two to three months. Think Christmas," Grady said. "But a bigger question needs to be answered. Who started it?"

Jim's face hardened. "I already have some ideas about that," he said solemnly. Then he pointed to the large maple next to the road near the entrance to his driveway. "My surveillance camera on the tree will tell us more. I'll grab the chip out of the computer in my study, and I'll take a look at it when I get to the office."

After a half hour of planning and discussion with the fire chief and insurance adjuster, Jim and Carol went into the house, grabbed some more clothing, cosmetics from the bathroom, a few of the children's favorite toys, and the computer chip, and headed back to Gladys Hanson's farm.

Sheriff Elaine Turnmile sat glumly at her desk holding her head in her hands as she re-read the newspaper article in front of her. The cup of coffee she'd gotten at Kwik Trip was cold, and the banana nut muffin only half eaten. *How long have I been sitting here?* she thought.

She reached for her phone and dialed the number of the *La Crosse Sentinel*. After several rings, an automated voicemail system listed several options. Irritated, Elaine punched a number. "You have reached the desk of Darin Woods, reporter for the *La Crosse Sentinel*. I am away from my desk and unavailable at this time. Please leave me a detailed message, and I'll get back to you." The machine beeped.

"Darin, Sheriff Turnmile here. I'd like to discuss the article you wrote in the newspaper this morning about the investigation of the robbery and murder at the Gas & Go in Stoddard. In that article—" A voice interrupted Sheriff Turnmile's message.

"Sheriff Turnmile. Darin Woods here. How can I help you?" the reporter asked politely.

"Well, for starters, you can print a retraction of the article you wrote in today's morning edition in which you mentioned a member of the sheriff's department."

"Are you talking about Sam Birkstein?"

Elaine scowled and continued. "Exactly. Some of your facts about Sam are skewed and uninformed—more opinion than anything. Did you actually talk to anyone within the law enforcement department before you wrote the article?"

Darin squirmed uneasily in his chair and leaned forward, placing his elbows on his desk.

"Well... no. But I went into the newspaper archives and read about some of Birkstein's cases. He's known for using some rather questionable tactics to apprehend the criminals he's chasing. Dressing in drag, cavorting at some pretty wild parties, and other stuff. That's all public information. What's wrong with that?"

Elaine ignored his attempts to placate her. Her dander was bristling, and she had no intention of letting the newbie reporter off the hook.

"You painted Detective Birkstein in a questionable light when you mentioned his past and called his service 'escapades,'" she said, her voice abrasive and condescending.

"That wasn't my intention—"

"Chasing down drug dealers and perpetrators in the area is not some pansy walk in the park," she continued belligerently.

"I understand—" Darin said apologetically.

Sheriff Turnmile continued as if he hadn't spoken. "It's dangerous and requires grit, determination, and patience." By this time, the sheriff's voice had turned frosty with contempt. "Using the word 'escapade' hardly paints Officer Birkstein's service to the community in a positive light. 'Escapade,' as described by Webster's is daring or reckless behavior. Sam has one of the best drug apprehension records of anyone on staff, largely due to his carefully planned strategies, patience, and street smarts. With the current attitude toward law enforcement and frequent accusations of police overreach, I would appreciate a retraction of the negative comment about one of my officers." A prolonged silence followed. "Darin? Are you still there?" Turnmile asked sourly.

"Yeah, I'm here," Woods commented weakly.

"I will be waiting to see a printed retraction in tomorrow's paper. Are we clear?"

"One hundred percent," Woods said.

"Thank you." Elaine Turnmile slammed the phone into the cradle, then sat back, her eyes flashing with anger.

"We'll see what comes of that," she said to herself. But despite her energetic defense of Sam's service, she doubted it would stave off the actions she'd have to take in the very near future. The robbery case was bogged down in a mire of seemingly unrelated facts and suppositions, and the resolution of the crime was like looking for a ghost in the fog. But sooner or later, Sam Birkstein would be arrested and charged with murder, and Elaine didn't know how she could stop it.

32

The investigative crew met Tuesday afternoon on the third floor of the law enforcement center. Lt. Higgins, Paul Saner, Mike Leland, and DeDe Deverioux were present, but Sheriff Turnmile was conspicuously absent. Jim was sure she was trying to fend off reporters who were demanding the truth about the robbery at the Stoddard Gas & Go and Detective Sam Birkstein's role in the crime. With each day that slipped by, the chances of bringing justice to Vicki Invold's family decreased substantially. Collecting information that would lead to a perpetrator seemed as preposterous as wringing blood from a turnip.

Jim stood near a third-story window that overlooked Vine Street and stared forlornly at the blur of traffic below, wondering where everyone was going in such a hurry. He'd considered the evidence of the murder and robbery at the Gas & Go so many times his brain felt like mush.

As he contemplated the lack of progress that his team had made, Jim heard a commotion behind him. He turned and saw Sam and Leslie Birkstein appear at the door of the third-floor classroom. Seeing the two detectives back in the building brightened his sour mood a little. Sam looked upbeat and well-rested—almost happy. Leslie just looked very pregnant. As the team eagerly welcomed them back, Jim's phone beeped. Bobby Rude was calling, and what he told Jim surprised him.

"Wait a minute! Let me get this straight. You think these thugs of Devon's are planning a jewelry store heist somewhere in the city?" Jim asked. *These kids are teenagers,* Jim thought. *A robbery of a jewelry store seems highly unlikely.*

Sam walked over toward the window and listened intently to Jim's conversation.

"I don't think. I *know*," Bobby said fervently. Jim could imagine his dark brown eyes and serious attitude. He had to admit that Bobby had a sixth sense about sketchy situations. *Probably comes from all those years living with an alcoholic father,* he thought, *picking him up off the floor and getting him to bed.*

"I was in the hall by Lyle's locker this morning," Bobby went on, "and I heard him mention some jewelry and coin place, but he didn't give the location. There can't be that many jewelry stores in La Crosse, are there?"

Jim did a quick mental survey. The establishments that sold jewelry were well-known in the city and were located in high-traffic areas. He doubted the two-bit thugs would have the bravado to plan a heist like that.

"There might be a dozen or so jewelry stores in La Crosse, but the ones I know all have sophisticated alarm systems. I doubt they'd try those. But there might be a few in quieter neighborhoods. I'll get somebody on it... and thanks, Bobby. You stay safe," Jim warned.

Jim turned to the group, but before he could begin, Paul interrupted. "Chief, what's the status of your house?" Sam and Jim walked over to the group and sat down.

Jim leaned over the table, weary and exhausted. "It's a mess, but it's not a total loss. Basically the middle of the house is burned out, but the garage, the bedrooms, and bathrooms are still intact. The reconstruction and clean-up will take a couple of months," Jim said, meeting the stares of the team. He looked down at his bandaged hands. "We're just thankful we got out with the kids before it was too late." Jim sighed and closed his eyes briefly, trying to block out the images of chaos from the previous night.

"Any ideas how it started?" Sam asked. He'd perched on the end of a table, his cool demeanor belying the intense frustration he felt about the robbery and the fire at Higgins's place. *The same perpetrator probably committed both crimes,* he thought, *but we don't have any proof.*

"Someone started the fire with a couple of gallons of diesel fuel. But the bigger question is *who* started it?" Jim said. Sam recognized the cold, deadly stare that often accompanied Higgins's questions. He recalled the way Higgins interrogated suspects, engaging them in casual conversation and then—bam! He'd ask a pivotal question, catching everyone in the room off-guard. *That's what he looks like now,* Sam thought, *like someone with an important question on the tip of his tongue.*

Truth be told, when Jim thought about the fire, he could hardly contain his anger. It threatened to overwhelm him like an ocean wave that hits you broadside and knocks you into the swirling foam. Jim could visualize a right uppercut to the chops of whoever had torched his house. Thankfully, no one knew the rotten thoughts he was having.

"So it was intentional?" Sam asked. "Is that what you're saying?"

"Absolutely. The fire chief confirmed from the evidence he gathered at the house this morning that the fire was arson. There's no doubt it was started intentionally—it wasn't an accident," Jim rasped, clearing his throat loudly.

"So now we're looking for an arsonist, too?" Leslie asked.

Jim leaned back in his chair, took a few deep breaths, and appeared calm, but deep down he felt violated. Everything about the fire, the threat to his family, made him long for revenge. It was that simple and that complicated. Somewhere out of the blue, the words he'd said to Carol earlier in the morning came back to him: "You can't fight evil with evil. You've got to fight evil with good."

"Vengeance is mine, saith the Lord." Jim harrumphed to himself. *Easier said than done.*

In a calm, clear voice, Jim began a recitation of the arson law as he knew it. "First-degree arson: The willful and malicious setting of fire to, or burning of, any structure in whole or in part when that building is occupied by another person... or persons," Jim recited flatly. His face looked like carved granite. He crossed his arms over his chest in a defiant gesture. He looked at each team member and continued. "Standing in my driveway this morning looking at my home, that's what it looks like to me—first-degree arson." Jim leaned forward, placing his elbows on the table. "Ten years to life if convicted." He paused for a moment. "I'm going to get this guy, whoever he is, and then I'm going to nail him to the wall for trying to kill my family!" he finished. Although delivered in a calm voice, the words had a startling effect on the team. Higgins's righteous anger was on full display, and in typical fashion, he'd announced his intentions with an understated attitude of confidence and aplomb.

After several moments of silence, Jim began again. He opened his laptop, touched a few keys, and brought up the images of his house from the surveillance camera near the driveway. He gestured to the team, and they gathered around the laptop.

"I thought you might be interested to know that my security camera recorded the arson event, although somebody disabled the motion lights on my pole shed before they started the fire, so it's pretty dark. You can still make out the perpetrator in the shadows, though." He started the home surveillance video. The team gathered around Jim and watched the security footage roll across the screen.

From the fuzzy images on the laptop, the group could see a person dressed in sweats, a hood pulled over his head, carrying a fuel can down the driveway toward the house. Although it was dark, a few moments later the figure retreated into the shadows from the house while dumping a trail of fuel down the driveway, striking a match, and running out of camera range. In a few seconds, the house was ablaze, the flames spreading rapidly. Jim punched the pause button to stop the video, his face pale as he recalled his family's narrow escape from the burning building. He quietly shut the cover on the computer.

"Okay, we've seen it. Now let's get organized," Jim said, shifting into command mode. "I'll conduct the investigation of the fire myself, but I believe the fire was meant to detract from the investigation into the robbery and murder at the Gas & Go. I can't prove it yet, but that's what I think. Whatever the perpetrator thought he was going to accomplish with the fire was a major screw-up." Jim stopped, his eyes blazing with determination. "Now more than ever, we've got to pull out all the stops. Establishing the motive, suspects, and persons of interest from the gas station robbery—that's your job. You all know the drill. We need a theory based on hard, solid evidence." Jim looked over at Sam, who stared back. "So… I want to hear what everyone found out yesterday," Jim said impatiently, loosening his tie. He leaned forward, his eyes hard and glittering.

Throughout the next hour, several significant pieces of information came to light. Paul reported that the gun was most likely stolen. He had a call into a gun dealer who'd had several firearm shows in the area the last few months. He planned to confer with the dealer about buyers of a Kimber 9-millimeter handgun.

Next, Paul told about his visit to Veterans Freedom Park where he discovered the houseboat that Devon Williams had been using over the last several months. He relayed the information about Devon and Vicki's argument behind a bar on Third Street.

"Who told you that?" Jim asked brusquely.

"Lyle Leverentz. By the way, Vicki was five months pregnant. So maybe they were arguing about the baby or an abortion—something like that. Anyway, that argument was pretty serious, according to Lyle—shouting, swearing, stuff like that. If Devon did kill Vicki, an argument during the robbery at the Gas & Go might have tripped his trigger, he lost his temper, and things got out of control. Something to think about." Paul leaned forward and continued building his case.

"Devon was rattled that Vicki stood up to him. Maybe she wanted to keep the baby; he wanted to get rid of it. He goes to the Gas & Go to rob the place and ends up in an argument with Vicki while she's working. It gets tense, and Devon gets angry. He rips the necklace off Vicki's neck, and when she fights back, he goes into some kind of a rage, loses control, and fills her full of bullet holes, effectively eliminating the need to abort the baby."

Jim and Sam looked at each other. "Could happen, I guess," Jim said calmly, tipping his head slightly.

"Hey, it's better than anything else we've got. Right now, it's the *only* theory we've got," Sam commented, "excluding the theory that *I* robbed the station, that is."

In addition, Paul told them he'd gotten a surprising phone call from Seth O'Connor, a Stoddard resident, who told him about an abandoned, expensive dirt bike he'd found in the alley near his garden shed. Paul drove to Stoddard and retrieved the bike. It was in the crime lab being checked for fingerprints and logged as possible evidence. "But we still have no eyewitnesses who actually saw someone leave the Gas & Go at around 11:40 that night," Paul finished dejectedly.

"Well, you've uncovered some things we didn't know before," Jim said. "The argument between Devon and Vicki is certainly feasible. We all need to keep digging." He turned his attention to Mike Leland. "What do you have, Mike?"

"I looked at the rate of petty crime in La Crosse. It hasn't changed much in the last year. Car thefts are up slightly—about 1.4 percent," Mike said, his finger moving down his typed report. Jim gazed at the newbie detective and waited.

"But I went through the juvenile court cases from last year and read the notes on the kids who were detained. Nine kids admitted they were coached into criminal activities by another more experienced perpetrator, some an older sibling. I met with five of them over at the juvenile detention center today. I think a couple of kids recognized

Devon from his mug shot, but nobody would admit it. He's got a hold on his little underlings, but somebody might come forward later. We'll see what comes of it." Mike looked at Jim for a long moment.

"Okay. Sounds good," Jim replied. He turned to DeDe. "And what did you discover on your trip to the countryside?"

"Not much. I talked to two farmers—one in West Salem and one in Holmen—who own donkeys. They manage their small farms themselves, and they didn't hire anyone who fit the description of Devon Williams to work on their farm. So..."

Jim looked up hopefully. "Yeah?"

DeDe shook her head. "So I think the donkey poop on the boots is a dead end, sir," DeDe said. "But on another front, Jude hired a young girl in the kitchen at Si Bon who's been telling him about some Black dude she met. She seems totally taken in by this guy, whoever he is. It sounds like Devon's MO. She didn't say where she met him, so I'm going to talk to her tonight when she's on duty at the restaurant. Jude suggested I work a shift with her to see if I can find out more."

"That's good," Jim said, encouraged by the team's work. "Bobby Rude just called. He overheard a conversation between Lyle Leverentz and another kid in the hall at school. Something about plans to hit a jewelry store." Jim turned to Sam and said. "DeDe and Leslie, this afternoon I want you to research any small jewelry establishments around town, maybe someone who sells out of their home. I want you to call every jewelry store in town and give them a heads-up about this rumor. Don't send them into a panic—just ask them to check their surveillance cameras and alarms to be sure they are activated before they leave their establishments tonight."

DeDe and Leslie nodded.

Paul asked, "So are we going to tail this Lyle kid?"

"We've gotta figure that out. We need to make a plan," Jim said. "We don't have any solid evidence that this kid is actually being directed by Devon Williams to carry out criminal activities, but he is a close associate of Devon's, so we're justified in watching him to see where he goes and what he does. Video surveillance or catching him red-handed would be great, but right now, that probably won't happen."

"What about getting a search warrant for the houseboat on French Island?" Paul asked.

"Yes, absolutely," Jim said, nodding vigorously. "With what you guys have found out, we can move on that. We need to look for drugs, drug paraphernalia, large amounts of cash, and any evidence that suggests illicit sex with underage girls, like underwear, condoms, and sex toys. Also any stolen items like weed whackers, lawn mowers, tools—typical stuff you might find in someone's garage."

"How much did they get from the till at the Gas & Go?" Leslie asked, frowning.

"The manager thought it was over two thousand dollars," DeDe said.

"You want me to get going on that search warrant, Chief?" Leslie asked.

"Yeah, let's get started on that, Lez," Jim said. He turned and stood up, motioning to Sam as he walked toward the row of windows overlooking Losey Boulevard. He turned to Sam and asked, "What are you doing here, Sam? I understood you were off duty for a while. Has something changed?" Jim asked.

"I can handle it, Chief. I'm feeling pretty good today," Sam said.

Jim shook his head. He hated these moments when a decision that had already been made was called into question and had to be reconsidered. He wasn't sure Sam was really prepared to head back into a full-blown murder investigation. Although he'd never known anyone personally who'd suffered a lightning strike, he'd read enough about it to know that side effects from the injuries could be long-lasting and debilitating. Sam sensed Jim's misgivings and rallied a defense.

"Really, Chief, I can handle it," he reiterated again. "My headache is gone, and my ribs are still sore, but it's not any worse than the spills I've taken on my bike."

Jim sighed and stared at the floor, trying to make a decision. Finally, he looked up at Sam. "I'll talk to Turnmile, but I'm telling you, she may say no. If you get in trouble and start having problems, you have to let me know. That's how I'm going to sell it to her, but in all honesty, Sam, I think you're pushing the envelope here. But I'll go to bat for you if you think you can handle it. Deal?"

"Deal," Sam responded.

Jim began walking down the hall with a wave of his hand. "Come on, guys. You're with me."

An hour later, Sam and Jim were huddled around a map of La Crosse that was thumb-tacked to one of the beige walls in Jim's office.

"You think this is gonna work?" Mike asked. Jim calmly met his gaze, but he could see the skepticism in Mike's eyes.

"No, I'm not sure it'll work, but we've got to do something," Jim said, frustrated. "We need to flush Williams out of hiding." He ran his hand through his hair. Jim had removed the bandages from his hands, and Sam and Mike cringed at the sight of the red, blistered skin.

"I'm not sure he is hiding," Sam said. "His cohorts seem to know where he is, but we haven't been able to locate him..." Mike gave Sam a look of confusion.

"I doubt that this is going to work," Mike mumbled.

"Just think of this whole plan as being proactive," Sam said sarcastically.

"Okay, I guess I can run with that," Mike said, raising his eyebrows. "One more question. Doesn't this whole plan border on entrapment?"

"No. We're not inducing Lyle to commit a crime," Jim explained. "He's been spreading the plan of robbing a jewelry store at school himself. We're simply acting on a tip from a citizen. Entrapment and citizen tips are miles apart," Jim explained patiently.

"Sometimes you have to create a little drama—kinda get things going in the right direction," Sam said. "It can get results, but it takes some coordination and luck." Sam's good mood had ground to a halt. Covering his eyes with his hand, he slid it down over his face, remembering other stings and ambushes that had gone south, leaving cops shot or hurt. Besides that, the hustle of the investigative process was overwhelming his senses. He could feel an intense headache building at the back of his head.

"What are the chances the kid will be armed?" Mike asked Jim.

"He'll be armed. You can count on it," Jim answered, "if the robbery at the Gas & Go is any indication. These little cohorts are getting braver. Whoever hit the station was armed and had no reservations about using a weapon. So, for starters, everybody wears their vests and swat gear, and we assume he'll be armed," Jim said.

"We're getting ahead of ourselves. First, we've got to tail this Lyle kid," Sam said. "Then we've gotta make sure he doesn't notice us, and when he makes his move at the store, we'll nail him."

"How confident are you that Bobby Rude got all this straight?" Mike asked. "All he overheard were some kids bragging by their locker, and sometimes the talk from these teenage hotshots is just talk—more bluff than actual plans."

Jim nodded in understanding. Beneath his calm exterior he was beginning to question his own judgment about this whole operation. From past experience, tailing a suspect and actually apprehending him in the midst of a criminal act was a complex balancing act—one teeming with complications. However, ignoring a tip from someone who'd heard the threat firsthand was also tantamount to dereliction of duty. It always boiled down to a delicate balance between duty and judgment. All these thoughts were running through his head as he composed a logical response to Mike's question.

"Okay, let's go over it again," Jim said, determined to calm his team members' misgivings. "First, one of you will be at school when it lets out this afternoon and tail Lyle's every move. We'll keep in touch via text. Second, we've contacted every jewelry store in the city and put them on alert. They know to call if anything seems suspicious. But I'm really thinking this kid is going to hit the shop over on the north side—"

"You mean the one on Monroe Street? That place that buys coins and old jewelry?" Mike interrupted.

"Yeah. Bobby said Lyle mentioned jewelry *and* coins. That's the one that makes the most sense to me. It's close to the houseboat, and it's in a quiet neighborhood. I just can't see an inexperienced teenager going for broke and breaking into one of the chain stores. The security alone would be a major logistical problem. They'd need too much sophisticated equipment to carry out a heist like that, and they would have to do some store surveillance. A teenager in a store like that is going to attract some major attention, especially if he doesn't have cash or a credit card. They'd need a lot of chutzpah to pull it off."

"Alotta what?" Mike asked, screwing up his face at Jim's use of the antiquated term.

"Chutzpah. It's a Yiddish term that means bravado, gall. You know somebody with—" Jim explained.

"Balls," Sam said sourly, rubbing his neck. Mike looked over at him.

"So, getting back to the plan," Jim interrupted, "Sam and I will be in constant contact with the shop on Monroe. We're planting Officer Helen Simons inside the business to impersonate the owner. She's done some other undercover work for us in the past, and we'll have another officer inside with her for added security. Plus we'll have the place surrounded."

"That's a lot of manpower for a sting on a home-based business," Mike said, looking skeptical.

"We better hope for a slow night then, although that hardly ever happens," Jim said as he studied the city map again. Pointing to the general area of the shop, he said, "There's an alley in the back of the shop. We'll post someone there, Sam will be stationed in an unmarked car outside on the street, and a couple more city officers in street clothes will be scattered throughout the block. We'll communicate by cell."

"Well, considering our options, which are few and far between, I think it's our best bet to rattle Devon's cage and flush him outta his hole—wherever that is," Sam said, rubbing his temple.

Mike looked at both detectives. "Okay. Whatever you say. I just hope it works."

"Usually it doesn't," Jim said flatly, depressed at the odds stacked against them. "But sitting here with our tail tucked between our legs is not an option. Be ready to rock tonight."

33

Jim drove back to Gladys's for dinner before the stake-out at Millers' Coin and Jewelry Store on Monroe Street. Gladys had outdone herself putting the evening meal together: roast pork with sage dressing, mashed potatoes and gravy, corn, cabbage salad, and apple pie for dessert. Jim pushed his chair away from the table after the meal and retreated to the living room feeling like a stuffed and trussed turkey. He thought about the exercise and moderation he'd been practicing and decided all of it had just gone out the window. Instead of going for a walk, he sank into a well-worn leather recliner in the living room that had belonged to Gladys's husband, Otis. While he read the *Wisconsin State Journal*, Lillie and Henri played a competitive game of Go Fish on the carpet. He could hear Carol and Gladys chatting in the kitchen while they cleaned up the dinner dishes.

Fifteen minutes later Jim's phone beeped with a text message.

"Tailing Lyle. Mike"

Tucking his phone in his shirt pocket, Jim continued reading the paper until a tapping on his arm interrupted him.

"Bapa?" Lillie said.

"Yes, peanut. How was your day?" Jim asked distractedly as he continued to read.

"Bapa, did you know that when Mozart was my age he was already traveling around Europe, amazing people with his musical talent?" Lillie asked. Jim quickly surmised that this little exchange was some kind of parental test, so he lowered his newspaper and looked directly into his daughter's eyes. *She's gonna kill the boys with those blue eyes,* he thought.

"Do you even know where Europe is, honey?" Jim asked, a sly grin curling the corners of his mouth.

"Yes, I do know where Europe is, but that's not the point," she said, crossing her arms over her chest. The frown that had been a little crease on her forehead a moment ago deepened.

"What's your point then?" Jim asked, waiting for Lillie to reveal her request.

"I need a piano here at Gladys's if I'm going to keep up with my lessons. Sister Maria doesn't like me to miss even one day of practice. Can you do something about that?" she asked, tipping her head. Her wild blonde curls framed her cherubic face as she held Elsa under her arm, and Jim felt a deep affection for her. Henri came up beside him on the other side of the chair, and Jim couldn't help but recall the near-death experience of the fire the night before. *We could be getting ready to bury our children,* he thought.

Jim considered Lillie's request carefully. His family had been uprooted once before when Jim's daughter, Sara, had been abducted by a crazed drug dealer, and they'd had to go into hiding at Gladys's. Now it had happened again, but this time their stay would be extended for several months until their home on Chipmunk Coulee Road was renovated.

"Well, I think I could rent a piano from Bowman's Music Store downtown and have them deliver it here to Gladys's place. How does that sound?" Jim asked.

Lillie nodded seriously. "That sounds good."

Jim expected a big smile, but instead, Lillie continued to stand next to the chair. He felt something brewing beneath the surface. By now, he'd learned that a conversation with Lillie could turn on a dime and become a major hoopla when she was involved. Uncomfortable with his daughter's intense stare, Jim ventured a question.

"Did you need something else, Lillie?" he asked.

"I was very scared last night, Bapa," Lillie said softly.

Jim laid the paper on the end table and opened his arms. Lillie wriggled into his lap.

"Hey, what about me?" Henri asked. Jim widened his arms, and Henri crawled in and cuddled up to Jim's chest.

"You had every right to be scared last night. I was scared, too," Jim said.

"You were?" Lillie said, her eyes widening at Jim's confession.

"Fires are really scary. The Lord protected us, or we wouldn't be here," Jim said softly. He loved the feel of the children's warm bodies scrunched against his chest as he wrapped his arms around them. He kissed Henri tenderly on the top of his head.

"Bapa, I was going to tell you something last night after the fire, but I forgot," Lillie said, her eyes downcast, avoiding Jim's direct gaze.

Jim's stomach tightened with misgiving. "Forgot what?" he asked casually, although the goosebumps on the back of his neck told another story.

Lillie locked eyes with Jim. "You know the guy who started the fire? He ran down the bank into the bushes across the road."

Jim froze. "What?" He sat up straight, jostling the children from their comfortable positions. "How do you know that, Lillie?"

"I saw him.

"Wait. Wait. You saw him? When? How?" Jim asked, shocked by this admission. Henri jumped down from Jim's lap and began gathering up the Go Fish cards.

"I looked out the window," she said, gawking at Jim as if he were dimwitted.

"Why were you awake? It was the middle of the night."

"I don't know. Something woke me up, and when I looked out the window, I saw some guy running across the road." Lillie squirmed uncomfortably as Jim continued to stare at her. "That's the truth, Bapa," she finished solemnly. "I was going to come to your bedroom and tell you, but then I thought I must be dreaming, and I lay down and went back to sleep."

Jim stood abruptly, leaving Lillie by the chair. He walked into the kitchen. "Carol, could I talk to you for a minute in the other room?"

Carol stopped her conversation with Gladys. When she looked at Jim, she could see the urgency on his face. Lillie was standing behind him wearing a look of guilt.

"Sure, I'll be right there." Carol finished wiping a plate. She laid the dishtowel on the counter and followed Jim down the hallway to Gladys's bedroom. Lillie trailed behind him. "Am I in trouble, Bapa?"

Henri crowded around Jim's feet. "Is Lillie in trouble again?" he asked.

Jim held up his hand in a stop gesture to Lillie and Henri. "Stay here," he said sternly. The children stood out in the hallway while he talked to Carol in Gladys's bedroom behind the closed door.

"What's the matter now?" Carol asked.

"Lillie claims she saw the arsonist across the road from the house," he said softly.

"What? You mean she was awake when he was actually starting our house on fire?" Carol whispered intensely, her eyes widening at the implications of Lillie's confession.

"Yeah, it sounds crazy, but we can't afford to doubt her, can we?" Jim said.

"Not really. We doubted her when she said she smelled smoke, and look how that turned out," Carol said sourly, rolling her eyes.

"Of course, there's always the possibility that Lillie dreamed the whole thing, and none of it really happened," said Jim.

"What are you gonna do now?" Carol asked.

I've got to go back to town. I may not be home 'til early morning."

"Okay. No problem," Carol said.

Jim turned to go, but Carol grabbed his arm and pulled him to her in a quick, intense hug. She gave him a long kiss.

"I'll be back later," Jim said.

34

It was a little after seven in the evening, and Jim had decided to drive to his home on Chipmunk Coulee Road. He couldn't ignore the nagging thought that he had missed something the arsonist might have left at the scene of the fire. The sun was hovering above the horizon, and the light left diffused streaks of gold across the lawn. Jim climbed out of his truck and stood in front of the sooty shell of his house. Somewhere above him, an owl hooted a lonely call, adding to the feeling of desolation. The clean-up company had come and wrapped the burned-out portion of the house in heavy, thick plastic. The work to restore his home had begun.

Jim ducked under the crime scene tape and walked up to the house to get a closer look. The front door was scorched, and the glass panes were cracked. A sign tacked to the door read "Keep Out—Private Property." It seemed so incongruous, Jim chuckled to himself.

He still could not believe the home where he'd lived for over twenty-five years was in such shambles. The memories of his children's laughter down by the creek just a few days ago left him feeling forlorn at the destruction of a place he held so dear. His house had been a shelter and a haven through all the blessings and storms of life. He thought back to the day he and Margie bought the house and the excitement they felt to own their first piece of country real estate. Other memories flooded in. The day Margie had died—how the neighbors had brought casseroles, hugs, and quiet affirmations of their support and love. His solitary nights trying to sort out the deep feelings of loneliness and sorrow without Margie. The joy of his wedding night with Carol and the long, intimate soaks in the deep tub. The arrival of Lillie, who never stopped asking questions, the birth of Henri, Jon and Jennie's engagement announcement, and Sara's wedding. He sighed and looked toward the sky, then turned and walked down the driveway, his shoulders slumped in defeat.

He walked across the road and looked down into the steep ravine across from his property. He'd rarely given this area near his home a second glance. Why would he? It was just a ditch by the road, but now it seemed weighted with importance.

In the receding light, Jim suddenly felt stupid, but then he reconsidered. In her own indomitable way, Lillie had tried to warn him of the impending fire that nearly destroyed their home and threatened their lives. He'd never forgive himself if he'd missed something that could help them find the lowlife who'd destroyed his home and tried to kill his family. The light was disappearing fast. If he was going to try and find something he'd better get moving.

He stepped off the shoulder of the road and began slipping and sliding to the bottom of the ravine. It was darker down here, and Jim flipped the switch on his flashlight, sweeping the light back and forth in a continuous arc, hoping that something would present itself. Surprisingly, people had thrown a number of items into the deep ditch. As he walked, he spotted Walmart bags, beer cans, an old tote bag, a microwave, and a dirty McDonald's coffee cup, but nothing that resembled something belonging to an arsonist.

He walked about a hundred feet along the bottom of the ravine. Not finding anything, he turned and headed back to his point of entry. He kicked at the grass and tall weeds as he walked, hoping to spot something he'd missed, but he came up empty He climbed out of the ravine and walked down the driveway to his Suburban. Sitting in the silence of the cab, he wondered how many times he'd searched for something—anything—to move a case forward to a resolution. Too many times to count. *It's all part of the process,* he thought.

Jim glanced at his phone—almost eight o'clock. Time for another rendezvous. He started the SUV and drove to the stake-out on the north side of La Crosse.

Sam Birkstein sat hunched in the seat of his Jeep along the curb on Monroe Street in north La Crosse. It was eight-thirty in the evening, and the neighborhood had finally quieted down from the bustle of people returning from work and school. Sam reclined in the driver's seat and closed his eyes. Returning to work and getting roped into a stake-out had been a bad idea. His head was exploding with pain, and his blistered feet, though healing, were still sore. *How am I going to chase somebody through the neighborhood?* Sam thought. *I can hardly walk. Coming back to work was a really stupid idea.*

In the span of a few quiet moments, he tried to relax so the Tylenol could get into his bloodstream. Suddenly, the passenger door of his car popped open, and Lt. Higgins slid into the seat.

"Hey. How're you doing?" Higgins asked flatly, glancing over at Sam.

"Not good. My head feels like it's going to split open any minute," Sam complained, still reclined in his seat. He threw his arm over his eyes and remained quiet. Jim glanced at him. He was pale and withdrawn like a wounded animal.

"Don't worry. Nothing's happening yet. Mike texted me about fifteen minutes ago. Lyle's cruising the city on his bike, biding his time." He paused for a moment, then continued. "Listen, Sam, you don't have to do anything physical. Just sit in the car and watch. Let us know if you see something suspicious."

Sam thought back to the evening before. He wasn't about to tell

Higgins that his sexual responses had been surprisingly unaffected by the lightning strike. Some things were better left unsaid. He sighed when he thought how relaxed he'd been after the lovemaking with Leslie. She'd been so understanding. How could he have ever doubted her loyalty and love? *Only an idiot like you,* he thought.

"How're things with Leslie?" Jim asked, his question eerily intrusive.

Does the guy read thoughts, too? Sam wondered.

"Actually, we're good," Sam said. "Now if I could just get rid of these stupid headaches. I'm not where I want to be yet, but I'm getting there. Physically, I'm coming around little by little. It feels like the edges of things are healing anyway. That's a good thing."

"Yes. Yes, it is," Jim replied. They fell into an easy silence. Jim sat in the Jeep for about an hour, scrolling on Facebook and Instagram while Sam napped. At nine-thirty, Jim's phone buzzed.

"Higgins." He listened carefully, the light from the phone revealing the worry etched on his face. Sam stirred next to him, sucked in a huge breath, and opened his eyes slowly. Disoriented, he sat up slowly, groaned, and leaned back in the seat again. Jim stuffed his phone in his pocket.

"It's a go," Jim said tersely. "Lyle called the shop on the pretense of picking up something for his mom's birthday."

Jim touched Sam's arm lightly and pointed down the street. Lyle Leverentz was riding a bike along the curb, heading in the direction of the jewelry and coin shop. Sam and Jim watched him weave around several parked cars until he came to the intersection of Monitor and Kale. Then he ditched the bike in a copse of trees along the street, emerging a few minutes later. He looked around nervously and walked across the street toward the shop, slithering along the side of the building to a back entrance.

Jim dialed a number, waited, then said, "Helen, Lyle's arrived. We have you surrounded. We'll provide support," Jim ordered. He hung up. "I'm outta here. Stay in touch," he said brusquely. He opened the passenger door quietly, slipped out on the pavement, and walked up the sidewalk. The trees arching over the street formed dark shadows on the ground. An outdoor light over the side entrance of the shop flicked on, illuminating Lyle Leverentz bouncing nervously on the balls of his feet outside the door. The door opened, and he went in.

Jim watched the action as he stood under a sprawling maple tree. His phone vibrated in his pocket.

"Higgins," he said softly.

"Chief, Mike here. I'm coming up the street, walking toward you. Two officers are in the alley behind the shop. We're closing in."

"I'll hang back in case he makes a run for it," Jim said. The connection went dead.

Jim walked past the house, then doubled back and snuck across the darkened yard, staying in the shadows along the wall until he was beneath a window. The light from inside created a geometric shape on the narrow strip of grass outside the window. From somewhere in the neighborhood, the odor of frying hamburger wafted on the evening breeze. Inside the house, voices ramped up in volume, but despite hovering under the closed window, Jim couldn't understand what was being said.

Suddenly, doors were banging, and a shot rang out. Jim tore around the house and cautiously approached the side door, which was hanging open on its hinges. He heard scuffling inside and shouts. With gun drawn, he hurried inside and down a hallway where sounds were coming from the front porch of the house.

Hugging the wall in the hallway, Jim shouted, "Everybody clear?"

"Yeah, Chief. We're okay. Come on in," Mike Leland shouted back.

The owner had turned a small enclosed porch in the front of the house into a jewelry shop. A few showcases of necklaces, rings, and earrings were on display. Another case held gold and silver coins. Lyle Leverentz, restrained with handcuffs, was sitting on an adjacent chair, his face pale, his expression dark and perturbed. Two city police officers flanked the chair.

"Thought I heard a shot. Everyone okay?" Jim asked. He locked eyes with Officer Simons.

"Shot went wild," Helen said, pointing to the bullet hole in the wall facing the street. "Nobody was hurt, sir."

"Right. Mike, you get Lyle downtown and book him. I'll interview him tomorrow. I'll get crime scene over here."

Jim was on his phone when Sam appeared wide-eyed in the doorway. "We're fine, Sam," Jim explained. "Mike's taking control of the scene here. You're coming with me." Jim turned and walked back down the hall and out the side door.

"Where are we going now?" Sam asked, limping behind Jim. They went outside and walked toward the Jeep. Jim stopped on the sidewalk and faced Sam.

"We're going to the houseboat where Devon Williams has been hanging out over in Veterans Freedom Park," Jim said.

How are we going to get in?" Sam asked.

"Easy. I've got my Leatherman. We'll take the screws off the hinges. We're going to take that place apart," Jim said intensely. "Let's go."

35

By the time Jim and Sam arrived at Veterans Freedom Park, a La Crosse police cruiser was parked near the river, its red and blue lights flashing in rhythmic blips. Jim noticed Paul's Ford F-150 pickup parked near the memorial.

Jim and Sam hopped out of the Jeep and ran over to the houseboat. Paul was pacing on the back deck of one of the houseboats, pale and angry. Conversing with Officer Lakowski, his finger wildly jabbed the air next to the officer.

"This is the work of Devon Williams," Paul said angrily. When Jim and Sam appeared on the bank by the houseboat, Paul looked up, surprised to see them.

"What's going on?" Jim asked, stepping onto the deck. "Rose Becker found her husband, Horatio, unconscious on the floor of their houseboat after she'd returned from the store to get groceries. He'd been punched several times, and the EMTs thought he might have had a heart attack as a result of a fight with an intruder."

"Is he dead?" Sam asked.

"I don't know," Paul said. "Rose found my number and called me about a half hour ago. When I got here, they were loading Horatio into an ambulance. But I talked to Rose, and listen to this—she smacked the guy with her cast iron frying pan. He took off. One guess who it was," Paul said, his face creased in disgust.

"Devon Williams?" Jim said.

Paul pointed at Jim's chest. "You got it, Chief. She identified him from a mugshot." Paul's head bobbed up and down in amazement. "Can you believe it? She hit him with a damn frying pan!"

"Maybe she should work for the sheriff's department," Sam said grumpily. "Let's hope the whack with the frying pan will slow him down a little."

"And he escaped?" Jim yelled, pointing to the door. "How'd he do that? Didn't anybody go after him?"

"Nobody was here to stop him," Paul said dejectedly.

Jim began talking in a rapid-fire fashion. "I'm issuing an APB on this guy, getting it on the morning news with a picture, and enlisting the help of La Crosse residents. If he's still around, somebody has to have seen him somewhere. How the hell did he disappear into thin air? Did this lady say what direction he went?"

Paul looked toward the sky, closed his eyes, and swore softly. He gave Jim and Sam a blank stare. "She was so shook up by the whole incident, I doubt that she noticed. But I'll go over to the hospital and talk to her."

"We're going to search that houseboat he's been using. You need to show us which one it is," Jim said.

"You'll have to bust the door down," Paul said, walking rapidly in front of Jim and Sam as they left the Beckers' houseboat and trotted along the river. "There's a big padlock on the door."

"Don't have to bust the door down. I've got my Leatherman," Jim said.

Paul led the way to the houseboat floating silently on the dark, still river. Jim jumped on the boat and walked up to the door. Sam and Paul crowded around him.

"Gotta flashlight? Can't see anything," Jim said.

Paul used his cell phone flashlight and pointed it at the lock.

"Guys, let's get the door open," Sam said seriously.

Jim dug out his Leatherman, unscrewed the hinges on the houseboat door, and flicked on the light. "Come on, guys. We're in. Let's get busy."

36

Si Bon restaurant on the south end of La Crosse was bustling. The huge refurbished barn, with its rustic atmosphere and sophisticated menu, was packed with customers, and more patrons patiently waited in the foyer for a table. The wait staff carried out their duties with efficiency and friendliness. Jude Delaney, DeDe's chef husband, was doing what he did best—coordinating the cooking of exquisite dishes, keeping the wait times for tables and food reasonable, and presenting elegant plates displaying culinary perfection that wowed the customers.

Off in the distance, the sky was burning with a kaleidoscope of brilliant pinks and reds. Several customers waited on the terrace under the pergola and absorbed the beauty of the smoky blue bluffs and the spectacular sunset. A few puffed on cigarettes, but most customers enjoyed a glass of wine and a charcuterie board of Wisconsin cheeses, crackers, and fruit while they waited for a table to open up.

Angela Fitzpatrick and DeDe Deverioux were working together plating salads at a long table off to one side of the kitchen. They had been extremely busy earlier in the evening, but now things were slowing down, and the girls had a few moments to talk.

"Is this your first night at the restaurant?" DeDe asked, leaning against the counter.

Angela shook her head vigorously. "Oh, no! I've worked here for about six months. Chef Delaney has a stellar reputation, and I'm gonna hook up my wagon to his star," she said. "Someday I'll be the owner and chef of my own restaurant."

"That's great. Do you really think he's a star?" DeDe asked. She was very familiar with the culinary prowess of her husband. He had built a reputation for fresh, innovative cuisine in New Orleans and won a James Beard award to boot, but she always found it interesting to hear what others from the Midwest thought about JuJu's food—its Southern influence and interesting spice combinations.

"Are you kidding? His food could walk off the plate and smack somebody over the head. It's that good!" Angela raved, carefully tearing lettuce and arranging it on a salad plate. She placed cherry tomatoes carefully on the salad, sprinkled on capers and thinly sliced red onions, and topped it with homemade garlic-infused croutons.

A picture formed in DeDe's mind from Angela's description of JuJu's food—a steak trotting across the table to madly embrace a baked potato in a passionate kiss. DeDe tried to get the comic visualization out of her head.

"How're things going over here at the salad station?" Jude said in a booming voice, walking up to the table. "And how's my favorite girl?" he asked, leaning over and kissing DeDe on the cheek.

Angela's eyes widened at the gesture, and then her nose crinkled. "Do you two know each other?" she asked.

"Angela, this is my husband, Jude," DeDe said, enjoying the young girl's dumbfounded look. Turning to Jude, she said, "And to answer your question, things are finally slowing down. Wow! We must have plated two hundred fifty salads tonight," DeDe said, wiping a paper towel across her sweaty forehead.

"Busy is good," Jude said. He looked over at Angela. "Hey, why don't you take a fifteen-minute break? DeDe can handle it by herself for a little bit."

"Really? That's great because I need to make a phone call. I'll be right back," Angela said, stepping through the patio door as she dug her phone out of her apron pocket.

"So, did you get anything out of her yet?" Jude asked quietly, popping a cherry tomato in his mouth.

"The atmosphere hasn't exactly lent itself to true confessions," DeDe said sourly. "What I've gotten out of this evening is a permanent image of lettuce, tomatoes, onions, and croutons appearing repeatedly in my mind. I swear I'll be making salads in my dreams tonight."

"Hey, no pressure. Just askin'."

DeDe's face softened. "I'm really proud of you, you know," she said softly, gazing into her husband's warm brown eyes.

Jude tipped his head shyly. "Coming from you, that means everything, baby," he said.

Suddenly, the door to the patio whipped open, and Angela hurried in, the cool night air gushing into the steamy kitchen.

"What's the matter?" DeDe asked. "You look upset." She studied the young girl carefully.

"A friend of mine got hurt in an accident. He needs me to come and... and take him to... to the ER," Angela stammered.

"He should just call 911," DeDe said, frowning.

"He doesn't have insurance, and he can't afford a big ambulance bill." Angela looked over at Jude, her eyes desperate and pleading. "Please, chef, it's important that I help him. Can I be done for the night?"

"Absolutely. You go take care of your friend," Jude said kindly.

Angela threw her apron on the chair and bolted out the front door of the restaurant.

"Well, that was terrible advice!" DeDe said, turning to Jude. Her sharp, staccato words bounced off the kitchen walls. "She's just a teenager. She probably doesn't even know any first aid."

Jude cocked his head to one side, staring at his wife with an intense expression. Finally, he shook his head and said, "Honey, I know you're a big, hot detective and all, but that girl is goin' to meet her man, and you better get your rear end in gear if you want to get in on the action. You get my meanin', darlin'?" he asked, folding his arms across his chest.

DeDe rolled her eyes and slapped her forehead. "Crawdads and gizzards! She's goin' to meet Devon. I'm outta here! Catch you later!" she yelled as she tore through the kitchen door.

"Be safe!" Jude hollered after her.

By the time DeDe ran out to the parking lot and got in her car, Angela's tires squealed on the pavement as she headed south on Highway 35. DeDe rammed her car in reverse, then peeled rubber onto the highway, accelerating until the speedometer hit seventy. Despite DeDe's quick response to the young girl's hurried escape, Angela had a heavy foot. She carelessly wove in and out of traffic until DeDe feared the young girl would be killed in a head-on collision.

While driving, DeDe dug her cell phone out of her apron and speed-dialed Jim Higgins. She put the phone on speaker and laid it on the seat. Up ahead she could see Angela's taillights in the distance.

"Higgins."

"Chief, I'm in pursuit of the girl I told you about who works at Si Bon. I think she's going to meet Devon. She said something about her boyfriend being hurt and needing help. Do you know anything about that?" DeDe asked. She tore around a car in front of her.

"Whoa, whoa, whoa! Be careful, DeDe. Devon beat up an older gentleman tonight who talked to Paul a couple of days ago. He's in the hospital. The wife of the older guy whacked Devon with a frying pan during the scuffle. We're not sure of his injuries yet, but he's desperate, and he's hurting. That's a bad combination."

"Really? A frying pan?"

"Yeah, really. A frying pan. Cast iron, no less. Where are you now?"

"I'm heading south on 35 along the river. So far I have Angela in my sights, but she's really movin', so there's no guarantee I'll be able to keep her on my radar. I need some assistance—anybody—if I catch up with her. What have you got on your end?"

"Keep your phone handy. I'll call you back in a minute." The line went dead. DeDe disconnected and concentrated her efforts on the road.

Up ahead, Angela flew through Stoddard, barely missing a delivery truck that pulled out of a side street. Her car skidded sideways and fishtailed as she tried to avoid a collision. As luck would have it, she maintained control and roared out of town.

DeDe tore up the road, trying to keep Angela in her sights. Two miles out of Stoddard, a semi-truck driver pulled into the highway and navigated his big rig in front of DeDe. Tromping on the brakes, she pounded the steering wheel in frustration. She tried to pass the semi numerous times, but oncoming traffic impeded her efforts. While she drove, she dialed 911, identified herself, and asked to be connected to the De Soto police. When they answered, she explained her situation and requested a car get down on the river road to keep watch for a beat-up tan 2010 Chevy Cavalier.

"Do whatever you have to do, but stop her," DeDe ordered impatiently. "She's involved with a guy who is a suspect in the Gas & Go robbery and murder last week in Stoddard. We need to talk to her and find out where this guy is holed up," DeDe finished.

When she finally managed to get around the semi, Angela's taillights had disappeared. DeDe groaned with frustration, slowed her speed to something more reasonable, and watched for driveways or turnoffs where Angela might have met Devon, but nothing presented itself. Angela had disappeared.

After fifteen minutes of desperate searching along the highway for the Cavalier, DeDe pulled her car onto the shoulder of the road and called Higgins again.

"Chief, I lost her," DeDe said, swearing softly. "Sorry, but she's somewhere between La Crosse and Victory, or she's met Devon, and they're out on the river making a getaway. I called the De Soto police and had them park a car down on the river road to watch for her. She hasn't shown up."

"I'm on my way. I'll drop Sam off at home, and then I'll meet you at Blackhawk Park. We'll make a plan for the morning. I called Darrell Schnider at the fish hatchery in Genoa to assist us with our search tomorrow. He knows the river between La Crosse and Lansing like the back of his hand. He might know where Devon would be hanging out," Jim explained. "There's a ton of islands and inlets in that part of the river, though, and it's gonna be really difficult to pin him down... but it's worth a try."

"That'll be a wild goose chase, sir. He could be from St. Paul to Iowa if he's on the river. I don't think we'll catch him once he's on the water," DeDe said, the doubt shading her voice.

"We gotta try. I think he's the guy who burned down my house. I'll be damned if I'll let him slip away that easily." Jim said sourly. "See you in fifteen minutes." The phone clicked off.

After Jim's conversation with DeDe, he dropped what he was doing at the houseboat since the crime scene crew had arrived. He grabbed Sam and ran to the Jeep. They crawled in and buckled up as Jim wove through traffic.

"Where's DeDe?" Sam asked.

"Down on 35 chasing some girl she thought was going to meet Devon, but she lost her. I'm going to meet her at Blackhawk, and we'll make a plan," Jim said.

Jim raced down the Great River Road, the dark water shining in the moonlight. Despite the lateness of the hour, traffic was steady. He turned into Sam's driveway, climbed the steep incline, and waited while Sam stepped out.

"I'll return your Jeep tomorrow," Jim said through the driver's window. He watched Sam hobble to the house. The overhead light came on above the side door, and Leslie waved him off.

Jim turned north on Highway 35 and drove for fifteen minutes until he reached the entrance to Blackhawk Park. The wind had picked up, and the trees swayed like drunken dancers. The winding Mississippi River flowed south, the dark outline of the bluffs illuminated by a moonlit glow. Jim drove to the first turnout near the park's entrance, where DeDe sat glumly in her car. Jim pulled up next to her, driver door to driver door, and lowered his window.

"So, tell me what happened," Jim said. DeDe noticed his exhausted look. The fire, the stake-out, and now the chase to find Devon Williams were taking a toll. He looked haggard. His tie was loose and hung crookedly around his neck. He yawned.

DeDe began explaining what had taken place throughout the evening.

"You mean she took off after the phone call on the patio?" Jim asked.

"Yeah. She said her friend was injured and needed help. She appeared to know where she was going, so I'm thinking they might have a rendezvous spot somewhere around here. Maybe a place they've gone to before."

"That sounds believable. If Devon is injured, then he's not going to go very far. That'll work to our advantage. Paul called the hospital and talked to the lady who hit him. She said she walloped him on the shoulder with her frying pan. He might have some broken bones. At the very least, he probably will need medical attention," Jim theorized out loud.

"So what's the plan?" DeDe asked, stifling a yawn. She was beginning to feel the long day catching up to her.

"We'll do a door-to-door search by land and a cruise along the river from Stoddard to the Lansing bridge in the morning," Jim said.

"Won't that take a lot of personnel?" DeDe interrupted.

"Not really. You and Paul can start below Stoddard. Mike and I will get together with the DNR guy and check out the residences along the river by boat. I'm wondering if Devon has access to a boat. Of course, we don't have proof of any of that." Jim sighed with fatigue, his brain fuzzy with weariness. "Anyway, we'll meet at the fish hatchery at seven-thirty tomorrow morning."

"Okay. I'll see you then," DeDe said. She closed her window and turned her car out onto the pavement. Jim turned around and followed her until he came to the turnoff to County K. Half an hour later, he rolled into the quiet farmstead of Gladys Hanson.

Jim climbed out of the Jeep and stood for a moment under the security light, thinking. They were closer to a solution than they were yesterday. Perhaps things would be resolved tomorrow, although Jim knew the answers to difficult crimes were usually never that cut and dried—or that easy.

A solution usually boiled down to collecting insignificant pieces of information and arranging them into a cohesive whole that eventually led to a resolution of the problem—with a few wild goose chases to boot. That seemed like a long way off.

He heard the door to the house open softly. Carol stood on the steps in her nightie, beckoning him with a wave. He walked toward her, climbed the steps, and stepped into her arms.

"I've been waiting for you," she said tenderly.

WEDNESDAY, SEPTEMBER 3

TAKING ONE DAY AT A TIME IS GOOD ADVICE, BUT DON'T BE SURPRISED IF SOMETIMES SEVERAL OF THEM ATTACK YOU AT ONCE.

37

Donavon "Doc" Wycowski slowly lowered the *La Crosse Sentinel* until it lay limply across his lap. He stared at the river from his small cabin window that faced west. He'd learned more about Sam Birkstein since their conversation on Monday evening. From Sam's own admissions, Doc knew he'd had an accident and was injured in a lightning strike, but the article buried on page twelve of the newspaper had been a revelation. The details Sam left out of his story caused Doc some consternation. He thought they'd had an honest exchange. Now he wasn't so sure.

For starters, Sam hadn't mentioned his job as a cop—apparently a rather colorful cop at the La Crosse Sheriff's Department—a detective no less. Maybe that wasn't such a big deal. After all, detectives frequently worked undercover, but there seemed to be more to it than that. For one thing, Sam hadn't mentioned the cloud of suspicion hanging over his head regarding the robbery and murder at the Gas & Go in Stoddard last Thursday evening. According to the newspaper article Doc read, Sam was a prime suspect, although the article mentioned his stellar record of drug and prostitution arrests throughout the region that had earned him the respect of police personnel and a certain scintillating reputation among the citizens of the Coulee region. From the facts about his service at the sheriff's department, it seemed highly unlikely that Sam would be involved in a murder and robbery.

Doc considered himself a pretty good judge of character, but Sam had been less than truthful during their conversation. Actually, that was a gross understatement, and Doc felt a tick of anger when he thought about the gracious empathy he'd offered Sam. Now the detective's precarious circumstances had come to light. From everything Doc had learned in the article, it seemed Sam's job, reputation, and freedom were at stake. This was troubling. But another question loomed: Why hadn't he been arrested yet?

As the minutes ticked by, Doc rolled the facts around in his head again. Then he stopped his thought process abruptly. Wasn't this exactly what others had done to him? Despite his innocence in the theft of his identity, no one had believed him. Rather, everyone looked askance at him as if he'd orchestrated the whole thing himself, which was ridiculous. He hadn't been stupid or careless. On the contrary, his reputation and honesty within the medical community were well-known. Yet his friends and his wife had believed the worst about him. It hadn't taken long after that for his life to unravel. Doc had operated under the mistaken premise that people loved and valued him, but, in the end, they'd deserted him to believe a pack of lies and innuendos.

As he reconsidered what he knew about Sam, he realized he was no better than those who had leveled judgment on him. He was filled with guilt and remorse for even having such thoughts. Whether Sam had withheld information from him was irrelevant at the moment. *To be honest,* he thought, *no one shares their thoughts completely with another human being, especially the first time they meet.*

This much was certain—the young detective was in trouble. Doc was convinced their meeting had not been an accident. He smiled. He thought about the meeting. Did he consider it a divine appointment? He chuckled at the incongruity of the situation. *Doc*

Wycowski—an angel on a mission. Now *that* was funny. But Sam's predicament wasn't the least bit comical. The guy needed help. Doc wasn't sure how to help him—yet. But his thoughts wandered back to the mysterious occupants of the high-powered boat yesterday and the conversation centered on the police. Doc felt a chill run up his arms. He realized that he may be in possession of certain facts that could have a bearing on the crime at the Gas & Go. The trouble was, he didn't know where Sam Birkstein lived, and even if he did, he didn't have a vehicle to get there.

38

A mild wind blew through the towering white pines along the border of the Gate of Heaven Cemetery early Wednesday morning, the fragrance of evergreen boughs a pungent reminder that life went on. Although the sky was a brilliant blue, it didn't make much difference to BJ LaPointe. The tall, handsome young man made his way through the tombstones to the freshly dug grave mounded with clumps of dirt, absent of a headstone.

Withered red and white roses lay on the grave in silent commemoration, and a few loose petals blew into the grass nearby. So many shattered dreams lay beneath the dense, black earth. After a few moments, the wind died down a little, and it became quiet. The stillness seemed like an invitation to the young man. He approached the burial site slowly, stumbling, his steps hesitant. His shoulders sagged, and his head hung in sadness. Standing at the graveside for several minutes, the teen searched for the right words, wondering if they would make any difference.

Bitterness engulfed him. *What you say won't make a difference now,* he thought angrily, arguing with himself. *Don't be stupid. Vicki can't hear you. She's dead, and there's nothing you can do about it. It's too late.* Despite his thoughts, he knew the words that were stuck in his throat needed to be said.

After several moments, he lifted his eyes and regarded the jagged mound of dirt. Underneath, Vicki lay silent and lifeless. All the hopes and dreams they'd shared were buried there—the baby, Vicki's quirky sense of humor, the love they'd shared, the plans they'd made—all of it six feet under. Tears coursed down his cheeks, and anguished, muffled sobs shook his body.

"I'm sorry, Vicki. I tried to help you, but I was too late. I'm so sorry," he gushed helplessly. The young man stood there awhile longer, trying to gain control of his emotions. He remembered the blood creeping across the concrete, Vicki's lifeless eyes as she lay dead on the floor of the gas station, the beautiful necklace he'd given her that had been ripped from her neck. Fear coursed through him when he remembered the gun, the round of the barrel pointed at his chest, the hard glitter of the murderer's stare. Panic welled up within him, and he gasped at the memory of that moment coming back to him in living color—the moment when his entire life had flashed before him with sickening finality.

Standing at Vicki's grave for several minutes, the young man's tears slowed and finally stopped. The outburst of emotion left him feeling empty, like a dry husk of corn rattling in the wind. He turned and walked out of the cemetery to his car. Sitting in the driver's seat, he struggled with memories of Vicki, torn by indecision, regret, and guilt.

Was there anything he could do now that would make a difference? He leaned his head on the steering wheel, his mind jumbled and filled with vague uncertainties. He sat up and thought again about the night of the robbery. From somewhere deep within himself, BJ felt a thread of resolve. Yes, there was something he could do, and he resolved to do it—today.

Meanwhile, across town, Lila LaPointe pushed the vacuum cleaner over the stained carpet in the hallway of her home on Adams Street.

She thought of her husband, Jack, and his love of their two purebred Brittany Spaniel hunting dogs, Sophie and Cash. He'd loved those dogs, and although they were beautiful animals and well-trained, Lila detested the mud and hair they left behind on the carpets and furniture after their romps in the coulees around La Crosse. Lately, BJ had been spending more time with the dogs. She supposed the outdoor adventures and the dogs' companionship were a healing balm for his troubled soul.

Lila was surprised when she knocked on her son's bedroom door at six-thirty in the morning, only to find he was already gone. She hadn't heard him leave and didn't know where he'd gone. *Probably just as well,* she thought. *He's got to make his way in this world sometime. Might as well get started.*

Lila finished vacuuming the hallway and moved into her son's bedroom. He'd updated his room after Jack's death. The athletic posters of his sports heroes came down, and in their place, he'd hung pictures of himself and his dad—deer and grouse hunting photos, their camping trip to Yellowstone last year, and favorites of them on the river fishing for walleye. Lila stopped her work briefly, gazed at the pictures, and remembered her husband's zest for life—always ready with a smile and an encouraging word. She still found it hard to believe he was really gone.

She started the vacuum again, buzzing around the room, picking up BJ's clothing as she went. She pushed the vacuum under the bed, but something blocked the machine's path. She got down on her hands and knees, peering underneath. A brown paper grocery bag was stuffed tightly between the floor and the mattress. She reached over and pulled it out.

Standing up, she opened the bag and looked inside. She sucked in a breath of air. *Whose clothes are these?* she wondered. *Where did BJ get a pair of Nike running shoes and an L.L. Bean jacket?* She was about to close the bag again when she remembered the news article in the *La Crosse Sentinel* a few days ago. She stared out of the bedroom window remembering the details of the article.

The robbery in Stoddard where Vicki was killed involved a policeman—a detective, the one who was a suspect in the case. Vicki looked in the bag again. *It couldn't be, could it? Were these the clothes the police were looking for? Why did BJ have them? What was going on?*

Lila swallowed hard. She knew her son was still reeling from the loss of his father and now the tragic death of his girlfriend. Shaking her head silently, Lila argued with herself. At the same time, fear threatened to grab her by the throat and choke her. *My son is not a murderer,* she thought, pushing down feelings of panic. *But he's going to have to answer some very difficult questions when he gets home.*

39

Angela Fitzpatrick marveled that she was still alive. After the chaotic chase down the Great River Road with another car in pursuit, she couldn't believe she hadn't had a fatal accident. Swerving recklessly around and between traffic at seventy miles per hour was not only capricious but foolhardy and downright stupid. *I could have been killed,* she thought remorsefully. *I still might be killed.*

She stared across the living room of the small river cabin near Victory, where Devon had told her to come. The cabin was for sale, but in its condition, it was doubtful anyone would want to tackle its restoration. It seemed to be disintegrating right where it stood along the banks of the Mississippi River. Angela was sure it hadn't had any prospective buyers for months, maybe years. Now, in the early morning, it was chilly inside, and Angela shivered and cuddled deeper beneath the old, moth-eaten quilt. Although the living room had a small wood stove, she couldn't risk building a fire. It might attract attention from fishermen cruising the river at dawn. Instead, she'd found some musty old blankets in the bedroom closet last night to keep them warm.

Devon and Angela used this abandoned place many times for their trysts, but now, in broad daylight, she noticed the outdated furnishings from the seventies and the dull, dirty windows. The smell of mothballs and stale sweat permeated the place. The carpet was filthy with dirt and grime, the ceilings stained with nicotine. *How could I have ever thought this was romantic?* she wondered. *What was I thinking?*

Devon had finally fallen asleep in an outdated brown tweed recliner, but only after she'd scrounged in the medicine cabinet of the bathroom and found some Tylenol with codeine to ease his intense pain. His shoulder was probably crushed. It was swollen and turning a very ugly purple. She'd torn some wide strips of material from a rotten pillowcase she'd found and made a type of sling to stabilize his arm. Her eyes drifted to the pistol that lay casually across his lap, his fingers loosely gripping the handle.

Angela's heart ticked faster as she remembered the confrontation with Devon when she arrived at the cabin. In his pain and desperation, Devon had aimed the pistol at her chest and threatened to kill her if she didn't help him. She wondered what her expression must have looked like when he shouted those threatening words at her. *That would have been a picture worth a thousand words,* she thought bitterly.

She had no idea how this of her life would end, but she was sure it would be dramatic, criminal, and probably deadly—things she wanted to avoid at all costs. She leaned back and rested her head on the back of the couch, staring at the brown-stained ceiling. *How could I have been so gullible?* She shook her head, silently chiding herself for her poor decisions. She realized now that infatuation was a dangerous elixir that blinded you to reality and set your feet on a dangerous path filled with stupid, perilous choices.

She'd met Devon downtown on Third Street six months ago. The famous boulevard in La Crosse was lined with bars and taverns populated by college patrons who were cruising for a good time. Devon had latched onto her immediately. He gave her a sultry glance, their eyes locked, and he walked through the crowded bar with a swaggering confidence. When she replayed the scene in her mind, Angela realized that Devon was nothing more than a very practiced and proficient actor who'd barged onto the scene and stolen the show. He was handsome in a dangerous kind of way. Smoldering dark eyes, beautiful brown skin that begged to be touched, tall and lanky in an athletic sort of way. It hadn't taken long for them to begin a series of secret meetings in which Devon introduced Angela to a world of sexual exploration.

Tears sprang up and rolled down Angela's cheeks when she remembered some of the things she'd done with Devon. *Can God ever forgive me?* she wondered. Forgiveness? Was that what believers called "amazing grace"? Because right now, she needed a healthy dose of it. Ironically, a small crucifix hung on the wall near the kitchen, and above it hung a calendar dated 1988. She concentrated on the small cross and began to pray. "Hey God, I'm in a terrible jam, and I need your help..."

40

Jim woke early Wednesday morning even though he hadn't gotten to sleep until well after midnight. He slipped from bed, went to the bathroom, took a hot shower, then returned to the bedroom and slipped naked into bed beside Carol. She stirred when he cuddled against her back.

"What time is it?" she murmured lazily.

"You mean you have to ask?" Jim said when she turned toward him. He kissed her tenderly, then deeply with an urgent desire, moving his kisses down her neck and back to her voluptuous mouth.

"I miss the foreplay in the tub," Carol said, responding to his kisses, running her fingers through his graying hair. "But this is nice, too," she purred, slipping off her nightie.

"Oh, so you like my moves?" he rumbled. Carol arched her back with pleasure as Jim kissed her breasts, and she rolled on top of him.

"There's no doubt about that," she whispered.

After twenty minutes of lovemaking and cuddling in the afterglow, Jim sat up and swung his feet to the floor. Carol was jabbering about furniture for the living room and other decorating minutiae.

"...and I found another swoopy, black chair," she said. "Do you believe it? I thought when it burned up in the fire, I'd never find a replacement."

Jim loved that chair, stupid as it was to love an inanimate object. As he listened to Carol chatter about the details of her furniture purchases, he mentally reviewed his plan for the morning—to hunt down Devon Williams, arrest him for the break-in and assault at the houseboat on the Black River, and bring him in for questioning in the robbery and murder of Vicki Invold and the torching of his home.

Jim stood by the bedroom window and looked at the farmyard below, thinking about the difficulties of a shoreline search. A thick, heavy curtain of fog had moved in overnight, which would make his plan even more challenging.

"Where'd you find another swoopy chair?" Jim asked, secretly rejoicing that Carol had located another one. He leaned his elbow against the window sash, thinking about strategies that might lead his team to Williams as he watched the resident rooster strutting across the yard, crowing with gusto.

"They had one at that international furniture place over on French Island. 'Course it cost about four hundred dollars more than the original one," Carol complained, grabbing her robe and tying it closed. She walked around the bed and headed for the bathroom. "And you could care less," she finished, giving him a sly grin. Nothing was going to ruin Jim's mood this morning, not even reminders of the devastating house fire.

Jim turned away from the window and grabbed her hand as she walked by him. He pulled her into his arms, cuddling her to his chest, enjoying the smell of her skin. Carol tilted her head back and studied the shadows that haunted her husband's face. Despite his insistence that the depression had waned over the last few months, she was skeptical he had truly gotten a handle on the problem. These afflictions were complicated and fraught with difficulties.

She noticed he seemed particularly tired lately, and his ability to rebound from life's rough and tumble situations was less elastic than it had once been. The workload at his job and the house fire added to his concerns. The fire especially seemed to elicit a particularly acute sense of loss, although she was sure the loss was more about the memories rather than the physical contents of the house.

As Carol thought about the perplexities of loving her husband, Jim took in her radiant skin, her captivating brown eyes, and glossy dark hair. He had to admit she'd adjusted well to life with a cop. The pressure of the job was something she was not prepared for when they'd married, but her independence and fighting spirit had served her well in dealing with the many sticky problems confronting them—some from the intrusive nature of hunting down criminals and some from the pressures of having two small children when they were well into middle age. Jim smiled down at her and met her concerned stare with gratitude. He couldn't imagine his life without her.

"You never disappoint me," he said affectionately. "You're so beautiful, and I need you so much." He kissed her tenderly and held her against his chest.

Returning his kiss, she leaned into him. "I aim to please. Although someday you might have to deal with a lot more wrinkles and a few more lumps and bumps, but… let's hope that's a ways off." She untangled herself from Jim's arms and cleared her throat. "However, there is one thing you'll have to deal with—a significant chunk of money missing from our checking account."

Jim groaned. "You mean the furniture excursion?" he asked. Carol nodded. "I knew that was coming. Our insurance will come through eventually… I hope. When is this stuff arriving? Will we have to store it somewhere?"

"No, they'll store it at their warehouse until the house is ready, but with the supply chain problems, it'll be a couple of months before the order gets here," Carol said. She noticed Jim's distracted look when he walked to the closet and scrutinized his minimized wardrobe. Since the fire, most of his clothing was still at the cleaners, especially his expensive jackets, dress slacks, and ties. "Anyway, while you're gazing at your pared-down wardrobe," Carol continued, "just remember a simplified life can be a good thing, especially when it comes to clothes. Don't forget the famous words of old Albert Einstein."

Jim stopped rifling through the scant selection of clothes and looked at her. "So enlighten me. What did Einstein say?" He straightened up, rubbed the back of his neck, and stood facing her.

"A table, a chair, a bowl of fruit, and a violin. What else does a man need to be happy?"

Jim chuckled. "Einstein said that?" He shook his head, made a sour face, and frowned. "Well, I can think of a few more things I'd need to make me happy, and it isn't a violin or an apple. My Irish wool suit coat and some decent dress pants, for starters." He lifted his eyebrows and grinned, looking into her eyes. "And, of course, loving you always makes me happy."

"Well then, you got what you wanted this morning," she said saucily as she turned and opened the bedroom door. "You should be a happy man."

41

By seven o'clock, Jim was racing along County K to U.S. Highway 35. The pungent woodsy scent of the oak and maple stands along the roadside wafted through his open window and reminded him of previous fall seasons. He passed a farmer pulling a load of straw with a tractor and a little old lady putting happily down the road, oblivious of her slow pace. Jim pulled around her, waved hurriedly, and sped on.

When he finally reached the river along Highway 35, it was shrouded in a ground-hugging fog. Jim turned onto the four-lane river road and traveled south. A half hour later he parked his truck at the Genoa Fish Hatchery along U.S. 35, where he planned to meet DeDe, Paul, Mike, and DNR agent Darrell Schnider. Schnider had agreed to assist Jim and Mike in a shoreline search with his government-issued johnboat. They planned to patrol the water from Blackhawk Park south to the Lansing bridge while Paul and DeDe visited the communities bordering the Mississippi River in search of a place where Devon and Angela may have hidden. Jim had called Les Talbert from Coulee Hills Realty, who had done a search of real estate available for sale or rent along the Mississippi River shoreline. Jim planned to pass the list along to Paul and DeDe, giving them a jump start on places where a desperate perpetrator might hole up for a few days.

As Jim got out of the Suburban, he noticed Paul, DeDe, and Mike standing around the hood of Paul's F-150 Ford truck talking quietly in the fish hatchery parking lot. He sauntered over to the group. They turned to face him, and for some unknown reason, Jim felt like a kid targeted for ridicule and rejection. *How's this going to go?* he thought.

"Hey, Chief. What's up?" Paul casually asked when Jim walked up.

Jim tilted his head back and studied the sky. "Well, this search would have been a lot easier without this fog. It's going to make it even more difficult than I anticipated. That's what's up," he said sourly.

"So what are we doing exactly?" Mike asked abruptly.

Jim reached into his jacket and pulled out the real estate listing from Coulee Hills Realty. "DeDe and Paul, here's a start on some properties that are for sale or rent along the river. Check them out while you're cruising properties along the shoreline." There was a moment of uncomfortable silence.

"Cruising? We're trying to find two people in a very big area, Chief. Cruising is kind of a misnomer to describe this operation, don't you think?" Paul countered, thrusting his hands in his pants pockets, frowning conspicuously. He hunched his shoulders and stared at Jim. Jim stared back.

"Well, you know what I mean," Jim said impatiently, tugging on his earlobe nervously. Turning to DeDe, he said, "Look carefully on that stretch of highway down toward Victory where you lost Angela. Devon could be holed up somewhere in that area. Don't forget to check out abandoned properties, too."

"This whole thing seems like a long shot, doesn't it?" Mike said, lifting his eyebrows in a skeptical glance.

Jim and Mike exchanged a stony glance. Jim was surprised by

the boldness of Mike's question considering he was a newbie on the team. Still, part of being a good investigator was asking questions and developing strategies. Jim pushed his shoulders back as if shucking off the challenge, crossed his arms over his chest, and took a big breath.

"Could we just try to run with the plan?" A look of defeat passed across his handsome features. Planting his hands on his hips, he said, "What else do you suggest we do? Anybody have other ideas? Now's the time to tell me, people." Jim waited in silence and looked at each team member with a challenging stare.

"We're not dissing you, sir, but it seems like an awfully big area to cover with only four people," DeDe offered. "That's all we're saying."

"I agree," Jim said, trying to sound reasonable, although the tightness in his chest and rapid pulse rate suggested something totally different. He calmed himself, and after a few moments he continued.

"As you already know," Jim began, "the sheriff has not volunteered any additional manpower, so I think that pretty much means we're on our own. We're in the second week of this investigation, we have few leads, and we have little or no actual physical evidence from the crime scene other than the obvious. Witnesses to the crime do not seem to exist. The clock is ticking toward the moment when this case will become old hat, and everybody will move on to the newest, hottest criminal event. Vicki Invold deserves better than that. Her parents and family deserve better; they won't forget her tragic death, and we shouldn't either. While this case gets colder and colder, the sheriff gets madder and madder—if that's even possible." Jim took a deep breath. "So, unless I missed something—we are it." Jim met his team's stares. "Comprende?"

Paul nodded, conceding Jim's points. Mike and DeDe simply stared at him.

"So let's get at it," Jim said as Agent Schnider strolled across the lot. Jim turned to Paul when Darrell joined the group. "Tell us what happened at the hospital last night after the houseboat break-in."

"Well, when I went to the hospital last night, Rose Becker positively identified Devon Williams as the person who broke into their houseboat and beat up her husband. Rose, in her pissed-off state, grabbed a frying pan during the kerfuffle and whacked Devon across the shoulder blade. Mr. Becker suffered a coronary during the struggle, but doctors are confident he'll recover. In the chaos that followed, Devon escaped, but we don't know if he was on foot or rode his bike or what."

Jim said, "After the houseboat incident, Angela talked to someone on the phone at Si Bon. She mentioned that her friend was hurt and needed help. Right, DeDe?" He pivoted and stared at DeDe.

She nodded. "Yes. I believe she was talking to Devon. She mentioned her friend had been injured somehow. Then she asked JuJu if she could be excused from work, and she flew down the river road to some unknown destination. I lost her somewhere around De Soto," DeDe informed the group.

Jim took over the narrative. "We're guessing that Devon is with Angela, possibly somewhere along the river. He's injured—thank God for little old ladies with cast iron frying pans. That hit must have slowed him down some. He's hurting and probably needs medical attention, which he can't risk right now. So holing up somewhere until things quiet down seems logical—to me anyway." Jim frowned and cocked his head at a jaunty angle. "Of course, most of the time, logic does not apply when it comes to desperate people." Looking at DeDe, he said, "Angela is driving a—what kind of car?"

"A 2010 Chevy Cavalier, tan in color, sir," DeDe said.

"So she escaped in a Cavalier, and as of now, they are missing," Jim said. "So we're deducing one of two things. They are either still in the area, or they've left." Jim shrugged. "Take your pick. We're banking on the fact that Devon is injured, and traveling would be too painful. Personally, I think they're still in the area someplace."

Mike nodded and said, "Makes sense."

For some reason, Jim felt vindicated by his comment.

The group gathered around the hood of Paul's pickup, where Schnider spread a map of the area. Discussing their options, they pointed to the map of blue water and green land, which was swirled together in random patterns and hemmed in by the linear black line of Highway 35. It was a big area, and they were at a distinct disadvantage with such a small crew. *Gotta keep on,* Jim thought. *Might as well get started. We've been outnumbered before.* They decided to meet at the Lansing bridge at noon after their search unless other developments arose.

Mike and Jim walked toward the office at the fish hatchery and then around the back of the building, where an eighteen-foot aluminum johnboat was tethered to a landing dock. Equipped with an eighty horsepower Evinrude outboard motor and a smaller trolling motor, the lightweight, flat-bottom boat had two bench seats and a captain's chair behind the steering wheel. The boat was filled with paraphernalia Jim supposed Agent Schnider used in his daily patrols along the Mississippi River.

"I cleaned it out as best I could," Darrell said sheepishly. "At least you'll have a place to sit."

Jim waved nonchalantly. "Not a problem. We'll be fine."

The men loaded up, and Darrell expertly guided the boat into the river's main channel. The morning fog created an ethereal atmosphere among the many inlets and islands, and the shoreline drifted in and out of view. It seemed like they were floating in the clouds instead of navigating the tricky backwaters of the Mississippi River. Wildlife was absent from view, and the morning air, usually teeming with birdsong, was ominously quiet. The scent of brackish water and the fumes from the boat motor mixed together, reminding Jim of excursions on the *Little Eddy,* the boat he inherited from his dad.

They moved slowly, deliberately, weaving in and out along the shoreline, paying particular attention to the small cabins along the shore. Jim didn't know what they'd see that would indicate something was wrong, but he hoped that pressure from the two teams working the water and land would flush Devon and Angela into the light of day.

At about nine-thirty, the johnboat approached the *Bernard H*, a huge dry cargo barge loaded with grain as long as two football fields. It sat low in the water off the main channel about two hundred feet out from shore, and in the murky fog it seemed strangely ominous and foreboding, like a floating, silent city. It was exceptionally quiet as Darrell positioned the boat close to the side of the push boat, sounded his horn, and waited.

Turning to Jim and Mike, he said, "I've gotten to know a few guys on some of the barges. It's possible they might have noticed something going on." He shrugged. "Worth a try."

"We need all the help we can get," Mike said. Jim silently agreed.

In a moment, one of the crew leaned over the upper railing and yelled, "Whaddya need?"

Jim lifted his arm and flashed his ID. "We'd like to come up and ask a few questions, if you don't mind."

The man waved. "Sure, come on up. The captain's in the pilot house." He turned and disappeared inside.

The three men disembarked from the johnboat and clambered onto the deck of the push boat, then climbed three sets of stairs to the pilot house. Opening the door, Jim was amazed at the incredible view. Twenty-five feet above the water, the scene in front of them opened up. It felt like a completely different world up here. The fog was just beginning to lift, and the surface of the water was as smooth as glass. As the curtain of fog shifted in the slight breeze coming off the water, Jim caught glimpses of the towering dark bluffs across the river on the Minnesota side, hunched in moody indifference. A fresh pot of coffee was brewing, filling the cabin with its irresistible scent, and Jim hoped the crew would offer him a cup.

"Boy, you can sure see a ways up here," Mike commented,

scanning the scenery. The fog was patchy and breaking up in the warm sunshine, revealing more of the river landscape as each minute passed.

The inside of the pilot house was sleek and technologically well-equipped. A huge steering wheel was unmanned at the moment, but a couple of crewmen were scanning computers and checking various gauges. Captain Jim LaSalle swiveled away from his computer in his leather office chair, stood, and greeted the men with a handshake and a shy smile. He had an effacing manner, but beneath the bushy eyebrows, longer hair, and two-day stubble of beard, Jim could sense an unflinching, calm resolve. He supposed navigating the largest river in the United States gave the captain ample opportunity to exercise his leadership and decision-making skills.

"Gentlemen? What can I do for you?" he asked, a hint of a Southern drawl beneath the soft, drawn-out vowels.

Jim stepped forward a few feet. "We're looking for a perpetrator who was injured during a break-in at a houseboat up near Veterans Freedom Park on the Black River near La Crosse. He may have taken a young girl hostage. Long story short—the girl tore down the river road and got away from an officer in pursuit, but we believe she's with the guy somewhere in the area. We wondered if you'd noticed anything out of the ordinary along the shoreline—maybe a deserted house where a car might be parked that wasn't there before or someplace along the river that is normally quiet but now seems to be occupied."

LaSalle was quiet for a moment. "That desperate, huh?" the captain said, looking at Jim with hooded eyes.

"Yeah, that's the gist of it," Jim said brusquely.

"Well, our focus on the *Bernard* is the river itself, keeping the channel in sight at all times, watching for obstacles and other boat traffic in the water ahead, checking water levels, and keeping the barge on an even keel. Right now we're waiting out the fog, and then we'll get moving again. Running a barge is a challenge with a river as serpentine and unpredictable as the ol' Mississippi. What's happening on land isn't always on our radar, so to speak," Captain LaSalle drawled.

"Yes, I can believe that. I'm sure you have other things to do," Jim commented.

"You can talk to some of the crew, but I seriously doubt they'd notice changes at the residences on shore. They're pretty busy attending to their duties. But if you think it's worth a try, then be my guest," Captain LaSalle commented laconically, making a sweeping gesture with his arm.

Jim stared at the floor for a few moments deep in thought. He looked up and said, "We're fighting the clock, so I guess we'll pass right now, but can we leave a cell number with you if you see anything suspicious?"

"Absolutely. I'll pass the word on to the crew," the captain said, taking Jim's card.

Schnider, Jim, and Mike retraced their steps down to the water again and stepped off the barge into the johnboat. Pulling away from the huge behemoth, Darrell motored slowly along the shore while Mike scanned the properties with binoculars, hoping to see someone or something that seemed out of place, but those possibilities seemed highly doubtful.

In the meantime, Paul and DeDe were moving among the residences along the river in the village of De Soto, knocking on doors, asking about possible sightings of a Black man with a young white woman driving an older Chevy Cavalier. It was tedious, painstaking work, getting in and out of the car, knocking on doors, asking the same questions, looking around at properties that seemed deserted, and talking to anyone who might have noticed something out of the ordinary. After two hours, Paul and DeDe met back at the pickup truck. Paul groaned loudly when he looked at the list of properties they'd ticked off the list. They still had a significant amount of real estate they had to investigate.

"This seems pretty impossible," Paul said as he checked off another property. He continued tapping the list with his pencil. "Why do we always get these flatfooted jobs?" He threw the paper on the seat. He could feel the lack of sleep creeping up on him, clouding his mind and thinking.

"I know. It does seem pretty hopeless, doesn't it?" DeDe agreed. She slumped in her seat and stared forlornly out of the truck windshield at a series of small cabins clustered along the river's shore just outside of De Soto. A sagging sign near the first cabin read, "Cabins for rent." An older man walked past the pickup carrying a fishing pole and bait pail heading toward the river. He wore a floppy straw hat, a white T-shirt, and a pair of worn OshKosh B'Gosh overalls. As he walked by the truck, Paul spoke to him.

"Excuse me, sir."

The older man stopped and turned toward the truck. He walked over, set his pail down, and leaned his pole on Paul's pickup hood.

Paul continued talking as he flashed his ID. "We're looking for a Black man who might be in the area, possibly renting a cabin. We think he might be with a white girl, early twenties, who was driving a Chevy Cavalier. Have you seen anybody fitting those descriptions?"

The old man squinted, looked down the road, and then locked his eyes on Paul. "Well... sorry to say, I haven't. Not too many Black people around here. Are they in trouble?"

"You might say that," DeDe added, leaning across the seat toward Paul. "The Black man is injured, and we believe the girl is being held against her will."

"No kidding?" the old man asked, his eyes disbelieving.

"No kidding," Paul said, frustrated with the dead-end conversation. "Have you seen anybody around here like that?"

There was a pause. "No, sorry, I haven't," the old man apologized. He turned, picked up his gear, and began walking toward the river again. Paul watched him as he disappeared around the end of one of the small cabins.

"Another dead end," Paul said disgustedly, leaning over to start the truck.

At that moment, DeDe looked in the distance, pointed, and said, "Wait! He's coming back."

Paul looked up. The older man was walking briskly toward the truck. He approached DeDe's passenger window and held up his index finger.

"I thought of something, but it probably isn't related," he said.

"Just tell us. We'll decide if it's relevant or not," Paul said brusquely.

The old man shrugged, but his eyes flashed with anger at Paul's impatience.

DeDe smiled at the old man. "Go ahead. I'm listening," she said gently. *You catch more flies with honey than vinegar*, she thought. "What can you tell us?" she asked politely. *Southern charm has its advantages.*

"My brother had a little place across the railroad tracks down by Victory. Just a small house, but he didn't take very good care of it. It's pretty rundown. He died last winter, and his kids have been trying to sell it, but they ain't had no luck. Just yesterday I talked to my niece, and she told me that someone had broken into the house, but nothing was missing. That's all I know," the old man finished.

What are the chances? Paul thought, briefly closing his eyes. "Do you have an address for this place?" he asked.

"No, but I can draw you a map," the elderly man said.

DeDe dug in her purse and retrieved a used envelope and a pen. The man began drawing a rudimentary map. After a few moments, he tapped the drawing with the pen. "Right across the road from the driveway is a house next to a slough that has a tire swing in a tree that hangs over the water. You turn right there," he said emphatically. He marked the driveway with an X and handed the map to DeDe. She thanked him profusely.

"We really appreciate your help," she said. The old man looked past DeDe, frowned at Paul, and tapped DeDe's arm lightly. He smiled, pointed to her, and said, "*You* are welcome."

DeDe threw Paul a deprecatory glance as the man walked back toward the river, which he ignored. He shook his head, rolled his eyes, and reversed the truck. He turned onto Highway 35 and headed south toward Victory. "Call Higgins and fill him in," he ordered. "They might want to meet us at this joint in case we need some backup."

"Right," DeDe said, punching Higgins's number in her phone. After a moment, she frowned. "The number isn't connecting. Must not have a good signal here. I'll try again in a couple of minutes."

42

While the two teams scouted the surroundings along the Mississippi for any sign of Devon Williams and Angela Fitzpatrick, Sam and Leslie Birkstein were spending a leisurely morning at their hilltop home near Genoa.

Sam had gotten up mid-morning after sleeping off a raging headache. Surprisingly, it hadn't turned into a full-blown two-day migraine, for which he was thankful. At about ten o'clock, Leslie came through the back door into the kitchen with Paco.

"Nice walk?" Sam asked. Leslie hung Paco's leash on a hook near the back door.

"A little foggy, but it was okay. Mmm, something smells good. Pancakes and bacon?" she asked, giving Sam a quick peck on the cheek.

Sam was hovering over the stove, flipping bacon, watching it carefully. Leslie noticed a bowlful of batter had been mixed together, and the waffle iron was heating up. He had taken time to cover the weathered picnic table on the patio with a nice tablecloth where two place settings of her grandmother's china, silverware, and wine glasses sparkled on the table. A carafe of orange juice was chilling on ice, and Sam had picked a bouquet of black-eyed Susans from the patch that grew near the bluff next to the back of their property.

Now he turned to Leslie and gathered her in his arms. He kissed her long and tenderly. When she pulled back, Leslie looked into his intense hazel eyes.

"And this is because?" She tipped her head in a curious pose.

"Simple. You're the love of my life. You're the one who has stuck with me through this stupid accident and all my bad behavior, and you're the moth—"

Leslie laid a finger across his lips. "Shh. I get it already. And thank you. The table is beautiful."

Her eyes softened with affection. Paco nudged her with his wet nose and licked the skin on her tanned leg. The black lab barked a single, sharp warning.

"Jealousy will get you nowhere," Sam said, looking down at the dog. Paco tilted his head and barked again. "I'll get him some fresh kibble. You sit outside and catch your breath while I make breakfast," Sam said.

They had gotten through the majority of their special mid-week breakfast when the doorbell rang. Paco tore through the house and stood alert in front of the door, his pink tongue dripping with saliva, his tail wagging like a metronome. His nose quivered with excitement.

"I'll get it," Leslie said, rising from her chair. She walked briskly through the kitchen and living room, calmed the big lab with a quick pat on his majestic head, and swung the door open.

A middle-aged man with dark hair and friendly brown eyes smiled at Leslie. He wore a pair of tattered cutoffs and an old T-shirt that was frayed at the neck. He smiled at Leslie and pointed downward at the front cement porch where he stood. "Is this where Sam lives?" Paco stood next to Leslie, his dark eyes fixed on the strange man. *Must be one of Sam's drug informants,* she thought.

"Yes, Sam lives here." Holding the door open with one hand, Leslie extended her other hand, which the man shook enthusiastically.

Her eyes swept the driveway, noticing the absence of a vehicle. "I'm Sam's wife, Leslie. Please come in." She stepped aside, and the man came in and stood inside the front door. Paco's tail wagged back and forth in recognition. The man offered the top of his hand to Paco.

"Is there something I can do for you?" Leslie asked tentatively.

At that moment, Sam appeared in the living room. His surprised expression and subsequent smile told Leslie Sam knew this man.

"Hey! How are you? How'd you find out where I lived?" Sam asked the man, holding out his hand.

"Checked around the neighborhood, and a man at the bar down the hill pointed me in the right direction," the man said, grasping Sam's hand firmly.

"Why do I get the feeling you two know each other?" Leslie asked, looking back and forth at Sam and the visitor suspiciously.

"We do know each other, Lez. This is the guy I met the other night in Stoddard when I was walking with Paco down by the river," Sam said excitedly.

"Well, aren't you going to introduce me?" Leslie asked, giving Sam a brazen stare.

Doc Wycowski beat Sam to the introduction. "I'm Donovan Wycowski, but people just call me Doc."

"Hey, come on in," Sam said, turning and waving. "We can sit out on the patio."

Though Leslie had not been privy to the meeting between the two men, she got the distinct feeling that the exchange between them had led to Sam's thankfulness for the death he'd dodged and gratitude for the life he still possessed. *What had these two talked about that had caused such a change in Sam's outlook and attitude?*

The trio settled in the Adirondack chairs around the campfire ring in the backyard. Sunlight filtered through a tall pine. Sam leaned forward, placed his elbows on his knees, and looked at Doc with keen interest. "So what brings you here?"

Doc paused a moment having second thoughts, not wanting to

burst the bubble of this happy couple. "I read about your problems in the *La Crosse Sentinel* and—"

Sam groaned. "Oh boy," he mumbled, and his face instantly became dark with anxiety.

Leslie's head jerked up at the mention of the newspaper article. The topic of the robbery had a dampening effect on the carefree atmosphere. "Are you referring to the Stoddard Gas & Go robbery and murder?" she asked. Her blue eyes suddenly became icy and cold, and her voice sounded tight and brittle.

"Lez, I'll handle this," Sam warned, sitting up straight, noticing her belligerent stare at Doc.

"You mean the way you've handled it so far?" she asked, her voice laced with sarcasm. "That oughta be interesting." She slumped in her chair and continued to stare at Doc.

Doc interrupted them both. "Wait. Just wait," he said, lifting his hands in the air. "I'm not here to accuse or find fault. Actually, I'm here because I think I saw something that might pertain to your case, but at the time I didn't realize it."

Sam and Leslie stared at Doc, their expressions reflecting confusion and curiosity. They looked at each other, and Sam shrugged.

"Okay, let's hear it then," Sam said.

Doc began to explain. "Yesterday morning—it was early—I was out on the river in my little fishing boat. I dropped the anchor at one of the tiny islands and put my lines in the water. I'd been there about a half hour when this big fancy boat came up along the other side of the island and dropped anchor. It wasn't more than a hundred feet away from me. There were two guys in the boat—a Black man and a white kid."

"Where was this exactly?" Leslie asked. Sam frowned at her for interrupting Doc's account.

"Right about where the Coon Creek dumps into the Mississippi," Doc said.

"I know where that is—between Stoddard and Genoa. Keep goin',"

Sam said, leaning forward.

"I didn't hear the exact words of the conversation, but I could tell it wasn't friendly. These two guys mentioned cops, and there was some reference to criminal activity of some kind, although I didn't know what that was at the time."

"So you're thinking these two in the boat were involved in the robbery somehow," Sam commented. He was skeptical it could be true. "Based on what?" he asked.

"Well, I didn't connect it all until I read about your supposed role in the crime. Then it kind of fell into place and made sense... sort of." Doc stopped. Doubt shadowed his face. "Course this is all speculation at this point—"

"But it could be related," Sam said, finishing Doc's thought. He turned to Leslie. "Whaddya think, hon?"

"It's pretty sketchy, but if it's related, it's a huge breakthrough. One of the problems with this Williams guy is we don't know how he's been getting around the area. We know he has a bike, but other than that, we've been stumped. We discovered he's been staying at a houseboat, so having a boat makes sense in the overall scheme of things, I guess... although I don't know how he could afford a boat if he's only involved in petty crime around La Crosse," Leslie said. She seriously doubted that the guy in the boat could be Devon Williams. It seemed way too easy, and when you're chasing criminals, easy doesn't usually happen.

"There's one more thing," Doc continued. "While I was baiting my lines, I noticed this same boat was over by one of the river buoys for quite a while. They were doing something by the buoy, but I was too far away to see what it was exactly."

"Which buoy?" Sam asked sharply.

"Six eighty-four," Doc answered.

"Describe this boat," Leslie demanded.

Doc stared at the bluffs behind the house. Then he said, "It was about sixteen feet long, a fancy, fast boat, blue and white." He leaned back and closed his eyes, trying to imagine the boat again. "There was a word on the side of the boat that started with a D..."

Leslie fiddled in her jeans and pulled out her phone. She brought up a mugshot of Devon. "Do you recognize this man?" she asked, handing the phone to Doc.

He studied the photo. "Looks like the same guy who was in the boat."

"Anything else you remember?" Sam asked.

Doc got a smug look on his face. "Yeah, the registration number of the boat was WI73904."

Sam and Leslie shot up in their seats. "What? You remember the registration number?" Leslie asked, her mouth dropping open in surprise.

"That's the number. I wrote it down on a scrap of paper after they left because I had a feeling the boat was special for some reason."

"How sure are you about all this?" Sam asked.

"I'm very sure," Doc said, smiling for the first time in the conversation.

"Better call Higgins," Sam ordered. "This could be big."

43

"I don't know, Viv. Jim's just different lately," Carol said, the phone pressed to her ear as she helped Henri adjust his backpack. "I don't think he's really recovered from his latest bout of depression."

Vivian Jensen listened carefully to her sister. Through the years, she'd advised her on a number of sticky personal problems and had always considered Carol to be a good judge of situations. From her first divorce to her sexual assault at Goose Island to her decision to marry Jim, Vivian had been Carol's confidante and counselor. Beneath Carol's concern beat a heart of gold. "What makes you say that?" Vivian asked.

"He's distracted and tired, he avoids talking about his condition, and he just looks sad," Carol lamented. "The sparkle in his eyes is gone... like a vacant stare."

Vivian heard some mumbling and rustling. "What are you doing?" she asked.

"Just getting the kids out the door for school. The bus just rolled up," Carol said.

"Okay, back to your concerns," Vivian continued. "It sounds like the observations you've made about Jim's demeanor are typical of men who are depressed. But Jim is not typical—I don't need to remind you of that. He's very intelligent, he works in a profession that is extremely demanding, and I'm sure he's well aware of his depressive state of mind. Of course, there's always the possibility he's in denial. But consider this: He—well, all of you—have had a very rough week. Investigating the murder of a young, vibrant teenager and losing half your house in a fire would send most people over the edge."

"That's true." Carol paused, thinking. "That's very true. So what can I do to help him?"

Vivian leaned back in the recliner, crossed her legs, and wondered what kind of advice she should give. Despite Carol's astute observations and good intentions, she knew her sister wasn't always willing to implement her suggestions.

"It sounds to me like you're already doing all the right things. Listening, encouraging him to talk about his challenges and concerns, being available, loving him where he's at. Those are all good things," Vivian emphasized again. "But I have to tell you, these problems are not easy to solve. They're sticky and persistent and take time. Nobody wants to hear that."

"So that's your advice. Be patient?" Carol asked, her voice gritty with impatience.

"Pretty much. And that's not something our culture is very good at. We want results right now, but I can tell you from a professional psychologist's viewpoint when you're dealing with things like depression, that attitude is unrealistic and not helpful in the long run. I could recommend a different medication," she suggested. "Is he taking his medication?"

Carol shook her head and shrugged, even though Vivian couldn't see the gesture. "I don't know, but I could ask, I guess."

"No, don't ask him about that. He might feel like you're spying on him or figure out we've been talking about him. Just continue to support Jim where he's at. Maybe find time to be alone. Go out to dinner, take a drive, do some shopping, go on a hike, plan a getaway.

In time, I have every confidence he'll come out on the other side stronger and more empathetic, if that's possible. By the way, how's the house coming?"

"Slow. Very slow. They've cleaned up most of the mess, and I guess next week the carpenters will start the reconstruction. I've ordered some replacement furniture, and soon we'll have to select kitchen cabinets and countertop materials." She sighed loudly. "But it's gonna be a long haul, Viv."

"Patience, Carol. Patience. Besides, the alternative scenario of losing all of you in that fire keeps me extremely thankful that you're all still in my life. If you need help with anything, you just call," Vivian said.

"Oh, I will. When it comes to paint colors, you'll be the first," Carol said, a hint of humor in her comment.

"It's nice to know my opinion is so valued."

"You have no idea," Carol said, laughing.

44

BJ LaPointe and his mother, Lila, walked solemnly behind the young female officer down the hallway of the law enforcement center. The officer stopped at Sheriff Turnmile's office door, knocked, and waited for the sheriff to acknowledge her presence. The sheriff looked up briefly from her paperwork and waited, a scowl on her face. Her irritation at being interrupted was palpable.

"A couple of people wanted to see you, ma'am," the officer said.

"Have them come in," Turnmile said.

The young female officer gestured to the LaPointes, and they walked in. Lila LaPointe looked around. The office seemed cold and devoid of any decorative appeal, and the woman sitting at the desk seemed aloof and intimidating. Finally, BJ walked forward and dropped a crumpled brown bag on the sheriff's desk. It made a loud thumping noise when it landed.

Without a word, the sheriff opened the bag, looked at the contents inside, and waited for an explanation. When none followed, Turnmile focused her attention on the two individuals standing in front of her. She rose silently, stood behind her desk, and waited some more. *This better be good,* she thought.

Lila and BJ LaPointe stood mute and pallid before the sheriff, but Turnmile could see from the mother's haunted stare and sober expression that she was worried. Very worried. The tall, handsome young man beside Lila seemed strangely calm, like the calm that comes from a resolute decision made in an agonizing moment of self-examination. *What's up with these two?* the sheriff wondered.

"Would you care to explain what this is all about?" the sheriff ventured, giving the two a calculated stare, but her standard intimidation tactic didn't work. Neither mother nor son were forthcoming with an explanation.

After several moments of uncomfortable silence, BJ stood a little straighter and began. "I thought the whole thing would just quiet down, and I could forget about what happened when Vicki was killed, but... I couldn't forget, so I decided to come in and confess."

Lila scrunched her eyes shut at the word *confess*. An uncomfortable thought came to her. *Maybe we should have brought our lawyer along.*

Sheriff Turnmile swallowed hard. If this kid was going to spill his guts about the Gas & Go robbery and murder in Stoddard, then nobody could have been more surprised than her. In all her years as a cop, she'd never heard an honest-to-God voluntary confession about a serious crime from any perpetrator. Never. It defied the laws of human nature—the human side that played the blame game, the denial game, the innocent victim game, the con game. The sheriff harrumphed and remembered the old axiom: "Honesty is the best policy." It seeped into her brain and sat there. *Does anyone even believe that anymore?* she wondered. *What is going to come out of this kid's mouth next?*

The silence in the office continued. Finally, Sheriff Turnmile said, "I'm waiting for you to proceed with your explanation." The mother and son exchanged an uncomfortable glance but remained silent. The sheriff decided to try a bit of kindness to move the confession along.

"Maybe you should sit down," she said as she moved around her desk. "Let me get you some chairs." She grabbed two well-worn, beat-up leather chairs from the corner and pushed them toward the LaPointes. They sat down. Turnmile went around her desk and plopped her generous butt in her office chair. The group exchanged a stony glance while Elaine discreetly pulled a legal pad across her desk. She opened a drawer, pulled out a small recording device, and laid it on the desk. If someone was going to confess to the robbery and shooting, she planned to record all the details. With a pen poised above the paper, she looked up at the teenager.

"You were saying?" the sheriff said, staring at BJ as if that might prompt him to soldier on with his account.

Instead, BJ's mother, Lila, took a deep breath and began speaking. "This morning when I was cleaning my son's room," she glanced briefly at BJ, "I found that brown paper bag stuffed underneath his bed." Lila pointed a shaking finger at the bag. "I remembered the article in the *Sentinel* about the detective's clothes that were missing, and when BJ came home I tried to get it out of him, but he insisted on coming to see you. He wouldn't tell me a thing."

Sheriff Turnmile nodded and stared at BJ. "All right. And now you're going to tell me how you got the clothes," she said emphatically, tucking her chin toward her chest and raising her eyebrows.

BJ closed his eyes briefly as if he were summoning some kind of courage. "I knew Vicki was working that night—" he began, squirming uncomfortably. The young man tucked his long legs beneath the chair as he sat forward and looked at the sheriff, his hazel eyes sparking with intensity.

"You're referring to Thursday, August 28. Is that right?" Sheriff Turnmile interrupted, sitting up straight. She began scribbling the date of the robbery on the top line of the tablet.

"Yeah, the twenty-eighth. I decided that night at about eleven o'clock to drive down to Stoddard and hang out with Vicki until she finished work. She was supposed to be done at midnight," BJ said, but he choked on the words, stayed silent for a few moments, and then wiped the tears from his cheeks in an angry gesture. "I stopped outside the south side Kwik Trip and got a Coke out of the vending machine, and when I walked into the Gas & Go about twenty minutes later, this Black guy was standing over Vicki with a gun in his hand. I kinda freaked out. But then he aimed the gun at me." BJ hesitated a moment, shuddering at the memory. "And why he didn't shoot me right there, I... I don't know, but he didn't."

The silence in the office was all-encompassing. It felt like they were wrapped in a cocoon of secrecy. Sounds from the outer office could be heard occasionally despite the closed door, but Lila remained silent. The shock on her face told the sheriff she had not heard this account from her son before. Her gaze remained fixated on BJ, her body stiff and frozen like a statue, disbelief written on her facial features.

"This person who was holding the gun. Did you know him?" Sheriff Turnmile asked.

BJ's eyes flicked to the sheriff's face. "Oh yeah. It was Devon Williams. The guy that Vicki had a relationship with over a year ago," BJ sneered, contempt darkening his handsome face.

I don't believe this is happening, the sheriff thought. "So Devon's pointing the gun at you. What happened then?" Turnmile asked dryly, continuing to take notes.

"He pointed to the door and told me I was gonna help him get away."

"He didn't have a vehicle?"

"Guess not, or he wouldn't have been asking me for help."

"And then what happened?" the sheriff asked in a patient tone, although the confession was riveting. *Nobody is going to believe this,* she thought again. *I don't believe it, and I'm sitting here listening to it.*

"We left the station through the front door, got in my vehicle, and he told me to drive toward Genoa on 35, which is what I did... like I really had a choice," BJ added, his tone bitter and resigned. "We'd only gone about five miles or so when Devon noticed someone lying alongside the road. He told me to pull over and stop and turn off my headlights. It was still raining. I remember because I kept my windshield wipers on the whole time we were stopped. Devon took the bag of cash he'd gotten from the robbery and fiddled around with this guy on the side of the road for a little bit. Took off his jacket and exchanged it for the one the other guy was wearing. Then he exchanged his shoes. That's all I could see. But when he got back in the car, he didn't have the gun anymore." BJ briefly stared into space, remembering the events of that fateful night. He seemed to have drifted into another world as he made his confession.

"Okay. And then?" the sheriff asked, pulling the teenager back to reality.

"He told me to drive down to the public boat ramp in Genoa, which I did," BJ said.

"So why did he go to the boat ramp?" Turnmile ventured, cocking her head at a curious angle.

"He handed me that bag," he pointed to the brown bag on the sheriff's desk, "and told me to get rid of the jacket and boots so they couldn't be found. Then he got out of the car, hopped in a big boat—some kind of a speed boat—started up the motor, and tore outta the harbor heading west on the river," BJ finished.

"A boat?" the sheriff repeated, leaning over her desk. *Unbelievable,* she thought.

"Yeah, a boat," BJ repeated. "You know, one of those fancy speedboats people use for water skiing and tubing," BJ said, slightly irritated by the sheriff's disbelieving questions. "A very expensive boat."

"This is crazy," the sheriff whispered. She took her cell phone out and dialed Higgins.

"Higgins? This is Sheriff Turnmile. Are you sittin' down?"

45

Jim, Mike Leland, and agent Darrell Schnider were slowly trolling along the shoreline of the Mississippi River in the DNR johnboat and had gotten beyond the village of De Soto. They'd stopped along the river to talk to boaters casting and baiting their hooks and fishermen wetting a line off their docks. Jim and Mike asked them questions about Devon and Angela, trying to discover their whereabouts. The sun burned through the haze about eleven o'clock, and the fog lifted. Despite the serious nature of the manhunt, Jim enjoyed the time on the water observing eagles and hawks and muskrats swimming in the marshes. Feeling the tug of the current on the small boat, he envied others who had time to spend on the big river.

When Jim's cell rang, he expected it to be Paul or DeDe. Instead, the gruff, irritable voice of Sheriff Turnmile came over the line. Jim bit down hard on his lower lip as he listened to her litany. *Why does she always set my teeth on edge?* He stopped thinking treacherous thoughts when she told him the latest news. Instead, astonishment took over.

"What? I can't believe this! Are you serious?" Jim responded, the cell phone pressed to his ear.

When Mike heard the surprise in Higgins's normally calm voice, he quit scanning the shore with his binoculars and fixed his gaze on

Jim, who wore a shocked expression. Higgins's lower jaw dropped, and his stupified expression told Mike something was up. Something important. As Higgins continued to listen, his eyes widened in amazement at the implausible account.

"This kid is in your office right now?" Higgins asked. Then he thought, *It's not often an eyewitness to a murder appears out of the blue and gives specific details about a crime that seemed unsolvable just an hour ago.* He swallowed and said, "I'll want to talk to them later today or early tomorrow." There were a few other comments, and then Higgins hung up.

Mike stared at Jim. "So, what's going on?"

"A bombshell we never expected," he said, shaking his head. He proceeded to explain the scenario the sheriff had told him—how BJ LaPointe had been coerced into helping Devon escape from the Gas & Go after the robbery and murder, how Devon had exchanged Sam's clothing by the side of the road, and how BJ kept the clothes hidden under his bed for over a week.

"The kid brought in Sam's clothes? What are the chances of that happening?" Mike asked.

"Slim to none. I never thought we'd find those clothes again. This puts a whole new spin on this case. And Sam is finally off the hook." Jim let out a sigh as if saying a prayer of thanks.

"So what's the plan now?" Mike asked.

Higgins held up a finger in a wait gesture, retrieved his phone from his jeans pocket, and dialed Paul. "Where are you?" Jim asked. He listened a moment and then said, "Meet us at the boat landing where 35 and 82 meet above Ferryville. We'll be there in about twenty minutes. We need to make a plan and coordinate all the new information we've gotten."

Jim no sooner hung up than his phone buzzed again. "Yeah, Sam. What's up?"

"I'm at home, but listen, I think we've got a break in the case," Sam said hurriedly. "Devon Williams has a boat—a sixteen-foot speed boat, blue and white—"

"How do you know that?" Jim asked brusquely. "Where'd you get that information?"

"It's a long story, but believe me, I think it's pretty reliable. Are you down on the river?"

"Yeah, we're below De Soto cruising along the shore. We're meeting with Paul and DeDe at the boat landing where 35 and 82 meet as soon as everybody can get there."

"I know where it is. We'll be there in twenty minutes," Sam said, and he abruptly hung up before Jim could tell him about the discovery of his lost clothes.

Mike Leland was a greenhorn in this murder investigation, but as he observed the flow of events the last few days, he was gaining a better understanding of the fluid, open-ended nature of hunting down a killer. Nothing they'd planned this morning had gotten them anywhere, but now possibilities had suddenly burst on the scene that would take the investigation in a totally different direction. Mike studied Higgins. The frown on the senior detective's forehead deepened, but the man had a preternatural calm that seemed to infuse his team with a confidence that was hard to explain. There was a sense of purpose linked with a thirst for justice that most people wouldn't understand unless they were actually involved in the process and saw it firsthand. Heck, Mike wasn't sure he fully understood it, but he was certainly observing the effects of Higgins's leadership now.

"Now what?" Mike asked.

"Things are coming together—I think," Jim said cautiously. "Or maybe they're coming apart. I'm not sure, but don't quote me on that."

Twenty minutes later, Agent Schnider eased up to the shore at the junction of the two highways. The boat banged against the dock, and Schnider jumped out and tied it off. A crow squawked at them from the high limb of a dead oak. Sam, Leslie, Paul, and

DeDe were waiting in the small parking lot adjacent to the dock, shuffling uneasily on their feet, looking tired and discouraged. Paco, the Birksteins' intrepid black lab, was running in circles along the parking lot, sniffing and investigating. Jim gave a half-hearted wave, stepped out of the boat, and walked toward the group of cops. Mike and DNR Agent Schnider trailed behind. Jim pointed toward a picnic table under the shade of a maple tree. Everyone wandered over and sat down. Paco sidled up to Jim, who ruffled his silky ears and thumped his side, the lab's tail wagging like a metronome.

"Okay, everybody. I need updates on whatever you've found out this morning," Jim began. He listened carefully as his team relayed the information they'd uncovered. Sam and Leslie explained the discovery of the speed boat that Doc Wycowski had seen a few days after the robbery and murder.

"Who's this Doc guy you're talkin' about? Is he a reliable source?" Jim asked, watching Sam's face carefully. "Or is he one of your drug goons?"

Sam squirmed impatiently and said, "No, he's not an informant. Doc's a unique individual with an interesting history, but I think what he told us is totally on the up-and-up. He saw the boat himself while he was fishing near Stoddard Tuesday morning, and he described Devon to a tee—also identified him from a photo on Leslie's phone. He said another teen was with Devon, and I think it was Lyle Leverentz."

Leslie jumped into the mix. "We've been wondering how Devon was getting around. The houseboat was a perfect hideout for someone trying to keep his criminal conduct undercover, and the speedboat could explain his ability to go undetected for so long. When things got intense on land, he took to the river and hid out. There's plenty of places to hide out here," she finished.

"We've gotten some good evidence from the houseboat," Paul said. "The team is still gathering up stuff there. Stolen property, tools from garages, that type of thing. There's more, but it will take a while to log all of it," Paul said.

"That's good. Back to the boat thing," DeDe said. "He's probably been getting help moving around the area undetected from people like Angela Fitzpatrick. But that boat sounds expensive. Where'd he get the money for that?" She squinted at Jim as she waited for an answer.

Mike piped up. "Well, there's lots of possibilities. It could be owned by someone else, could be stolen, could be his own if he used drug money and the money from all his stolen property that he pawned." He leaned over the table. "This business about hanging around the buoy. What's that about?"

Jim offered an explanation. "The Mississippi River is the largest water highway in the country. Don't think drug dealers aren't taking advantage of it and plying their trade up and down the river. They're probably dropping drugs at certain buoys and counting on dealers like Devon to pick it up and distribute it. Crazier things have happened. Remember the stolen antiquities a couple of years ago? That stolen museum stuff was getting into the country through New Orleans and coming up the river to Galena, then being transported by truck to La Crosse, so drug traffic on the river should be no surprise to us."

Everyone thought about that for a moment.

"We need to check out buoy number 684 and see what the heck is there. Devon sure was interested in it," Sam said.

"We will, but right now we've got to apprehend Devon before he hurts Angela," Jim said. "If he hasn't already."

Paul spoke up. "You're right, Chief. But listen, DeDe and I got a possible lead when we talked to an old codger in De Soto. His deceased brother has a dilapidated cabin below Victory. It was recently broken into. Since Angela disappeared in that area, it might be worth it to investigate this place. Maybe those two are holed up at this cabin."

"We've got nothin' else at this point," Jim said, shrugging his shoulders. "Where is it?"

DeDe pulled out the crude map the old man had drawn for her and laid it on the rough surface of the picnic table. Everyone gathered around and studied the wrinkled envelope. DeDe interpreted the map, explaining the landmark the old man had emphasized—a swing over the slough on one side of the road and a driveway across the highway over the train tracks that led to the rickety cabin. After a few minutes, they made a plan.

"Everyone, you need to gear up—vests and helmets for sure," Jim said. "This guy's dangerous and desperate. We're not taking any chances. When we get to the cabin site, we'll proceed with our plan. Cell phones on vibrate and keep in touch." Jim turned to Leslie. "Lez, I want you out of the line of fire. You're going to coordinate with the local law enforcement out of De Soto. You're our point person for information. You'll be up on the highway, and we'll keep you informed about what we're doing." Paco barked a single woof. Everyone looked at the big black lab, who had an uncanny sense of duty, and his tail began wagging furiously.

"Paco wants in on the action, Chief," Leslie said, grinning.

"That dog has saved our butts more than once," Jim agreed. He straightened up, signaling the end of the meeting. "Leslie and Sam—I need to talk to you."

As the small group broke up, Paul, DeDe, and Mike returned to the truck and began putting on their vests and holstering their guns. Darrell walked toward the boat parked at the nearby dock while Jim walked a short distance from the picnic table. Leslie and Sam followed him, then stood next to Jim, waiting for him to speak. He looked directly into Sam's hazel eyes and said, "A young kid named BJ LaPointe came to the sheriff's office this morning and turned in your missing clothes."

Sam's mouth fell open, and a look of incredulity passed over his face. Then his features hardened again. "Well, he sure as hell waited long enough. How'd he get them?" Sam asked gruffly. Jim noticed the anger flaring in his eyes. Jim held up his hand in a calming gesture.

"He told the sheriff that Devon Williams hijacked him when he went to the Gas & Go to see Vicki. He walked in just after Vicki was shot. Devon forced him into his car, and when they saw you lying next to the road, they stopped, and Devon exchanged the clothes. BJ hid your jacket and Nikes under his bed until this morning when he decided to bring them into the sheriff." Jim paused a moment, letting Sam and Leslie absorb the news. Then he quietly said, "We've got him, Sam. BJ was an eyewitness to the aftermath of the crime. He can identify Devon, who was at the scene, literally holding the smoking gun. This proves you weren't involved in the robbery and murder of Vicki Invold—" Jim held up his hand, then continued, "not that we ever thought you were. You're off the hook, buddy." Sam noticed Jim's eyes misting with tears as he turned and walked toward the johnboat. His heart swelled with admiration and love for the senior investigator.

For a moment, Sam and Leslie just stood frozen in shock. Sam swiped his hand through his hair and looked at Leslie, awestruck. He suddenly felt a huge weight disappear, a tension that had been unseen lifted from his chest. Leslie smiled and kissed him. "Someone heard my prayers after all," she said.

46

Paul, DeDe, Mike, and Leslie hopped in Paul's crew cab Ford pickup. Paco rode shotgun next to DeDe. The canine's ears blew backward, and his pink tongue lolled in the breeze as Paul drove north on Highway 35 toward the tiny, unincorporated village of Victory along the river. The small hamlet's main street ran parallel to the river road highway. Paul turned onto the main street, a collection of houses strung out along a couple of blocks. In addition to the houses was a collection of buildings, including the First United Methodist Church and a general store, Victory's Variety, which sold fishing licenses, bait, tackle, and essential groceries. The century-old building contained the post office with eighty-five mailboxes, of which only thirty-five were currently in use. Out in front of the store was a gas pump and a place to inflate tires. Down the street, a small tavern called Victory Lane overlooked the Mississippi River, and next door to it was a defunct cheese factory that had been remodeled into an antique, art, and curiosity shop.

Ironically, Victory was named after the defeat of Chief Black Sparrow Hawk (shortened to Black Hawk) on August 1–2, 1832. After a chase by U.S. Army troops over the top of the bluffs, Black Hawk maneuvered his way down the steep hills to the river with a band of about a thousand members of the Sauk and Fox tribes. In the chaos of the battle that followed, a group of three hundred women, children, and elderly natives were chased into the Mississippi River, where they drowned or were shot trying to escape capture in what was known as The Battle of Black Axe. At the battle's end, only one hundred fifty natives, including Black Hawk, survived the onslaught.

The sleepy little town had a dramatic backdrop in the form of Battle Bluff, which rose to a height of four hundred eighty feet above the tiny village. Leslie and Sam had spent time hiking across the top of the bluff, which featured limestone boulders, sandstone outcroppings, and a few stunted red cedars, but the reward of the climb was the view from the top where you could see the great river weaving its way through the valley for twenty miles. Sam closed his eyes, briefly remembering their foray on Battle Bluff earlier in the summer before Leslie became too heavy with her pregnancy to enjoy it. In his mind he could still see Paco reveling in the atmosphere, his nose to the ground and his tail in high glory.

"So where is this place we're supposed to be going to?" Paul asked.

"About a mile out of town. Watch for the tire swing. That's where we turn," DeDe reminded him.

The tire swing appeared a minute later, moving gently in the breeze over the slough.

"The driveway is right across from the swing. Slow down. You'll have to do a U-turn and park on that side of the road. We'll hike down to the cabin and check it out," DeDe said. She turned and said to Leslie, "You can stay up top on the highway with Paco while we three head down to the cabin and see what's up."

"Sounds like a plan," Leslie commented.

"It's a plan all right. I just hope it works," Paul said in a soft, tentative voice.

"We'll find out soon enough," Mike added as Paul turned the pickup around and stopped the truck across the road from the tire swing.

At the same time out on the Mississippi River, Higgins, Sam, and DNR Agent Schnider were in the johnboat patrolling the shoreline.

They passed the Victory boat landing, and Schnider slowed the throttle to low, watching for a blue and white speedboat secured to a dock somewhere above Victory. Jim consulted the map he'd sketched and tried to pinpoint the cabin's location as they cruised slowly along the water's edge. It was a stab in the dark—mostly guesswork. Jim didn't know if the cabin had a dock or not, although most river cabins had them.

"Slow down, Darrell," Higgins said, quietly warning the DNR agent. "We're coming up to the place where this cabin is supposed to be."

They putted around a bend in the river where a piece of land jutted out from shore, almost like a thumb. Darrell slowed the boat motor to an idle and cautiously floated around the bend where a steep bank rose upward from the water's edge. There on top of a hump of land stood a small dilapidated cabin, its wooden siding gray and weathered. Five wooden steps led down to the shoreline, and at the bottom of the steps was a dock where Jim spotted a blue and white Discovery speedboat tied to an upright post. Darrell cut the engine. Jim retrieved an oar tucked inside the boat and began quietly paddling, staying close to shore, using the overhanging bushes and undergrowth along the river to stay out of sight.

"See anything moving?" Jim whispered.

Darrell shook his head. "Nope."

Jim made a quick decision. "Mike and I will get out here and hike up that incline toward the cabin. You stay in the boat. Keep your phone on. We'll call if we need assistance."

Jim edged the boat next to the shore where he tied it to a clump of sandbar willow. He jumped out into the thicket of willow and buckthorn, and Mike followed suit. A huge basswood spread its shade over the shore. They climbed through the bushes toward the tiny cabin, slipping on the uneven ground. Jim tripped once and landed hard on his knee, but the ground began leveling out as they walked up the steep slope. They approached the cabin cautiously, stepping quietly through the overgrown grass. When they were about fifty feet away, Jim held up a hand and stopped, then lay flat on his stomach using a copse of elderberry bushes as cover. Mike crouched next to him, huffing a little.

They had come up on the south side of the cabin, which blocked their view of the driveway, so they stayed where they were. A moment later, Jim's cell vibrated in his pocket, and simultaneously, he saw a flash of color to his left in some tangled undergrowth next to the overgrown lawn.

"Yeah," Jim said quietly in his cell.

"We're approaching the cabin," Paul said softly. "I don't see any vehicles. We'll go up to the house and see what happens."

"Be careful," Jim warned. "Devon's boat is tied off at the dock. If he isn't here now, he was here recently. We're off to your right in the bushes. Stay on your phone."

Jim and Mike continued crouching beneath the elderberry bushes. They heard pounding on the door of the cabin, then silence. After a few moments, DeDe opened a window on the south side.

"There's nobody here, sir."

"We're comin' in," Jim said, getting off the ground and trotting around the cabin. Jim and Mike entered the musty cabin and looked around. Paul was in the tiny bathroom and came out with a waste basket. He peered into it, and everyone gathered around.

"Looks like bandages of some kind. A little blood. Not much else except some Tylenol that's sitting on the edge of the sink," Paul said.

"We need to get the crime scene guys down here. I'll call them," Jim said. He stepped away from the group and, after a few minutes, began giving orders over the phone. Everyone else walked carefully through the cabin and observed rumpled blankets, bandages, and the painkiller. Someone had been here, probably as recently as this morning.

"Whaddya think?" Paul asked Sam as they waited for Higgins to finish his conversation.

"They've ditched this joint—for now. But the boat is still here, so they haven't gone far. Maybe they went to get some food," Sam said, shrugging his shoulders. "Don't know. It's all a crapshoot at this point."

Jim walked up to the group. "Crime scene is on the way. They'll cordon off the cabin. If Devon and Angela were planning on coming back here, that option is no longer viable."

"God, we were so close," Sam said through clenched teeth. "A half hour earlier, and we might have had them."

"Sometimes failure is disguised as opportunity," Jim said.

Mike looked at him, a confused expression on his face. *Another one of Higgins's arcane statements,* he thought. *That's about as clear as mud.*

"Well, if that's the case, then we missed our opportunity," Mike said.

Jim looked at his sagging, dejected team. The day had been long and, up to this point, unproductive. He could have given them some more interesting quotes to ponder, but they would have been lost on them at the moment.

Save your quotes, Jim thought. "Anybody up for Plan B?"

"Plan B?" Sam asked. "Isn't it more like Plan F?"

47

The wind on the top of Battle Bluff was steady and unabating. Ancient red cedars, the venerable elders of the bluffs that overlooked the Mississippi River, were unfazed by the wind. Their gnarled roots clung tenaciously to the rocky soil. In their dense tangle of branches earlier in the year, the uncommon juniper hairstreak butterflies had staked a claim and mated—each male occupying one tree during the mating season. High above the bluffs, raptors soared on the recurring warm drafts, their wings outstretched as they floated above the hilly bluff countryside. The stubborn cliff-dwelling red cedars, some a thousand years old, populated the goat prairie near the top, and a hiking trail led upward to the precipice of the bluff. Along the edges of the trail, bluestem grasses, milkweed, wild bergamot, and prairie phlox shifted in the wind. At the lower levels, where the bluff began to rise, there were forests of oak, birch, and basswood.

Devon Williams and Angela Fitzpatrick had visited the Victory store earlier in the afternoon and bought a few groceries. When they approached the driveway to the cabin, they noticed an unfamiliar truck parked along U.S. 35. Suspicious, they turned around, drove to Battle Bluff Road, and ditched the car in a deserted turnout at the bottom of the bluff. Then they began their climb up over the top of the steep bluff. All of the wonders of nature were wasted on the two hikers who plodded up the trail on the rough gravel path, their attention focused on the steep terrain. Despite the brilliant sunshine, the shade from the dense woods that surrounded them seemed pervasive and impenetrable. Angela felt a chill run up her spine.

"Tell me why we're doing this again?" she asked, huffing. She stopped hiking, trying to catch her breath. The straps of the backpack, loaded with water and groceries, was heavy and dug into her shoulders.

Devon stopped and looked sideways at Angela with a look of exasperation. "Do I need to spell it out for you? We can't go back to the cabin. The cops are all over it. Besides they know the make and model of your car, and they'll be looking for it. My boss has a camper off Kumlin Road. We can get there sight unseen if we hike over the bluff and connect to the road on the other side of this friggin' hill," Devon explained impatiently. "Besides, the cops will never be able to track us in these bluffs."

"You think you can make it that far?" Angela sneered. Devon roughly grabbed her arm and pulled her up to his face. "Ow! You're hurting me!" Angela cried, tears misting her eyes.

"Now you listen to me," Devon snarled, the grip on her arm biting like a piece of steel. His irises were like black holes and reminded Angela of a pit viper. "Nothing about this is goin' to be easy. This ain't no walk in the park, so quit your damn bellyaching and get truckin'." He pushed past her in a huff and began climbing the trail again. Every step was steeper, and the loose rocks along the path made the ascent tough and exhausting. They climbed steadily for fifteen minutes until Angela stumbled when the strap on her flimsy sandals slipped off the side of her foot. She stopped and bent down to fix it. Devon halted, looked back at her, and collapsed on the ground, breathing heavily while resting his hands on his knees. His shoulder throbbed with a steady, unrelenting pain, and the grimace on his face revealed his discomfort.

"We bring any water?" he huffed.

"Yeah, I've got a couple of bottles in my backpack," Angela said. She dug around in the pack and handed him a bottle of water.

While Devon quenched his thirst, Angela considered the possibility of her escape. Seemed unlikely. Despite Devon's injured shoulder, he appeared to have an untapped reservoir of strength. He wasn't likely to let her out of his sight. But what did he have planned exactly?

"So what's so great about this camper?" she asked tentatively. Maybe he'd slip and let her in on his plans. She drank a swig of water and watched his dark, brooding face.

"Nothing, really," Devon responded, "but it will give us a chance to hole up somewhere until things quiet down. I'm counting on the cops giving up the search, and then we can get out of here. Maybe go south to Texas," he finished, looking off in the distance.

"Texas?" Angela's eyes widened at the suggestion. "I'm not goin' to Texas!"

Devon got to his feet quickly and pushed his water bottle into Angela's chest. The shove sent her slipping and sliding down the steep slope. "You got two choices: You can come with me, or you'll be buried six feet under somewhere on this bluff."

A shiver of horror crept through Angela, chilling her to the bone. She carefully reconsidered. "Well, when you put it like that..." She adjusted her backpack and began to climb.

48

After securing the cabin near Victory, the crime scene crew started gathering and recording evidence. Jim began developing a Plan B. They were standing in the shade of an old white pine outside the small, rundown cabin. Pine needles and cones lay scattered underneath the huge tree trunk, and Jim breathed deeply of the pine scent wafting in the air. In the distance, the Mississippi River shimmered in the late afternoon sun. Barges plowed through the water, and a speedboat towing a skier cut curved slices into the surface of the river. DNR agent Darrell Schnider had joined them and listened carefully to the conversation. Jim glanced at his phone—3:28 p.m. Before long, the day would be spent, and the search would have to be called off.

Standing next to Mike Leland, Jim leaned over and said quietly, "Are you getting some idea of the nature of an investigation, Mike?"

Mike nodded, and his expression reflected a dogged determination. "We'll get 'em, Chief. They're gonna screw up somewhere along the way, and then—"

"Atta boy," Jim said, cutting him off. Personally, Higgins had serious doubts about capturing the two perpetrators. As the hours ticked by, it seemed very unlikely. But his team had succeeded before, overcoming tremendous obstacles. *A miraculous apprehension of a desperate murderer?* Jim clucked his tongue at the thought.

"What are we gonna do now?" Sam asked grumpily, tipping his water bottle for a long drink.

"Good question. Anybody have any ideas?" Jim asked.

"I say we split up again, keep combing the countryside. We can zero in on the Victory area and move outward if that turns out to be a dead end," Paul said. "We've already got an APB out on Devon and the description of Angela's car. We could get lucky, and somebody might spot the car." Jim stared at the ground, listening carefully.

"True. Any other ideas?" Jim asked, looking around the circle of cops. He knew that dogged determination usually was the determining factor in the apprehension of fugitives. It seemed Paul was determined enough for all of them.

"Have we impounded the boat?" DeDe asked. "We don't want Devon to have the opportunity to escape in it. Frankly, I don't understand why he didn't head south on the river, but sometimes criminals just make stupid mistakes. We need to take advantage of that," she finished.

"Agreed. The crime scene crew will be here for a couple of hours yet," Jim informed the group. "And yes, the boat is now in the jurisdiction of the La Crosse Sheriff's Department."

Sam was leaning against an old, rusty boat trailer, his arms crossed over his chest, his face somber. Above his dark hazel eyes, his brows were furrowed in concentration. He hadn't contributed much to the conversation. Clearly, he was ruminating. Ideas were percolating to the surface, and Jim wondered when he was going to erupt with one of his famous theories. He didn't have to wait long.

"All right, everybody. Here's what I think," Sam began. "We know Devon is hurt, possibly seriously. But he's young and tough, so the chances of him lying down and giving up are unlikely. According to DeDe, Angela fled the restaurant last night, presumably to help him, but by now he's probably revealed his true colors, and they're no longer on friendly terms. She's most likely become his prisoner. Not exactly a romantic scenario." Sam paused briefly, collecting his thoughts. The rest of the crew considered what Sam said in silence.

"They were at the cabin last night. The evidence in the wastebasket suggests Angela propped Devon up with some kind of first aid. They left the cabin this morning—probably hungry—so maybe they went to get groceries. That was risky, but here's my question. Why is Devon sticking around here? What's motivating him to stay in the area when Angela has a roadworthy vehicle to get out of here? That doesn't make sense to me."

"His injuries?" DeDe suggested. "He might be in a lot of pain."

"Possible," Jim responded. Mike nodded in agreement.

After a moment, Sam continued. "Doc Wycowski told us he saw Devon hanging around one of the USATON buoys in that blue and white boat. I think that's important. If someone is using the buoys for drug drop-offs, then maybe a big shipment is scheduled to come in and Devon is committed to delivering the cache to his boss somewhere in the area. He probably needs the money to get out of here. We need to go out and look at the buoy, Chief. Maybe we could do a river stake-out. Watch and see if someone shows up."

Darrell interrupted. "I took the liberty of looking up the boat registration number. Belongs to someone named Tony Howser from Milwaukee."

Jim nodded. "Thanks, Darrell. That information will come in useful when we put this all together. But first, we've got to catch this guy." Jim thought Sam's idea of a river stake-out had merit, but he was wondering who would be willing to sit in a boat along the shore and watch the traffic come and go on the river—at night, no less.

"So since you suggested observing the buoy on the river, are you volunteering for duty?" Jim asked, locking eyes with Sam.

"Do I have a choice?" Sam sighed loudly, shuffling on his feet. "Yeah, I guess I'm in," he finished.

Jim leaped into action. "Okay. To my way of thinking, we've got two missions: someone has to head up the search for Devon and Angela—"

Paul interrupted. "Got it, Chief. DeDe and Mike, you're with me," Paul said.

"Wait," Leslie interrupted. "I think Paco could be helpful if we find Angela's vehicle. So I'll go with you, Paul." As if on cue, Paco wandered into the middle of the group and barked a single woof as if to say, *Come on, guys. What are we waiting for? I'm ready to hit the trail and catch me a criminal.*

"Fine by me," Paul said.

"And Sam and I will hunker down in somebody's boat," Jim glanced at Darrell, who nodded, "and set up a stake-out near the buoy downriver between Stoddard and Genoa. We'll tow Devon's boat behind so if somebody shows up at the buoy, we can use his boat to approach whoever drops the drugs. Everyone keep your cells on; communicate what you find. This is going to be a nightmare to coordinate, but we've done things like this before."

Everyone looked serious, but Jim smiled and said, "Come on, guys. Lighten up. It's time for a little rodeo action."

49

The johnboat gently swayed in the current of the Mississippi River. Jim, Sam, and Darrell had constructed a boat blind from Darrell's equipment stash, and now they sat hunched together behind the blind, drinking coffee from a thermos, keeping an eye on buoy 684 in the main channel of the river between Genoa and Stoddard.

Jim was confident the boat looked like part of the landscape being only fifty feet from shore and camouflaged. Barges had passed by in the afternoon and early evening hours. It was close to eight o'clock now, and the sun was sinking in the west, billowing the sky with a rainbow of swirling pinks, oranges, and reds. Boaters and fishermen were returning to shore. Jim watched the scenery and thought about Carol at home with Gladys and the kids. Anchored to the johnboat was Devon's sixteen-foot Discovery cruiser. Jim decided he'd use it in case someone actually showed up at the buoy. *Fat chance,* he thought.

Late in the afternoon, after they'd solidified their plans, the three men had gone to the Stoddard Kwik Trip and packed sandwiches, candy bars, and water in a small cooler, along with a couple of thermoses of strong coffee. Sam had taken a nap earlier in the evening, but now he rummaged through the supplies and found the night vision goggles and binoculars. He noticed Jim watching him.

"Gonna need these in a while," he commented.

"Yep. Still can't believe we found that empty cooler weighed down with rocks tied to the buoy," Jim said. "Would have been nice to get this over with in one fell swoop. But your idea that the buoy could be a drug drop-off site was right on target... thanks to your mystery friend."

"Help comes in strange forms sometimes," Sam said philosophically.

"Can't argue with that," Jim commented. He thought again about BJ LaPointe and Sam's clothes and now the discovery of the cabin where Devon and Angela had hidden. *What are the chances?* he thought. But he didn't question it for long. Instead, he watched the sun sinking on the horizon and pondered the many cases when his team was stumped, but perseverance and pigheaded grit had won the day.

Darrell stretched out along the back seat of the boat and made himself comfortable by tucking a flotation cushion behind his back. Since he usually worked alone and made his own decisions about different situations he was in, he found the investigative process among the detectives very interesting. He thought it was a little like the explorers who set out for the New World without a map, thinking they might sail off the end of the earth. So many things could go wrong. Here he was in a johnboat conducting surveillance on a USATON river buoy, waiting for drug dealers to show up. Go figure. Sometimes life is stranger than fiction. He hoped nobody would get shot. "From my observations of your operation today, I'm assuming things are probably never easy when you're trying to catch criminals, right?" Darrell asked.

"Nope, it's not easy," Jim answered, "but you know that from your line of work. Sometimes someone makes a really stupid error in judgment, which has happened a few times in my career. But if anything goes wrong, you can count on it happening during a sting," He thought back to a raid they'd made on a small cabin in Avalanche, Wisconsin, when his team and a group of officers from the Viroqua Sheriff's Department had hunted down a desperate fugitive hiding deep in the woods. Paul Saner had taken a shot in the leg and ribs. The image of the young detective lying in the grass screaming in pain, bleeding profusely, came back to Jim in living color. He shuddered at the memory of that horrible moment. Most cops had memories like that from their years of service. "We've had some pretty intense situations over the years. Thankfully, everyone came out okay... for the most part."

"Lots of those situations could've ended up a lot worse, that's for sure," Sam said. He remembered the day he'd been shot at close range in the chest while walking toward a desperate murderer bent on revenge. His Kevlar vest had saved his life that day. He looked toward the darkening horizon. "Desperate people do desperate things."

"You married?" Jim asked Darrell.

The question caught Darrell off-guard. He shook his head and said, "Engaged, no wedding date yet."

"Does your girl know what you're doing tonight?" Sam asked.

"Didn't tell her. I just explained that something had come up at work, and I needed to be out late," Darrell said. "She didn't ask any questions, and I didn't offer any other information."

Sam nodded in agreement. "Probably just as well. All she'd do is sit home and worry."

After a moment, Jim and Darrell began talking about fishing—the differences between river fishing and fly fishing along a creek, various makes of lures and fishing poles, and certain techniques guaranteed to snag a catch. Sam listened halfheartedly. Fishing was not something he had ever done much of. Their technical talk, however, provided a backdrop that he found relaxing, and their chatter filled the void as they floated in their fortress, waiting for some kind of action to develop.

After an hour or so, everyone fell into a quiet spell, each man lost in his own thoughts. Darkness had descended. Sam fiddled with the night goggles and kept an eye on the river traffic around the buoy. Jim dozed intermittently; Darrell scrolled through his Facebook contacts and read his messages. Sam fidgeted to keep himself awake.

Meanwhile, around five o'clock in the evening, DeDe, Paul, Mike, and Leslie, accompanied by Paco, began an intense search for Angela's Chevy in and around Victory. They drove from one end of the hamlet to the other, which took about five minutes, and ended up at the Victory Variety store, where they talked to the owner, Bud Casleford.

Bud studied the photos of the two fugitives carefully. "Yep, they came in here about eleven o'clock this morning and bought a few groceries—bread, sandwich meat, cheese, couple of apples, a pack of Oreos, some bananas, and water—then they left in a hurry."

"Did you see what direction they went?" DeDe asked.

"No. My phone rang, and all I saw was them driving back north along the river. Sorry," he apologized.

The team crammed in Paul's truck and drove north toward Genoa. They came to Battle Bluff Road and the brown sign for the Battle Bluff Prairie State Natural Area, which was a 338-acre refuge located between the Genoa Fish Hatchery to the north and the Lansing bridge to the south that led into Iowa. Leslie tapped Paul's shoulder from the back seat and suggested they swing in and look around.

"Turn up there, Paul, into that prairie area," Leslie directed, pointing to the sign.

"What for?" he asked, scowling.

"I have a hunch. You got a problem with that? Just run with me on this. Ya never know. They might have come in here to get off the main highway," Leslie said, noticing the dubious look Paul gave her. "Hey! We're conducting a search. That means anything is fair game. Besides, Paco needs to pee."

Paul turned right on Battle Bluff Road and proceeded down a tree-lined gravel road that led to a rudimentary parking lot. A couple of small log buildings that served as restrooms sat off to one side of the lot.

"Oh boy!" DeDe said softly. Angela Fitzgerald's Chevy Cavalier sat directly in front of them. Paul stopped the truck. He looked into the back seat where Leslie was sitting. His mouth gaped open in wonder. Leslie leaned forward. "You never know when a hunch will lead you in a new direction," she said playfully.

"Yeah, one that will probably get us shot," Paul said, touching the vest over his shirt. His hand wandered to the pistol strapped under his arm.

Leslie reached across the seat and clipped on Paco's leash. Jumping out, she opened the front passenger door, and Paco leaped to the ground. Paul and DeDe got out of the truck.

"Now what are we goin' to do?" DeDe asked Paul. As they talked, Leslie peeked into the vehicle and circled the car. Paco seemed agitated, barking noisily, pulling on his leash, and prancing back and forth in front of Leslie.

"I thought you said he had to pee," Mike reminded her.

Leslie checked the doors. All locked. "You got a clothes hanger in your truck?" she asked Paul, ignoring Mike's comment.

Paul walked to the truck and returned with a clothes hanger, which he inserted into the seal around the driver's door window. A minute later, Paul pulled on the hanger, and the door snapped open.

Leslie leaned over and gingerly lifted a sweater off the front seat of the Cavalier with two fingers. "Paco! Look here, boy!" she said. The black lab zeroed in on Leslie, then stopped abruptly when she pushed the sweater at his nose. He buried his face in it, sniffing intensely. His eyes fixed on Leslie, waiting for a command.

In a quiet voice, Leslie said, "Paco, find Angela." Paco tilted his head in puzzlement, and Leslie offered the sweater again. He sniffed it again.

Leslie repeated, "Find Angela."

The spirited black lab put his nose to the ground and began tugging Leslie toward the trail that led up the hill. She yelled over her shoulder," Come on, you guys! Paco's picked up a scent!"

50

At about one-thirty in the morning, Sam spotted a pair of red and green sidelights on a boat slowly proceeding up the channel about a half mile away, heading in the direction of USATON buoy 684. Sam kicked Jim's foot. He startled awake, forgetting for a moment where he was. Jim, in turn, shook Darrell's arm, then placed a finger across his lips.

Jim crawled over to Sam, who was looking in the direction of the buoy. "What's up?" he asked softly. There was enough ambient light to make out distant shapes.

"Someone's coming," Sam said cautiously, peering through the blind. He had the night vision goggles on, but the boat was still too far away to make out specifics. "It looks like it might be some kind of cabin cruiser. Sits high in the water. We'll have to wait and see what happens." Jim stretched and let out a puff of air. His shoulders and neck were stiff from trying to sleep sitting up.

Darrell quietly slipped into the Discovery while Jim and Sam closely watched the buoy. They intended to approach the boat at the first sign of activity.

"You say something, Chief?" Sam asked nervously.

"Nope. You got your vest on?"

"Ready to rock."

"Anything happening?"

"Not yet," Sam said quietly as he peered in the distance toward the direction of the buoy.

Several moments passed, the intensity and anticipation growing. Finally, Sam held up his hand, his index finger pointing toward the horizon. "They're at the buoy, Chief."

Jim nodded. "All right. Let's load," he said brusquely.

Darrell started the inboard motor on the Discovery. Despite the loud rumble of the engine, Jim was sure it couldn't be heard farther out on the river. Jim and Sam jumped on board. The men shuffled nervously as they approached the cabin cruiser in the main channel.

"Slow, slow," Jim said softly into Darrell's ear. "We don't want to spook them."

"You forget, Higgins. I've done this several times before in my career," Darrell replied, "and usually by myself."

Jim looked at the DNR agent and noticed the determined line of his firm jaw. *All right. We got another one in our corner,* Jim thought.

"Well, I'm glad somebody's done it before, because I haven't," Jim said. His stomach felt like it was in his throat. His first arrest as a rookie, he'd been so nervous and scared. Since then, whenever he was in the moment before an arrest, he got a strange sense of déjà vu—the same plots of wrongdoing with different characters accompanied by a strong sense of heightened danger and distress. Now he felt the same way. *You never know what's gonna happen,* he thought. *You could get blown away.*

Jim squeezed his hand around the portable bullhorn Darrell kept handy in the johnboat. It steadied him for some reason. The night air was cool, and Jim felt a chill on his arms. They were just about a hundred feet from the cabin cruiser when Darrell turned on a brilliant white spotlight and illuminated the vessel. Jim raised the bullhorn.

"This is the La Crosse Sheriff's Department. State your intentions, please!" he said.

Silence.

Darrell slowed the motor as he approached the cabin cruiser off the starboard side. Then he grabbed the bullhorn from Jim. "This is Darrell Schnider, DNR agent for Pools 7 and 8 of the Mississippi River. Please identify yourself."

Silence.

"We're coming on board," Darrell stated. Jim could hear the waves lapping against the hull of the boat. A slight breeze came over the water and ruffled the U.S. flag attached to the back of the boat.

The silence dragged on. Jim continued. "We have reason to believe you are delivering drugs to USATON buoy number 684," Jim continued. "When we come on board, we will be searching for drugs on your person and on the boat."

Silence.

Darrell slowly approached the cabin cruiser, threw a cushion between the two boats, and tied the powerboat to a cleat. Jim, Sam, and Darrell heaved themselves over the side of the speedboat and boarded the thirty-foot cruiser. As they stepped onto the deck, they noticed two men—one at the steering wheel inside the dimly lit cabin and another man calmly sitting on one of the upholstered benches at the rear of the boat. He sat quietly, his arms outstretched along the top cushions of the seat. Thanks to the bright light from the powerboat, Jim could clearly see the features of the man sitting before him—slight build, black hair streaked with gray, cold, dark eyes, and an arrogant attitude that was reflected in his posture. He wore faded jeans, a T-shirt, and a dark windbreaker. The man stared at the law enforcement officers with disdain, and a cruel smile curled the corner of his lips. Finally, he spoke. "Can I help you, gentlemen?" he asked softly, tipping his head slightly as if he found the whole scene amusing.

Jim stepped forward and stood in front of the man. "State your name, please, and tell us what you're doing here."

"I could ask you the same thing," the man said coldly, his stare cutting through Jim. *Gonna be a tough customer,* Jim thought.

Jim tamped down his impatience. He reached into his jacket and retrieved his ID, which he flashed at the man. "Jim Higgins, La Crosse Sheriff's Department. Your turn."

"And who are your companions?"

"Sam Birkstein, detective, and Darrell Schnider, DNR agent for Pools 7 and 8 on the Mississippi River," Jim informed him. The guy's superior, arrogant attitude left Jim feeling impatient and angry.

"Your name and your crew member's name," Jim insisted, his blue eyes hard in the white light.

"Christopher Ravel. My co-pilot is Tim Slade."

Jim nodded. "We're going to conduct a search of this vessel, and we expect your full cooperation, or we'll take you into custody."

"As you wish," Ravel said, shrugging his shoulders. Sam walked a few steps toward the cabin, opened the door, and asked Tim Slade to join Christopher on the bench. The man squeezed past Sam, brushing against him briefly before he sat on the bench. He was short but powerfully built. His furtive eyes searched his boss's face, but Christopher remained impassive and sullen.

Jim was jumpy and nervous. This whole scenario seemed contrived and easy—way too easy. Where was the resistance? Either these guys were truly innocent, or they were extremely disciplined when under pressure. Whatever it was, Jim sensed something was off.

Darrell began to search the cabin. Rifling through drawers and cupboards, he removed everything, looked carefully through the items, searching through plastic containers and other boat paraphernalia. While Jim assisted Darrell, Sam frisked the two men and, finding them clean, directed them to sit down. After an hour, they still had nothing to show for their efforts. By now, it was almost three o'clock in the morning. Darrell and Jim left the cabin and stood on the deck in front of the two men.

"Please move to the other bench," Darrell said, directing the two men with his thumb.

Christopher and Tim stood, but as Darrell stepped toward the bench, Tim threw a punch at him. Darrell sidestepped, but not quick enough, and Tim's fist glanced off his jaw. Darrell tackled Tim, and they struggled toward the edge of the boat. Before Darrell could pin Tim against the side and handcuff him, the surly co-pilot lost his balance and fell over the side of the cruiser. He splashed unceremoniously into the dark river, went down below the surface of the water, and reappeared a few seconds later, spitting and shouting, "I can't swim! Help me!"

In the meantime, Jim and Sam had restrained Christopher and put him in handcuffs.

Christopher sat back on the bench and remained dark and brooding. Jim walked over to the side of the boat and joined Darrell. Tim continued to sink below the surface and reappear, shouting and flailing. Jim found a life preserver ring attached to a rope and threw it to the drowning man, who grabbed it and hung on. He looked like a drowned rat; his breath came in loud, heaving rasps. He clutched the ring and shouted, "Get me outta this river!"

"We'll assist you, Mr. Slade, when you tell us where the drugs are."

The man in the river let out a stream of curse words. Darrell rubbed his chin where Tim had punched him.

"Flattery will get you nowhere, Tim. Neither will foul language. Tell us what you know about Devon Williams," Jim continued.

"I don't know Devon Williams."

Jim jerked the rope, and the ring slid away from Tim. He made a desperate attempt to grab it, but he quickly disappeared under the surface of the water again, popping up a few seconds later in a full-blown panic.

"Help me!" he sputtered. "I'm drowning!"

"Devon Williams. Do you know him?" Jim asked.

"Help me. Please," Tim said weakly.

Jim threw the ring back out to the man. "This can all be wrapped up if you'll just cooperate," Jim said reasonably. "Devon Williams.

Do you know him?"

A voice behind Jim interrupted. "We don't know a Devon Williams," Christopher said.

Jim turned and stared at him.

Christopher made a wry face. "The less we know about each other, the simpler it is," he said.

"Get up," Jim commanded. Christopher got up and stood next to Sam. Darrell popped open the bench top and shone a flashlight in the interior.

"Oh boy," Darrell whispered. Inside the covered bench were several large ziplock bags of what appeared to be cocaine stored in a cooler. "Must be about a hundred pounds, give or take."

Jim walked over, looked briefly at the stash of drugs, then turned to Christopher. "Mr. Ravel, you are under arrest for possession of illegal drug substances with intent to deliver. Further charges will follow if evidence shows you aided others in a conspiracy to deliver illegal drugs. This boat is being confiscated by the La Crosse County Sheriff's Department. You have the right to remain silent…"

When Jim finished reciting the Miranda rights, he walked back to the side of the boat and hauled Tim in on the life ring. As he stood on the deck dripping wet, Jim handcuffed him. Sam stood facing them, his pistol in full view. Jim called the law enforcement center and asked for assistance in transporting the men to the La Crosse jail.

"Meet us at the Genoa Fish Hatchery in half an hour," Jim ordered. He turned to Darrell and Sam. "I'll take Devon's boat and meet you upriver at the hatchery."

51

By the time Jim had traveled up the Mississippi River in Devon Williams's speedboat and transferred the two perpetrators and the two bags of cocaine to officers from the La Crosse Sheriff's Department, it was inching toward four o'clock in the morning. Jim and Sam were standing in the office of the fish hatchery leaning against a counter so they didn't fall over. Higgins rubbed the back of his neck and rolled his shoulders, getting the kinks out. After a few moments, he tipped his head upward toward the ceiling, then closed his eyes for a moment, pondering all that had transpired. He was dead-on-his-feet tired.

"You heard from Paul?" Sam asked, worry etched on his face. "We should have heard something from him by now."

"Not a word," Jim said. "Don't know if that's good or bad, but I'll call him and see what's going on." Jim punched in Paul's number and waited. No answer. Jim frowned. From what he'd remembered, his instructions to the team had been clear—keep your phone on vibrate. Stay in communication at all times.

Sam leaned against a counter in the office noticing Jim's troubled expression. "They haven't checked in, Chief. I don't like it," he said, his mood dark. "That's not good."

"I don't like it either," Jim commented. Just then his phone vibrated in his pocket. "Paul?"

"Chief. I see you tried to call," Paul whispered.

"Why are you whispering?" Jim asked. Sam straightened up and leaned in close to Jim so he could eavesdrop on the conversation. Jim put his phone on speaker and laid it on the counter.

"We're lying in the weeds next to a crappy, old camper which is parked off Kumlin Road. Devon Williams and Angela are inside. We trailed them this far, thanks to Paco. We've got a plan. We're going to wait until daylight, then advance and try to take them alive. But we might need some backup."

"Why didn't you call earlier?" Jim asked impatiently.

"We tried, but you didn't answer."

"Well, we were a little busy. I'll explain later. Sam and I will come down and assist. Keep your phone on. We'll call you when we get close to Kumlin Road."

"Is Leslie okay?" Sam asked.

"Yeah, she's fine," Paul said. "Paco led the charge. We're not goin' anywhere. Talk to you when you get here." Paul's phone went dead.

Sam's eyes were wide with anxiety. "What now?" he asked hoarsely.

"You heard it. The crew is hunkered down outside a camper parked off Kumlin Road. Devon and Angela are inside. Paul wants to take them at daybreak."

"Sounds like a shit show to me," Sam said roughly.

"Been there, done that," Jim said, trying to keep the anger out of his voice. "Come on. Looks like the rodeo is far from over," he said as he turned and walked briskly through the office to his Suburban outside.

The tiny, decrepit camper Paul had referred to in his conversation with Jim was parked about twenty-five feet off Kumlin Road. It had two tiny windows, the aluminum siding toward the bottom had practically rusted off, and the blue metal door was scuffed and faded.

Surrounding the little mobile home was a thicket of dead weeds and scattered branches from a copse of birch trees that had been blown off in the recent storm a week ago. For all practical purposes, it looked deserted and unoccupied.

Leslie and Paco were huddled together beneath a grove of pine trees on a hillock overlooking the tiny camper. DeDe had cleared a spot of dead brush under a huge white pine and was lying on her side, her head resting on her backpack, catching a few winks. Occasionally, Paco raised his massive head and emitted a low growl. Leslie calmed him with a gentle touch, but the black lab remained vigilant, staring through the undergrowth toward the camper. Leslie noticed the blue light from Paul's phone screen flickering in the dark a short distance away. Although she couldn't hear the words, she could tell he was talking to someone—probably Higgins. She relaxed and pulled Paco close to her to keep warm from the chill that had settled over the valley during the night.

Paul and Mike sat on the ground leaning against a massive oak trunk about thirty feet away from the women. Mike dozed infrequently, and at one point, he woke in a panic when Paul snorted loudly in his sleep. Right now, Paul was having a whispered conversation on his phone. Mike tapped his arm.

"What's up?" he whispered. Paul held up his hand and finished his conversation.

"Higgins and Sam are on their way."

"Jeez, you'd think we were taking on Jesse James and his gang. It's just one guy and a girl that I'm sure are basically harmless. We'll have enough people down here to—"

Paul interrupted, his words brusque and intense. "Hey, this guy is a bad player. He already killed one innocent girl. He's probably armed, injured, and desperate. That's all I need to know. He'll come out of that trailer with his guns blazin'—you can count on it. Wait and see."

Mike studied Paul's somber profile and decided to stay quiet.

Better to let Paul think he was intelligent than to open his mouth and remove all doubt. After all, Paul had conducted BOLOs and ATLs for over five years. *Don't forget you're the rookie,* he thought.

Mike leaned back against the tree again and reviewed the night's activities. The hike to the top of the bluff at dusk with Leslie and Paco leading the chase had left him breathless. It was steep and rugged, and despite his excellent physical shape, he was winded and tired by the time they finally reached the top. They'd barely caught their breath when Paco caught the scent again, and they were scrambling down the other side, slipping and sliding through dense woods without a clear path, falling over logs, and trying to avoid depressions in the landscape. After a harried descent, the team had slipped into the overgrown brush above the camper. They hiked uphill behind the camper and settled at a spot where they could watch the action. Thankfully the recent downpours of rain had softened the dead vegetation around the site, so their footfalls remained quiet.

Keeping Paco contained took all of Leslie's physical strength and dog-handling expertise, especially when they got close to the camper where Devon was hiding. Mike was fascinated with the control Leslie exerted over the black lab. The dog hadn't let out one bark since they'd approached the camper. It was almost as if he knew the perps were inside. If his sense of smell was accurate, the perps *were* inside the camper. After all, the dog could sniff out gunpowder residue with downright spooky accuracy. The word *stealth* had taken on a whole new meaning as Mike watched Leslie and the military dog work together.

Around four o'clock in the morning, Angela opened the camper door, and the dim light from a flashlight bobbed up and down as she headed for the bushes, where she relieved herself. When she stumbled back to the camper, she paused on the steps and stared at the hill where the team was hiding as if she'd heard something. After a few moments, she opened the door and went back in.

Now in the darkness, Mike wondered what awaited them in the morning. It was still dark, but in an hour or so, dawn would begin brightening the sky to the east. He fingered his Kevlar vest and touched the pistol tucked in his shoulder holster. He was counting on the team's experience and determination to apprehend Williams. Somewhere in the darkness, an owl hooted, and Mike felt shivers race up his back. *Steady. Calm. All will be well,* he thought. *I hope.*

THURSDAY, SEPTEMBER 4

IT OFTEN REQUIRES MORE COURAGE TO DARE
TO DO RIGHT THAN FEAR TO DO WRONG.

ABRAHAM LINCOLN

52

Jim eased the Suburban onto Kumlin Road. The gravel crunched beneath the truck tires, and the night air cooled the truck's interior until Jim felt chilled. Sam was on high alert, leaning forward, trying to locate the dilapidated camper in the darkness.

"There it is," Sam said softly, pointing to his left. The camper sat on a low rise, looking forlorn and dark. "Drive farther down the road. We'll ditch the truck, walk back, and find a place to hang out until sunrise."

Jim followed Sam's directive and drove another quarter mile down the road, pulling the SUV onto a farm lane. He shut off the engine and dialed Paul. Listening carefully, Jim made a few nonchalant remarks, then put his phone back in his jacket pocket.

"The team is situated up on the hill behind the camper. The girls are under some big pine trees with Paco, and Paul and Mike are waiting under another tree. We'll find a position across the road with a clear view of the entire operation. Takedown will be at first light. Maybe another half hour or so," Jim commented, glancing at his phone.

"And then?" Sam asked.

"We hope all bloody hell doesn't let loose," Jim said. He glanced at Sam, who looked back at him with firm resolve.

"We've had that happen before," Sam said darkly. The silence in the truck seemed to grow, weighing the two men down with memories of other apprehensions.

"We were lucky that the arrest on the boat didn't go bad," Jim said. "This situation might be pushin' our luck."

"My pregnant wife's out there," Sam finally said, popping open the passenger door. "Let's do this."

The two detectives exited the Suburban and began walking down the gravel road toward the camper. Night sounds accompanied their footsteps. Crickets chirped in the high grass along the road, the single hoot of an owl floated above the dark trees, the oak leaves rustled in the gentle breeze, and the distant noise of traffic from U.S. Highway 35 reminded Jim that life went on despite the actions of a few lowlife desperadoes. The sky grew lighter, and a faint pink glow appeared on the eastern horizon and turned golden as the moments ticked by. Sunrise was only a half hour away.

Once Jim and Sam were close to the camper, they ducked into the ditch along the road. They walked slowly until they found a position that gave them a clear, unobstructed view of the tiny trailer.

"Here," Jim whispered, pointing toward the ground. "Let's hunker down here."

They got on the ground, lying prostrate on their bellies, and tried to get comfortable, which was almost impossible. The ground was damp and rough, covered with sticks and mounds of weeds. They pushed the natural undergrowth down to get a clear view of the camper and its surroundings. Then the wait began.

During the moments before sunrise, Jim thought about his team. He was proud of the grit they'd displayed in hunting down Devon Williams. Of course, having BJ LaPointe drag Sam's lost clothing into the sheriff's office and plunk it on Turnmile's desk had been a breakthrough of major proportions and had given the team the impetus they needed to complete the job. Never in a million years had Jim imagined that things would turn out as they did. He was just thankful they were on the cusp of apprehending Devon. Hopefully they could take him down with minimum force and protect Angela from further harm.

Twenty minutes later, Jim's phone vibrated in his pocket. He answered and, at the same time, noticed the outline of the trees becoming visible in the early morning light.

"We're ready. What's the plan?" Jim asked. He listened carefully, then replaced his phone in his jacket.

Sam looked at Jim for direction. "We'll form a ring around the camper," Jim explained. "Tighten it up until we're twenty feet out. I'll knock on the door and see what happens."

"That's the plan?" Sam asked, his eyebrows arched in surprise.

"You got a better one?" Jim asked crossly.

"Not really," Sam said. "Let's go." He stood and suddenly felt vulnerable and exposed. Devon could be watching them, waiting to pick them off, one by one. Jim began climbing out of the ditch. He looked back at Sam. "You comin?"

"Yep. Right at ya," he whispered.

Out of the woods above the cabin, Sam could make out Leslie and Paco coming down the hill in the early morning light. He waved silently at his wife. *She shouldn't be doing this,* he thought.

DeDe appeared at Leslie's side and then stepped in front of her as if protecting her. Paul and Mike came down from higher on the hill. Everyone looked rumpled and tired. When they were all within visual proximity, Jim lifted his hand in a stop gesture. He pointed to his chest and then the door of the camper. Everyone waited while Jim approached the rickety little shelter.

There were no steps, so Jim stood next to the trailer and beat on the door with his fist. Three loud pounds. *Boom, boom, boom.*

"This is the La Crosse Sheriff's Department, Lt. Jim Higg—"

Gunfire erupted from the camper. The tiny window in the door above Jim's head shattered and pelted him with shards of glass. He hit the ground and rolled beneath the trailer. Sam ran to a nearby tree. Jim had no idea where the rest of the team had scurried to.

"This is Lt. Jim Higgins," he yelled in an angry voice, louder this time. "Come out, Devon, and surrender. You will not escape—"

More gunfire shattered the silence of the early morning, but the shots seemed aimless. Jim heard a tussle inside the trailer. Something fell on the floor of the camper with a thud, and Jim saw Sam run toward the camper at an oblique angle. Two more shots rang out. A few seconds later, Sam crawled along the edge of the trailer toward the door. He was panting more from fear than exertion, but his voice was calm.

"Gotta get him out of the trailer, Chief," Sam said nervously. He heard footsteps inside and a desperate exchange of angry words. The noises continued along with the sharp sound of breaking glass.

"You're surrounded by six officers of the law, Devon. You have no chance of escape. Come out! Now!" Jim yelled again with authority.

Sam heard some rattling at the door. Angela appeared, shaken, but in one piece. She ran away from the trailer toward the road.

Sam cocked his head at an angle and watched the door carefully. It was flung open and hung crookedly on its flimsy hinges. The silence that followed the gunshots was unnerving. Sam rolled away from the trailer, sprang to his feet, and with his gun extended in front of him, he carefully approached the door.

"This is Detective Sam Birkstein. I'm coming in, Devon. Throw out your weapon."

Silence.

Jim crawled out from under the trailer and followed Sam, his pistol cocked upward in front of him. Sam stepped up into the trailer. It was dark, but there was enough light to see Devon lying on the small bed in front of the trailer, holding his side, bleeding onto the mattress.

"That bitch shot me!" he exclaimed. "She shot me!" His surprise seemed genuine.

"Maybe you deserved it," Sam spat sarcastically. He walked toward the bed, leaned over Devon and checked his wound, then turned to Jim. "He'll need an ambulance, I guess. Somebody needs to check on Angela. She took off down the road."

Devon grimaced in pain and sputtered a string of obscenities. "Good riddance."

Jim recited the Miranda rights as he stood over the wounded perpetrator. "Devon Williams, you are under arrest for the robbery at the Stoddard Gas & Go and the murder of Vicki Invold. Anything you say can and will be used against you in a court of law…"

53

Carl Ettinger, one of the CSI technicians from the sheriff's department, drove down Kumlin Road in the early morning light. Pulling off the road, he stopped suddenly when he spotted the ramshackle trailer and the other police vehicles. Ramming the van into park, Ettinger opened the door and unfolded his long, lanky body from the cramped seat. Outside the CSI van, he stretched his arms upward to the sky and yawned. He looked around and spotted Jim Higgins standing outside a beat-up, ancient camper that looked like a home for vagrant gypsies. Carl walked up to the senior investigator.

"Hey, Chief. When is this gonna end? I've got so many crime scenes to investigate it's gonna take a month of Sundays just to scratch the surface," Carl said. "You're going to have to hire some help so I can get it all done."

Higgins looked rough. His clothes were wrinkled and smeared with dirt. Black circles under his eyes and a whiskered face made him look vaguely criminal. He barely acknowledged Carl's complaints.

"This whole deal is a lot bigger than any of us thought, but all I know right now is if I don't sit down, I'm gonna fall down," Jim said. "You need to go through the camper and do what you do. But first, I need you to take me down the road to my truck—about a quarter of a mile that way." Jim pointed down Kumlin Road. "Then I'm driving home, taking a shower, and I'm gonna sleep for at least twelve hours. Let's go." Jim began walking toward the crime scene van.

"Where's the rest of your team?" Carl asked.

Jim stopped and turned toward Ettinger. "The sheriff brought a van and took them all back to their cars. They're on their way home," Jim explained. Sheriff Elaine Turnmile had arrived on the scene twenty minutes after the shoot-out with fresh recruits and promptly excused the detectives.

"Go home and get some rest," she said. "We'll put this all together later." Her eyes softened as she looked at the weary, bedraggled team. "Good job. I'll take care of the scene here and tie up some loose ends. You all go home. You look like hell." A fleeting grin passed over her lips.

Ettinger knew it was futile to try and converse with Higgins. From the looks of it, he needed a serious dose of sleep, food, and downtime.

He dropped Higgins at his Suburban, and Jim drove straight home. On the way he met a school bus, and in his brain fog, he thought of Lillie and Henri on their way to St. Ignatius school in Genoa. He'd missed their daily routine this morning—a breakfast of chitchat with a few childish arguments thrown in for good measure, the hurried last minutes of getting backpacks and lunch boxes gathered up before the bus came, fist bumps and kisses, and then the glorious quiet of the dining room where a second cup of coffee and a thorough reading of the *Wisconsin State Journal* could be savored.

The morning was beautiful—the sunshine filtering through the woods along the road—but Jim's mind felt like a blank slate. He was having trouble absorbing everything that had happened in the last twenty-four hours. The turn of events that had sealed Sam's innocence and Devon's guilt was miraculous. His mind wandered to the brief congratulatory speech from the truculent sheriff. *Maybe she's getting the hang of the job,* Jim thought. Then another thought crept in. *Don't count on it.*

Jim drove slowly through Chipmunk Coulee enjoying the familiarity of the route. Then he suddenly slapped his head in disgust. He'd forgotten he was living with his family at Gladys Hanson's farm. *I guess my mind is on auto-pilot,* he thought.

"I must be losin' it," he mumbled softly, but as long as he was so close to his home, he decided to take a quick look at the progress. He drove in his driveway and shut off the engine. Sitting in the Suburban, he stared out the windshield at the roof of the house and was somewhat pleased that it had been replaced and shingled.

Jim stepped out of his vehicle and walked slowly toward the front door of his home. Noises from inside—hammers pounding, saws whining—brought a level of comfort that progress was being made. He went inside and found a carpenter studying blueprints in the dining room on a makeshift table slapped together with sawhorses and a piece of plywood. The carpenter turned and greeted Jim.

"Can I help you?" he asked.

"Looks like you already are," Jim said. He stepped forward and shook hands with the man, noticing his calloused, rough grip. "Jim Higgins. This is my house."

"Les Johnson. I'm the lead carpenter with Coulee Builders." He paused and took in Jim's rough appearance. The guy looked like he'd been on an all-night bender. "You've got quite a mess here. It may not look like it right now, but we're making good progress. We've removed all the burned materials, and things will start to look better when we get the walls framed up and the sheetrock on."

"Mind if I look around?" Jim asked.

"It's your house," the carpenter said. "Have at it." He turned his attention back to the documents on the table in front of him.

Jim slowly strolled through the living room, which had been enlarged to include a baby grand piano for Lillie. Jim smiled when he thought of the music that would grace their home and bring comfort and happiness. Looking through the large sliding door to the patio in the back of the house, Jim could see stone masons repairing the terrace, enlarging the area to accommodate more outdoor living space. The kitchen looked rough, but Jim envisioned the new kitchen cabinets and appliances they'd selected, and the dining room with the added skylight would fill the space with bright sunshine.

"Thanks for your work," Jim said when he'd come back full circle to the dining room. "It's been a rough couple of weeks, but seeing the progress gives me a little hope."

The carpenter nodded and smiled. "My pleasure. It's a beautiful house. Hope you can get back here real soon."

Jim walked out of the house, got in his Suburban, and arrived fifteen minutes later at Gladys's farmyard. She was just coming out of the chicken coop, an empty pail in her hand. She looked at Jim.

"We missed you last night," she said simply. Her wide girth was embellished with an old apron in a faded red rose pattern that covered her ample chest. Her flyaway white hair encircled her wrinkled face, and her inquisitive blue eyes gazed at Jim with unabashed affection.

"Been chasing crooks," Jim said with a weary grin.

"And did you catch them?" Gladys asked, setting her pail down next to her.

"Yeah, we did."

"And you're still in one piece?"

"Last time I checked, I was still in one piece, but I feel like I could sleep for a year. Thanks for asking."

"Carol's waiting. She's been worried."

"I'm home now," Jim said, rolling his shoulders to relieve the tension.

"That's good."

"Yeah. It's real good."

MONDAY, SEPTEMBER 8

LET IT BE, LET IT BE,
LET IT BE, LET IT BE,
WHISPER WORDS OF WISDOM,
LET IT BE.

THE BEATLES

54

Jim walked to the outer reception area from his office on the third floor of the law enforcement center early Monday morning and poured himself a fresh cup of coffee. As he walked by Emily's desk, he stopped briefly and leaned over her high counter. Emily looked radiant in a pair of cream slacks and a muted rust pullover that accented her auburn hair. As usual, she was pulled together and looked professional. Jim had never really seen her any other way. She looked up at him as he stood near her desk.

"I was wondering, sir, if you'd gotten around to the mound of paperwork stacked on your desk," she said, observing a shadow of exasperation pass over his face. She tipped her head in a jaunty fashion as she waited for his answer.

"Haven't been here enough to even think about it, but I'll get to it in the next few weeks," Jim answered bluntly. He didn't mind his heavy workload when conducting an investigation, but his dislike for the bureaucratic side of detective work was the one aspect of his job he dreaded. Still, he also knew the paper chase frequently revealed hidden details that could make or break a case. Emily's gentle reminder about the mountain of paperwork didn't diminish his appreciation of her legendary efficiency, even if nobody else in the department seemed to notice. He moved to another subject. "The team is coming in about an hour. We're meeting down the hall in the large classroom."

Emily continued typing, then looked up briefly with a soft smile. "Should I point them in that direction then?" she asked.

"Yes, please... and Emily?"

She stopped typing and held her breath. "Yes, sir?"

"Thank you for what you do every day."

Emily's eyes softened. "You're most welcome, Chief. I love my job," she said simply.

By ten o'clock, Jim and his team had gathered around the whiteboard in the classroom down the hall from Jim's office. Everyone looked alert after a long weekend of recovery and rest. Jim was glad that Sam and Leslie had joined them, although Sam was technically still on medical leave.

Sam leaned over and spoke a private word in Mike Leland's ear. "So... have you recovered from your first murder investigation?"

"Recovered? Oh, yeah," Mike said, exasperated at the reference to his newbie status. Then rather sheepishly, he reconsidered. "I have to admit, I really learned a lot. I don't think I've fully absorbed all the ins and outs of the whole process. All I know is, chasing a killer is pretty unpredictable, and you better be able to think on your feet and change your tactics at a moment's notice."

"True and—" Sam began, but he was cut off mid-sentence.

"All right, let's get started," Jim said in an assertive tone. "We need to sort out the evidence from the murder and robbery and fine-tune the timeline. Paul and I will be interviewing Devon this afternoon, and I'll be going to the LaPointes later to talk to them about Sam's clothing and BJ's eyewitness account of Devon's escape from the crime scene."

Sam got up, walked to the whiteboard, and grabbed a colored marker from the pen holder. "Ready, Chief," he said seriously, slipping into the role of scribe.

In the next hour, the details of the crime were rehashed, arranged in order, then rearranged by the team as they solidified the evidence that had been gathered from multiple crime scenes: Jim's security footage of Devon's shenanigans at his house on Chipmunk Coulee Road, the stolen property stored in the houseboat on the Black River, the ancient camper near Victory that had served as an impromptu escape hatch, Devon's boat tied to the dock on the Mississippi River, the cabin cruiser and the drugs that were confiscated near river buoy 684, the surprise return of Sam's clothes by BJ LaPointe and his subsequent eyewitness account of Devon's escape and, of course, the Gas & Go convenience station in Stoddard. As the facts filled up the board and spilled toward the edges, it was apparent that it would take weeks, possibly months, to consolidate all the evidence they'd gathered to construct an air-tight case against Devon Williams that would hold up in court.

Sam listened carefully and scribbled information about the crime on the whiteboard with due diligence, feeling an urgency to get the facts in writing as if that alone would be proof to everyone that he was not the perpetrator of murder and robbery.

"Honey," Leslie had told him earlier in the morning over their second cup of coffee, "nobody in the department ever believed you were involved." She tucked her feet underneath her as she sipped her coffee on the couch and carefully watched her husband's reaction.

Sam frowned ominously, his face shadowed with dark thoughts, disinclined to believe the nightmare he'd been through was really over. Leslie could see his recovery would stretch on into the future. Somewhere in the process of the lightning strike and investigation, Sam had lost his cocksure confidence. Leslie thought that perhaps the events of the past few weeks had forever marred the casual optimism Sam had so easily adopted in his life before the strike.

"Your dedication to law enforcement and your character and core beliefs are well-known to anyone who's really bothered to get to know you," she continued, trying to comfort and convince him.

"That's easy for you to say," Sam said, glowering, staring out the window at the Mississippi River in the distance. His eyes drifted back to his wife's face. Paco, who was sprawled on the living room floor, let out a sigh as if he was bored with the whole conversation. "You didn't wake up in the hospital in different clothes suspected of committing a murder." He shivered involuntarily.

Leslie set her coffee cup on the end table, knelt in front of him, and grasped his hands. He looked into her clear, blue eyes and felt a level of comfort and love he knew he couldn't find anywhere else. "It hasn't been easy for me either, Sam," she said tenderly. "I had to watch you try to make sense of the whole thing when your memory was fried to a crisp. But now—"

"Things haven't changed all that much, Lez," Sam interrupted crossly, pushing her hands away. "People in the department still look at me cross-eyed with suspicion." He spat the last word out with a vehemence that surprised—and worried—Leslie.

"Look, let's just go to the meeting today and let the chips fall where they may," Leslie said, tenderly kissing him. "Don't forget, I'll always have your back."

Now as the team gathered around the whiteboard and reviewed the details of the long list of criminal offenses, Leslie watched Sam's demeanor closely. He seemed stalwart, determined to absorb all the facts of the case, and, she hoped, sanguine about the opinions of those on the law enforcement staff about his possible involvement. *What a ridiculous bunch of crap,* she thought. *How could anyone possibly believe Sam would be involved in such a heinous crime? When the facts of the case become widely known,* she thought, *Sam's trepidation will ease, and he'll return to work and recover his sense of confidence and enjoy the admiration he's earned in the department over the last five years.* A small voice nagged inside Leslie's head. *I hope.*

"Why the hell did that stupid kid keep my clothes so long?" Sam asked loudly, the marker poised in midair as he waited for an answer. "Didn't he realize how important it was to turn them over to the police?"

Jim did a double-take when Sam barked his questions. At the same time, he noticed a pink blush spread across Leslie's face at Sam's abrasive outburst.

Paul shrugged his shoulders nonchalantly. "He's a kid. He was probably scared out of his wits. He'd been threatened within an inch of his life. He'd never confronted a criminal before—take your pick. It's hard to tell, Sam, how an innocent bystander will react to a violent crime, but the chief and I will find out more about it this afternoon."

Sam glared at Paul, obviously finding his answer inadequate. *Nothing like giving the kid a bunch of excuses,* he thought. He tamped down his impatience. "I'd like to be there when you interview BJ, Chief."

Jim studied the top of the table where they were seated, weighing the wisdom of granting Sam's request. "I'll think about it," he finally said, meeting Sam's insolent stare.

A knock on the doorframe of the classroom interrupted the discussion and caught everyone off-guard. Emily stood in the opening of the door flanked by two men dressed in cheap gray suits off the rack and plain white dress shirts. One had a blue tie, and the other had a red one. Jim stood.

"Lt. Higgins? May I introduce FBI Agents William Hersey and Tom Vanderveld," she said primly, pointing to each man as introductions were made.

Jim nodded. "Hello. I'm Jim Higgins. My team, Paul Saner, Sam and Leslie Birkstein, DeDe Deverioux, and Mike Leland." The men entered the room, and Emily took the opportunity to escape. With a sweep of his arm, Jim motioned the two men to vacant chairs. The FBI men walked toward the table, grabbed the empty chairs, and sat down. Everyone shuffled positions and got comfortable again. "How can we help you?" Jim asked politely.

The one agent, Bill Hersey, was dark-haired, graying at his temples, and had a swarthy complexion with a five o'clock shadow.

He cleared his throat noisily. "We'd like to know how you put two and two together to make the drug bust by the buoy. We've been trying to track these drug drops for a long time and haven't had much success. We never dreamed they'd use a USATON buoy in the river to do their drops. That's pretty unbelievable." The agent's low voice rumbled around the room, bouncing off the white walls. The team stared at the two unfamiliar men.

Jim contemplated the wisdom of revealing their own naivete about the magnitude of the drug operation. Paul looked over at Jim as if to ask, *Are you really going to tell them how we found out?* The silence in the room grew until Jim felt compelled to speak.

"Through a couple of contacts within the community, it became clear that a local hoodlum was hanging around buoy 684 out on the river between Genoa and Stoddard. It seemed unusual since he wasn't fishing, so we thought it was worth looking into." Jim made a wry face. "We'd been chasing the guy down for a robbery and shooting at a local gas station when we discovered this other connection. It seemed pretty crazy to us, too, but I guess we got lucky."

Tom Vanderveld, the other FBI agent, jumped into the conversation. "We're putting a team together who are familiar with water travel, boats, scuba diving, and surveillance—that type of stuff. They're not that easy to find in the Midwest, but we're working on it. We were wondering if there's anything specific we should know about this drug operation—from your standpoint, that is." Vanderveld leaned forward and placed his elbows on the table.

"Navigating the river is tricky," Jim began. "The current is swift and strong, and you have to be constantly aware of weather and river traffic. It's a whole other world out there. Other than that, I really can't offer much."

"Well, this whole thing shouldn't be surprising, I guess," Hersey responded. "If they use our freeways and interstate highway systems to transport drugs, why wouldn't they use our rivers?"

"Our thoughts exactly," Jim added.

The group talked shop for another half hour, but Jim was feeling the pressure of continuing his team meeting. "Is there anything else we can do to help?" he finally asked.

Hersey shook his head. "Not really." He looked around at the team. "We'll be taking over the drug operation on the river."

Jim nodded. "I'm not surprised. I figured you would."

Bill continued. "Our department in Madison heard about your team in La Crosse and some of the work you've been doing up here. Frankly, we thought the stories about you guys were overblown—more hyperbole than reality. We never really believed it was all true. The busts you've made are pretty legendary, but this latest discovery has me reconsidering my opinion."

Jim bit his tongue. *Like we need you to tell us what kind of a job we're doing,* he thought sardonically. But being the gentleman that he was, he simply smiled while having treacherous thoughts about state and federal law enforcement agencies who come in with their high-powered personnel and make the local guys feel like hicks in the sticks. Then he thought about what Abe Lincoln said: "Whatever you are, be a good one." He sighed. *Yeah,* he thought. *I think we're pretty good at what we are.* He smiled at no one in particular.

55

In the quiet of his office early Monday afternoon after the staff meeting, Jim spent some time preparing for an interview with Devon Williams. Devon had been hospitalized for his gunshot wound and his damaged shoulder. He was recovering at Gundersen Lutheran Hospital. Angela Fitzpatrick was interviewed by DeDe and Paul. It became apparent during the interview that she had been forced to cooperate with Devon Williams in exchange for her safety. She was released on her own recognizance until the time of the trial.

Jim turned off his cell to get in some critical thinking time. He wondered how the interview would go. As he thought of all that had transpired during the week, he jotted down questions, but, in the final analysis, it was no good. He just couldn't get past the upheaval of the house fire that had upended his family and threatened their lives.

Lillie and Henri were still having nightmares. Jim and Carol were trying to juggle life at Gladys's farm while attempting to ease their children's real fears and simultaneously overseeing the renovation of their home. *Are we ever going to get back to normal?* Jim wondered. He tossed his pen on the desk and wearily laid his tablet aside. He thought he'd gotten enough rest over the weekend, but the bone-deep exhaustion that had plagued him during his depression had returned. He leaned back in his office chair and stretched his arms toward the ceiling, feeling the tension in his shoulders and neck ease a little bit.

After the house fire, thoughts of revenge and hatred for the man who had tried to kill his family came roaring out of the blue and left Jim breathless, like he'd been punched in the gut. When he thought of his beautiful family perishing in a house fire, the desire for retribution was overwhelming. He wanted justice. At the same time he was haunted with a desire for vengeance that left him reeling in a sea of guilt. He knew from past experience the secret to peace of mind in the wake of insensible violence was to give it to God and let his plan unfold, whatever that was. Now Jim worried that in the interview with Devon, the feelings he'd carried around for days would override his common sense approach and derail the interrogation before it even got started. He thought about Lillie and Henri. He wished he could erase the worried frowns on their innocent faces from his mind. Their expressions haunted him at the most inopportune times—like right now when he was supposed to be completing a critical component in the murder investigation of Vicki Invold. He seemed to have lost his ability to concentrate. He'd prepared for interviews of known perpetrators who had committed serious crimes for years. *This should be a piece of cake,* he thought. But the distraction of the house fire robbed him of energy and clouded his concentration.

After a few moments savoring the quiet of his office, Jim reached down, opened the bottom right-hand drawer of his desk, and pulled out a well-worn leather Bible.

King David was one of Jim's biblical heroes. David was flawed, passionate, a man of many moods who loved the Lord deeply. Despite his many failures—the most well-known, his torrid affair with Bathsheba and the subsequent murder of her husband to cover up the scandal—the Lord forgave David but allowed him to experience the consequences of his sinful choices. *Nothing new under the sun,* Jim thought. *That story, and so many others in the Bible, read like something out of a modern novel.* Although Jim hadn't had any affairs or blatantly knocked off the husband of an illicit lover, he deeply identified with the flaws of King David. Jim could identify with many of David's traits—impulsive, prone to repaying those who wronged him, indulgent with his children, protective, and proud.

He laid the Bible on his desk and turned to Psalms. Flipping through the thin pages, he stopped at Psalm 91. In the quiet of his office, he savored the words and let them sink into his heart. "Because he loves me," says the Lord, "I will rescue him; I will protect him, for he acknowledges my name. He will call upon me, and I will answer him."

Jim closed his eyes, took a deep breath, and meditated on those words. Just then, there was a quiet knock on his door.

Emily peeked her head around the doorframe. "BJ LaPointe is here, sir. He'd like to talk with you."

"Give me a minute," Jim said. He straightened his desk with a few quick strokes, then stood up and walked to the door. BJ LaPointe was a tall, well-built young man, but at the moment, he sagged wearily against the wall in the hallway, staring dejectedly at the floor, his arms crossed over his chest, deep in thought.

"BJ?" Jim said. "Come on in, son."

The young man straightened and pulled himself away from the wall, then walked with determination into Jim's office, where he found a chair and pulled it up near Jim's desk. His brown eyes scanned Jim's office walls—the numerous awards, citations, and photos; Jim's collection of arrowheads and tomahawks; and an oil painting of a rugged red barn by Wisconsin artist John Schneider. Jim didn't rush him. BJ's eyes fell on the open Bible on the desk, and after a few moments, the young man focused his attention on the senior investigator sitting in front of him.

"So, what did you want to talk to me about?" Jim asked, easing his shoulders back in his chair.

"I already told my story to the sheriff. Do you want to hear it, too?" BJ asked.

"I just have a few questions," Jim commented.

"Sure. Go ahead," BJ said.

"When you arrived at the gas station, had Vicki already been shot?" Jim asked.

"Yep. She was on the floor, and she probably wasn't dead yet, but from the way she was bleeding, I knew she wouldn't live long." Jim noticed BJ had clenched his fists in his lap, and his jaw formed a hard line, making him look much older than he was. Tears welled in his eyes, and he swallowed hard.

"I'm very sorry you had to witness that, BJ," Jim said quietly. "What did you do then?"

"Well, for a few seconds, I thought I'd entered another universe—you know, it was so unbelievable—and then Devon turned the gun on me and told me I had to help him."

"Which you did?" Jim asked.

The sudden anger in BJ's brown eyes left Jim with no illusions. This young man had suffered a terrible trauma. "What choice did I have?" BJ rasped angrily. "When somebody's ramming a gun in your face, you don't argue."

"No, you don't. That was wise on your part. What about the manager?" Jim queried. "Did he come out of his office? Did you see him at all?"

"No. We hightailed it outta there and jumped in my car."

"So the manager never saw you?"

"Nope. Not that I'm aware of," BJ answered.

"And then what happened?"

"I drove Devon down 35 until we came to that guy by the side of the road."

"And you stopped?" Jim asked.

"Had to. Devon had his gun poked in my ribs."

"You waited in the car?"

"Yep."

"What was Devon doing while you were in the vehicle?" Jim asked.

"He got out and walked to the man on the side of the road. He exchanged his jacket and boots and put them on the other guy. He stuffed the rain jacket and the Nikes under his arm. He came back to the car and grabbed some of the stolen money. Then he walked back to the guy again, lifted him up, and tucked some of the money under him. When he got back in the car, he didn't have the gun anymore."

"So he gave you the jacket and the Nikes that he'd taken off the man by the side of the road?"

"Yeah. He told me to get rid of them."

"Anything else?" Jim asked.

"I drove him to the marina in Genoa, and he jumped out and took off down the river in some big powerboat."

"Yes, we discovered the boat near Victory," Jim explained.

It was silent in the office then, like the air had been sucked out of the room. Jim waited for a few moments before he continued. "Do you have any questions for me?" He looked at BJ and noticed his brown luminous eyes were turbulent with confusion and anxiety.

"Yeah. I got a couple. What about Vicki's baby? Have they found out whose it is?" BJ asked.

Jim shuffled through some papers on his desk until he came to the coroner's report. He scanned the pages until he found the paternity reference. "Well, from what's written here, I can tell you it's not Devon's baby, but until you give us your DNA, the paternity of the baby cannot be determined. Sharing your DNA is a decision you'll have to make." Jim looked up and locked eyes with BJ. "If you're interested in doing that, here's Luke's card. You can contact him." BJ grabbed the card from the desk and deposited it in his wallet. "Any other questions?" Jim asked.

"I have so many questions it will take an eternity to ask them all," BJ said despondently.

"Try me," Jim said simply.

"Okay, I will. Will I be charged with something? Like hiding evidence or something?"

"We haven't determined that yet. We understand you were under duress from Devon to keep the exchanged clothes a secret, but in the end, you did the right thing and came forward. So as far as I'm concerned, I will recommend that no charges be filed against you." Jim watched BJ carefully. The young man was certainly a bundle of emotions. "Any more questions?"

"Yeah. One you probably can't answer. Why did this happen?" BJ asked, his voice hoarse and cracking with emotion. "Why did God do this?"

Jim sighed. *Theology 101,* he thought. *Better get started. This might take a while.*

"God didn't do this," Jim started to explain. "Somebody with evil in their heart—namely Devon—acted on an evil impulse, and because of that, your girlfriend lost her life. But God spared you, BJ. You could have been killed, too, but you weren't. Despite the fact that Vicki lost her life, God spared yours. That's no accident."

"You mean like… God was kind to me?" Jim nodded.

BJ screwed up his face in disbelief. "Really, lieutenant?" The young man's expression was a mask of indignation and outrage. "What am I supposed to do about all this? Vicki was all I ever really wanted," he croaked hoarsely. "And now she's gone forever."

"Yes. Yes, she is gone forever, and we can't change that fact," Jim said, leaning forward in his chair. He paused, thinking through his response. "Listen, BJ. I don't know exactly why you're still here. But make no mistake," Jim said, his voice firm and his eyes flashing, "God has a plan for your life. Unfortunately, you've seen and experienced a horrible crime that I wouldn't wish on anyone. Your life will be forever changed because of this. But you still have choices. You can choose to use this event as a springboard to do good—to love people, to help people, to care about people. Or you can capitulate and let this evil have the final say."

"That sounds all warm and fuzzy, but what about justice, huh? Where's that?" the young man spat.

"Your choice to bring those clothes into the sheriff's office and tell your side of the story helped justice along. You gave us some solid eyewitness testimony and identified Devon as the perpetrator of this hideous crime. In doing that, you're already fighting the evil that befell Vicki." Seeing the fury on the boy's face, Jim doubted his little speech was having the desired effect. The teenager was still distraught.

BJ roughly wiped the tears from his cheeks. He looked exhausted and terribly sad. Jim's fatherly instincts welled up within him. He just wanted to take the hurting young man in his arms and comfort him like he'd comforted his son John when his first wife Margie had died. *Do it,* a voice told him.

Jim stood up and walked around his desk until he stood before BJ.

"Stand up," he said.

BJ looked up at him, a confused expression crossing his face. Cautiously, the strapping young man rose from his chair. Jim took a few steps toward him and wrapped his arms around BJ and pulled him close. Jim could feel his strong, warm body melting into his own. Soon, muffled sounds came from BJ's throat, and then heart-wrenching sobs escaped and filled the small office. Jim continued to enfold the boy in his arms until his emotions were spent. Finally, BJ straightened and pulled away from Jim, who stepped back a few feet.

"My dad died six months ago. You remind me of him," BJ said softly, crying.

"I have a son who's a little older than you and one who just started kindergarten," Jim said.

BJ's eyes widened at the revelation. "Really? A kindergartner at your age?" he asked.

"I've had some surprises in my life, too," Jim said, a grin crossing his face, "but just believe me when I say that God is the God of second... and third... and fourth chances."

"I guess I never really thought about it like that," BJ whispered.

Jim gently patted BJ's shoulder. "God is for you, BJ. He's got your back, and He's watching over you even though you probably haven't realized it."

"I don't know if I believe that, but thanks, Lt. Higgins. This really helped." The young man stood awkwardly in front of Jim, more a child than a man. But the circumstances at the Gas & Go in Stoddard had pushed BJ into the real world of crime and violence in a way that was frighteningly real, and BJ LaPointe had no choice but to grow up fast. Jim had seen it time and time again in his line of work. He wished it wasn't so, but that was the stark reality when violent crime left its calling card.

"It will take time to process all of this," Jim said. "Don't hurry it. Be patient with yourself, and call me if there's anything I can do to help." He stepped back and gave BJ a last pat on the back. "Maybe we can go trout fishing sometime down in Timber Coulee. Just call me."

"I'd like that," the young man promised, and then he walked from Jim's office, shutting the door quietly behind him.

56

By late afternoon, Jim Higgins and Paul Saner were headed through busy traffic along South Avenue on their way to Gundersen Lutheran Hospital to interview Devon Williams. After parking, Jim and Paul sauntered through the front entrance, took an elevator to the surgical ward on the third floor, and stopped at the nurses' station. A heavy-set nurse looked up from her computer and directed the men to Devon's room. A police guard stood outside the door, and Paul and Jim exchanged some light banter with him. Before entering the room, Jim touched Paul's arm lightly and pulled him aside farther down the hallway.

"Hey. True confession time," Jim said seriously. Paul's stomach turned over when he gazed into Jim's crystalline blue eyes.

"Uh-oh. You're not gonna tell me Carol's pregnant again, are you?" Paul said, assuming a cocky attitude in an attempt to ward off the somber gaze of his boss. He grinned foolishly.

"Come on. For Pete's sake! That's not even possible anymore," Jim said sarcastically.

"That's what you said five years ago."

"Could we move on?" Jim said, the irritation bristling.

Paul held up his hands, and his grin faded. "Just trying to prepare myself for whatever it is you're gonna tell me." The sober look on Jim's face made Paul hesitate, and his cheeks flushed with embarrassment at his earlier comments. He wisely decided to give Jim his full attention. "Go ahead. Spill your guts. I'm listening."

Jim looked down the hallway for a moment and noticed the blue sky reflected through the window at the end of the hall. His mood was dark despite the sunny day, and he struggled to put words to the range of feelings he'd had in the last few weeks. "Well, as you might have guessed, I've been pretty torqued about Devon trying to kill me and my entire family—notwithstanding the fact that he burned down my home. I've never met the guy, but I'd just as soon deliver a right hook to his chops as to talk to him. Just so you know."

Paul nodded noncommittally. "I hear you, Chief. I'm not surprised. I've been wondering how you've been dealing with all of this. Nobody blames you for being angry, you know," Paul commented wisely.

"Yeah, well, if I get out of line with this guy, you're going to have to keep me in check. Just jump in if I go off the rails," Jim directed.

Paul had never really seen his boss out of control despite the many desperate situations they'd found themselves in, but he was sure there was a limit to Higgins's command and mastery of his emotions. He supposed the torching of your home and the possibility of the death of your wife and children would be considered well outside the range of normal detective activities—even for Higgins.

"I've got your back, Chief," Paul said as they started back down the hall to the hospital room.

"Why don't you conduct the interview, and I'll jump in when it's appropriate," Jim suggested.

"Sounds good. Ready then?" Paul asked.

Jim straightened his shoulders and pushed the door open. "No time like the present."

Devon Williams woke up from a drug-induced haze when the two detectives entered the room. His shoulder and chest were wrapped in white gauze bandages, and his arm was supported with a sling. The perp sat in a reclining position, his lunch tray pushed to the side of a hospital cart, the food cold and shriveled. When Jim locked eyes with Williams, he felt a subtle heat on his skin that felt like a mild sunburn. He gritted his teeth, and his jaw tightened with anxiety. *Face to face with the lowlife who tried to kill me and my family.* Jim walked to the edge of the room near the window and leaned against the wall, hoping the distance would defuse the anger he felt toward this man. Meanwhile, Paul quietly set up the camera close to the hospital bed so he could record the interrogation. Jim prepared to listen, assuming his classic pose—head down, arms crossed over his chest, eyes downcast, studying the floor.

"Devon, I am Detective Paul Saner, and you know Lt. Jim Higgins. I'm going to ask you some questions related to the robbery at the Gas & Go station in Stoddard on August 28 and the subsequent shooting and murder of Vicki Invold. I'll be recording your responses," Paul began in a steady but uncompromising tone. "Do you understand?"

"Yeah, I got it," Devon said sourly. "But you don't have any proof I actually did it." Paul ignored his claim and began questioning Devon about the incident at the gas station.

During the interrogation, Jim studied the young man lying in the hospital bed. Williams was a handsome man. Jim could understand the charm he might exert over women who were unaware of the subtle fabrications and lies of an experienced con man—like Vicki Invold and Angela Fitzgerald. Although Devon was handcuffed to the hospital bed, his extraordinary self-regard continued unabated as he rambled on about the trials and adversities he'd experienced in his early life as if that was a legitimate excuse for his criminal activities. His voice floated through the room, slick and smooth as silk.

"...and then my dad took off and left my mom alone to raise five kids in the inner city of Milwaukee," Devon droned on.

You can't believe anything this guy says, Jim thought bitterly.

"Let's get back to your relationship with Vicki Invold," Paul said.

Devon began painting a picture of perceived wrongs done to him by Vicki. "Do you know that she left me high and dry for some high school kid? Some BJ LaPointe. Can you believe that?"

Jim's head popped up, and he felt his heart begin to tick faster. *Is he really talking about insults from an eighteen-year-old nursing student—trying to justify the shooting based on some smack a college girl gave him?* If Devon had misinterpreted Jim's silence as acquiescence, the lieutenant's entrance into the conversation removed all doubt.

"So you're telling us that the shooting at the gas station was because Vicki had insulted you by ditching you for someone else?" Jim asked harshly, his eyes sharp and penetrating.

Paul looked over at Jim, his eyebrows raised ever so slightly. *Easy, Higgins,* he thought. *So much for jumping into the conversation when it's appropriate.*

Devon grimaced as he shifted in bed. Then he focused his full attention on Jim, who was still standing by the wall. "Vicki claimed she was pregnant and the kid was mine. I didn't believe her, but she kept threatening me with paternity tests. I don't take shit like that from some snot-nosed little clerk in a gas station," Devon sneered.

Jim stood to his full height, staring at Devon until he squirmed uncomfortably. "So you're not man enough to just walk away from the accusations? Instead, you ripped the necklace from Vicki's neck and then filled her full of bullet holes!" Jim yelled. He took a few steps toward the hospital bed, but Paul intercepted Jim by grabbing his arm.

"Easy, Chief. I've got this," he said quietly.

Jim's face was flushed, a mask of disgust and loathing. Paul stood in front of Jim. "Chief. I have this. You need to back off. I can handle it," Paul reminded him again, his voice taking on an authoritative edge.

Jim jerked his arm away from Paul and took a few more steps closer to the bed. "You do realize that BJ LaPointe walked in the sheriff's office yesterday with the clothes you took off Detective Sam Birkstein," Jim said firmly, his blue eyes flashing.

Devon paled significantly at the news, and suddenly he looked terrified.

"He gave a full account of the scene at the gas station," Jim continued, "shortly after you shot Vicki Invold to death. He also told us what you did when you found Sam along the road. I'm afraid your claim of no proof just got shot to hell."

Paul watched Jim carefully. Then he said again, "Chief, I'll finish up here."

"Not 'til we talk about the fire," Jim spat.

"Fire? What fire?" Devon asked, but beneath the innocence, a hardness had crept into his voice.

"The fire in which you burned half of my house down! The fire that almost killed my wife and two children!" Jim shouted. "Don't play stupid with me. I have you on my home surveillance camera carrying the gas can from the scene. You're a pretty sloppy crook, Devon, and I won't rest until I see you behind bars for a very long time." By now, Jim had stepped to the end of the bed. His face was white with rage. "Believe me when I say you will pay a high price for the chaos you've caused."

"Where's my lawyer? I need to talk to my lawyer!" Devon yelled at Paul. He refused to make eye contact with Jim.

"We'll end the interview at this point until your court-appointed attorney can be present," Paul said.

"Well, we might end the interview, but this is just the beginning of your long slide into a prison cell," Jim said angrily. He turned and walked from the room, banging through the door into the hallway. Jim walked to the window that overlooked the hospital parking lot and stood there for several minutes getting a handle on his emotions and his outburst in Devon's room. He did experience a certain vindication in delivering the news of BJ LaPointe's critical testimony. The young man's account would help cement the DA's case in bringing a variety of charges against Devon. Jim breathed deeply and sighed. *Good*, he thought. *This case is on the way to the court system. Now maybe I can get on with my life.*

At that moment, his cell vibrated in his pocket.

"Higgins," he answered brusquely.

"Bapa?" a high voice said on the other end.

"Hey, peanut. What's up?" Jim asked, mellowing the tone of his voice.

"Mom wants to know if you'll be home by dinnertime," Lillie said, "or will you be late again?"

Jim smiled. "I'll be home in about an hour. See you then, toots."

57

"I can't believe you did this," Jim commented as he looked at Carol across the dining room table in Gladys's kitchen. From his expression, Carol couldn't decide if he was ticked, unpleasantly surprised, or in disbelief at her bold move. Maybe it was all three at the same time.

"Well, believe it. We need a break, and we had some money in our savings, so... I just did it."

"But Paris, honey? We're going to Paris in October?" Jim asked, dumbfounded.

"It's all cleared through Sheriff Turnmile and the department. I thought it was about time we introduced our kids to the City of Light. I even managed to book a suite in the same hotel where we spent our honeymoon. Besides, I saved quite a bit of money on some special buys on furniture so..." Carol's voice faded and stopped as she studied Jim's face. She could see the exhaustion seeping from his pores, and his sparkling blue eyes were dull with the burden of his responsibilities. "Please say you're all right with this, Jim. I just wanted to surprise you. I love you, babe."

The silence in the kitchen seemed to permeate every nook and cranny. Carol could hear the cuckoo clock ticking away in the corner near the hutch. Jim leaned back in his chair and crossed his arms over his chest. After a few moments, Carol could see the beginnings of a subtle grin tickling the corners of his mouth.

"You always said you liked my spontaneity," she reminded him nervously, her brown eyes wide with apprehension.

"I was referring to our love life, honey," Jim reminded her.

"Oh," Carol said softly.

Jim leaned forward and grabbed Carol's hands. "Hey, it's fine, really. I think it's a great idea. If you hadn't gone ahead and bought the tickets and made the arrangements, it would never have happened."

"Really? So you're okay with it?" Carol said, relief flooding over her.

"I love the whole idea, sweetheart," Jim said tenderly.

"It'll give us some time away from the remodel and the memory of the fire, and it'll give Gladys a break, too. We'll only be gone ten days. I've got it all planned..." Carol rambled, pulling out *Rick Steves Pocket Paris* handbook of places and events she wanted them to experience. "We'll do a day at the Eiffel Tower, and there's a very accessible museum near there that the kids will enjoy. I've scheduled a nighttime boat cruise down the Seine—just for you and me. We'll take bike rides and do a couple of picnics, and I've even planned a couple of days on a farm south of Paris. The kids can ride horses, feed the goats and chickens while we sample cheese and wine. We'll just let loose."

"Sounds great, sweetheart," Jim said. Carol's excitement oozed from every pore, and as Jim watched her, he felt the anticipation of the trip take root. "The whole trip sounds really great, but don't forget to add at least a day for some shopping. Remember that mall with the glass and steel canopy on the Rue Cler—I bought a couple of sport coats in that little men's shop near there. I need some new clothes, and the kids should absolutely get something to wear from Paris, even if it's just a T-shirt. And, of course, you deserve some Parisian haute couture."

Now it was Carol's turn to be silent. After several moments, she said, "All I want is to see the sparkle back in those blue eyes again. Whatever it takes to make that happen will be worth it."

Jim got up and pulled Carol from her chair, embraced her, and placed a tender kiss on her lips. "You always have my back, don't you?" he said, burying his nose in her brunette hair.

"Like nobody else," she said.

THURSDAY, DECEMBER 18

THE WORLD IS CONSPIRING IN YOUR FAVOR.

58

The sun was slow to penetrate the haze over the Mississippi River. The cold had burrowed in and hunkered down during the month of December. Several inches of snow left the ground blanketed in white. The Mississippi River was a steely gray with patches of ice at the edges and predictably quiet except for the wildlife that inhabited its shores. The cold, mute bluffs were whiskered with frost. Sam Birkstein walked to the large living room window of his home along U.S. Highway 35. He lifted a pair of binoculars to his eyes and gazed at the snowy river scene. A convocation of eagles was strutting on the shoreline, fighting over hunks of fresh fish, gobbling them ravenously. In the corner of the living room, the Christmas tree lights twinkled steadily. Cuddled against his chest, his new daughter, Karina, squeaked a little and wormed her tiny arm from the blanket. Sam lowered the binoculars, grasped her little fingers in his hand, and kissed them gently.

Becoming a father in mid-November had sent him into a new emotional landscape. He felt elation, pride, a tender wistfulness, and love so strong he knew he'd protect this little one with his very life if he had to. He looked again at Karina's beautiful little face. It reminded him so much of Lez. Blue, blue eyes, a fuzz of dark hair covering her head, and a distinctive nose reminiscent of Sam's mother. The genetics of the whole experience left him in awe—a new life, but one tied strongly to two parents and the line of DNA passed on by each one of them.

"Sam?" a voice said from behind him.

He turned. Leslie stood watching him. "Just watching the eagles down by the river," he said, holding up the binoculars. "What's up?"

"I need to run into town for a few groceries. I shouldn't be gone more than an hour. Karina just nursed, so you should be fine. Remember, we're going to Higgins's housewarming tonight," she finished.

"Yeah, that should be fun. I hear the house turned out really great. At least that's what Higgins has been telling us," Sam said. "We'll be fine. You just go. Don't hurry back. I can manage."

"Yes, I know you can," Leslie said. She reached over, glanced at Karina, and gave Sam a peck on the cheek. "Be back in a bit."

Sam watched Leslie back the Jeep from the garage and proceed down the steep driveway to Highway 35. She headed north toward La Crosse.

As Sam watched the Jeep speed down the road, his thoughts turned to the Devon Williams case. Since the capture of the perpetrator at Battle Bluff in mid-September, the collection of evidence continued full steam ahead. Sam thought the case would probably come to trial sometime in early spring. The account by BJ LaPointe had been the pivotal moment when Sam's innocence had been proven beyond a shadow of a doubt by the testimony of an actual eyewitness to the aftermath of the crime. Since that time, Sam had been coming to terms with the suspicions and innuendos swirling around the law enforcement department about him. But recently, it seemed the shadows had taken flight, and his colleagues and fellow officers had rallied around him. Sam's status as the top narcotics officer in the La Crosse Sheriff's Department had been restored.

Now he enjoyed the quiet atmosphere of the house. Walking into the kitchen, he poured himself a second cup of coffee. Paco, ever vigilant, appeared at his side. Sam leaned down and patted his side, stroking his silky ears. The black lab had adjusted well to the baby's presence, and he waited patiently for an opportunity to sniff and lick the newborn.

"So, Paco, what's up, buddy?" Sam said to the intrepid canine.

Paco barked and sat obediently at Sam's feet.

"Treat time?"

Another bark.

Paco leaped in the air when Sam threw him a liver biscuit. "Oh, that life should be so simple," he chuckled as the dog hungrily chomped on the biscuit, scattering crumbs onto the floor.

Sam walked to the living room with Paco trailing behind him. He sat on the couch, nestling his baby girl on his lap. Reaching over to the end table, he opened a drawer and took out the envelope with the return address of the Minneapolis Police Department. He slid the letter from the envelope, unfolded it, and scanned the contents again. It was an offer he'd only dreamed about: an invitation to apply for lead investigator of the Drug and Alcohol unit at the Minneapolis Police Department.

Apparently his reputation had caused bigger ripples on the law enforcement pond than he'd imagined. He hadn't told Leslie about the opportunity yet. Maybe he'd interview and see where it went. As tempting as the job was, he'd been contemplating all that he'd leave behind in La Crosse, and it tugged at his heartstrings. He and Leslie had begun to build a life here in the Coulee region, and he couldn't imagine policing without Lt. Higgins by his side. Furthermore, the challenges facing the Minneapolis Police Department were intimidating and well-known among law enforcement in the tri-state region. Besides, it wasn't like they didn't have their share of challenging cases to solve here in La Crosse. Something always seemed to fall into their laps that caused provocation and major headlines. There was plenty of work to go around in the Coulee region.

Paco trotted up to Sam as if sensing his angst. Sam breathed deeply, patted the big lab's head, and muttered, "Oh, that life's problems could be solved with a liver biscuit."

Later that same afternoon, Jim Higgins perched on a stepladder outside the front porch of his house on Chipmunk Coulee Road, stringing Christmas tree lights along the eaves. Lillie stood below him on the sidewalk untangling strands of lights and jabbering a mile a minute.

"... and Sister Julianne wants me to start a new Bach piece for the spring recital. It's pretty hard, but I think I can learn it, Bapa."

Jim squinted in the bright sunshine, struggling to see the nails he'd pounded into the eaves earlier that morning. "That's great, Lillie, but could you run into the house and get my reading glasses? They're lying on the hutch in the dining room. I can't see these nails to save my soul."

"Okay. Be back in a minute," Lillie said as she dropped the lights in the box.

Carol appeared at the door. "Jim, are you going to have these lights done by tonight?" she asked, her voice grating with exasperation.

"Honey, Lillie and I will have them done. We're almost finished, but I needed my glasses." Jim looked down at Carol from high on the ladder and marveled at his wife's ingenuity and persistence. The last week they had been decorating the house, unpacking and assembling furniture, hanging pictures, and living in a chaos of tissue paper, bubble wrap, and cardboard boxes. Finally, this afternoon the paper garbage was hauled into the garage, and Carol was putting the final touches on their remodeled and restored home. It sparkled with beauty and creative energy.

In the living room, the large Christmas tree in the corner glittered with ornaments and white lights. Carol had tastefully arranged the furniture, including the new baby grand piano in the expanded space, and she'd been busy preparing a buffet of finger food for neighbors and friends joining them for the housewarming party at seven o'clock.

"Believe me, honey. Everyone who saw this house in September will be overwhelmed by it tonight," Jim commented. Lillie appeared and handed Jim his glasses. "See, hon. We've got everything under control." Jim waved his hand in front of him in a sweeping motion and plopped the glasses on his nose. "Right, peanut?"

"Right. We've got it covered, Mom," Lillie declared.

Jim smiled down at Carol and said, "Now, just go do your thing inside."

"All right. I'll leave you to it." Carol turned and scurried back into the house.

By seven that evening, the Higgins home was bustling with friends and family who had been invited to their new dwelling. Paul and Ruby were there with their children, Melody and Max. Sam, Leslie, and Karina made it, along with Jude and DeDe and Mike Leland. Emily and the office staff had all cleared their schedules to join Jim and Carol in celebrating a new beginning on Chipmunk Coulee Road. In the corner, the ladies from the Hamburg Lutheran Church, including Gladys Hanson, were bantering back and forth. Vivian and Craig Jensen; Jerome, Sara, and Bobby Rude; and John and Jenny Higgins filled out the family side of the guest list.

Christmas tunes blasted from the newly installed surround sound system, and later in the evening, Melody Saner and Lillie Higgins entertained friends on the new baby grand piano with their rendition of "Silent Night." When the wild applause let up, Leslie took the opportunity to step forward.

"Jim and Carol," she began, "we have a little surprise for you. Since the fire, we know you've been looking forward to getting back in your house. Earlier this fall, Chief, we talked about a painting for your wall. I've been working on it, and this seems like the perfect time to give it to you." Sam appeared at Leslie's side with a large, rectangular shape covered in brown paper. Leslie held it up to Carol and Jim and said, "For you."

Jim and Carol walked across the room and began removing the

paper from the package. They gasped with wonder and amazement when the painting was revealed. Along the misty shoreline of the Mississippi River, cattails poked their way toward the sky. Nestled among them, a weathered gray boat floated in obscurity on the rippling water. The early morning sky rolled away in hues of gray, purple, and pink, and in the background, a mother duck and her baby ducklings paddled peacefully. It was just the kind of scene that kindled Jim's great love for the river and the people who lived along its banks. Jim's eyes suddenly misted with tears, and he could not find his voice.

Carol stepped forward. "Since Jim is obviously tongue-tied," she began, wiping away tears, "let me say, this is precious beyond words. You have all stood beside us during these long months of recovery, and we are so thankful for every one of you. We love you."

Everyone clapped, and there were a few whistles. People began moving around again, getting drinks and snacks. The music ballooned in volume, and after a few moments, Leslie felt a gentle touch on her arm. She turned, and Jim engulfed her in a hug.

He whispered, "The painting is beautiful. Thank you so much."

"You're welcome, Chief. I was glad to do it for you."

"I'll get the check in the mail," he said solemnly as he stood in front of her.

"No, you won't. It's already been paid for. Everybody chipped in," Leslie informed him.

Once again, Jim was overwhelmed. "It's okay, Chief," Leslie said, noticing his misty eyes.

Sam sidled up to her, draped his arm around her shoulder, and said, "Yeah, it's okay, and it's worth it to see you speechless. That doesn't happen too often. Better mark the calendar," Sam said, grinning widely.

Leslie drifted away. The two detectives stood shoulder to shoulder for a while, watching the crowd until Jim finally asked, "Have you made a decision about the Minneapolis thing yet?"

"Not yet."

"Leslie know?"

"Nope."

"Gonna tell her?"

"Eventually."

"If it were up to me, I'd give you a big raise," Jim said softly. "Keep you in La Crosse."

"Well, it's not up to you, so I guess you can kiss that idea goodbye."

"Yeah, I guess I can. Merry Christmas, Sam."

"Merry Christmas, Chief."

THE END

ABOUT THE AUTHOR

Sue Berg is the author of the Driftless Mystery Series. She is a former teacher, and enjoys many hobbies including writing, watercolor painting, quilting, cooking and gardening. She lives with her husband, Alan, near Viroqua, Wisconsin.

The Driftless Mystery Series set in the beautiful Driftless region of the Upper Midwest does not disappoint. With complex characters, intriguing plots, and surprising twists and turns, this series will delight you with its ability to entertain while upholding the values we all treasure; love, faith, loyalty, and family. It is destined to become a beloved and enduring legacy to the people and culture in this unique part of the country.

COMING IN MAY 2026

JIM HIGGINS'
ADVENTURES
CONTINUE...

Look to the next page for an excerpt
from *Driftless Reflection*.

"EVIL IS UNSPECTACULAR AND ALWAYS HUMAN, AND SHARES OUR BED AND EATS AT OUR OWN TABLE."

W.H. AUDEN

TUESDAY, MAY 15

1

The sun was dipping toward the western horizon, painting the pink sky with gold and fuchsia swirls. La Crosse, Wisconsin, a small college town nestled along the Mississippi River, is long and skinny, squeezed between the river on the west and the sandstone bluffs on the east. Delta flight 57 banked over the river to prepare for a landing at the city's municipal airport located at the wide end of French Island and in the middle of the river southeast of Lake Onalaska. Geoff LaSarde inhaled deeply and leaned toward the tiny window to catch a glimpse of the wide, winding waterway as it snaked its way through the steep forested bluffs on either side. In the distance, the sandstone landmark of the majestic limestone promontory called Grandad Bluff reflected the golden rays of the setting sun.

Geoff was a professional art critic with an intense interest in history, specifically the history of architectural and decorative arts in the United States. His field of expertise was the art and craft of Louis Comfort Tiffany, which included jewelry, decorative items for the home, including stained glass lamps, glassware, and church windows, an area of mastery of which most Tiffany aficionados were woefully ignorant. Geoff was the exception.

LaSarde made Tiffany-stained glass windows an area of particular emphasis in his doctoral thesis. After investing years of study, he'd finally earned a degree in history of decorative arts from the University of Chicago with high honors. In addition, LaSarde had published several articles about Tiffany windows in *Architectural Digest, Luxe: Interiors and Design,* and *Metropolis*. He'd traveled to The Mabel Tainter Memorial Theater in Menomonie, Wisconsin, to study the Tiffany-stained glass windows there and made several trips to Chicago, where Tiffany church windows were being rediscovered and restored to their former glory. A few months ago, he'd made a trip to St. Paul's Episcopal Church in Milwaukee where he stood transfixed by the glorious radiance of eleven of the country's rarest and most valuable Tiffany church windows.

Regrettably, La Crosse could not boast about any Tiffany church windows within its city limits. However, Geoff hoped to change all that with the construction of a new art gallery, Feast for the Eyes, on the south side in the old Fleischstad meat facility. He'd been involved in the planning of the gallery and had suggested the addition of a modest Tiffany window to grace the entryway. The committee had wholeheartedly approved. Yet he had to locate and acquire a window for inclusion in the gallery's design scheme.

Currently he was unemployed, but a generous inheritance from his wealthy parents made worries about a job pointless. Tall and lanky, LaSarde wasn't exactly handsome, but his narrow face held a pair of inquisitive green eyes, and behind them burned an innate curiosity and a sharp intelligence that drove him in his quest of all things Tiffany. His brown wavy hair was cut in a classic mullet, but it was rather attractive on him and frequently earned him a second glance from females he met on his architectural expeditions. He dressed modestly in muted colors except for a red T-shirt he'd bought at a convention of interior designers, which flaunted the saying: "It's a Tiffany Thing… You Wouldn't Understand."

Three rows behind Geoff on the Delta flight, a distinguished-looking gentleman flipped through a magazine with indifference. Lewis Borden uncrossed his legs and waited patiently as the flight attendant walked down the aisle, preparing the passengers for deplaning. The man's dark gray business suit was finely tailored, his fingernails were clean and clipped, and his mustache and beard expertly trimmed, but his cold, gray eyes lacked any warmth that would attract anyone to him. He remained aloof and unapproachable even to the friendly flight attendants.

As the plane descended for landing, trays were snapped into place, and people began gathering up their personal items, placing them in their briefcases and bags. The older man had been watching Geoff LaSarde since the luggage auction at Chicago O'Hare International Airport late yesterday afternoon. From everything Borden could deduce, LaSarde had no idea he was being followed, nor was he aware of the important information he carried in the luggage he'd purchased at the auction.

The luggage was part of the estate of Howard Ellison, a lumber baron from Oshkosh, Wisconsin, who had built a lavish Victorian home in the city from the profits he'd made at several sawmills in and around Oshkosh. The suitcase, a vintage calfskin throwback, had disappeared and recently come to light when a historical society in the city discovered it at an auction. They purchased it and then sent it by plane to a museum curator in Chicago who was preparing a display about the historical significance of the lumber industry in Wisconsin at the turn of the century. Unfortunately, the curator failed to pick it up at the airport, and it was added to the rest of the unclaimed luggage. Eventually, the suitcase was sent to a room on the lower level of the airport, where luggage auctions were regularly held every couple of months.

Locating the luggage had been a challenge for Lewis Borden, but last week, using bribery and threats, his contacts found the elusive suitcase with the valuable information at the airport's huge unclaimed baggage area. Learning that the luggage would be sold at the auction, Borden had been dispatched to the airport by his boss but had gotten stranded in Chicago traffic and arrived late. He missed the bidding on the suitcase. The realization that he'd failed in his mission left him with a dull ache in his stomach, but he was determined to redeem himself. He'd followed Geoff LaSarde to the boarding area and listened to a conversation he was having with another young thirty-something. When Geoff mentioned La Crosse, Wisconsin, as his destination, Lewis Borden went quickly to the ticket counter and bought a standby ticket.

Waiting to board the airplane, he called his boss and explained his dilemma. The contents of the suitcase held a special interest for his boss, and Borden's orders from his employer when he'd admitted his screw-up were to "keep that young kid from doing something stupid with the suitcase he bought. We need what's in it, and I will not accept failure. That's why I'm sending you. Don't disappoint me again."

Lewis Borden smiled to himself. *I am an efficient taskmaster capable of convincing anyone to do anything with the right amount of deadly force.* Geoff LaSarde was about to find out just how convincing Lewis Borden could be.

Geoff LaSarde put on his backpack and grabbed his carry-on from the overhead rack, got off the plane, and walked to his 2019 Subaru in the airport parking lot. The air smelled of river water and spawning fish, freshly mowed grass, and the sweet, intoxicating scent of lilacs. May was a glorious time of year in Wisconsin, and this spring had delivered a streak of fabulous mild weather, gentle rainfalls, and burgeoning vibrant greenery among the coulees and bluffs of the Driftless Area. Geoff unlocked his car, opened the back hatch, and placed his backpack and the old suitcase he'd purchased at the luggage auction in the vehicle. Then he crammed his lean frame in the front seat and drove to his home on the north side of La Crosse near Red Cloud Park.

After negotiating through light traffic, he turned onto his driveway on St. Cloud Street. As an only child of doting parents who were now deceased, he'd inherited a small fortune from the patents of his father's medical inventions. He lived comfortably, yet modestly, in his parents' home on a tree-lined boulevard in one of La Crosse's northside neighborhoods. The house was a low, cozy gray bungalow with a small greenhouse attached to the back. Perennial flower gardens surrounded the small residence and added to its charm. Geoff parked his Subaru in the garage, walked through the breezeway connected to the house, and unlocked the kitchen door. His cat, Sir Lancelot, a huge tabby male, greeted him with cold, yellow eyes and a husky meow.

Despite the cat's aloof nature, Geoff had a deep affection for the ornery feline. The young man leaned down, affectionately fluffed the cat's ears, stroked his smooth coat, and then refilled his bowls with fresh food and water. He walked through the small kitchen and dining room to the living room, turned the thermostat up to sixty-five degrees, and heard the furnace kick in.

Dusk had fallen. Geoff switched on the Tiffany lamp next to the leather couch. The dragonfly pattern glowed as light passed through the intricate pieces of glass, making the insects radiate with an otherworldly luminescence. He walked down the hall to his bedroom, unpacked his clothes, threw his underwear, shirts, and socks in the laundry basket, set his Dopp kit on the bed, and placed the backpack on a hook behind the door.

He always traveled light when he went to luggage auctions. You never knew what your luggage might include, and since you were not allowed to open the bags before bidding, your purchase could be a surprise, but that was part of the fun of the hobby.

Sometimes he bought more than one piece. In February, he'd traveled to Cincinnati and bought two huge Samsonite suitcases. One had been loaded with expensive, tropical clothing, including Tommy Bahama and Vineyard Vines watercolor shirts, Tiboyz Hawaiian shorts, and Driftwood cargo shorts, all with the tags still on them. Unfortunately, Geoff wasn't in the market for a tropical wardrobe in February—it was still in the lower thirties at night in Wisconsin—but he was able to take the upscale clothing to one of the many secondhand resale shops in Rochester, Minnesota, where he sold the merchandise and made a quick thousand dollar return on his purchase. Not bad for having paid only twenty dollars for the suitcase. The other piece of luggage yielded a collection of cameras and recording equipment, which Geoff stashed on a shelf in the spare bedroom. One of these days, he'd examine it and determine its value.

He strolled back to the kitchen and picked up the vintage suitcase from the O'Hare auction. Something about the luggage appealed to his sense of style. It was a reminder of a time when high-quality materials and craftsmanship were a priority. Made of tanned calfskin and accentuated with brown trim around the edges and corners, it had a fancy brass key lock beneath the leather handle. Geoff leaned down and read the label affixed near the lock—Anthi Leoni—an old well-known Italian name in quality luggage. The clerk at the auction had to drum up interest in the old suitcase, and after a short, intense exchange with another bidder, Geoff had won the luggage for one hundred dollars. He chuckled to himself. The luggage alone might be worth that in a store that specializes in vintage items.

Geoff carried the suitcase to his bedroom and plopped it on the bed. He carefully opened the luggage, his hands shaking in anticipation. Unfolding the suitcase, he peered at the contents inside.

At first, he was disappointed. He saw nothing but some musty, yellowing papers. But then, as he sifted through the paperwork inside the case, his disappointment turned to amazement. A newspaper article caught his attention. He stood stock still for several minutes reading the article about a horrendous fire at an Oshkosh, Wisconsin, lumber baron's mansion in 1904 which resulted in some Tiffany windows that had disappeared. One of the windows depicted a Knights Templar figure in full armor, and the others featured various

Templar iconography. A search for the windows by the Oshkosh police after the fire had come up empty. Now, the windows were still missing over one hundred years later despite intense interest by other Tiffany experts and amateur sleuths.

Geoff gazed across the room thinking about the information. He'd read about these windows during his research for his graduate thesis. The Ellison windows had been missing for a long time, and their whereabouts were still a mystery. He could never have known the suitcase held such intriguing information. It was almost as if a stranger had reached over and tapped him on the shoulder, saying, "Look at this. It's right up your alley. Missing Tiffany windows." What were the odds? *About a million to one,* he thought. Geoff grabbed the top papers along with the newspaper article and quickly walked into his study, opened his roll-top desk, and deposited them inside.

Just then, his landline rang. He was tempted to let it go to his answering machine so he could get something to eat, but he was sure there were several messages to answer already, so he quickly walked back into the kitchen and answered.

"Hello. This is Geoff."

"Hey, buddy. Where've you been? I've been trying to get a hold of you for two days."

"I could ask you the same thing, Jamie. But to answer your question, I went to another airport luggage auction in Chicago, and I just got back," Geoff replied. Jamie Alberg was an archaeologist friend. The two young men had been on numerous digs together throughout the tri-state region.

"You know we discovered another vein of buried pottery at Fish Farm Mounds down near Lansing. The items we're finding are pretty significant—more Oneota pots, some pipestone tablets, bone awls, some turtle shell rattles. Cool stuff. I'm getting a crew together. Can you help us excavate for a few days?" Jamie asked.

Geoff could imagine the excitement in Jamie's eyes, and he heard the quiver of anticipation in his friend's voice when he spoke about the new discoveries buried in the river silt.

"Well, I guess I could help for a few days," Geoff replied reluctantly, "but I've got a couple of pressing projects that I need to finish in the next few weeks for the new art gallery. I can help until Friday, but then I have other priorities."

"Great! I'll call you tomorrow and explain how to get to the site. See ya," Jamie finished, and the line went dead.

Geoff hung up and stood by the phone, thinking about his friend. Brilliant and determined to make a name for himself as a famous archaeologist and treasure hunter, Jamie Alberg was demanding and obstinate. He'd also been involved in a number of cases at the La Crosse Sheriff's Department as a self-proclaimed consultant in a couple of mysterious predicaments involving gold coins and ancient Native American ball clubs. He believed the police needed his expert opinion, even though they hadn't solicited his knowledge and expertise. Instead, Jamie had just audaciously inserted himself into the investigations and had come close to being killed both times. His social awkwardness and bravado notwithstanding, Geoff had formed an authentic friendship with Jamie, and he looked forward to seeing him again.

At that very moment, Sir Lancelot let out a loud mewl, and his hair puffed out and stood on end. Simultaneously, Geoff heard a rustling noise behind him. A strong arm grabbed him around the neck in a choke hold. Despite his resistance, within seconds, Geoff slumped into unconsciousness, and the perpetrator lowered him roughly to the floor.

The darkly attired man walked rapidly through the small house, searching for the vintage piece of luggage. Finding the case opened on the bed, he shoved the loose papers lying next to it inside, clicked the lock, and walked back to the kitchen. Looking down at the young man who lay crumpled on the floor, he was momentarily tempted to send him into oblivion. Instead, he reached into his pocket and retrieved a syringe of potent benzodiazepine, which he promptly injected into Geoff's rear end. The young man groaned, then fell silent.

Sir Lancelot, however, had other ideas. The feline suddenly gripped the intruder's leg hard with his front claws and sunk his sharp teeth into the man's calf. The perpetrator stifled a scream and kicked at the cat, who scampered away unscathed. Lewis Borden turned hurriedly toward the door and silently slipped into the night with the antique suitcase in his hand.

DIRTY BUSINESS MYSTERY SERIES

DEATH at the DENTIST

A Sonja Hovland Adventure

SUE BERG

NEW SERIES

The author of the award-winning Driftless Mystery Series presents a new series. *Death at the Dentist* is now available for purchase at your favorite bookstore, Amazon and Ingram.

**CLEANING UP MESSES IS HER JOB—
SOLVING MURDERS IS JUST A BONUS.
BUT THIS TIME, THE DIRT RUNS
DEADLY DEEP!**

Meet Sonja Hovland, entrepreneur of the Dirty Business Housecleaning Services. In addition to her cleaning skills, Sonja often makes inquiries for her clients of a personal nature. As Sonja often says, "There's nothing wrong with killing two birds with one stone, is there?" But when Sonja goes to clean a swanky new office in downtown La Crosse, she finds a dentist dead in his chair. Things heat up fast, and Sonja finds herself in the throes of a full-blown murder investigation. Join Sonja, her husband, Trygve, and La Crosse Police Chief Tanya Pedretti, as they pit their investigative skills against a murderer who is determined to rid society of the evils of capitalism. A rousing new series sure to capture the reader's attention!

Printed in the United States
by Baker & Taylor Publisher Services